The
FIELDS
of
EDEN

The
FIELDS
of
EDEN

RICHARD S. WHEELER

A TOM DOHERTY ASSOCIATES BOOK
NEW YORK

THE FIELDS OF EDEN

This book is printed on acid-free paper.

Design by Heidi Eriksen

A Forge Book
Published by Tom Doherty Associates, LLC
175 Fifth Avenue
New York, NY 10010

www.tor.com

Forge® is a registered trademark of Tom Doherty
Associates, LLC.

Library of Congress Cataloging-in-Publication Data

Wheeler, Richard S.
    The fields of Eden / Richard S. Wheeler.—1st ed.
        p. cm.
    ISBN 0-312-87309-3
    1. McLoughlin, John, 1784–1857—Fiction.   2. Hudson's Bay
Company—Fiction.   3. Immigrants—Fiction.   4. Oregon—
Fiction.   I. Title.
PS3573.H4345 F45 2001
813'.54—dc21

                                                        2001018948

First Edition: May 2001

Printed in the United States of America

0 9 8 7 6 5 4 3 2 1

For my bride, Sue Hart, with everlasting love

1842

1

John O'Malley dragged Mary Kate out of the river more dead than alive, upended her, pumped water out of her lungs, crying at her to live, and was rewarded with a cough, a gasping, and a pulse that steadied into life. And then tears.

He yanked off her soaked shoes, then her lisle stockings, and undid her sodden skirts and wrung them dry. Her white cotton petticoat clung wetly to her icy flesh. He pulled off his soaked woolen coat and shirt, which were bleeding the heat from his heart and belly. Then he wrestled off his sodden boots, and drained the water out of them. His bare feet hurt. He stretched her out upon the wet rock and rolled over her, and damned if he cared what the rest thought.

Now she lay beneath, quaking, but breathing regularly, still dazed. Her warmth was rising to him, helping them both stay alive—for the moment.

"We'll live, Mary Kate," he cried. He wasn't so sure of it. The sleet in his hair had frozen. His whole being ached with cold.

She didn't reply but her arms tugged him down. If she hugged him hard enough, she might find warmth.

He ventured a glance, at last, toward the rest. Some were staring at him. Let the fools stand there and die of cold.

"Jesus, Joseph, Mary," she whispered.

That politician named Reese was staring. John O'Malley had long since had his fill of politicians, clerks, officers of the law, and all those who peered down their long noses at him. Back in Independence he had taken one look at Reese and knew the type.

And now Reese and the brand-new widow sat yards apart on the rock, dripping ice water, turning blue, envying him. He pitied them.

Mary Kate shivered, and he buried his head upon her neck, willing his warmth into her. His trousers were freezing stiff but he ignored that. His body was warming her. The sopping cotton between them gathered the fragile warmth and held it. An embrace was keeping them alive, and damned if he would let go just to avoid a scandal.

This was the end of his honeymoon. It had started long ago in Waterford, where his father ran a small glassworks that made fine crystal tableware. The little shop supported the O'Malley family adequately, though not on the scale of the lords whose grasping hands lay upon all of Ireland.

He scarcely wanted to think about all he had left behind, especially the Troubles. There were always troubles in Ireland, but none so terrible as the present ones, where paid spies tattled on conspirators and bystanders alike, and men vanished off the cobbled streets and ended up in Van Diemen's Land.

He had few choices: he could be a rebel and get himself hanged or trans- ported to the penal colonies, or he could leave. He had always had larger visions than killing English dragoons, and so he had left, taking his bride, Mary Kate. His father had paid for the passage, and not mean passage either, but a private honeymoon cabin on a good Liverpool brigantine, where he and his bride had discovered passion to the rhythm of the seas.

Now she was pregnant, and he was keeping her alive with his own warm body—at least for the moment. They would find land and liberty in Oregon, not at all like the cramped, stone-walled half-acres of Ireland, but real land, as far as the eye could see, a lush valley filled with kine or sheep, in a new settlement, in a new nation. If they lived.

He glanced again at the rest. The gaunt missionaries had artfully turned their backs on him and Mary Kate and had even turned their children's gazes away from the scandal. They sat or lay like isolated stumps, chattering with cold.

They had earned their misery. All the way from Independence they had walled off the Irish Catholics, never warming to Mary Kate, the sweetest and brightest lass in all the world, their sour gazes leveled upon the small silver crucifix at her breast, the shine in her brown eyes, the sway of her hips. At night, he and Mary Kate had scandalized them, crooning in their tent, yet rising to meet each toilsome day more filled with energy than the rest.

Two thousand brutal miles had worn them down to sinew; uncountable steps, a thousand brief and unsatisfying stops to rest, a few hundred miserable meals full of sand and flies cooked over buffalo-dung fires, and frightful thirsts. A hundred pious Protestant pilgrims walking to Oregon that year of 1842, and two young Irish among them.

Electra Reese knew she would not last. She trembled within the heavy, sodden mass of her skirts and could not stop the shaking. Her feet, pinioned in her soaked shoes, tortured her. Oh, God! Even around her heart she felt her own heat ebb away and her body tighten toward death.

She had watched in horror as Warren, her husband, had teetered on the bucking raft and then slowly tumbled into the gray torrent of the Columbia. She saw him bob up once, death upon him, and then the raft spun around, threw her and the others into the river, and foamed away.

Oh, God, Warren lost in a froth of white.

She had been thrown into a tumble of slippery rock and battered there by the current until she dragged herself toward shore. Then Garwood Reese, her brother-in-law, had yanked her into the quietness of the eddy, and they clambered up to a small shelf of black basalt streaked with green slime, and began to die of cold, ice water pooling at their feet, their body heat along with it. He had tugged off his soaked boots, but she would not let him pull her shoes off.

She would depart this world. Electra Clewes Reese, born on January 12, 1820, departed November 28, 1842, along with her husband. The uncaring river churned between slopes so forested with pine that not even someone on foot could thread them.

Sleet fell lazily, but only a few hundred yards higher in the Cascades, snow was settling on pine boughs.

Convulsion rattled her jaw and chattered her teeth. Her breath came raggedly.

"Got to walk," Garwood said, trying to tug her up. "Keep warm."

"Oh, I can't. I can't!"

They weren't alone. Three rafts had capsized, leaving the living on that rocky shelf and the dead tumbling toward the Pacific. So close, so very close. Seventy or eighty miles to reach succor.

They had nothing. No flint and steel, not that it would do any good in a place where every stick and bough dripped water. All their worldly possessions were churning down the Columbia toward the sea. No food, no dry clothes, no shelter. No fire.

No one else had anything either. She felt a great sadness. Some lay so grotesquely she thought they were dead. As she soon would be. Like Warren.

Garwood Reese tried to run, the madness driving him, his clothing still spraying water, his blued feet dancing on rock, and then he groaned and tumbled to the obdurate stone, his breath irregular.

"So cold, so cold . . ." he muttered.

Electra begged her body to stop shaking. All she wanted was to command her body to stop but it didn't stop. It had a will of its own, defying her. Sleep beckoned. If only she could slide peacefully into sleep.

"Oh, oh . . ." she cried.

The Irish couple lay nearby hugging each other, hugging shamelessly, half naked, barefooted. Electra diverted her gaze elsewhere, away from the shocking sight.

The missionaries refused to touch one another, the parents huddling separately in misery, their two boys twisting and trembling with walls of icy air between each, their teeth rattling, their shoes sloshing water. The other child lay still and white on the rock, water oozing from her thin green skirts, a blueness under the splash of bold freckles across her pinched face.

Garwood Reese knew he must get up, walk, jog, flail his arms, but he couldn't. He felt a weight creeping over him. His limbs refused to work and he found himself not caring. He stood near Electra, burdened with regret.

They had warned him: if you're going to Oregon, never stop, never waste a minute, because he who tarries will be lost to the winter. It wasn't his fault: the captains had been slow. He had upbraided them for fifteen hundred miles, blistering their ears with his complaints, to no avail. No one else in the company would listen to reason, and now he and Electra were paying the fatal price for the stupidity of the captains.

God knows there had been warning enough: there would be two thousand miles of grassland, heat, desert, roaring rivers to cross, swarming flies and gnats and mosquitoes, and at the Blue Mountains the wagon road would end and nothing but pack animals, foot traffic, or boats could get through. All vessels had to be portaged around the falls of the Columbia and innumerable rapids.

The promise of a new Canaan had lured them. Land aplenty in the lush Willamette Valley, where a small colony of Americans had already put down roots. A new Zion, a new land, a chance to be in on the beginning, become an important man, organize the settlers, drive out the British, write a constitution, be appointed to high posts, lead the people to statehood. He had fancied that a title, governor, would precede his name someday. Maybe senator. But Warren had had more modest dreams: attorney, landowner, pioneer.

They were bold and ready to adventure two thousand miles ago. Now Warren was dead and he and Electra soon would be, at the very gates of Eden. His mind wasn't clear. The same force that had numbed his limbs was addling his brain. Where were they? Was there a cheerful cottage with a blazing fire in the hearth just around the bend?

Seventy miles from Fort Vancouver, but it might as well be seven hundred. The grim Cascade Mountains hemmed them in. Trapped. No one on that rocky shelf would survive to see the next dawn. He felt the last of his heat ebb from him, felt his heart clutch, felt ice in his belly, felt his pain ebb into numbness. He stared absently at the new widow, Electra, slumped on the barren rock.

Stupid. Everything that the fur traders had said was true. Make haste! By the time they had reached the desert chasmed by the Snake River, they were running out of food. By the time they reached the Hudson's Bay Post of Fort Boise, they had footsore oxen, their hooves ground to bits on the volcanic rock. They traded these for a few packmules.

They had been able to get a few supplies at Fort Walla Walla at outrageous Hudson's Bay Company prices. But by the time they reached the Methodist mission at The Dalles, which was also the end of the road, they were all worn to shadow. The mission could not help them much. So many Americans had come through. There were no boats to take them downriver.

Reese stared bitterly at the Irish couple, lying together shamelessly, trading heat at the cost of their decency. Honeymooners, he had gathered, and now honeymooning, their bodies pressed tight, warming the soaked cotton chemise that alone was sandwiched between them.

Reese stared at his sister-in-law, wanting to do just that, for both their sakes, and couldn't. So they gaped at each other, numb and shaking and dying, six decorous feet apart, a wall rising so high they could never scale it—even though he ached to.

What did it matter: in an hour or two they would all be dead, and he would never be the governor of Eden.

2

Jasper Constable quaked. The Lord had consigned them to doom, there on a rock beside the river, only a few dozen miles from help.

He did not understand the fickleness of the Lord, especially toward his own faithful followers. The Constables had been both the luckiest and least lucky of these stranded people. Their log raft, bearing their worldly goods in a wagon box, had struck rapids and careened into the tumble of rocks projecting from the shore, dumping them all into the eddying water only yards from the bank. Swiftly he had gathered the children and heaved them upward onto the wet black rock. Then the raft had twisted out into the current and vanished downriver.

All three children and Rose lived—for the moment. He himself had been less lucky, skinning his hand and bashing his head on the knife-edged rock, but eventually he succeeded in pulling himself from the water. Sleet mixed with the blood on his hand. The cold shocked him. His feet, in their soaked boots, ached.

Now they were chattering, whimpering, enduring the sleet and waiting for the night to stop their hearts.

He had wrung Rose's woolen skirts as decorously as time and place permitted, and squeezed water out of the clothing of his children as best he could. But little Damaris lay numbly, while Matt and Mark dipped and whirled and wasted their energies in their skinny bodies running from the ice demons that were stalking them.

"Be still; conserve your strength," he commanded, but they ignored him.

There was nothing he could do, at least nothing that was not scandalous. He eyed the embracing Irish couple almost enviously, but swiftly pulled back from that temptation. Better to die obedient to every command of the Lord than to surrender even one particle to the wiles of the devil. His conduct would be impeccable, even unto death.

Rose hugged herself and stared bleakly, her face white, a cruel blueness showing just under the skin. She looked at him with haunted eyes that begged for life. He could do nothing for her. Beyond the ledge, forbidding pine forests catapulted upward, dripping logs and branches, thick fern and brush, every steep step treacherous. Across the pewter river, dour dark slopes lifted into haze and then vanished. Someplace not far beyond rose the awesome Mount Hood, the cynosure of their gazes for days.

In the heat of summer on the endless plains they had jettisoned everything in their overburdened wagon to lighten the strain on the weary oxen. A hutch, half a theological library, heaps of winter clothing. Surely Rose could sew new things when they reached the Willamette Valley, or so they thought.

But now the children trembled in their cottons. Poor Mark, eleven years old, stared at him from eyes set in black holes, his mouth twisted.

"You boys sit quietly and pray to God. Don't waste energy. Damaris, you go hug your mother tight as you can."

The girl failed to move. He clambered to his feet, lifted her with aching hands that refused to function, and half dragged her to her mother's lap. Rose gathered the child into her soggy lap and stared accusingly at her husband.

"Please hug me, hug me," Rose said, tears in her eyes. "Jasper, please . . . gather us all together."

Her eyes accused him.

"Pray," he said. "Pray for delivery in our time of need."

His throat had stopped up so much he could barely rasp out his instructions. They would have to pray on their own. He could not utter one.

He was an ordained minister, but had never had a church or congregation. Theology absorbed him. He had, after graduating from Ohio Wesleyan, fashioned himself into the watchdog of the Methodists, a pamphleteer, journalist, upbraider of the straying, and overseer of faith and morals.

He had burned to go to Oregon, the place of holy mystery, burned so much that he was willing to subject himself and his family to an appalling journey through mud, cold, drenching rain, fierce heat, parched plains, sullen rivers, gnats, mosquitoes, thirst, and sleepless nights. Burned to walk across a continent to build a new heaven on earth; burned to raise a City on a Hill, far from the corrupting wiles of the world; burned with a vision so intense that the Methodist mission board could not refuse him, and reluctantly let him go.

Now they quaked and died on a riverbank ledge as the daylight began to fade. If only someone, anyone, had flint and steel, a bit of tinder and a hatchet with which to cut dead limbs in the thick forest not ten yards distant. If only someone could rub sticks together and make flame, or weave a shelter, or hollow a warm hole in the ground. If only God Himself would descend, or send an angel of mercy, or drop manna from the darkening heavens, or wash a trunkful of dry clothing from out of the river, a trunk that would be discovered by his faithful, and not those wantons hugging each other in plain sight.

"You got to help us," Matt cried.

"Pray."

"I can't stop shaking."

"Pray."

"We're going to die, aren't we."

It was not a question.

"Whatever the Lord chooses to be our fate, we must accept it."

"Why?" The boy's face crumpled into tears. He could barely talk as convulsions swept through him.

The others were watching him, too numb to respond.

That other American, Reese, stepped over. "Walk, run, don't just sit there. Do that and you might warm up. And take off your shoes. The wet shoes are worse than the cold air."

"Thank you, sir, but we prefer to trust in the Lord," Constable said.

"Use your head. The Lord doesn't object to it."

Constable glared at Reese.

Matt rose stiffly and began trotting in a small circle, around, around, his arms flailing.

"Pray, Matthew," Constable commanded.

"Look at me, Father. I'm not shaking so bad."

Rose peered fearfully at her husband, and her son, and said nothing. Rarely had a child defied Jasper Constable.

The minister closed his eyes and stilled his own shuddering body. He could feel death creeping up his limbs. The heat was out of him, his innards had lost almost all of it. His feet had vanished from his mortal coil. He could not feel them.

"We must prepare ourselves," he said. "Not a soul here will see the dawn. Tonight we will pass from this vale. I beg of you all, prepare. Repent. Make your peace with one another and with God, and surrender to him in brotherly love."

The others stared. The Reese woman, the Irish.

The air thickened in the long twilight.

Far out upon the slate waters, a lantern bobbed.

Jasper Constable watched it, fascinated. The devil's snare, false hope, trumpery.

Male voices, in song.

"Allô, allô," came the faint voice across the dull waters.

"Well, say something, Constable. I can't. My throat doesn't work." That from Reese.

"It's the devil's mischief, Reese."

Reese tried to yell, but the sound crackled and died in his throat. The woman, Electra, emitted only small sobs.

Then the Irishman sprang to his feet.

"Hello the boat! Hello the boat!" His cry had music in it. Music answering music.

A pause. The song died. The light bobbed. And then the oarsmen turned the vessel toward the north bank. Mary Kate stood. The children, all but Damaris, clambered up. Even Rose forced her body to rise.

"Hello the boat!"

Half a dozen brawny men rowed. Someone manned a tiller. The low flatboat shot straight toward the riverbank. And then, incredibly, Constable discovered a second boat, not far behind, also making for shore.

Someone was coming. Someone with fire and heat, food and comfort. God had answered his prayers. He had prayed through to victory, while all the rest had faltered. He felt a sublime and heady sanctity about him. They had been lost in the wilderness, and found.

Carefully, cagily, the swart boatmen eased the craft toward the bank, dipping red paddles into the river, a tricky business because of the tumble of rocks that could punch the bottom out of their bateau.

Constable could see they were foreigners. Some wore stocking caps. Others sported great black beards and looked sinister. But the man at the tiller was blond and stocky, and not a foreigner.

As the little craft slipped into the quiet pool created by the rockslide, two of the oarsmen nonchalantly jumped over the side with ropes in hand, clambered up the bank, and beached the slanted prow of the barge.

"Bonsoir, bonsoir," they said. "We are come, oui?"

Miraculously, they began handing out blankets, first to the children and women, and then to the men.

Constable saw they were thick warm blankets, beautifully carded, some creamy with green stripes at either end, some gray and red, some gray and black. Hudson's Bay company blankets, renowned over all the world.

Swiftly he tucked the first one around Damaris, and pulled a second one over his ashen wife and rolled Matt into a third, and Mark into a fourth, and finally drew one around himself.

The others had received blankets as well, and were huddled in them, wrapped in them, clutching them as they were clutching life itself. The Irish were weeping.

Constable felt no warmth, and yet he knew it would come, grudgingly, painfully. He stared at Damaris, hoping against hope the girl lived. Rose was fighting back tears.

Then the burly blond man stepped over the slanted prow.

"Peter Ogden here," he said in a high-pitched voice. "John McLoughlin heard you were in trouble and sent us at once. Are there any others?"

Constable shook his head.

"We were the last, as far as I know," Reese said. "Thank God for you. We owe you our lives."

The other Hudson's Bay bateau hove to, this one with another crew of voyageurs, and several other Oregon immigrants in it, snugged into their own blankets.

"Well, let's get you warm," Odgen said.

Jasper Constable had never heard such heavenly words.

3

Peter Skene Ogden felt good, even though every muscle in him ached. Pluck-ing people from the abyss did that to him. He had rescued trappers scores of times as a brigade leader for the Hudson's Bay Company. Indeed, the safety of his men was always the most important thing.

Now he visited with these shivering Yanks while his exhausted voyageurs made camp. They knew exactly what to do. Some had struggled upslope to hack enough dead, semidry limbs to feed two hot fires all night. They were only minutes away from full darkness and had to hurry. Others had coaxed a hot fire to life with tinder and pitch, and now they were setting up an iron tripod with a kettle hanging from it, and soon would be heating some beef broth.

Others of his weary French Canadians were hefting the two bateaux up to the rocky bench and turning each of them into a shelter against the sleet, using sailcloth they had brought along. They were almost as cold and worn as these emigrants, having paddled hard for a night and a day.

The Americans in the other bateau, a family of four named Brownell, the parents, a girl and a boy, who had been rescued earlier, wandered across the rock, wrapped in their Hudson's Bay blankets. They were luckier than these because they were dry. They had beached their disintegrating log raft long enough to step onto the riverbank without a soaking. Nonetheless they, too, had lost everything save what was on their backs.

Thirteen starved Yanks rescued in all, the last of the migration from Mis-souri. He did not understand them. Why did they choose Oregon, half a continent from their frontier? Why did they walk fifteen hundred miles be-yond the settlements when they could homestead on superb cropland in Io-way beyond the wide Mississippi, or nest in the lush hills of Wisconsin, raise a house and barn in the oak-dotted Illinois country or plow the mighty plains beyond the Missouri, with black loam thirty feet thick, ample rain, and a long growing season—cropland close at hand, all virgin land and there for the taking?

Why did they scorn the vast empty territories their country already possessed? What myopic vision, what madness, what odd epiphany drove them to pack up, endure unspeakable hardships, and hike to this brooding and mysterious wilderness called Oregon, far beyond their national borders? And why had they ignored the warnings of the company traders and built rafts? Stupidity or desperation, one or the other.

He knew only a fragment of the answers: Oregon wasn't a geographical place for these people, but a shimmering vision. Their Oregon was not in the temporal world. He had questioned scores of them, asking why they came so far from the settlements, and what they expected to find in Oregon. He never got the same answer, and rarely got a sensible one.

They didn't know much about the temporal Oregon and its forested wilds and rushing rivers; they saw, in mist, Taj Mahals, Egyptian pyramids, Alexandrian libraries, Camelot, the Pearly Gates, the Eden . . . Oregon was a Dream, or maybe a harlot.

Ogden squatted down on his heels, a position known to every man of the wilderness, and addressed the missionaries. "Would you like some spirits? A sip will stir the blood, drive out cold."

Constable, wrapped in the creamy wool, jerked backward. "Sir, ardent spirits will never touch our lips, nor stimulants like tea or coffee."

Ogden absorbed the rebuke and stood, wearily. "We'll have broth in a bit. It warms a body." He gazed at the too quiet girl swaddled in the blanket. "How is she?"

"We don't know, Mr. Ogden. But with God's help, she'll make it."

The Hudson's Bay factor nodded. Chances were, a girl that frail would succumb in hours to pneumonia.

"I hope so," he said gently. "You are bound for Jason Lee's mission?"

"Yes, sir, we are. I don't know what'll happen now."

"We'll be taking you to Fort Vancouver tomorrow."

"And then what?"

"And then you'll decide what to do, Reverend."

"We can't pay for this, Mr. Ogden."

"You don't need to. Dr. McLoughlin's willing to extend credit to those who can pay, or lend a hand to the needful. You may get what you need from our store."

The shivering minister nodded, his gaze upon the still, blue child.

Ogden rose, checked his busy voyageurs, who were miraculously turning the barren flat into a habitation. Sleet still drifted in but the two bateaux, durable five-foot-wide plank boats light enough to portage, were propped at an angle with canvas hanging from them to form a shelter. The Brownells were already under one, staying dry.

He found Garwood Reese shaking inside his blanket, and the blond woman, Electra, looking miserable.

"Not much warmth yet, eh?" he asked.

"We'll never be warm again."

"Let me suggest that you remove as much wet clothing as possible. We'll dry it later at the fires."

The woman looked shocked. "I couldn't do that. Not with all those dirty Frenchmen . . ."

"They're fine men, madam."

"Catholics."

Ogden slowly considered that. "They are tired, madam," he said. "Seventy miles of rowing upstream as hard as they could, in sleet, singing all the way . . . to help you. They never stopped to rest. They are brave and great-hearted men."

Reese intervened. "She just lost her husband, my brother, a scant hour ago, Mr. Ogden."

The factor sighed. "I'm sorry. How?"

"Drowned, swept away as we tried to reach shore." Reese paused. "We owe you our very lives. We will be eternally in your debt. Because of you, we have breath in our bodies. You'll forgive us if we're distraught."

Ogden nodded.

Reese tugged the blanket still tighter around his body. Not even months on the trail had reduced his paunchy belly. "What are you going to do with us?"

"Warm you first, feed you, stay here tonight, and take you down the river tomorrow."

"What's your price?"

"Nothing."

"We're destitute."

"You'll work that out with our chief factor, Dr. McLoughlin. He'll equip you."

Reese brightened. "This is not the Hudson's Bay Company we've heard so much about."

"Mr. Reese, I don't doubt that if I were to show up at your doorstep in desperate straits, you would do what you could for me."

The Yank nodded, and coughed. He would likely catch catarrh unless he got dried and warmed.

Ogden slapped him on the back. "Get out of those wet duds, man. And madam . . . do what's necessary."

She swiveled her head like an angry osprey, spraying water from her yellow hair.

Ogden pointed at one shelter. "That'll be for women. Go do it before it's too late. For your sake. You'll still have your blanket."

Electra Reese simply sunk deeper into her gray blanket and would not look Ogden in the eye.

Ogden stood again. Would they not save their own lives at the cost of some minor degree of modesty?

The Irish couple stood, wrapped like red men in their blankets, their arms about one another. Ogden sensed they were enduring better than the rest.

"Mr. and Mrs. O'Malley, my men will have good hot broth in a bit. Are you warm enough?"

"I will never be warm again," the raven-haired woman whispered.

"Oh, Mary Kate, I would dispute that," O'Malley said, and laughed.

"You'd best get out of your cold duds. It may be the difference between health . . . and pneumonia or catarrh. That shelter's for women—"

"I will do it," O'Malley said. A small smile built around his lips.

Mary Kate stared primly, her gaze shifting from her husband to Ogden.

"Are you an Englishman?" O'Malley asked.

"Canadian."

"And these are French Canadians? And is this Dr. McLoughlin an Englishman?"

"Canadian, Mr. O'Malley."

"But the Hudson's Bay Company, now, it is English?"

"It has a Crown charter, yes."

"And who runs it?"

"Governor George Simpson."

"At Vancouver?"

"No, usually York Factory or Fort William, and more and more from Montreal now."

"Is the governor about?"

"No, he's east."

"I have neglected something, Mr. Ogden. To thank you for saving the life of my bride and me. May you and this doctor who runs the post be blessed by God, and all the host of angels above, for we were dead and now we live, and we had lost hope, and now we have hope. And bless you especially, for you rescued three, not two."

Mary Kate seemed to shrink into herself with that revelation, but then smiled wanly. She was a comely woman, and not even the numbness of her flesh extinguished the brightness in her brown eyes.

Ogden sensed there was much happening inside the man's head that related to the Irish troubles, but eventually O'Malley nodded, tugged at his wife, and they crawled into one of the shelters, making mayhem of the idea of separating the sexes.

The sleet whipped into Ogden's face. A night breeze was picking up, driving needles of ice into this desperate company. The two fires wavered, radiating little heat, but that would change soon. Above, on the black slopes, he heard the whack of axes and the shouts of his voyageurs as they dragged limb after limb out of the darkness and heaped it near the fires. It had turned black, and he could scarcely see the river a few yards distant.

Orange light wavered through the camp, making the shadows bounce and bobble like clattering skeletons. Heady aromas, hot meat broth steaming out of the kettle, wafted through the air.

Thirteen Americans. Probably twelve by first light. Maybe more to bury later.

The voyageurs jabbered in French, making bold comments about the helpless Yanks, and saying things they shouldn't about the pretty Irish woman, and Ogden hoped none of the Yanks could translate. He did not rebuke them.

"Alors," said Pierre Bey, who was stirring the pungent broth, sniffing it, dancing around the small pot like a skinny dervish. He dipped a tin cup, poked a finger in it for temperature, and carried it tenderly to the pale-cheeked Mrs. Constable.

He pointed to the girl who stared upward almost lifelessly.

"Drink, drink," he said.

The woman took the cup and tried to help the girl sip the steaming broth but most of the liquid slid down her chin and neck and dripped into the blanket.

"You must drink some, Damaris, you must!" she whispered.

Ogden watched his voyageurs carry cups to the shivering boys, who gulped down the hot liquid gratefully, and another cup to the Reese woman.

"No, it's dirty," she said.

"For heaven's sake, drink it, Electra," said Garwood Reese.

"But I saw him put his finger in."

Ogden sighed.

4

Garwood Reese could not remember a worse night. None of those on the long trail from Missouri matched this one for misery. The sleet had not let up, and the next day they rose to an iron-gray world, as bleak as any he had ever witnessed.

No one had slept except perhaps the voyageurs, who seemed impervious to the insults of nature. Reese's every muscle remembered the imprint of gray rock. No soil separated his sagging body from the basaltic bed upon which it had spent the night, and now he hurt. His throat ached; his head pounded.

The sleet had formed a murderous curtain, forbidding entrance to Oregon. They had come so far, for so long, only to run into walls of half-frozen water barring passage to the promised land.

At the barest gray light of dawn, he had heard the voyageurs stir.

"Levez-vous, levez-vous," someone shouted.

The French had camped upriver fifty yards after building a hot fire against a wall of rock that would reflect the heat outward upon them. Ogden had joined them, and Reese suspected that camp had been much more comfortable than the emigrant one, even though nothing sheltered the Hudson's Bay men from the elements.

The Yanks had not segregated themselves by the sexes, preferring to huddle in family groups and endure their clammy clothing beneath the Hudson's Bay blankets. All that night Electra had clutched a blanket around her, trembling beside him, her eyes accusing him. She had not wanted to come west.

The missionary Constables had gathered in the other flatboat shelter along with the four Brownells. Reese envied the Brownells, who had abandoned their disintegrating raft without getting soaked. They, at least, were dry even if no one else was.

Reese had gotten to know Abel and Felicity Brownell on the long overland trip, and had marveled. Abel had succeeded at everything he had put his hand to in Boston, and was simply looking for new worlds to conquer, new ways to live, new things to believe.

The Irish couple seemed comfortable, snugged tight in blankets while their outer garments soaked up the fire's radiation, drying steadily. But the woman's face betrayed something bleak. Reese wished he had found the courage to dry his and Electra's garments as well.

"Levez-vous, levez-vous," bawled a Canadian, stirring the weary and miserable Americans.

Reese crawled into the dawn, feeling the icy sleet wet his face. His bones quaked.

Ogden appeared, looking cheerful.

"Up, now. Up, up! If we leave now, we'll make Vancouver before dark."

"That far in one day?" Reese asked.

"That far, Mr. Reese. It's downstream."

"Your men perform miracles."

Voyageurs were building up the fires, while others were starting some gruel heating in a cast-iron pot. There would be a hot, albeit bland, breakfast for the travelers. Pungent woodsmoke filtered through the camp, and Reese found himself heartened by it.

The Irishman, O'Malley, retrieved his and his wife's garments and retreated to the dark shelter. The man looked haggard, but who didn't? Not even those Canadians, inured to the weather, seemed comfortable.

Reese ducked under the canvas and into the shelter.

"Up, Electra."

She stared at him from her blanket, and shook her head.

In a corner, the O'Malleys were struggling into their outer clothing under their blankets with awkward good humor.

"We'll be at Fort Vancouver tonight, Ogden tells me."

Electra didn't reply. Was it grief? Weariness? Sickness? Surrender? Indifference? He decided to give her a few minutes and then carry her to the boat if that was what was required.

Over in the other shelter, people were stirring.

Then Jasper Constable appeared, staggering under the weight of a child in a blanket, staring into the dawn. Sleet dripped from his beard. The minister stumbled toward Ogden, carrying the burden.

"We need to bury her," he said.

"I'm sorry," Ogden replied.

"Didn't last the night. Rose said the girl was gone before we took to the shelter . . . she was a sweet and pure child."

Constable slowly settled the child on the wet rock.

"Have to comfort Rose," he said. "Will you take care of this beloved child in a decent manner?"

"We'll take her to Vancouver. We've a burial ground there, and you can have a proper funeral."

Constable nodded. His eyes were creped in black.

The Canadians stared. One made the sign of the cross. Reese discovered the Irish couple peering from the shelter, absorbing the news.

O'Malley approached Constable.

"It's a hard thing, Reverend. A wee little girl. Oh, the pity of it. May God watch over you, and draw her up to him. And we'll be praying for you."

The minister nodded, looking discomfited by O'Malley's tenderness. There it was, in plain view, the difference between the Irish couple and the rest.

Mary Kate O'Malley, wrapped fetchingly in her red and gray blanket, approached the dead child, knelt, and drew a cross with her finger, whispering things beyond Reese's hearing. Then the young woman prayed while the Constables carefully gazed elsewhere.

Slowly the rest emerged from the shelters, staring at the limp bundle on the wet rock. Sleet began collecting on the blanket.

Last to appear was Electra, who ignored the rest. She seemed so lost that Reese wondered if she had fled to some private landscape back East.

"It's the Constable girl," Reese said.

His sister-in-law gave no sign of understanding, not even a nod, and Reese wondered whether the woman had slid into her own madness. It had not been twenty-four hours since she had lost a husband.

The voyageurs began handing out tin bowls of steaming oat gruel and spoons. Electra declined, but Reese took a bowl and ate heartily, the hot gruel warming his innards.

"Eat now; it's all you'll get until Vancouver," Ogden said. "We'll have a noon tea stop so my men can rest, but we haven't time to spare."

Even as they ate, the French Canadians were dismantling the shelters and carrying the bateaux toward the riverbank.

The company had been uncommonly decent, rescuing them all at some cost, but Reese was not fooled. It was good business. Count on the shrewd factors at Fort Vancouver to turn all this into profits for the London company. For them, this was simply markets and cash. The more Yanks in the Willamette Valley, the more business to be done in tools, grains, livestock, and supplies.

No wonder Ogden could be so pleasant. The Crown monopoly was merely gathering in another wave of Yank serfs to exploit. Reese knew that someday he would make something of all that when he ran for office.

No one talked. This wasn't a morning for conversation. The overcast stretched endlessly west, sawing off the mountains north and south of the river, depositing snow above, and the maddening sleet below. All around them, the voyageurs broke camp, hauling packs down to the boats. Then one of them wrapped cord around the blanketed girl, tying it tightly under the somber gaze of the Constables.

Reese studied Rose Constable, seeing not the slightest sign of grief in her composed features, except for black bags under her eyes. And neither did the boys reveal the slightest sense of loss. A most admirable fortitude, he thought. Or maybe not. Would she weep if her husband weren't present?

A warm-eyed Canadian gracefully lifted the shrouded girl and carried her into a flatboat, settling the child gently near the prow, and stood, head bowed, for a moment. Ogden nodded for the rest to hurry up with their feeding.

There were no joyous boatmen's songs that morning. This time, the Frenchmen silently lifted the first boat into the gray water, holding the lines fast while the Constables and Brownells settled themselves in the center. Then the Hudson's Bay men pushed off, their red paddles flashing, and the current caught the boat and shot it westward, while the boatmen began a rhythmic stroking, their blades pulling the boat forward through gurgling water.

"Well," said Ogden, "let us be off."

The boatmen lowered the second craft into the Columbia, loaded it with a heap of gear, and then invited the O'Malleys and the Reeses to board. Electra stepped in and settled on a large canvas pack. The rough boatmen, attired in coarse wools and stocking caps, settled themselves on either side and picked up their red-dyed paddles. Ogden was the last to step in, and nodded.

"Allons, mes amis," he said.

Reese felt the frightful current whip the boat past the rocks and out into the river, and then the voyageurs began their metronomic paddling, each stroke like a heartbeat, carrying the Yank emigrants ever westward, through cruel sleet, over an iron-gray river to their destiny.

He had not intended to arrive in Oregon in a Hudson's Bay boat, indebted to the company for his very life.

5

Ogden was back. The limping clerk, Ryland, had informed the chief factor that two bateaux were even then docking on the riverfront, with several Americans.

There was a time when Dr. John McLoughlin would have hastened down the long path from Fort Vancouver to the Columbia to greet his guests. But no longer. Rheumatism stayed him. A great tiredness had overtaken him this year and some of his exhaustion could be ascribed to the Americans. Night had fallen and the late November chill discouraged any impulses he might feel to greet his guests out there, so he opted to wait.

He would receive these, the last of the emigrants of 1842, in his warm parlor. Over the years he had received amazing people in his home, some of them vicious, hostile, greedy, or plain mad. He had welcomed them all, visionaries, lunatics, spies, naturalists, scientists, and missionaries, as well as rollicking mountaineers, business rivals, and vagrants. He had entertained them all as best he could, usually delighting in that rarest commodity there in isolation, the good company of others.

He rose painfully, seeking Marguerite. These desperate people would no doubt have needs. He found her sewing in her room, a half-finished shirt held close to the oil lamp.

"Ogden's back," he said.

She nodded, poked the needle into the primrose linen, and rose. She was older than he and feeling her years. She radiated a quietness that had been won over a lifetime of absorbing John McLoughlin's mercurial moods. Marguerite smiled, her warm brown eyes revealing an ancient understanding with him, and headed for the kitchen. There would soon be Darjeeling tea and scones for the exhausted travelers if some embers remained in the kitchen range.

She plodded heavily out of the room, her stocky Cree body wrapped in purple shantung. Actually, she was half Swiss, but the white blood had vanished in her warm Indian features. She was his wife at last. Until a few days earlier, at least by the standards of the church, she had not been.

McLoughlin felt sore. The winter damp had inflamed his arthritic joints. He had not even noticed his pain until this year, when he had lost a son and was wrestling with company burdens too heavy to shoulder, and discovered his own amazing age.

He examined himself briefly in the looking glass, knowing he had a bad habit of being careless about his person. He found himself neither more nor less presentable than usual in his black broadcloth suit and gray silk stock, and beyond that he didn't care. But these days he saw pain and weariness upon his face. In earlier times he'd seen determination and an imperious will.

He heard a commotion at the gate and knew he would soon hear boots upon his porch, so he headed that way, lamp in hand, and threw open the door. The immigrants had passed the trading post and stores and were streaming across the vast yard to his house, guided by Ogden. Little did they know what a good man was guiding them, he thought.

Around a hundred Americans had arrived in the past two months and he suspected they were harbingers of mightier immigrations to come. Among the first to arrive this fall was the energetic Dr. Elijah White, Methodist missioner and leader of this splintered group of Yanks. But that was weeks earlier. These last, laboring across the yard, were the laggards, or so McLoughlin had been made to understand.

He had gotten the story from Lansford Hastings. White's imperious ways had soon fostered a rebellion in the ranks, and the company had elected Hastings as their captain. They had proceeded across the continent peaceably until they had reached Fort Hall, the Hudson's Bay post on the Snake River. Advised not to try to take four-wheel wagons further, they fell to bickering and soon the immigrants were making their own decisions, some trying to push through with wagons, and others heeding the advice they had received and turning the wagons into carts. Most had come to disaster.

And now the last of them, on the eve of December.

Ogden, looking worn, herded these people up the stairs.

"Ladies, gentlemen, please come in, make yourself warm," Dr. McLoughlin said. "My goodness, come in, come in."

They clutched their blankets about them, and McLoughlin knew that these thick, finely carded, English-made blankets had saved their lives.

"This is Dr. John McLoughlin, and he'll see to your needs," Ogden said. "I'll join you shortly, as soon as I see to the boats and my men."

The Americans gasped at the interior of the chief factor's home, graciously decorated with fine cherry and mahogany pieces shipped all the way across the seas. McLoughlin led them to his spacious parlor, noting their haggardness. These were mostly families. Why they came to Oregon he could not imagine.

"Sit down, sit down," he said, when he saw most of them hesitating. "There's nothing a little mud can do to our furniture. You must be tired. I'm a physician, and while I don't normally practice, I'll see to your ills if you have any, or have our post surgeon do so."

They settled hesitantly, still uncertain, gaunt, exhausted, desolate.

But then a thin, potbellied, balding one offered a hand. "Garwood Reese, sir, and my sister-in-law Electra. Much obliged. You and your company saved us from certain doom. All but two of us. We lost my brother, and there's been one other loss . . ."

"Oh, I am so sorry."

Gradually, McLoughlin learned the story, which he coaxed from the Brownells and Reeses first, and then the grief-stricken Constables, and lastly, the Irish couple, O'Malley was their name, who had scarcely arrived in the New World before plunging westward to pursue a dream.

He saw Marguerite appear with a tea cart. "Ah, here now, meet my wife, Marguerite, and have some tea and scones. Something warm to lift the spirits."

"No tea for us, sir," said Constable. "But we'll have a scone. Methodists, you know. No stimulants, no spirits."

"As you wish, Mr. Constable."

"It's *reverend*, sir."

"Yes, thank you. You're on your way to Jason Lee's mission, are you?"

"We were. I'm not sure we'll stay now. . . . Mr. Ogden said there would be room in your graveyard—"

"Certainly. I'll put men on the task first thing."

"We brought her with us. The cold took her. She fell into the river, and there wasn't a bit of shelter or anything dry . . ."

Rose Constable clutched her blanket and wept quietly, then ruthlessly wiped away her tears as if they were shameful.

The awkward conversation stalled while Marguerite poured steaming tea to the guests and passed the scones around, along with butter and marmalade.

Their gazes followed her, absorbing her heavy Cree features, looking no doubt for signs of savagery and finding none. What they did see was the daughter of a Swiss trader, though probably none of them knew that. McLoughlin had often watched the frank curiosity of his visitors as they studied her, or studied his part-Indian sons and daughter. She accepted it better than he did, because he was all too familiar with certain attitudes about the native peoples of North America.

"Butter! Jam! We've not seen that since last May," Reese said. "You have a dairy?"

"A few milch cows, yes. We've a small breeding herd of Mexican cattle, too few for so many people, so we rarely slaughter them."

Marguerite smiled. "Is anyone hungry?"

The Constable boys nodded. The Brownell girl and boy looked starved.

"Give me a little time," she said, and vanished into the dark regions of the great house.

"Now, is anyone in need of attention?" McLoughlin asked.

Rose Constable nodded. "A fever," she said.

The widow, Electra Reese, nodded also. "Sir, a fever takes me also. And I have chills too."

He pressed a hand to her forehead, and then to Mrs. Constable's, and found nothing very alarming.

"I'll send our post physician later if you wish. Bed rest. You're exhausted. Not much at hand but cinchona bark, and that's for intermittent fever. But we've a warm bed for you, and Mrs. McLoughlin will supply some dry things to wear, and we'll see what a night's rest brings, eh?"

"You have saved our lives, sir," Mrs. O'Malley said.

"It is only what any Christian would do, madam. I will not allow anyone to die in the wilderness if I can help it." He turned to the Americans. "And I trust that you good people would do just the same for me. A different nation, yes, but one tongue to bind us. I consider it my duty and honor to help anyone of any race or tongue."

They nodded, some dubiously.

"Mr. Constable, I'll summon Jason Lee at the mission. It's not far up the Willamette, you know, and they'll take you into their care. Shortly now, we'll put you up in our guest chambers. We have two, one for the ladies, and one for the gentlemen. Is there anything you need?"

"Only information, Doctor. What of the rest? Did they all arrive safely? White and Hastings? Did anyone die?"

McLoughlin was glad the man asked. "They arrived, a few as desperate as you are now, some ill, most without means. I believe none died, so far as I've been in-formed. The Methodist mission took many of them in and my company assisted them in certain ways. Now, a question for you. Didn't our traders warn you about the Columbia rapids? Grant at Fort Hall, and Pambrun at Walla Walla?"

"Yes, they did," Constable said.

"I asked them to warn you in the sternest possible manner. Rafts can't make it. Only boats or canoes that can be portaged. I was afraid you didn't get the message."

"We thought—"

"Yes, I heard it from the others. You Americans thought that our warnings were really meant to discourage you, get you to turn back, so they, ah, weren't taken seriously. Yes?"

Constable nodded.

"I assure you all that our traders were instructed to help you in every way they could, and provide the best advice we could offer about the perils before you. We offered every bateau and every canoe in our possession to those who came ahead of you. How much I grieve that no boats were left for you."

They stared at him, exhausted and miserable and still suspicious of the Hudson's Bay Company, in whose bosom they now rested. He did not know where this distrust came from; only that it had driven so many of these Americans to reject the warnings of the company traders as self-serving and invalid. And for their dark suspicions, they harvested misery and death.

"That brings up a question, sir," said Abel Brownell. "We've little but the clothing on our backs. How are we to survive in a wilderness?"

That was, indeed, the thorn of all thorns and a source of contention between John McLoughlin and the governor, Sir George Simpson, and the directors of the company in London, all of whom directed him in the harshest terms not to encourage the Americans, other than missionaries.

"Are you farmers?" the chief factor asked.

It amazed him that not one of these people intended to farm. Reese offered no occupation. O'Malley confessed he didn't know what he would do. Brownell turned out to be some sort of entrepreneur, but it was all rather vague. Was this last lot of emigrants nothing but misfits without a useful trade?

"And why did you come? Why are you here?" McLoughlin asked.

"Just looking Oregon over," Reese said, to the nodding of his sister-in-law.

A shrouded answer, the chief factor thought. A man with veiled purpose.

"Opportunity," said Brownell.

A business rival, the chief factor decided.

"Founding the City on the Hill," said Constable.

A religious utopian, God help us, the doctor mused.

"Because of a dream," O'Malley said.

"And what might that be, Mr. O'Malley?"

"A refuge and a hope to my people," the Irishman said, wariness in his eyes.

A bard or a poet, McLoughlin thought.

"I am always curious what Oregon means to you Americans," McLoughlin said. "And so I ask. In the morning I'll make myself available to discuss your plans, and offer assistance where I can.

"To survive here, you'll need to be flexible and resourceful. Mark my words. Oregon will transform every one of you. You'll be changed, whether you want to or not, for good or ill. You've come to subdue a wild land, but it'll subdue you. It will test you; test everything you believe in. The wilderness will put you on your mettle. You've walked and ridden and rafted to Oregon, but that's just the beginning of your journey into a new life.

"Do you suppose you've arrived in Eden? Do you suppose there'll be laughter on the hills, surcease from toil, and peace on earth? Ah! Now comes the hard part. You've arrived here with little but the clothing on your backs, but believe me, you brought your mental baggage with you and it'll weigh you down. I'll tell you what succeeds: work, work, work, night and day. That, and courage and virtue. Nothing else does. Welcome, friends. I will help you get started."

They stared at him uneasily.

6

A clanging bell summoned John O'Malley from a dreamless sleep, and after some confusion he concluded it was a breakfast gong. He and the other males had shared a humble room, while the women had received much finer quarters. The two small bedsteads had been appropriated by rank, at least as this party perceived rank, which meant that Abel Brownell commandeered one, and Garwood Reese the other.

The rest, including all the Constable males, the Brownell son, Dedham, and himself, occupied straw-stuffed ticks which were indescribably luxurious after months of bedding on hard ground.

He sat up swiftly, seeing little light in the sole window, which actually was glassed. The post breakfasted early. He felt rested for the first time in weeks, though the underlying exhaustion of walking across a continent would take months to abate.

The others stirred, tugging on their newly dried clothing brought by courteous Hudson's Bay functionaries. He stood and stretched luxuriously, feeling game to take on the world, and itching to see Mary Kate. But he swiftly realized that his entire body ached, as if it had been pummeled by fisticuffs, and his ankles had swollen.

He saw, outside the window, the rain-streaked outlines of the fort, which lay oppressed by a sullen sky. Was this how it would be in fabled Oregon? Cloudy and gloomy day after day? Perhaps he had been sold a bill of goods. All across the continent, as he and Mary Kate had toiled west on aching and blistered feet, the vision of Eden inspired him, this Oregon where flowers danced in zephyrs and a man could be anything he chose. The closer he got to Oregon, the more his heart danced, but for Mary Kate it was quite the opposite: with every footstep from Ireland, the land of her birth tugged all the harder.

He was first out the door and into the damp gloom. The others had monopolized the pitcher and basin so he would wait. A stillness lay upon Fort Vancouver. A towering stockade surrounded the post. The numerous unpainted frame buildings within appeared to be stores for grain and peltries, dormitories for the toilers, a kitchen, a chapel, a smithy and carpenter shop, bakery, washhouse, and the trading store next to the great gates. A wilderness post had to be its own city.

Most of the structures were rude, but John McLoughlin's enameled house was an elegant exception.

He discovered in the yard a wash tank probably employed by the help, and scrubbed his face, determined to wait for his wife. The other guests limped past him to a mess room, from which the heady odors of fried bacon and fresh bread reached his nostrils. He saw no sign of any women, and imagined they would eat separately, so he entered, and found himself in the company of about twenty men, mostly post employees. Judging from the leavings, others had breakfasted earlier.

He kept to himself, speaking little but listening, trying to fathom what this strange wilderness fortress was all about. He devoured mounds of sidepork and heaps of yeasty bread with churned butter and several jams and preserves and even blessed marmalade imported from England for flavoring.

Then a swart and vaguely mysterious man in immaculate black attire appeared, as if from a whirlwind, asked for quiet, and spoke to them.

"Friends, I'm James Douglas, chief trader here and second in command. Dr. McLoughlin has arranged to conduct graveside services as soon as you're done here. The Reverend Mr. Constable has asked him to officiate." He pointed. "Go out the gate and turn right."

O'Malley knew he would go out of respect, though the Constables had not deigned to traffic with him and Mary Kate.

He hadn't the faintest idea what he would do in Oregon, or how he might support Mary Kate, and for that reason had paid close attention to the post and its industries. He doubted that the powerful Methodist mission up the Willamette would assist an Irish Catholic. Nothing that he and his bride had experienced on the long trail led him to believe he would find a welcome there. But what did it matter? Surely this virgin land would offer a finer future than brooding and weary Ireland.

He drifted outside the post with the others, wondering where the women might be. The dark-bellied overcast seemed scarcely a hundred feet above his head, and he supposed it might soon rain.

And so had the women who were gathered at an open grave in a small burial ground half a mile from the great fortress, sharing two borrowed black umbrellas. His gaze met Mary Kate's searching one, and he knew she was well enough to endure this burial. He found a place beside her and squeezed her hand. The two women on the sick list last night seemed well enough this day, though Rose Constable, whose daughter they would bury, clutched her husband's arm heavily. She wore a borrowed veil. Electra Reese, widowed just two days earlier, stood unsupported and pale beside Garwood Reese.

Chief Factor McLoughlin arrived, along with Douglas, and a small contingent of clerks all arrayed in black, and somehow that pleased O'Malley. This generous viceroy of a great company had come to pay his respects to a wee girl he never knew, and for a family he had not met until the previous night. What an electrifying figure was McLoughlin; massive, perhaps six and a half feet, with a fierce thatch of white hair framing a ruddy face no man would ever forget, a face that radiated power and pain.

John O'Malley had learned a few things just by listening, and one was that the Scots-Irish chief factor, and his Cree-Swiss wife, had converted to the Roman church days before, and had their civil marriage solemnized by a priest. O'Malley did not see Marguerite, but didn't really expect to. Back a bit from the grave, two Canadians rested on their spades, awaiting the moment they would shovel the wet earth over the small, tightly shrouded child now lying in the bosom of Oregon.

It did not surprise O'Malley that McLoughlin would conduct the funeral. The bulky man settled his black beaver hat on the grass, and then stood at the dewy head of the grave, truly the White-headed Eagle the Irishman had been hearing about ever since Missouri.

"We are gathered to pay our last respects to Damaris, daughter of Jasper and Rose Constable, and to Warren, husband of Electra Reese, and brother of Garwood. Now, then, let us pray."

The chief factor opened an Anglican prayer book and began his service with that liturgy, comforting the bereaved as best he could, departing from it whenever he felt the need.

At last tears welled from Mrs. Constable's eyes and she slumped heavily upon her solemn husband. O'Malley felt a strange relief, welcoming the tears, having come to the conclusion that no public display of feeling was countenanced among those stern missionary people. Mary Kate tightened her arm about his, her thoughts the same as his thoughts about these people they had traveled with for half a year, yet who remained strangers.

He thought of that wee little slip, Damaris, eight years old, as quiet as her parents, a child too afraid of being unseemly just when life's sweet joys were bubbling within her small breast. Only Rose wept. And neither of the Reeses revealed the slightest emotion. Did Electra care so little for Warren that she could not grieve?

Each time O'Malley glanced her way, he beheld a woman locked in icy calm, her face a mask, her blank gaze settling neither here nor there, and her mein forbidding. Lord in heaven, he couldn't fathom her! If she focused on anyone at all, it was McLoughlin, and his King James Bible and Book of Common Prayer, almost as if these things didn't suit her and she was enduring them because she had to. He felt, in a moment of epiphany, that nothing at all would ever suit Electra Reese.

O'Malley allowed himself a moment of levity because he knew, somehow, that was exactly what she was feeling. Nothing measured up here in wild Oregon, and especially the newly Catholic lord of a Crown monopoly, reading an Anglican liturgy that appealed little to her godless and discontented heart.

McLoughlin was brief. In a few minutes he was reciting a last prayer, and then he closed his prayer book.

"Mrs. McLoughlin and I will receive you in our parlor," he said to the assembled immigrants.

The assemblage drifted away, and O'Malley had a chance, at last, to find out about Mary Kate's night.

"Did you sleep well, my darling?"

"Ah, John, John, it was better than a feather bed in a lord's manor," she said. "I cannot tell you how it felt."

"Who got the beds and who got the floor, Mary Kate?"

She frowned softly. "And who would you suppose?"

"I would suppose you were the only grown woman who did not."

"A thick straw tick and a real pillow, John, was all I needed. That and the blanket they have given us."

"What about the fevers?"

"A bit of sleep does wonders, my darling. The ladies are well enough."

"You ate before the men did?"

She glared. "Yes, and Electra asked me to serve! 'Bring me a plate, dear,' she says. 'I'm so tired.'"

"And did you?"

She squeezed his arm. "We are strangers in a strange land, love, and I do not mind."

"I mind."

"You are a caring man, O'Malley. And you will need all your wits about you now. There is no glass factory making crystal here, you know, and you have never held a plow in your hand."

He laughed.

They wandered through the massive riverside gates and into the post, which hummed now with life he had not seen earlier. The doors to storerooms stood open and the pungence of heaped furs drifted across the yard. He discovered various Indians from tribes whose names he didn't know, lounging about, especially on benches before the trading post.

They climbed the steep stairs to the McLoughlin house and found the front door wide open. Within, the last of the immigrants of 1842 had gathered, subdued and pensive in an alien refuge. Marguerite had filled a punch bowl and laid out pastries, which the Reeses, Constables, and Brownells nibbled.

"Ah, here you are," said McLoughlin, leaning on his black cane. "Marguerite has prepared a few sweets with some sugar from the Sandwich Islands. Whenever you're ready, we'll discuss your future."

7

Abel Brownell suspected he was quite mad. Maybe *daft* was the word, or *tetched*. Possibly *deranged* or *demented* or *lunatic*. In fact he was certain of it, though not ready to confess it to the world, and not even to Felicity.

Yes, mad as a hatter. He had only recently discovered it and was now mulling the whole business in his head. *Lunatic,* that was a good word, *peculiar, odd, reckless* . . . Ah, but *reckless* wouldn't work because that word implied that he knew what he was doing, and in fact he didn't.

Mad it must be. Only deep, advanced, incurable madness could account for his conduct. He could blame it on nothing. He was not far gone in drink, not an imbiber of opium, nor a devotee of some secret and bizarre cult. The only thing he could make of it was that his friend, the Boston ice merchant turned adventurer Nathaniel Wyeth, had gotten to him and softened his brain. Wyeth was certainly mad, and now the madness had affected Brownell.

Why would any affluent Bostonian, living in vast comfort, ditch the civilized world and drag his family to a little-known dab of wilderness across an entire continent? In Boston, he had nimbly leapt from success to success. He had been a merchant capitalist so lucky he couldn't fail. If he bought shares in a China enterprise, money poured into his vaults. If he bought into a rum or whaling venture, he profited. If he purchased shares in a cotton looming mill, he reaped a harvest.

He had a fine brick home, servants, the respect of Boston's aristocracy, health, the city's diversions, and every comfort. And yet he had pitched it away and dragged his suffering wife, and his eleven- and twelve-year-old children, Dedham and Roxanne, out of Boston Latin School and Miss Porterfield's classes and into a continental bunion-builder, through mud, ice, furnace heat, chapping wind, clouds of insects, and vile swamps. The entire family was limping.

He could not explain it. He had simply done it. That treacherous Nathaniel

Wyeth, with all his mad stories about the mountain men, fur trade, and especially the wilderness Eden called Oregon, had addled Brownell's mind. A curious thing. Wilderness, he'd discovered, was emptiness, a place forgotten by God. Better to turn the world into a garden or a Brook Farm, like Ripley's experiment back East.

Addled. Now there was the *mot juste*. Mad, perhaps, but addled, certainly. Addle-headed. Poor Felicity. No wonder she had taken to staring reproachfully at him and dodging kisses and complaining about her knees. And Roxanne, who usually worshiped him, had turned squinty and skeptical and secretive. Dedham was doing fine. He prospered and bloomed into young manhood, free of the slateboards and raspy lecturers of the brick schoolhouse, but Abel doubted that he could now spell C-A-T.

The luck of the mad. How else could he explain his safe arrival at this post after months of trudging through plains, deserts, mountains, and forests? They had stepped off a bobbing wreck of a raft onto a spit of rock, scarcely wetting a shoe, and only hours later a passing scow picked them up like a Boston omnibus en route to Beacon Hill. Only the mad could be so fortunate.

But all of that was dwarfed by the reality that now confronted him: he had never done a lick of muscular work in his life, had no trades, scarcely knew a plowshare from the rear end of a mule, and hadn't the slightest skill with which to support his hungry family. In short, only madness could explain his abysmal conduct, and so madness he must confess.

The McLoughlins circulated quietly, comforting the bereaved, offering pastries, heartening those present. The doctor was taking his time, though certainly he was a busy man. Brownell had not even known this day's date until he drifted past a fine glassed bookcase and secretary with a desk calendar on it. This day was Thursday, the first of December, eighteen and forty-two. A weekday, in which the caesar of a fur empire that embraced a quarter of North America should be about his numerous duties instead of consoling the flotsam of the Oregon road. Indeed, through much of the reception, company clerks pulled McLoughlin aside for whispered conversations and then hurried off bearing the master's decision.

About mid-morning James Douglas appeared, as suave and bland as the previous evening, and then Peter Skene Ogden too, dressed in rough outdoor wools, red-haired and clean-jawed and willful. Here were the three lords of Hudson's Bay Company's Pacific Department, each so different that Brownell marveled that they could work amicably.

Then McLoughlin summoned them all to the parlor, where he waited before a cheerful crackling hearth.

"You are in grave straits," he began without preamble. "Most of those ahead of you managed to preserve some of their goods, either portaging around the falls by themselves, or hiring Indians to do it, or by purchasing pack animals at Fort Walla Walla or The Dalles mission. About thirty arrived with nothing, like yourselves. We urge you to find means among your American brethren in Jason Lee's mission."

The immigrants were listening attentively, because life and death hung in the balance.

"I've arranged for a bateau to take you up the Willamette to the mission. I'm certain that those at the mission will see to your comforts.

"But the Methodists lack shelter, and what they have is crowded by those who arrived ahead of you. The women in particular will find such cramped life difficult."

So that was it, Brownell thought. The HBC was going to shuffle the burden of these penniless immigrants onto the mission. But there were those, like himself, not connected to the Methodists, who wouldn't go upriver. Would the company proffer a hand?

"Somehow, you'll need to get a living," the chief factor continued. "That means farming the land or raising livestock. Starting orchards. This is a fine land for that, mild and well watered, and we've found that crops flourish abundantly."

He paused again.

"Every manufactured item here has come thousands of miles from its source. Some around the Horn, some on the backs of our voyageurs from Canada, who canoe and portage amazing loads from York Factory and Fort William. These men hoist ninety-pound packs on their backs, and carry them for miles from one stream to the next. I don't know how they do it.

"Some of our goods come from the Sandwich Islands, the great commercial crossroads in the Pacific, in foreign bottoms. We have very little, and most of it necessary to trade to the Indians for peltries, which is our chief business. The prices for all goods are necessarily high, for each mile a product is carried from its source, the higher its cost to us, and the more we must ask.

"This post has grainfields and gardens and fisheries and a livestock business, and yet it scarcely feeds our people. We cannot support you. But we can do this: we can lend you some things and sell you some things. We can sell you a bushel of seed wheat for your plantings, and lend you a breeding pair of cattle long enough for you to obtain calves. We have a few plows, enough to be helpful.

"These we will sell or lend on credit. As soon as you have means, you can repay us. For now, at least, we'll accept wheat or other grains in payment, as well as pelts and certain produce. As much as I wish the company could simply meet your wants out of charity, the directors require a return on their investment.

"So what I am suggesting, friends, is that any of you who can find succor among your missionary colleagues, please do so. And the rest of you, if you wish a private interview with me, I will be in my office the rest of the day.

"One more thing: the conditions are such that some husbands may prefer to keep their wives here while they claim land, measure out its bounds, erect a homestead, and build bedsteads and furniture. The company would be honored to shelter women here at Vancouver while you men settle."

"How does one take land?" Reese asked.

"Ah, a vexatious question, sir. This is a country disputed by your nation and mine. You can claim acreage, but you will not have title. I myself have claimed land at the Falls of the Willamette, and hold it as first possessor. I'm erecting a gristmill there, and parceling up the area into city lots. We've hired a surveyor to come up with adequate metes and bounds, and I know that the mission has such people."

"What if we have no cash?" Brownell asked.

"I expect you to pay, Mr. Brownell, as honorable men must. The company has no policy permitting loans, so I carry the loans at my own risk, though it is still the company you owe. The company discourages such credit, preferring not to encourage American settlement. Governor Simpson has made that very clear."

"What does passage around the Horn cost?" he asked.

The question obviously did not surprise the chief factor. "Hudson's Bay operates several ships, and leases other bottoms, Mr. Brownell. Your passage would depend on what you can negotiate with the masters. Are you thinking of returning?"

"Perhaps to an asylum. I'm addled, sir, and if not that, then mad. That's what three thousand miserable miles have shown me. I not only have sore feet, but also cold feet."

Felicity Brownell seethed. Abel had dragged her all the way to Oregon, only to turn tail. Was this the man she had married? How blind she had been! He was a vainglorious fool without the slightest feeling about the wishes of others. Even Roxanne was upset at her father, something of a first in the Brownell family.

That afternoon the various emigrants had met privately with Dr. Mc-Loughlin to negotiate some means of survival. When it came Abel's turn, he tried to exclude Felicity from the meeting in McLoughlin's office, but she insisted on being present, speaking so sharply that he surrendered.

Unlike the chief factor's handsome home, McLoughlin's office exuded a spartan aura, and its whitewashed austerity somehow made the chief factor all the more formidable, like some periwigged cosmic judge resolving questions of life and death. Here was the very heart of empire, a plain oak desk and plain cabinets and a single window overlooking the barren yard. The post's window glass was the first she had seen since Independence. The decor was curios, Indian things such as bows and arrows, black spears, tan and ocher medicine shields. Also curiosities: a gray buffalo skull with an arrow point embedded; a curious brown antler; an odd fossil. But she sensed that in this lair great events took place, the fate of posts and forts and ships were decided; prices negotiated, receipts and losses tallied.

"Mr. Brownell, sir, if you want to catch an American coaster, your best bet is to continue south to Yerba Buena, and do so swiftly before snow closes the passes. There are mighty mountains between here and Mexican California."

"I have no cash."

"That can be dealt with. We've a trading store there, and I can give you a letter of credit if you'll give me a letter of credit negotiable upon your Boston bankers."

"Don't coasters ever come here?"

"Rarely. The currents and sandbars at the mouth of the Columbia put ships in great peril, and only the most determined masters negotiate it."

"What if we were to go to Fort Astoria and wait for a passing ship?"

"That old Astorian post is a ruin, sir. We manned it for a while, but no longer. You'd wait forever."

"I think it's our best chance. I don't know what possessed me to come here. Daft, you know. I listened to Nathaniel Wyeth and you know how he spins dreams."

McLoughlin smiled. "We enjoyed Wyeth. He wintered here, and gave us much good company."

"Credit, then, from Hudson's Bay. Thank you, Doctor. I'm sure I'll be able to reimburse the company in good time—"

"Oh, tut. Don't belabor it."

"What are the others going to do?"

"I think it's up to them to tell you, Mr. Brownell. I respect the privacy of our arrangements with settlers."

"Well, back to Boston, then!"

"No!" Felicity snapped. "You turned me into a savage, and now you want to turn me back into a Boston lady. I won't. I'm not going anywhere."

"A savage, Felicity?"

"A savage. Life in Boston wasn't good enough for you, so you decided we all needed to become savages. Well, you succeeded. No comfortable brick home on Louisburg Square, no Athenaeum to enjoy, no Latin School for Dedham, and no Harvard either. And what are poor Roxy's prospects? What oaf will she marry? No literature or ideas, because this isn't the Athens of America. No lectures by Emerson or Channing or anyone else. No Paris fashions, no serving girls or cooks or help.

"And what did we receive in exchange? The life of the noble savage that caught your fancy! A grimy ship to New Orleans. Riverboat to Independence. Then two thousand miles of walking until our feet and legs gave out. I can't walk a step without hurting. Sunburnt skin, blisters, bunions, cuts, chafed hands, headaches, nightmares, and stomach complaints.

"Two thousand miles of cooking over buffalo dung, baking our flesh in the summer sun, freezing ourselves in the mountain passes, gulping sand. Two thousand miles without a pillow or a tick, and rattlesnakes for company. Two thousand miles without a book or an edifying sermon. Two thousand miles without a bath, or privacy. Two thousand miles of rainstorms, mud, filth, rags, flies, mosquitoes, bugs and worms, and vile food.

"You decided we would become savages, and so we have. And Mr. Abel Brownell, my lord and head of the family, I'm not going anywhere. I'm not sailing around the Horn. I don't care where you go. Go anywhere. Go to the Sandwich Islands. Go to Whampoa. But I'm not going anywhere."

They gaped at her and she didn't care. Just one word out of them and she'd recite her litany all over.

Abel stared, aghast. "Do you really mean it?"

"Stupid question," she shot back.

"But how would you support yourself?"

"I'm a savage now. I can wash pots and pans. And how did you ever expect to support yourself? You've never held a plow in your hand."

"There's always something," he mumbled.

"What?"

He grinned. "My, my, you are in a temper, aren't you, Felicity?"

For an answer she stood abruptly. "I'm not your chattel, Abel. And from this moment on, I'm not your obedient wife either." She turned to the factor. "Dr. McLoughlin, I'll make my own way here. Supply me with necessaries and I'll offer my labor. I'm good with a needle. I'm a terrible cook, but I can be taught. You may employ me in any manner you choose."

For once, the formidable chief factor looked nonplussed. "Ah, ah, madam . . . this is something to think over, sleep upon, decide after you are rested and refreshed following a long ordeal, eh?"

"I've become a savage, Dr. McLoughlin, and there's nothing to think over. I've been handed to Oregon entirely against my will, and in Oregon I will live or perish."

She stormed out of the office, her temper at white heat, her worn-out body taut and fierce. Another overcast day met her, adding to her darkness.

She didn't need a night to think things over. She had just traveled for most of a year over oceans, up rivers, and then on foot until her shoes wore out and her body too. She had started slim and fashionable; now she was gaunt and windburned and rough-handed. No one had ever walked to Oregon and arrived fat.

She didn't need time, but Abel did. She'd give him a few days. If his plans didn't alter swiftly, she would sever her bonds. Yes! It had come to that! The children would stay with her; they had turned into savages too, and every shred of the Boston Public Latin School education and boarding school manners they had been absorbing all their lives had vanished. If Abel had for one moment thought beyond his own boyish dreams, he would have known he would end up with three savages!

She examined her worn brown dimity dress, her sole possession now. Maybe the trading store would have something better. She drifted across the post's rank-smelling yard, eyeing the forbidding skies, and entered the store. Half a dozen dusky Indian women shyly poked and probed among the bales of cloth, blankets, hardware, dyes and paints, and beads, under the watchful eye of a junior clerk. She thought that clerking here was something she could do if the HBC would let her. She would take out her pay in these savage goods and complete her transformation to savagery.

She fingered silks and nankeen from China, fine English cottons from Manchester, Shetland wools, American gingham, ribbons and threads. What good was any of it here? What would she do? In some chambers of her heart, her spontaneous outburst horrified her; in others, she rejoiced, even laughed. How presumptuous of Abel to inform his family one sunny day that he was hauling them all to Oregon, on the far side of a wild continent, for . . . for the sake of doing it. How dutiful had been her smiles, and what a mask! How much she had grieved the uprooting from all her beloved and familiar things, and the ordeal of travel.

If only she didn't feel so guilty. Had she been a faithful and loving wife: wherever thou goest, there will I go? Not now.

While thus musing on her fate, she discovered Electra Reese, now dressed in black linen so severe it made her blond features ethereal, almost unworldly.

"Electra! Where did you get that?"

"It's suitable, isn't it? For widowing?"

Felicity nodded. Electra Reese obviously intended to wear stylish widow's weeds.

"I found it here, cast off by Mrs. Peacock—remember her?—for some seed or something her husband needed. A few tucks did it."

"Are you well? You've borne such burdens . . ."

"I don't let myself think about Warren. At least he knew the front end of a horse from the rear, and we would have gotten along. But Garwood! He's no more suited for wilderness than a Tammany politician. But he thinks he can plat a town site and sell lots, and that's what he's up to. He's negotiated a loan from Dr. McLoughlin, more shillings than I care to think about, and he's hiring a guide."

"That's rather generous of the factor, isn't it? I mean, helping the rival?"

Electra gazed levelly at Felicity. "There's never anything generous about Hudson's Bay Company. It's all business, and they'll reap fat profits out of our misfortune. Think of the interest on our loans. That's what Garwood says."

"Well, they did save your lives . . . didn't they?"

"What did it cost them? A bit of food and some blankets. And now they have us at their mercy."

That astonished Felicity. "Would you prefer not to be at their mercy? To have died of exposure there, or starve to death here?"

Electra smiled sourly. Felicity noted the odd turn of the woman's lips, and didn't much like it.

"We Americans will have our day, that's what Garwood says. It's just a matter of time, and then we can drive these people out of the territory. There's hardly a white man in the company, just savages and mixed-bloods and French. Did you see that James Douglas? I'd bet my last shilling there's African blood in him. And McLoughlin's wife!"

"I didn't know you had a shilling to bet with," Felicity responded, but the harpoon sailed right past its target. There were savages everywhere.

She sniffed. "Garwood is going to sell lots somewhere until we can organize a government and make Oregon our own. So don't you feel sorry for Hudson's Bay."

9

Restlessly, John O'Malley awaited his turn with Dr. McLoughlin. What would a penniless man say? That he had no skill or trade other than his knowledge of glass and some accounting he'd done for his father?

Nay, he would say little of that. He and Mary Kate had a dream, and if he had nothing else to tell the chief factor, why then, a dream it would be. A man with a dream needed little else. Give a man a dream and all would follow in some natural order.

He occupied his time prowling the brooding post this dour day, feeling its power and its arrogance. This was an outpost of bloody England, but more. This man he would be leveling with was a Scottish Canadian, and the half of them hated England more than the Irish did. Last night, just at dusk, he'd heard the piper and could scarcely believe his ears. The rest of the immigrants were in McLoughlin's parlor, but he had ducked out a moment to see the sight. Sure enough, slowly pacing the stockade in the dusk was a Scot with a bagpipe, wailing an evensong that shot wildflowers and ice through O'Malley's soul.

A clerk found him. "Dr. McLoughlin will see you now, sir."

"Good. Have you seen my wife? I want her with me."

"It's not necessary, sir. A man's business—"

"We have a dream," he said. "I will find her and report directly."

A minute later he opened the massive door to the chief factor's office and found it plain, a fine reflection of the wild-haired man who occupied a wooden chair behind an orderly desk.

"Mr. O'Malley . . . and Mrs. O'Malley, please come in," McLoughlin said. The factor rose, towering a foot higher than the Irishman. Were it not for those amiable eyes, O'Malley would have felt fear crusting around his heart like rim ice on a pond.

"Are you comfortable? Do you have any needs?" McLoughlin asked.

"We are comfortable." O'Malley settled his bride in one chair and he took the other. He had been preparing for this and knew just what he wanted to say. "You saved our lives, sir. Without your timely help, we would be wolf carrion now, and the dreams gone. So we've come not to ask, but to offer. A life, sir, two lives, nay three lives, if you know what I mean. So we will repay you, Mary Kate and I. The true accounting for three lives is not possible, but we have decided to place ourselves in your service for two years if you will have us."

McLoughlin stared, astonished. "What are you saying?"

"Indenture us, sir, for the payment of a priceless gift, which is life, love, hopes, and dreams. We sit here now, alive and well, entirely due to your charity and diligence."

"Any good man would have done as much, Mr. O'Malley. Do not even think of binding yourself to the company for that."

"But we owe you for our very lives."

McLoughlin peered down that eagle beak of his. "You can repay us in full if, in the future, you will offer the same help to others. That is the sum total of your obligation. It is Christian charity, Mr. O'Malley, which binds civilized men everywhere, and especially here. I'm sure you'll be called upon."

"I will assume that burden as an obligation, sir."

"Well, good. Now what about getting a living?"

"I have no great skills or trades, sir. I know glass, but what good is that here? My father had a crystal glassworks in Waterford. Cut-glass goblets, tumblers, vases, dishes. I helped him, and did some books, and oversaw it all when he was not about."

"Glass," said McLoughlin. "The rarest treasure here. We have no glass. Every window in this post was fashioned in England and shipped around the Horn, with twenty percent loss. Glass, man, can you make glass?"

O'Malley laughed. "Make it? Here? I know how, but where is the silica sand, the crushed lime for flux, the coal and a brick furnace, just for starters? It takes a large works, sir."

"Yes, yes, of course. Well, what have you in mind?"

"Land, Doctor. The land is all snatched up in Ireland and carved to miserable pieces, and there are a dozen hands wanting a slice of every potato. Who can fill bellies on half an acre? Land, and a place without lords, sir. A place where humble people have a chance. A place not all eaten up by the grasping titled and the rich. A place to practice our faith, raise a family, be secure. Do you know, sir, that schools for Catholics are illegal? Only the Protestants have them. They keep us dumb, sir, to keep us under their foot.

"I swore when we set foot on that brigantine, I would do whatever it takes, learn what needs learning, master whatever trade that would earn our keep. I have never held a plow, and never harnessed a mule, and never owned a horse, but I would master all that for the dream. We will have green meadows, and sheep, and a big white house, and room for the babies, and gardens, and garlands of flowers, and a fine carriage, and a harpsichord and good company and a little ale."

The chief factor absorbed all that pensively.

"There will be no lord's spies seeing if our religion is right and if our shilling is true, and if our land is something they can steal. That's what Oregon is. A place where they do not spy on a man or throw him in jail if he tells his landlord the rents are too high, or ship him to Van Damien's Land if he steals a cabbage to feed his starving family. And no more cunning estate laws that favor the Protestants, and disinherit a Catholic son.

"There is a dream, Mr. McLoughlin. And there is more. When we have a little, we will bring others. We will send some money back, pay the rents of the desperate, start little outdoor schools, give what we can to our friends and neighbors . . . and settle them here."

McLoughlin sat stock-still, unspeaking, his brow furrowed.

"No young man dreams in Ireland, Doctor. You cannot have dreams there, not if you are Irish and Catholic, and if they hear you dreamin' they will come after you for your dreams. Here it is no crime to dream, to think of better tomorrows, to own some land that no one on earth can take away—"

McLoughlin raised a hand. "Ah, Mr. O'Malley, there's not a holding in Oregon that might not be ripped away from us. It's ungoverned land. England claims it and so does the United States, and it's not settled who'll get what. Now, I'll tell you this much. If you want land, and you don't want to be a subject of the Crown, you'd better stake it south of the river, because we're pretty sure that's where the line will be drawn."

O'Malley smiled. "A subject, never. A citizen, yes. Forgive me, sir, but we will not live under the Crown. Now I will tell you the rest of it. We are not going into debt. Not ever. These other people, they have borrowed from you, they are beholden and that makes for bad relations. You know the worst thing about Ireland? Debt. A man scratches the earth and never earns enough to pay his rents to his lord, and each year he is worse off than before, and when he dies his wife and babies are put out of the cottage, and everything is taken to pay that debt.

"I come from one of the few families in Ireland not ridden with debt. No lord's land agent came tapping on our door demanding rents. No lord's bullies swooped down on us and threw us out of our house. Ah, but I saw it aplenty. My father and mother, they helped our kin. Most of the men in our factory, they were kin pitched out of their crofts because of perpetual debt. Always some lord, or his manager, demanding shillings and pounds until they broke a man and then another. So, sir, we will not sign an agreement for a shilling. We will work for our food. Mary Kate can sew, and I can do most anything a post needs done."

McLoughlin nodded. "That's admirable, Mr. O'Malley, but debt's not a bad thing. It's the capital you need to start a business. You can't just start a business out of nothing, *ex nihilo,* as the Latin has it. You'll need something. If you don't accept some sort of help, if only to buy a plow or nails or planks or a draft animal, then you'll just deny yourself that dream."

"Not a farthing, Doctor. Not a bloody pence."

The chief factor sighed. "May I remind you that you've nought but the clothing on your backs . . . and two blankets?"

"We need no reminding. And we will pay for the blankets."

McLoughlin shook his head. "You needn't."

"We will. How, I don't know. What we are hoping, sir, is that you will board Mary Kate for a while, while I go roaming. The land is free! They told me I could stake a square mile; that is what the American Congress is talking about."

"Yes, and before they have possession of the territory," said McLoughlin dryly. "But Canada will probably recognize all claims in much the same fashion. Go stake your land."

"I can sew," she said. "I can keep house. I can cook."

"You don't need to do that to stay here, Mrs. O'Malley. We'll enjoy you as our guest."

"Then we will go elsewhere," she said. "We would not be indebted."

"And as for me, put me on day wages," O'Malley said. "A woodcutter? A laborer? Say the word. And when I have enough for an outfit, we will go look for our Eden."

"There's no paradise in Oregon, sir. Wolves, catamounts, frosts, rot, cold, rain . . . and some mean people."

"The paradise is the dream, not the reality, Doctor. It is in the dreaming that life is good."

McLoughlin stirred. "I'm going to *give* you a kit, including those blankets. All these Yanks, they've emptied our shelves. Wheat, plows, horses and mules, cattle, hogs, fruit, apple trees, saws, hammers, nails, planes, chisels, preserved salmon, weapons . . . We've drawn up a few contracts, and soon we'll see, we'll see . . . I am trusting them. I have little choice but to trust them. But if my judgment is bad, it'll be the ruin of me."

O'Malley saw that McLoughlin wanted to help. Very well, then. Help was one thing. Debt another.

"We will accept a kit, sir," he said.

"Good. And there's no monetary obligation whatever. You won't owe a pence. Just help others as you've received help. Is it agreed?"

"God bless you, sir. I will take a small outfit and head up the valley to claim some land."

McLoughlin scribbled a note to the clerk at the company store, and stood. "There's one small obligation, Mr. O'Malley. You must agree to tell me before next winter how it all worked out."

10

DECEMBER 4, 1842

It satisfies me that I have, again, had the honour of being the instrument of salvation for a number of people who might otherwise have perished. I wonder how many lives have been spared by the prompt attentions of the Company to their distress.

Now, it appears, this year's migration is over, and a hundred or so Americans are fanning through the area finding means to survive. This last group seemed the most ill-fitted for the wilderness, and no doubt their ineptitude was the reason they straggled in behind the rest.

Most of the hundred have gone up the Willamette to Mission Bottoms, finding succor in Lee's establishments. Some of the more able managed to arrive here with their goods intact, having portaged them and their boats around the falls, The Dalles, and other rapids. But even these sought loans and goods from the Company; seed wheat especially, but plows, harnesses, draft animals, cattle, nails, timbers, boots, and other gear. And I have supplied them, though I vex the directors and governor by doing so.

I both welcome and fear the Americans. For the most part they are good and honourable people with high purpose. Yet I fear them too, because their settlement is inimical to the Company as well as the Crown. I am helpless to stem the tide, and can only take what small measures avail themselves to further our interests.

Why do they come here? They arrive without the slightest grasp of the nature of Oregon. But something drives them. Is this a Promised Land, the Canaan of their imaginations? Is this a misty place beyond the western horizons where the curse of Adam is suspended and the lion will lie down with the lamb? I cannot get an answer out of them.

They have pursued a chimera, fragments of nonsense peddled by that mountebank Hall Kelley and others, bits and pieces of fluff they have worked into a Golconda. But that doesn't explain it either. At bottom, I cannot explain to myself why they abandoned all they knew and headed here. Consider Abel Brownell, a gifted financier who threw it all over, and dragged his family into the wilds. Why, why, why?

I steer them southward on the assumption that the Columbia will someday divide British America from the United States. So far, I have successfully discouraged settlers from heading north, though I am helped in that enterprise by land less fertile or well watered until one reaches Puget Sound and our plantations there. I've tried to reserve all that for the Company. Meanwhile, I've employed a surveyor to plat a town site at the falls of the Willamette. When he's done we'll sell lots. Since Oregon is in dispute, title will be shaky, at best.

Simpson upbraids me with every express about helping the Americans, and reminds me that the directors in London are quite adamant against it, apart from assisting the missionaries. And I reply, as always, that I do what any Christian man must do: rescue the travelers from certain doom and give them the means to survive in a wilderness that is no Eden. The directors give me no answer, not wishing to be on record as neglectful of human life or opposed to saving mortals in peril.

But it is as if my reply goes unheard, and they tax me with dire warnings that I imperil the Company and verge on defiance. Thus has arisen a great tension, one of several festering now, between me and the Company, and I wonder how long I shall remain at this post.

What is clear is that I undertake this ordinary charity at my own risk. I draw up a simple contract for these Americans: we will supply goods at such and such a price, and they will repay as swiftly as possible when they have broken sod and reaped harvest. The language empowers them to pay us in wheat or other grains, or with other products such as hides or sawn lumber. I have decided to trust them and believe the best of them.

I am particularly anxious about foodstuffs because even the cultivated fields about the post will not suffice to feed our own complement as well as starving settlers. So every bushel of wheat or plow or harness I proffer to them I deem essential to the survival of us all.

They protest the prices, and not even my explanation of the difficulty of bringing manufactured goods to this outpost in a wilderness suffices. And they protest as well our use of the imperial bushel, which is slightly larger than their own. It does no good to remind them that when they received a bushel of seed wheat, it was an imperial bushel and more than they had bargained for, thus increasing their plantings. But all this I endure amicably, for the sake of peace and neighbourly conduct.

I am sore troubled that this burden is my own to bear. Jason Lee's Methodists are honourable, and I have already received partial repayment from those few hands who came here earlier. But that crowd he brought in around the Horn last year—the Great Strengthening, he calls them—those are another story. Like the rest, they drew heavily on the Company for essentials and have fanned out in the valley to stake their 640-acre claims, which is what they believe will hold if and when their government comes into possession.

A certain Reverend Waller, who arrived in that company last year, supplicated me for the cut timbers I had stored on our claim at the falls of the Willamette, so that he might build a mission store. I granted him his wish, desiring in all ways to further their godly work among the Indians. But now the man has erected his building on Company property, and the matter is vexatious in the extreme.

I intend to hold the land for myself, if not HBC, and have made considerable improvements on it to strengthen the claim. Oddly, I get no satisfaction from Jason Lee, and find the matter worrisome. In a vast and virgin land, could they not select some other site?

I have, so far, lent the Americans about two thousand pounds' worth of grain and goods, and that liability weighs heavily on my shoulders. To some small extent it weighs on Douglas and Ogden, who have occasionally authorized the sale of goods from the store to needful immigrants entirely on credit.

Just what Douglas feels about all this rescuing of Americans is well concealed from me by his bland manner. I fancy that I could do something that would utterly offend or alarm him, and yet learn nothing of his private thoughts, because he lives so totally behind that inscrutable visage that he is unknowable. Ogden is more open.

Like me, he deplores the influx of Americans, but he is an honourable Christian gentleman and would do as much as I to relieve misery and foil the Reaper.

There are now well over two hundred Canadians and Americans living in the Willamette, and the best farmland is already gone. I don't know what these new migrants will do. Our retired employees and their families are well established on Frenchmen's Flat, and have the best land in the area. I hope that is not a source of future friction, especially if that country should go to the United States.

These last few seemed an odd lot, the first of the Yanks I am not comfortable with. I interviewed Constable at length, and discovered a man of the strictest theological view, intent upon erecting some sort of Utopia, a sort of Paradise insulated from the wicked world by a thousand miles of wilderness. I pity him and his wife the loss of a beloved child, and hope that in some small way we have eased his misfortune. I sent them at once up the river to Lee's mission on a company bateau after supplying them with coats and some small provender against the December cold.

I assigned half a dozen voyageurs to the trip, certain that the immigrants would not know how to portage the boat around the falls. I will wait and see about the man. Something about him stirs caution in me, and I would guess it is a barely concealed loathing of Catholics. Such a man could bring grief to our retired French Canadians, at present so comfortable in their farms and holdings.

But the Reverend Mr. Constable worries me less than Reese and his sister-in-law. I ended up lending the man a large sum so that he could stake out a town site—I hope somewhere well removed from the Company's—and sell lots. I had the sense that Reese engages in business only by necessity, and that his real intent is to heat up the passions of the Americans—no doubt against the British—and agitate for United States territorial status. He paid but scant attention to what we were doing for him, or the cooperation he has received from the Company. He will require looking after.

Electra Reese is a handsome woman, I must say, but with the soul of a goldfish. I could not help but notice the dark stares directed toward our people, including Marguerite. I heard no thanks from her for the small matter of saving her life, and I imagine she believes it was only her just due. Ogden tells me the woman declined even to drink some broth she found contaminated by a thumb of one of our Canadians. What a pretty pair those two make. I only hope I am witnessing nothing but her natural grief at losing her husband, and not an intolerance directed toward others because of their beliefs or flesh.

I should like to have known her husband, Warren. I looked in vain to discern grief in her face, or in her conversation, during the memorial services and after, and am frankly wondering what sort of woman she is, and what sort of man he was. Well, time will tell.

And the Brownells. A plunger for a husband, but Mrs. Brownell shows courage and mettle and a fine-honed temper too. He wanders about, unsettled in his mind, while she is making herself useful to our women, sewing and cooking and cleaning pots. That is a great decline in her natural station, but I admire her all the more for her industry. I'll offer our hospitality to Abel for a while, and if he comes to no good I'll make sure he ships out.

Brownell strikes me as a romantic chock-full of absurdities, but Felicity's grasp on reality is obdurate and strong and shrewd. Already he is grumbling about the quarters we've assigned him. They are rude enough, all right, but he has shelter and food, along with his children and wife. Meanwhile, he, too, has borrowed a goodly sum for necessaries.

Still, this account is not all gloom. The O'Malleys have fled an oppressed land with little more than a dream, and a very fine dream at that. Unlike the rest of this lot, they're willing to work. I'd wager that John will find a splendid piece of bottomland, and the two will build the dream that has inspired them ever since they set foot on a barque for the New World.

Mrs. O'Malley is here, of course, helping our people when she can. She is not at home here, and seems lonely and lost, and it is plain that she finds all of us guilty of the crime of not being Irish. O'Malley left with the others for the Willamette Valley. I hope he acquired enough survival lore on the long Oregon Trail to keep himself out of trouble. I'd bet on it.

I thought to confide my other burdens to this sporadic journal, not least my mounting anger toward Governor Simpson, but that will await some other day. I will not cease until the murderers of my son are brought to justice and the directors are apprised of Simpson's unconscionable treatment of the whole affair.

11

Rose was disconsolate and Jasper Constable didn't know what to do about it. She huddled in the bateau, her blanket tight about her, staring into fog. She had been like that ever since Damaris had passed from this vale.

He leaned toward her with earnest concern.

"Let us rejoice that the child is safe in the bosom of God, and not let grief overwhelm us," he said.

She nodded. "You are so strong," she said.

"We shall be comforted," he said. "Who are we to question the wisdom of God?"

"But Jasper . . . I'm not questioning. I'm so lonely for her . . ." Her worn face was crumpling and she looked ready to weep.

"Rose! Don't!"

She smiled wanly. "Whatever you say, Jasper."

He dreaded a scene, with unseemly tears. But she calmed herself, somehow, and he ventured to believe he had narrowly averted public mortification.

The swart voyageurs pulled their red paddles with fine metronomic rhythm, driving the Hudson's Bay Company flatboat up the bends of the Willamette River. At odd intervals they chanted some French boatmen's song to spur themselves along, their bodies bending to the task. Constable was grateful he could not translate the words, which he suspected were impure.

"Soon we'll be there, my dear, helping Jason Lee with his great work."

"I wish we hadn't come," she mumbled, so softly that no one else heard.

"We have two stout sons."

"Yes," she said, and then smiled bravely at Matt and Mark. "But the loss of one diminishes us all."

"Damaris isn't lost! She's the littlest angel."

"Oh, Jasper, I'm sorry to be so . . . faithless," she cried. She pressed her eyes shut.

That was good, he thought. She was listening and open and receptive. He nodded to the boys, who were observing alertly.

The Constables were not the only passengers. Before them sat that heathenish Garwood Reese, who probably had never seen the inside of a church, and the slouching Irishman, O'Malley, full of Romish superstition and bad doctrine. Let them listen. Maybe they would get a lesson in faith, or their souls would get a good birching.

Constable stared at the dark landscape, bleak in the snowless winter. Was this the fabled land of milk and honey? Someone had been exaggerating. The Reverend Mr. Lee was a man of great probity, so it must have been some of his followers, men of softer clay, who painted landscapes of some unearthly paradise where the sun shone perpetually except for brief rains, and the soil begged for seed, and a man could wear shirtsleeves almost all year.

"Rose, I've been weighing matters." Weighing was a better word than thinking, and it always evoked a certain acquiescence in her, so he used it frequently. "You know, if the Hudson's Bay Company had been more diligent and aware of its duties we would still have Damaris with us."

Rose looked doubtful. "I think they tried," she said, tentatively.

"No one at Fort Hall or Walla Walla warned us about the rapids. I remember that loathsome trader, the one with the French name, Pambrun, I guess. He just shrugged when we asked. Said he had lent his two flatboats to the emigrants ahead of us, and we'd have to find other means."

"No, Jasper. Quite clearly he warned us. We would have to portage around dangerous rapids and falls. There were Indians who'd help, for a price. I heard him. We were all standing there in his store. He said he'd already lent his boats and sold his horses to those who arrived earlier. That's how the others got through. With those bateaux, like this one. He talked about canoes, maybe getting some from the Indians."

"I don't recall it."

She seemed to shrink beside him. "Maybe my memory is flawed," she said, fading into weariness again. "I don't know. Ever since we lost Damaris . . ."

She was being dutiful. He had scarcely known her to resist his gentle leading, and that was her crowning virtue. She was a true helpmeet, a pious and virtuous woman, loving and reserved, subordinating her will for the well-being of the family, well fit to be a minister's spouse. Now he would draw her away from the sentimental weakness that had afflicted her.

Others were staring but he didn't much care. The French voyageurs wouldn't understand a word anyway. They paddled in unison, propelling the boat in small hard surges against the relentless downstream flow, toilers possessing admirable muscle but nothing more to offer the world. He was glad there were some brutes about to spare him the pain of hard labor.

The Irishman stirred, and soon was presenting his face to the Constables instead of his back. "I think the company did all it could, and did it without a second thought," the man said. "Peter Ogden told me that the moment the doctor heard of us—that very moment—he put his men to the rescue. They paddled a night and a day to reach us, never stopping except to rest their limbs. What more can we ask?"

Constable didn't know whether to respond or not, and simply sniffed.

Reese turned, and added his observation. "Oh, yes. They tried, more or less, so no one could fault them. Made all the right motions, you know. Stiff upper lip, help the poor devils. Appearances are everything for the English."

He eyed them solemnly.

"Here's the straight of it. It's a calculating company. It's not charity that inspires them but profits, fat profits, twenty percent a year, year after year. And what does that require? Markets. People to sell to and buy from. Now McLoughlin might put a fine lofty veneer on it, Christian charity, mercy, salvation, but dig a little and you'll find some good old John Bull avarice. Ah, yes! Avarice! That's all it was. Rescue the Yankees, put them in debt, and sell them goods at preposterous prices, and collect praise while pocketing the booty."

"No, sir," said O'Malley.

That was all. He didn't argue. The Irishman simply sat there resting his case on pure assertion. *No, sir.* Well, what could one expect? Just off the boat.

Constable thought the man was a simpleton. Reese had the better grasp of things. Commerce, cold commerce.

"I shouldn't have tried the raft," O'Malley said. "Mary Kate and me, we didn't have much, nothing we couldn't have portaged around the fast water with a few trips. I don't blame the company."

"You didn't lose anyone," Jasper Constable retorted.

O'Malley nodded. "Losing a wee girl's a terrible thing," he said. "We've prayed for you and for the sweet child."

Prayers uttered by rote instead of from the spirit, and from the likes of O'Malley, would not move God an iota, Constable thought. What good did the Romish think they were doing, uttering the same prayer over and over like some clockwork machine? Boring God? What did they hope to do? Wear Him out until he gave in?

They came upon a goodly river rushing in from the east, where the country lay flatter than the rising slopes of the western bank, and the voyageurs fought rapids that jarred the flatboat.

"Clackamas," said a burly boatman, pointing. "Soon, the falls."

The roar reached their ears before the sight of the horseshoe-shaped falls of the Willamette. The boatmen steered the bateau toward the near bank as the tumultuous water boiled underneath the little scow.

"We portage now," the man said. "You carry, eh?" He pointed to their few goods, mostly items purchased from the company store.

The voyageurs pinned the little vessel tight to shore while the passengers stepped onto a much-used landing. Constable helped Rose out, and the boys gathered up their goods. Then the burly boatmen, knee-deep in icy water, lifted the flatboat out, turned it over, hoisted it up, and carried it on their shoulders, a feat that amazed the Yank observers. Cheerfully, they manhandled the flatboat upslope to a point above the cataract.

They could see some structures on an island, and a building on the riverbank.

"Hudson's Bay gristmill. Dr. McLoughlin building it," the warm-eyed voyageur said, as the rest settled the bateau in the quiet river upstream. "Zat cabin, on ze island, zat was a carpenter the bourgeois make to leave because zis is company land. Zis here, Methodist store, yes? Now zere are lots, see, many stakes in the ground. All company land, some people living here already. Ze bourgeois, he calls it Oregon City but the Yankees, they call it ze Falls."

Reese hiked around, looking at the staked lots. The town had been plotted on three levels, separated by sharp cliffs. "Who owns this? The company? What right have they? This land doesn't belong to anyone."

The voyageur shrugged, suddenly guarded.

"How did they get this?"

The voyageur struggled for a word. "Preemption," he said, suddenly pleased with himself. "Zey make first claim. You can too."

"What if I want this? McLoughlin's a foreigner, not an American."

The boatman smiled, turned to his work, and soon the craft was readied above the falls.

"How far now?"

"Dans la soirée," the boatman said.

Soon they were being propelled once again against a swift current. The gray hills to the west looked forlorn, and except for the passage of a few honking ducks abrading the lonely silence, the world seemed empty. A vast plain ran eastward, and Constable believed it was Frenchmen's Flat, where Hudson's Bay men and their families had been allowed to retire on small holdings by the powerful company.

"A monopoly, that's what it is," Reese said. "They arrived here and preempted everything of value. There's a fortune to be made at that falls with a milling company. If this is good wheat land, think of what a gristmill could earn. But the company snatched it from us. The company grabbed these flats ahead of us. Frenchmen's farms, and by what right? Nothing but the arrogance of a commercial enterprise holding a Crown monopoly. Well, some day we'll fix that." Reese peered hawklike at the passing shore, plainly assessing the worth of the country.

Then suddenly he turned. "How much are you in debt to the monopoly?" he asked Constable.

"Considerable. I have four people in my charge. We've our blankets, and sundry other items I selected for our survival, and it came to fifty pounds. I don't know what that is, American."

"Over five dollars to the pound. And you, O'Malley?"

"I don't owe a cent except for the blankets, and Mary Kate's working us free of that."

"You didn't shop in the store?"

"I have this," he said, pulling his thick blanket about him. "It will do."

Constable couldn't imagine how. A man needed more.

12

In that bleak twilight John O'Malley discerned that the Methodist mission on the right bank of the Willamette was more than a church and schoolhouse; it was a settlement mostly built of sawn wood. Fallow grainfields, slumbering through the mild winter, surrounded it. If there were mountains eastward, he could not see them in the December haze.

The passengers hastened toward the complex but O'Malley lingered, nodding occasionally to the silent boatmen. They were the outsiders here. He wanted to take his time, absorb what might be absorbed, understand all he could. The voyageurs doffed their knit caps, piled into the Hudson's Bay vessel, and paddled quietly into the current, singing their way north, going home with the flow of the river. The songs had somehow ceased during the upstream leg.

Here is where virtually the entire overland party that year had come. This was American soil, or so they thought. And it was good soil, a rich dark loam that promised heady yields of wheat and oats and barley and maize, as well as plentiful garden vegetables. And this wasn't the whole of it. The Reverend Jason Lee was building an entirely new mission complex farther upstream, at Chemeteka, where already a saw- and gristmill operated and farms were staked out.

There were paid jobs here. The mission employed mechanics and carpenters. A man could earn something, get ahead. With some patience, a man could go as far as he wanted. They had passed the sleepy crossroads of Champoeg, and he had seen the Catholic mission there, St. Paul's, which served the French Canadians. But he had not stopped. He did not wish to donate his labor to the fathers or live in a slumbering village.

So he had come to the Methodists with a boatload of Protestants. He identified the squat schoolhouse and the prim church, and some residences, but couldn't discover the purpose of other buildings. He saw no Indians, and wondered where they might be. He had picked up hints about that. Lee, over the years, had concluded that the Indians first must be civilized before they could fathom Christian religion, and was now bending the mission to a new purpose: serving the spiritual and physical needs of white American settlers.

Something here impressed him. In this quiet outpost he sensed a sacred task. It shone in the sturdy but unadorned buildings, in the harmony, in the simple church. He even saw it in the naked trees that adorned and shaded this place. This was no castle, but a place given to God, and given as well to Indian children.

He wondered if he would feel the same way a few months hence. He thought he might. This was a Protestant version of a monastic society; nothing but dedication and sacrifice could bring these people two thousand desperate miles, across rivers and mountains and deserts, to minister to the savage tribes.

Of people O'Malley saw plenty, some of the men at work on a new structure even in the last light of day. That encouraged him. Any able body, even an Irishman with few skills, could find gainful employment here where labor was so scarce. He lingered at the riverbank a while, simply observing. A comfortable and well-adorned clapboard house he took to be Lee's. A barracks affair which probably held single men. There would be quarters for single women, or those separated from their men temporarily. He discovered a communal kitchen and mess hall, and a dormitory probably intended for Indian children who could not simply walk home, schoolbooks in arm.

Best of all, he spotted many a person he had come to know on the long weary trail. He could name names, address people familiarly, maybe find work among them—if they would traffic with the alien in their midst. Even now, Reese was gadding about, shaking hands, renewing the Oregon Trail bonds he had fashioned for two thousand miles.

Well, if he wanted dinner and a roof over him, he had better proceed. He wrapped his red Hudson's Bay blanket tight and wandered toward what appeared to be an office, or headquarters, or perhaps a rectory. He wasn't sure how Protestants named things.

He approached a hurrying man, roughly dressed and unknown to any barber.

"I am looking for the Reverend Lee," he said.

The man looked him up and down. "There, in that office," he said. "What is it you want?"

"Employment."

"What can you do?"

"I kept books, oversaw men in a glass factory . . . I will do whatever is required. Chop wood, nail up boards, saw planks . . ."

The man looked dubious. "Carpentry. We need that. Go talk to the missionaries. I'm Cal Tibbetts, the mission mechanic, and I need anyone I can get. We've much to do. Where are you from?"

"I am John O'Malley, Waterford."

Tibbetts squinted. "I thought so. Well, good luck."

O'Malley mounted rough stairs and entered a quiet building, asked again for Lee, and was directed to a doorway.

He knocked, though the door stood open.

"I am looking for the reverend," he said.

"I'm Lee." The rawboned man staring intently at him exuded energy and strength. From his narrow-set eyes, parted by a long thin nose, he seemed to absorb everything knowable about O'Malley.

"I am John O'Malley, sir. I came west with this year's migration. I am looking for work."

"Ah, yes, the Irishman. I suppose your wife's at Vancouver?"

"She is, sir."

"We're desperate for skilled labor. What can you do?"

O'Malley grinned. "Whatever I set my mind to. Would you like some crystal goblets?"

Lee paused only a second and then laughed. "So you've come to work in the mission. You're healthy after the long walk?"

"Stronger than ever, sir, if you do not count my blistered feet and a felon on my finger."

"Sickness decimates us here. Exhaustion. Half of our newcomers lie abed."

"I talked to your mechanic, sir, a Mr. Tibbetts, and he—"

"He kidnapped you on the spot."

"Very nearly, sir."

"We're Methodists and our mission is to the Indians." There was question in his voice, things unspoken.

"I plan to stay a while, save what I can, and make my own way with my wife, sir. Claim some land. I am looking for a position."

"All right. If you work out, you have employment. We'll see about that. I've no place to put you. Well, ah, perhaps there's a place. With the Indian boys. There's a spare bunk or two. You may eat with them. They're fed separately, of course. Fifty cents a day, six days a week, Mr. O'Malley?"

"Sixty cents."

"This is a mission, built on sacrifice and love of the Good Lord, Mr. O'Malley. Funds are desperately short."

"Well, my good reverend sir, supposing it is fifty cents cash, three American dollars a week, but ten cents a day credit toward timber or wheat or whatever produce you might have about that I can claim in the future."

Lee smiled and nodded. He was not a harsh or narrow man, O'Malley thought. He'd find plenty of hostility here, but not in this good and energetic soul.

"First of the month is our payday."

"Day labor, sir."

"But we don't have coin. There's no legal tender here."

"Then a receipt each day."

Lee nodded, not happy.

"I'll have our schoolmaster, Solomon Smith, settle you. And tomorrow you report to our mechanics."

Lee stood, and the handshake was hearty.

Moments later O'Malley found himself being escorted through the dusk to the austere Indian dormitory, and shown an empty wooden bunk with a straw-filled tick. "Here's where you put your duds, Mr. O'Malley."

"I have none, Mr. Smith."

"None at all?"

"Lost everything on the river, and I would not borrow a pence. That is a debtor's trap for any Irishman."

"But you'll freeze."

"Then I will have to work harder to stay warm."

"The boys are all at supper. You'll want to join them, I imagine. It's the building just across. The boys eat separately. I often join them, for instruction never ceases and the good shepherd stays with his flock."

"What tribes? Where do these boys come from?"

"Oh, they've come from the whole area. Wishram, Kalapuya, Clatsop, Tillamook . . ."

"Can they speak to each other?"

"Oh, they get along. And they use English as a lingua franca."

"How do they feel, being here?"

"It's a great honor among their people. Let's eat now, before we miss our supper."

"I will wash myself and join you shortly, Mr. Smith."

The schoolmaster nodded, shook hands, and parted.

O'Malley laughed. They had put him in with the Indian lads, the other heathen. He peered about the dusky room, lit by only two small shuttered windows, the glass too precious to waste on the students. The walls were whitewashed and unadorned except for two plain crosses that seemed to overlook the boys. Each boy had a wall peg above his bed, and spare white men's clothing hung on each. But few had white men's shoes. Moccasins were tucked beneath each simple bunk. Gray blankets and small pillows covered each bunk, and the blankets were neatly drawn over the straw-filled ticks. He saw no books or school supplies, and supposed most of the instruction was done on slate-boards.

They were not allowed to be Indians in this place.

He looked about for a basin and pitcher, and saw none. How did they keep clean—or did they? He drifted out the door and found a wooden wash trough in the yard. He splashed the much-used water over his face, wanting soap, and then scrubbed his hands, and shook them for the want of a towel. He discovered a two-hole outhouse set back a ways.

He made his way to the students' dining hall, a low log affair with a great wooden cross overlooking the room, and found Solomon Smith and about twenty thin, coppery, high-cheeked boys at a trestle table, eating stew in utter silence, glancing at him covertly with warm black eyes.

For reasons he couldn't fathom, he felt aglow. He was half a world away from home, but here among these solemn youths his happy heart found a new home.

13

John O'Malley settled happily onto the wooden bench, and an Indian woman promptly set a wooden bowl of beef stew before him. The boys eyed him curiously but continued to spoon the stew into their hungry bodies. Horn spoons were the sole implement they had. Solomon Smith occupied the head of the table, a gentle lord over these lads.

"Boys, this is Mr. O'Malley. He'll help us build the mission," said Smith.

They nodded, or eyed him boldly, or glanced covertly in his direction.

"I will be enjoying your good company for a while," he said.

The youths didn't reply.

O'Malley wondered whether the lads were forbidden to speak, which meant he would be too, so he held his peace. He wolfed down the flavorless stew, which filled and satisfied him more than anything he had eaten in weeks. He knew the wee boys were eyeing him covertly, just as he was eyeing them. They ranged from seven or eight up to their teens, though he couldn't put ages to these coppery lads. They all were thin as posts and had prominent cheekbones and jet hair, but beyond that they varied sharply, some hawk-faced, some moon-faced, some dark red, others rather tan or yellow. Jesus, Joseph, how could he tell 'em apart?

He helped himself to the bread heaped on a wooden platter, and dipped it into the juices of his stew. It was a fine meal.

Smith wiped his face and settled into his spindle chair, the sole chair at the trestle table.

"Mr. O'Malley, these are our charges. We hope to school them in the three Rs, and help open the Bible to them and bring them the gifts we have received. They understand English but don't often speak it. I've taught them their ABCs."

"Ah, it is a good thing, lads," O'Malley said. "I will tell you a bit about myself. I come from an island called Erin in the great seas, a big island as green as ever was green with a great plenty of rain and fog. And on this island there is not a snake, not a big snake or a little snake. Not a rattlesnake, not a garter snake. It was because our patron, Saint Patrick, drove out the snakes long ago. So you be thinking about God, and the good things He can do for you."

"No snakes?"

That came from the smallest of all the boys.

"Not a one."

He discerned awe in their faces.

"Are you a holy man?" asked an older boy.

"No, lad, just a working blighter."

"Why are you with us? Are you in school too?"

"Ah, we are always in school. Maybe it is because I am an Indian like you."

"Ah! What People? Like the Clatsop?"

Smith, at the end of the table, suddenly wore a mask.

"A wild, savage tribe called Celts, lad. We howl at the moon, dance our hearts out, tell big foolish stories about ourselves and make songs."

The boys laughed.

"Mr. O'Malley's making a good story," Solomon Smith said.

The men exchanged glances briefly, but O'Malley did not quite retreat. "When these good people look at me, they see an Indian like you," he said. "So I will be staying with you."

Smith concluded the supper with a reading from each of the Testaments, elaborated and translated into simpler form that the lads could understand.

Then the boys stood for a brief vespers, and drifted into the evening.

"They'll be in bed by eight, Mr. O'Malley. We give them one candle a week, and they have to conserve it. No need for you to join them if you'd rather stay up. I'll light a lamp and we'll play chess or checkers if you'd like."

"Thank you, but I am done in from a long day's travel, Mr. Smith, and not far from the catarrh. And tomorrow, I will be carpentering at dawn, I imagine."

Smith nodded. "We try not to confuse the boys about things they can't yet grasp," he said.

"I should not have called myself an Indian, is that it?"

"Yes."

"It was a way of saying that I am one of them."

"How is that?"

O'Malley decided to venture out on a limb. "You have a crowded mission, with your immigrants crammed into every corner, anything with a roof over it, especially for women while their men are out putting up a farmhouse. And yet, Mr. Smith, there are four empty bunks in the boys' dormitory, and the reverend put me in one."

"I see."

"So I am an Indian."

Smith laughed, and O'Malley suddenly liked the teacher.

The Irishman found most of the boys in bed, and the rest about to climb under their blankets. The single candle burned in an iron lantern hanging midway in the barracks.

"Well, my boys, you are about to blow out the candle. I will take just a moment here," he said, pulling off his shirt and britches. He laid his own blanket atop the gray one.

An older student, probably appointed a leader, stood next to the lamp, ready to blow it out. The moment O'Malley clambered into the incredibly comfortable bunk, or so it seemed after months lying on hard ground, the boy blew, and the barracks vanished into restless darkness.

"Tell us more stories," said a reedy voice.

"It is stories you want, is it?"

"From across the sea."

"Ah, stories! Well, now, I will have to think on it. Tonight it will be a short story because I am tired. But I like stories, and I will tell you one every night.

"Now, then, there was a man and woman from my sea-girt island traveling far, far away, going to a new home. They were strangers in a strange land, and humble people. The humblest of all those they traveled with.

"And then they came to a great barrier, a range of mountains cut by a big river, and they could drive their cart no farther. All they could do, to get to the place of their dreams, was to build a raft of logs and try to float down the big river to their new home.

"So they chopped wood and made a raft and put everything they possessed on it, and the others did too. And they set sail on the big river, and for a while everything was fine, and the river took them where they wanted to go.

"But they soon encountered rapids and big waves that tossed the rafts like little sticks and broke them apart. The people from the island were washed ashore, along with others, and they were very cold because sleet was falling. All the woods were wet and they could not make a fire or find shelter from the wind and sleet. Their very clothing began to freeze solid. Soon they would die.

"But at the last moment before they died, the lord of the new land sent his men up the river and rescued the poor ones from the sea-island and all the rest. They gave each person a thick blanket, and built hot fires, and then after the danger had passed, took them to the lord's castle where they were fed and warmed and given many necessary things, and allowed to borrow others.

"And so the young man and woman were saved, to begin to live out their dreams, and the good master of the great house was much honored as a merciful man. And the man and woman from the island vowed never to forget that kindness that saved their lives, and to repay it if they could, somehow. We should do unto others as we want others to do unto us. That is the end of the story tonight."

O'Malley settled into his blankets.

"That was a good story. I like the master, and I like the humble ones from your country who said they would never forget. You teach us good things, Mr. O'Malley, and we will learn from your stories how to be like you and receive the gifts of God."

The voice was probably that of the elder boy, the one who was lord of the lamp.

O'Malley thought of Mary Kate, and hoped she was as comfortable as he, and that she yearned for him as much as he yearned for her. And the next thing he knew, it was dawning and the boys were stirring.

When he reported for work that chill and overcast December day, shivering in his thin coat, he soon found himself peeling bark from logs, hard work that kept him warm all day. Then he found himself chopping notches in the logs so they would dovetail together, and then cutting windows in the logs, using a big two-man bucksaw.

The hours flew. That evening, he held a chit for fifty cents in his hand, and something stirred his heart.

Some days later, he learned how to split shakes from big cedar rounds, and soon a great heap of them lay ready to use. He kept a sharp eye on the rest of the workmen, making a quick study of all they did, and mastering what he could as fast as he could. The mission had no glass except in Lee's house, but deerskin scraped thin and tacked into the frame offered a soft light to the interiors, and shutters kept out cold at night.

They didn't toil on Sundays, but every daylight minute of every other day they wrestled the new building into readiness. They paved the floor with stones artfully set in the earth, completed a fieldstone fireplace that would throw heat into the room, and then they built simple bunks, very like the ones in the Indian dormitory.

O'Malley did a little of all of these things, his natural curiosity helping him master the whole frontier art, and his finely muscled young body garnering skills.

Each day he showed up in Jason Lee's office, and each day the missionary scratched the fifty-cent day wage into a ledger with a quill pen, and gave O'Malley a chit. On cold or rainy or snowy days, his fifty cents had been hard earned, but on the rare sunny day he had enjoyed the toil.

His sole shirt and trousers were in tatters. One day, feeling indescribably rich, he bought fabric from the mission store and employed two women to fashion clothing for him. If they hurried, they could finish the work before Christmas and a trip downriver to see Mary Kate. He was not a shilling in debt, and soon would have the skills and money to strike out on his own, his bride beside him.

And he never stopped telling stories to the boys.

14

Electra Reese spent her days examining Fort Vancouver and finding it wanting. Hudson's Bay Company might be a royal monopoly, but it utterly lacked taste.

She did not waste time grieving Warren because there was nothing to grieve. He had been a weak, vacillating, pusillanimous man. Warren had demonstrated his weakness by getting himself drowned in the Columbia, and that justified everything that Electra had long ago concluded about him. She marveled that she had agreed to come west, but what was a wife to do?

He had been just such a mouse in every facet of married life, which had left her bored and restless. He was also the very prince of ineptitude, greeting scullery maids with the same affability he might have greeted a senator. In fact, he would actually have befriended these English cretins if he had lived to meet them.

She had spent little time wondering whether she might now marry Garwood, and decided not to tax the question. He had a roving eye. At least Warren didn't do that. Garwood aspired to be Oregon's first senator, and that was something she might enjoy. Governor was another matter altogether. Who would want to be stuck in a wilderness being governor to a pack of rustics, living in some sort of ill-conceived palace that looked like a Roman ruin, and smiling at toads. Yes, she would just wait on that issue. She was destined to be the queen of Oregon, given her slim blond beauty, her chiseled features, and her knowing ways. In a place desperate for women, what a prize she would be. Yes, let Garwood go to the rear of the line—for now.

The Hudson's Bay Company amused her. What a mockery was Empire! Here were half-castes and dusky savages and the flawed fruits of miscegenation working in high positions for the company. Here were white men shamelessly consorting with fat squaws and toothy tarts from the Sandwich Islands, not to mention the unwashed French.

Apart from Dr. McLoughlin's well-appointed home, she could not find the slightest evidence of taste. The company store shelved barbarous goods, such as those blankets with the ugly stripes at either end, designed obviously for the savage aesthete.

Electra perceived that she had some immediate problems to resolve, and the foremost of these was that she had no clothing other than the tattered skirts in which she was rescued and the funeral dress she had acquired. She was living in borrowed rags. The trouble was, HBC had scarcely a yard of stylish fabric in its store, and whatever she chose would be a laughingstock back East.

Still, she had to do something. She was not well, and blamed the lack of clothing for it. She needed a shawl and dresses at once, plus all the underthings and accouterments. Two would be for everyday wear, one warmer than the other. One would be a ballgown. And the other one would suffice for afternoon entertaining.

She would have to find a seamstress, and since there were no white women, she would either have to sew the dresses herself or hire one of the half-castes. She didn't have the inclination to sew, which meant enduring the barbarous stitch of the breed women.

She finally settled on the least offensive fabrics, nankeen and calico, and added some ribbons and hooks and buttons and thread.

"It comes to three pounds six," said the half-breed clerk, no doubt some brat spawned by some trader's liaison.

"Debit my brother-in-law's account," she said.

He frowned, pulled out a ledger, and shook his head.

"Mr. Reese has no credit. You'll have to talk to the chief factor."

"You will do as I say, and right now!"

The clerk stared, nodded, and recorded the entry in Garwood's account.

She distributed the fabric among seamstresses imperiously, along with charcoal sketches of what she wanted—she was rather clever with all that—and insisted on the utmost haste.

"It will be three dollars, Mrs. Reese," said one.

"I'll pay you when I'm satisfied, and not before."

"Very well. You will be satisfied, madam. In ten days, come for fittings."

"Ten days! I need these in three."

The woman pushed the six yards of fabric back at Electra.

"No, keep it. Do it in a week; I can't wait a single minute beyond that."

The warm-eyed woman sighed and nodded.

And so it went.

She needed shoes also, but there were none to be had in that wilderness outpost. Women wore small, petite moccasins, sometimes whited or dyed. She found the moccasins rather enchanting, and found some available at the store. She bought the entire stock that fit her, three pair.

"That's two pounds eleven, Mrs. Reese."

"On the Reese account. You know that."

"I'll do it this one last time, but no more. It's only because the factor doesn't want to be bothered with small matters that—"

"I'll talk to him myself, and you need not consider the matter."

The toadying clerk nodded. How easy it was to impose her wishes on these breeds, who were plainly defective by birth and blood.

She had yet another matter that required immediate and resolute attention. She had been settled in a small guest room along with two other women. One was a Mrs. Corporal, a pipe-smoking matriarch with whom she became acquainted during the long ordeal of the overland journey. The Corporals had negotiated the trip successfully, using pack and saddle horses the last lap, but the matriarch had taken ill with pleurisy, and the Corporals elected to keep her at Fort Vancouver until they could provide comfortable circumstances for the woman.

Electra and Mrs. Corporal shared the two narrow cots supplied by Hudson's Bay Company, but there was a third woman crammed in with them, the Irish twit, on a straw pallet in one corner. That was a source of pain and mortification to Electra. Imagine such a creature in her own bedchamber! But removing the young woman would require delicacy. Dr. McLoughlin had taken a shine to her and her husband, probably because they were all papists.

This creature seemed to grasp that nothing was beneath her, and she spent her days finding ways to lighten the burdens of company people, though McLoughlin never paid her a shilling for it. One day, quite on her own, she cleaned and dusted the entire trading store. Another, she volunteered to serve the employees' mess, and do the pots and pans afterward. On another, she helped make soap, and another time she dipped candles all day.

Then McLoughlin gave her a gift of wool broadcloth, and the Irishwoman fashioned a dowdy winter dress, employing a fine stitch. At last the creature had a change of clothes. So that was it: trade her labor for a few favors. Electra wondered just what sort of favors.

Three in that small room was one too many. But there were always ways:

"Mrs. O'Malley, the chamber pot requires your attention."

"Mrs. O'Malley, the beds are a muss."

"Mrs. O'Malley, that straw tick, it just exudes something quite offensive. Please get fresh straw, and wash the tick. Maybe you should scrub yourself . . ."

"Mrs. O'Malley, please don't snore. It drives Mrs. Corporal to distraction."

"Mrs. O'Malley, can you not understand that we need some privacy? Three's too many. Find something to do and let us rest, please."

"Mrs. O'Malley, the pitcher's empty again. And when you throw out the basin, don't splash it on the path right where we walk. All right?"

"Mrs. O'Malley . . ."

"Mrs. O'Malley . . ."

"You're being too peckish on the girl," Mrs. Corporal said one day.

"Not hard enough, I'm afraid."

"Well, she doesn't protest, so she must accept it."

"I'm hoping she does protest! Then I'll talk to the doctor."

Winter lowered over Oregon. Snow collected in the mountains. Mount Hood glowed white, even on dull days. Light fled. The relentless overcast lowered the spirits of everyone, and especially Electra.

"I fought coming here. I fought it! Warren didn't care, but Garwood insisted, and so we came. Now look at us!" she exclaimed to Mrs. Corporal.

She visited the company store again, purchased a tasseled shawl and a gray blanket which she intended to be made into a greatcoat. She took it to a seamstress she didn't owe, the wife of one of the French Canadians, and asked that it be completed by Christmas.

"Three American dollars it will be," said Madame Thereaux.

"After I accept it."

"You did not pay Lisette Robideaux."

"I must have this coat! I'm cold. I lost everything."

The woman shrugged, unmoved.

"I will arrange credit for you at the store, on my brother-in-law's account."

She did just that: three American dollars of credit for Madame Thereaux; three dollars added to Garwood's considerable debt.

Shortly before that Christmas of 1842, she received word, at last, from Garwood. He wrote that he was making progress, and that he would come to Fort Vancouver for Christmas. He asked that she see Dr. McLoughlin about rooms.

She caught the chief factor in his office, looking solemn about something. She had heard he was warring by mail with Governor Simpson and even the directors of the company in London, but she wasn't sure about what. The tales that had trickled into her ears were too bizarre to believe. Murder, death, neglect, suicide . . .

"Mrs. Reese? I trust all is well and you are content?"

"Oh, I manage. Garwood's coming for Christmas, you know. I learned just today. Could you put him in a guest room?"

"I'm afraid not but he'll find warmth and shelter here among our employees."

"But he's a man of station."

"So are many others, Mrs. Reese."

She wasn't getting anywhere with that. "Actually, I have a favor to ask. We're so crowded, you know. There's really no room for three, for a tick on the floor—"

"Mrs. O'Malley's tick."

"Yes. Could you move her? I'm afraid things just aren't clean, you know. She lacks clothing, and her habits . . ."

He shook his head.

"Well, could perhaps you and Mrs. McLoughlin see fit to receive a guest?"

McLoughlin stood, and the act of standing amazed her as his body unfolded out of the chair and his head shot higher and higher until he gazed down at her from his full height.

"Good afternoon, Mrs. Reese," he said.

15

Back East, Garwood Reese had given much thought to what he would do and how he would prosper when he reached Oregon. He had spent his life in public service, employed in custodial posts for the state of New York and dreaming of entering politics. But the political ladders of New York were crowded and steep, and he knew that his best bet would be to go somewhere unsettled, and get a good grasp on the bottom rung.

Getting a living in Oregon had perplexed him. No government existed, and indeed, the area belonged to no nation, so he could not work for a city or a county or a state. But wasn't that the ideal circumstance for him? Make it American! Make it a Territory and then a state! Drive out the British!

Still, it was one thing to entertain dreams and quite another to make a living in a wilderness. But there were always ways, and the one he had hit upon, one memorable day, was to organize a town site out there and sell lots to arriving settlers. He knew nothing of surveying, of course, but his brother could draw up deeds, help draft claims that would withstand the vicissitudes of statehood, and make sure it was properly surveyed and done right. Warren had agreed, and would handle those aspects for twenty-five percent of gross sales.

Then, with lots surveyed, staked, and ready to sell, he would have an income without much work, and could devote himself to the things that really engrossed his mind, such as agitating for American sovereignty, and then statehood, and ultimately winning elections and entering high public office. The sale of town lots would succor him until he could become Oregon's first senator, or governor, or at the very least, congressman.

It all had made sense. Even before he set off for the West, he knew what he would look for: a good site along the Willamette River, a natural place for a town. But when he arrived in Oregon, Warren was dead and the whole business seemed shakier. He had, moreover, some responsibility to care for his widowed sister-in-law.

None of this did he explain to John McLoughlin when Reese petitioned the chief factor for the outfit he needed to examine the surrounding areas to find commercially valuable land, such as forests, farmland, pasture, fisheries, or minerals. He did not mention a town site among his objectives. The Hudson's Bay man listened carefully, seemed reluctant, but finally consented to let Reese outfit himself. It was plain to Reese that the chief factor did not like him.

Reese ended up not only with a good camping outfit, suitable for cold weather, but also with a saddler and three packhorses that he leased from the company. He had arranged with McLoughlin for these to be delivered to him at Frenchman's Flat, up the Willamette, where the company had a warehouse and a livestock operation. He intended to launch his exploration from that point, in the heart of the valley, after he arrived with his saddles and camping outfit, and from there he would explore the entire area.

The weather had turned cold and wet, and Reese feared he would catch catarrh or something worse, but he believed that the town site was his only option and he had to act fast. He knew nothing of frontier trades, even less of farming, and would swiftly find himself in dire poverty if he could not sell lots to incoming Americans. Thus energized by his fears and straitened circumstances, he set out at once through an icy mist to discover the ideal place for a future city. What he really wanted was a perfect town site, but one hidden from the cyclops eye of John McLoughlin, a refuge for the Yanks swarming into the valley.

He wasn't at all sure of what he was doing, but he would deal with all that one step at a time. He wandered along a well-marked trace, sodden in the monsoon season, that took him through the Willamette Valley, sometimes at river's edge, but more often back a way, on higher ground, the road cutting the river's bends and corners.

He was not a gifted camper, and many a night he could not manage to get a fire going, or keep one going through a night. He sometimes swallowed tasteless oatmeal mush to sustain himself because he could not cook anything better. After a few nights of trying to sleep in icy, sodden blankets, he learned to select his campsites with care and pay attention to drainage. He developed a harsh cough and sore throat, and at times felt feverish, but he knew he could not abandon the chase. And so he stumbled on, cold and soaked, famished for a hot meal, examining a saturated land which lay gloomily under cast-iron skies, all of it immersed in frightful silence.

Then one mid-December day, after weeks of wandering upstream without success, he realized he didn't know anything about staking out a future town. He stared at one gloomy prospect after another, witlessly trying to envision a shining city, bustling streets, river commerce, happy cottages, but all he saw was soaked grasses, somber pines, and overcast heavens. It was time to quit, time to turn back. The silent and secretive reaches of Oregon had defeated him, at least for the moment.

Eventually he reached the horseshoe-shaped falls of the Willamette, which dropped forty or fifty feet and raised a thunderous roar and a great mist at their base. Here was civilization, what little of it existed in the valley. A building, nay, two or three or five, welcomed him. Not just a building but a *store* of some sort. And yet another structure out on an island above the falls. And still more houses just beyond, with smoke drifting from their chimneys. A hamlet. In his haste to collect his livestock at Frenchmen's Flat and begin his quest, he had paid little attention to the settlement nestled below the falls.

He arrived late in the afternoon and soon the long winter's night would be upon him. But this night he would sleep warm and dry, and maybe his cough would get better. He hurried toward the buildings ahead, and then noticed something that shocked him to the bone. Lots! Rows of lots, neatly staked out, an orderly procession of rectangles of land, awaiting their owners. A frightful depression swept him. He detoured, wandering through three streets of lots at riverbank level, and then he hiked up a steep slope to a bench and discovered more lots, and more, all staked out, their wooden rain-washed posts glinting in the failing light. Hundreds of lots! As if someone were expecting a great migration!

The terrible reality was that someone had beaten him to it. Here was a city-to-be, awaiting the oncoming pilgrims. But who? Was this the place called Oregon City by the company? He hurried down the treacherous benches in the last of the light and made his way to the store, his lodestar the dim orange light from a window paned with linseed-oiled cloth.

He dismounted and tied his horse to a hitchrail, and then his packhorses as well. No one greeted him, and he heard only the relentless roar of the cataract.

He opened a leather-hinged door and pierced into a quiet, dark room lit only by a hearthfire. A few goods rested on rude shelves, or in casks, or simply on the plank floor.

"Hello!" he yelled.

"That quacks like a duck!" someone replied from a rear room. A young, fair-haired youth entered and surveyed his guest.

"Nasty night," the lad said. "What can I do for you?"

"Just answer a question. Whose lots are those out there?"

"John McLoughlin's. He's calling it Oregon City."

"Then all those lots are the company's?"

"He says they're his own, but he's just fronting for the company. Everyone knows that. And who are you?"

"Garwood Reese, from New York. I arrived here a fortnight ago, tail end of the emigrants, and I'm just looking over the country." He decided to say no more. "And who are you?"

"George Abernethy. I clerk here. This is the mission store, 'cept we hardly got anything to sell."

"You with Jason Lee's mission?"

"Sure am."

"Well, how come you have a place here?"

"This is an upcoming place, waterpower and all, and we wanted a store and a branch of the mission here."

"But these are McLoughlin's lots."

"He gave us some. Mr. Waller, he's one of the ministers, he asked the old bird for some lots for the church, and McLoughlin, he forked over five to us, and gave Waller some timbers too. He'd do anything for the church, that's what he says. This here building is made from them."

"And what about the water power?"

Abernethy grinned. "That's about to change hands."

"The mission's buying the mill site?"

"Nope. We've organized a milling company and we'll claim it. The company blasted a millrace but never did nothing. It's there for the taking. No one has any right. You can take whatever you can hold because there's no law says you can't."

Water dripped from Reese's capote. A faint heat warmed him. Being indoors was a voluptuous experience. "No claims are worth a thing, eh? Then how come you let him stake out all those lots?"

Abernethy shrugged. "Fact is, we need the company. Jason Lee's a friend of McLoughlin. We can't hardly stay alive without help from the British. So it don't pay to push too hard. Least not now . . ."

Reese nodded. "You got a place a man can stay? Can I put up my horse and mules?"

"Sure. Two bits for you, two bits for the livestock."

"I . . . left my funds at Fort Vancouver."

Abernethy grinned. "You got something to trade?"

"Not much now, but give me a while and I'll reward you beyond anything you've ever dreamed."

"Need something now, Mr. Reese."

Reese surrendered. "Sure. Help me with my animals and I'll find something in my outfit."

The grinning youth put the animals in a rude pen and fed them some hay while Reese dragged his heavy packloads into the store and dug out a square piece of discarded linen sailcloth he had gotten at Fort Vancouver. The rain was turning into snow, and Reese was delighted to be indoors.

The storekeep returned, scraped snow off his head and shoulders, and examined the piece of cloth.

"That'll do," Abernethy said. "I'll sell it for a dollar."

In the rear room of the store, the clerk dipped a ladle into a kettle of stew warming at the hearth, and handed a bowl to Reese. Nothing had ever tasted better. Except for his cough, Reese felt just fine.

Warmed and comforted, Reese was in an expansive mood.

"I'm thinking maybe we can work together, George," he said. "I'm going to start a town myself, sell lots, an income, you see. Maybe you can give me some ideas about where to locate one, and what's available for the taking."

"It's all available," Abernethy said. "Ain't nobody got a claim to anything yet. No one really owns the land under this here store. No one owns the land under Fort Vancouver, though the company says they own it."

"You familiar with the whole valley?"

"Sure am."

"Then tell me where to look! I'll give you a share."

"Best places all taken up, Garwood. The Methodists have the good ones; the company's got the others. Right here's the best."

Garwood Reese felt a sinking disappointment. "But surely there's some place in this big valley, some place not staked out, where a town should be some day."

"Down there where the rivers join, that's the best. But the company chases off anyone tries it there. A few have tried it, and the company just finds way to defeat them. Nope, the only good place is right here."

"Then I must get these lots here!"

Abernethy was visibly startled, and then he grinned. "Stick around a few days. This place is the future."

16

Jasper Constable remarked the ever-cheerful Jason Lee filling the doorframe of the mission's accounting room, where Constable had carved out some space for himself.

"Jasper, Dr. McLoughlin's requested a clergyman for Christmas at the fort. Would you go?"

"Why, ah . . ."

"They've got one of Father Blanchet's priests coming; they'd like someone for the Protestants."

"A priest?"

"Yes, from St. Paul's. It serves the Frenchmen at Champoeg, and a few Indians, of course."

"Well, that decides it. We must be represented."

Lee grinned. "I knew I could ask you."

"Yes, yes," Constable said. "I will go where I am called."

The mission's leader vanished. He rarely wasted a moment.

Constable didn't want to go, not one bit. He wasn't well, for one thing. The damp Oregon winter had evoked a runny nose and a sore throat. Rose still grieved the loss of Damaris and had settled into perpetual gloom. He had hoped a good warm Christmas would stir her to happiness. Ah, yuletide, with its warmth and sacredness! That would bring Rose about.

They had suffered not just a loss of a child, but pure misery. The mission had little room for anyone, much less the hundred or so newcomers. So the Constables had been farmed out; the boys into a family who were building a farmstead a mile distant; and Rose and Jasper crammed in with a joiner, Cavendish, and his wife and children, sleeping in makeshift bunks in one of the two rooms, along with three little children. Rose was almost beside herself, desperate for privacy and quiet, and constantly sick.

And now this, a Christmas torn asunder.

He had volunteered.

It would mean an all-day journey each way, whenever the post's voyageurs ventured upriver or down with their ubiquitous bateaux.

Gloomily he contemplated the task of telling Rose he must carry the Word of God north this holy season, to be planted among the post's heathenish and loose denizens. The more he contemplated the Hudson's Bay Company, the more aghast he had become at its gross neglect of even rudimentary religion and morals. They all had red or mixed-blood concubines, with whom they lived flagrantly, without the slightest benefit of the sacrament of marriage. And that included the Catholic French Canadians too. Hudson's Bay Company was good at begetting bastard half-breeds, and begetting profits for the lord directors in London, and nothing else. And the notorious chief factor set the tone, openly cavorting with his old squaw.

Constable pulled a borrowed shawl over him and plunged into the gloom. He had not seen sun in ten days, and was keeping careful tab, as a private reproach toward Oregon and the madness of missioning here.

He found Rose in her chair sewing, as she always did. She had completed outfits for the boys, and was finishing a black cutaway coat and trousers for him, quite suitable for services, and had started a white bib shirt too. He and she had purchased the fabric at Fort Vancouver, along with thread and needles and a sewing thimble, and a few other necessaries. The company had readily extended credit.

She met him with an upward glance as he loomed over her.

"Jason Lee wants me to minister at the fort on Christmas," he said. "It is a burden I cannot refuse."

"You won't be here?"

"Jason's planning to have a joyous yuletide here, with a candlelit tree and midnight services. You'll enjoy it."

She nodded and sewed. She had never complained. Not one word.

"You're a brave soldier, Rose. You will wear a crown of glory someday, beside God."

"Thank you, Jasper."

"Next Christmas, we'll feel better. We'll have our own snug home, our family back together, our hearth warm, our little gifts given to one another in honor of the Christ child, and your eyes will shine."

She smiled doubtfully.

The Cavendish children were napping with their mother, Agnes, and Rose was relishing the rare quiet. But soon they would come tearing in again, and her peace would be shattered.

"Will my new black suit—"

"It's done, but for a few buttons."

"Good. I'll take it. We still have a few days. You're a soldier."

But Rose was troubled. "Couldn't Jason Lee have gone himself? He's the one who knows those Canadians."

"He asked me. There was some urgency about it. You see, they'll have a priest coming."

"Oh, then you must go. You, better than anyone, can steer people away from superstition."

Her little compliments always cheered him.

He had always known that one of his missions in clerical life was to bury the Romish church in America. Father DeSmet himself had come with them partway west, with the mountaineer Tom Fitzpatrick as his guide, but then they had turned north at Fort Hall to the Bitterroot country and his St. Mary's Mission there. The Belgian Jesuit had impressed Constable with his energy and courtesy and his wondrous knowledge of the Northwest tribes. They had danced around the theological issues that divided them, mostly letting their differences remain unacknowledged, and the Methodist knew by the time they parted that the Jesuits were a formidable force in the Northwest, and must be checked ruthlessly.

He sighed. "Are you getting a little peace today?"

"The Cavendishes are quite solicitous of my comfort, Jasper. You go up to the fort, and they'll take good care of me, and we'll have a very holy Christmas."

Her courage caught and held him. What a brave helpmeet was Rose! Apart from her melancholic ways, he was quite fortunate in marriage. She had always hovered about, making his world comfortable. When he had proposed to go west, she had replied with Scripture: "Wherever thou goest . . ."

"How are the boys? I haven't seen them for days."

"Matthew's not happy. Mark doesn't seem to mind, but he has headaches. He knows we're only a little walk away. I do wish the mission would start a school for white children too. I've thought some about enrolling our sons with the Indians, but it wouldn't do, it just wouldn't do. No one does, you know. So they're falling behind. Matthew can barely read. But at least they're getting plenty of fresh air helping the men."

"We need a house! I'll press Jason Lee once again. Here I am, a minister of the Gospel, and we haven't a place to lay our heads! Sometimes I am vexed beyond endurance. I'm going to tell Jason that we insist! Insist! We must have a place at Chemeteka in one month, not a day longer. They mustn't do this, separating us and farming us out like orphans. I've put in seven years since Wesleyan, seven years, and we're poorer than ever."

"Yes, please petition Mr. Lee," she said.

He promised he would. But after Christmas. Just now, things were too hectic.

He plunged into the gloom again and hastened back to his cubbyhole in the mission's offices. Once, in the East, he had wondered why the Oregon mission consisted of so many carpenters, masons, joiners, and ordinary laborers, and so few clergymen and teachers, and now he knew. Before he had started west, he had sternly told the board that he would cut back the secular people and increase the number of ordained and skilled missioners. But now he had come to a broader view: one could scarcely run a mission from a tent. Workmen were required to build the mission and homes for the missioners.

Still, this new wave, the very ones he had joined for the walk across the continent, wrought some concern in him. For these were scarcely religious people at all, and they were flocking to Oregon for the getting and spending and every worldly pursuit, and not for the Christianizing of the tribes. He would deal with that soon. Oregon should be reserved as a great religious enterprise protected by the surrounding wilds.

In his cubbyhole he was penning the first of his forthcoming circular letters exhorting the mission and its numerous denizens to abandon worldly things and commit themselves to the Lord. Paper was frightfully scarce, especially because the ample supply he had carted from Missouri had vanished into the Columbia River, but McLoughlin had given him a few sheets and let him buy a blank ledger book at the company store. And by writing fine and avoiding margins, Constable could fit whole volumes of admonition into a small page or two.

Of admonitions he had plenty. In a tiny hand, to conserve paper, he had penned a list of future topics for his letters. There would be fortnightly epistles, very like Saint Paul's, dealing with the pursuit of Mammon in Oregon, the problem of foreigners, the need to drive a British monopoly from the region, the need to check the incursions of priestly faiths, especially Catholic, but not excluding Church of England and Orthodoxy.

He planned epistles about the moral cesspool entrenched just across the Columbia, the need for civil government to prohibit and punish fornication and other vices, the need to civilize the tribes on a far greater scale than was currently under way, the need to petition Washington for territorial status, and much more. Little by little, he would found his City on the Hill, a wonder to the world.

All these dreams whirled in his mind as he contemplated his trip down the Willamette. The more he pondered it, the more he realized that this was a God-given opportunity to pierce to the bosom of the Hudson's Bay post, and raise the scepter of righteousness inside the walls of the enemy. And suddenly his trip to the post took on an aura of sweet beauty. What did a sore throat matter?

There were moments when he reminded himself that he owed his own life and the lives of his family to John McLoughlin and the royally chartered

Lion of the North. That was a source of endless confusion and anguish, and he had moments when he wished he and his family might have died, martyrs of the church, rather than be rescued by those rough and wicked men. Where did his loyalties lie?

But those moments always passed. He owed the company something, and the best way to repay the debt was to draw the rascals away from their wicked ways.

17

Mary Kate O'Malley loved to slip through the front gates of Fort Vancouver and gaze across the vast plain to the distant foothills of Oregon. It didn't matter that the prospect was monotonously gray, and that the pewter river far afield looked nothing like Ireland. She didn't feel quite so homesick out in the open; but inside the post homesickness savaged her heart, and she could barely breathe the air of the New World. All she wanted was to go back home.

Come here, come here, John O'Malley.

He wasn't far away, close enough so that she could walk the path to her husband. If she had walked across a continent, she could manage a walk to the Methodist mission.

She could not go home, not ever again. She would never see her father or brothers, or visit the graves of her mother and Robert and Ann. So there was no point in being homesick, and she didn't know why she sometimes mooned about, or even wept, wanting what she could not have.

She had no friends. One of her roommates abused her. At first she had tried accommodating Mrs. Reese; she was a new widow, was she not? So Mary Kate had silently done all that the woman had demanded, offering a smile and service and a curtsy, and receiving only more abuse and grosser demands. Then she had tumbled to what was really happening. The woman scorned her and was deliberately trying to drive her out.

That wouldn't be so bad, actually. Electra Reese was not good company. But there was no place to go. Guests jammed Fort Vancouver, most of them wandering about doing nothing. At least she was determined to sing for her supper, and had found ways to help out in the big kitchen, the dining hall, and among the breed women whose task was to mend and darn the tattered clothing of the voyageurs, and sometimes even the factors and traders and chief factor himself. She received no pay, but at least she was returning to the Hudson's Bay Company some labor for what it was providing her: food and shelter.

But of course the mighty John McLoughlin scarcely knew she existed, and she didn't see him at all. She desperately needed clothing. Everything had been sucked into the river. She had a change, loaned by some of the half-breed women living with the voyageurs. She fought dirt constantly and lost ground: it caked her skirts and shoes, which didn't help when it came to the assessing eye of Electra Reese.

Then one bleak night Electra Reese began to badger Mary Kate mercilessly.

"You're filthy. You're not welcome here. Go sleep in the kitchen," the woman said.

"Mr. Douglas put me here," she replied patiently.

"I'll have you removed. I'll see Dr. McLoughlin in the morning."

Electra Reese lay abed, taunting the young woman, while Mrs. Corporal just sat and clucked, unwilling to take sides.

Mary Kate's Irish was up. "Not another blooming word, Mrs. Reese, not another," she said so softly and darkly that it gave pause to the frail blonde.

For a moment, Mary Kate thought she had, at last, stopped the faucet of bile.

"The mulatto put you here? I suppose that makes sense. Mr. Ogden put me here. Why don't you go share your charms with Mr. Douglas? A perfect union, yes, quite sublime."

Mary Kate closed her eyes a moment, then rose from her pallet, loomed over Electra Reese and whispered softly. "It is you who will be leaving now. Get out or I shall pick you up and throw you into the yard."

Electra Reese gaped.

Mary Kate felt her blood coursing her body, felt the heat rise, felt a wild joy.

She grabbed the front of Electra Reese's cotton wrapper, lifted her bodily while the woman shrieked, set her upright, and wrestled her to the door. The woman's feathery flapping didn't deter Mary Kate in the slightest. Electra Reese had scarcely lifted a cook pot all her life, and now she offered no defense except the lashing of her sharp tongue.

"Stop that, you witch!"

"A witch, is it? Now I am a witch? Out you go, m'lady, and don't come back."

Mary Kate yanked the door open. A dank night breeze drifted in. She shoved the Reese woman through, into the icy night, listening to her squawk and screech, and then slammed the door and dropped the latch.

She heard howling, and then the howling faded into the night.

"Mercy!" said Mrs. Corporal. "Aren't you the one!"

Mary Kate poured water from the pitcher into the bowl, commandeered the Reese woman's lavender-scented English soap, and scrubbed furiously at her face and neck, and then the rest of her until she felt clean. Up until that moment, she had never used the pitcher and basin because Electra Reese wouldn't let her.

She climbed into Electra Reese's bed, knowing this was not over, and lay quietly waiting for the rest of the night's story to play out.

She was not disappointed. Ten minutes later a sharp rapping at the door informed her that things had come to a head. She opened to Peter Ogden, who held a candle lamp, and peered at her, faint amusement in his face.

"Mrs. Reese seems rather distraught," he said.

"I did what I had to."

"A bit drastic, perhaps?"

She bristled. "She got what she deserved. No! She got less than she deserved!" She drew herself up and glared at him. "You may put me outside if you wish. It will be better than in here."

Ogden grinned. "Stay where you are. Mrs. Ogden and I have settled Mrs. Reese on our sofa. But tomorrow, we'll see."

Mary Kate slept soundly.

Nothing much happened the next morning, which was sunny for a change. She didn't catch a glimpse of Electra Reese. She ate her porridge and set to work in the kitchen with the Indian women, scrubbing pots and dishes. But she knew a reckoning loomed.

At about ten, a clerk took her to James Douglas, the post's factor and second in command, who occupied an elegant office next to Dr. McLoughlin's. A fire crackled in a fieldstone fireplace, casting a faint heat into the cool room.

"Close the door, please," he said smoothly, dabbing his runny nose with a handkerchief.

She did, and sat down across from him.

"It is not my intent to adjudicate a quarrel, Mrs. O'Malley. So we'll simply separate you and Mrs. Reese. We've given you the hospitality of the post, and expect a certain decorum in return. We do our best to alleviate hardship, and that means sheltering people at some cost to ourselves and the company. On occasion, we've refused to welcome people. Not long ago we prohibited a Yankee horse thief from abiding here.

"Mrs. Reese alleges you've laid hand on her, ejected her from the room we provided her, and have behaved—well, she went on at great length about your offenses to her person, and the abuse she's received from you. Very distasteful, I must say. You may reply if you wish."

"I am Irish."

"How am I to interpret that?"

"I think you know."

He stared. "I'm a man of several bloods. It does not affect my conduct."

"You do not understand."

"Oh, I suppose I do. I imagine Mrs. Reese is a trial."

She nodded.

He sighed. "You don't deny that you pitched her out of the door?"

"With both hands, one on the front of her wrapper and one on the' rear. And with a kick too. And I would do it again, mind you. And if you treated me just as how she did, I would pitch you out the door too, I would."

Some faint amusement lit his sallow features.

"For the time being, we'll move you into the pantry off the kitchen. Not very private, but a roof over you. At five in the morning, the cooks come in to start breakfast, but you'll manage, I'm sure."

"That is what she wanted. Exactly."

"We're out of space."

She laughed. "Out of patience, I would say!"

Not a muscle flickered in his face. She realized she hadn't the faintest idea what James Douglas was thinking of her, of the episode, or of Electra Reese.

"You might wish to contact your husband at the mission, Mrs. O'Malley. Perhaps he's ready to receive you."

There it was, bland as the man himself, smooth and polished but plain. The boot, wrapped up in velvet.

"He is coming for Christmas. We have not had the sacrament in a year, almost."

Douglas nodded. "That will be an opportune time to discuss your future."

She stood, stiffly, undefeated. "There is a little thing you should know, Mr. James Douglas. Every day I have been here I have found work to do. We have borrowed nary a shilling, John O'Malley and me, and I have won my board and room by mending, and scullery work, and cleaning. And not for a pence either. Not for a wee little credit in your store either. Just for the food and a roof.

"I will not trouble you or Dr. McLoughlin any more. When John O'Malley comes, we will go to the Christmas mass and receive the blessing, and then we will leave you on Christmas Day. And we will owe you not a farthing. We are proud; we are not going to mire ourselves in debt. We will make our way.

"I am wondering, Mr. Douglas, whether you can say as much about any other immigrant stranded here. Your Mr. Ogden and his boatmen saved our lives, and John O'Malley and me, we have been thinking how to repay you. So I thank you for the roof over my head, and the food, and the chance to escape the torments of Mrs. Reese."

She didn't have the faintest idea how bland Douglas took that.

18

John McLoughlin read the express from Sir George Simpson—the queen had recently knighted the governor—with horror, and then with bitterness. Even as he read, he felt his bones ache.

He had never read anything quite so callous. Not only did Governor Simpson offer not a word of condolence or sympathy, but he refused to bring the murderers of his son to justice, and coldly advised McLoughlin that if he wished to bring the malefactors to trial in London, he could do it at his own expense, which would be about ten thousand pounds, because the company wouldn't bear the cost.

There was still more, but McLoughlin put down the lengthy diatribe and rubbed his temples. In June had come the horrifying word that his son John, the factor in charge of Fort Stikine up near Russian Alaska, had been murdered by his own men. Simpson had hastily investigated and ended up believing the self-serving story told by the very ruffians who had killed John, men who were the worst of all those brutes employed by the company.

John had been a dissolute wastrel, according to Simpson's icy analysis; a weakling and bumbler. His ledgers weren't in order. And he had been shot during one of the many drunken brawls at Stikine. Therefore, Simpson had concluded, there wasn't much to do about the matter; the two culprits weren't worth prosecuting.

That cold news had torn the chief factor to pieces. He didn't believe what the governor had said about his own son, and he resented Simpson's unusual callousness.

That bitter summer he had dispatched his most gifted and trusted men to look into the matter, and soon enough the truth had come out: young John's conduct had been exemplary. He didn't even use his liquor allowance. His books were in order. He had had trouble coping with the unruly older *engagés,* many of them French Canadians, who increasingly took advantage of the young man. These had taken to pilfering the company store for trinkets with which to buy the favors of the local Indian women, and when John had sternly put a stop to it, the response had been bloody murder and coverup.

All this Dr. McLoughlin had conveyed to George Simpson and the London directors in harsh and acrimonious tones, but he got nowhere with his petitions, and the governor had never varied from his original conclusion that the fault lay with young John. His ripostes to McLoughlin grew colder and more arrogant with each exchange.

There was more, much more. Simpson was insisting on his mad plan to close all the trading posts McLoughlin had established along the Northwest coast, and to rely instead on the miserable *Beaver,* the cumbersome wood-eating steamboat that was to replace the posts. It didn't seem to matter that it took two days of woodcutting to fuel a one-day trip by the steamship, and that the cost of operating the trouble-prone craft greatly exceeded the cost of the posts.

Nor was that the end of it. Simpson once again admonished the doctor not to assist the Americans, not to encourage immigration, not to lend supplies, but to resist the foreigners in every way. The company would in no way assume the burdens of doing so, and if McLoughlin did so, it would be against the company's express direction, and at his personal risk and expense.

And still more. Simpson could scarcely write a letter without its running pages and pages, mandates from on high, Ten Commandments, a letter from Mount Sinai, a papal bull, and damnation upon the slightest failure to comply.

McLoughlin's antagonism toward the company he had nurtured for two decades now burned deep and bitter. The feeling was new to him. For all those years, he had rejoiced in his work, and his company.

"James," he said, upon spotting Douglas at the door. "Read this."

He handed the lengthy epistle to the chief trader, who read it calmly. Douglas was always calm. Douglas would be calm en route to hell.

"He offers no solace," Douglas said.

"You always say exactly the right and careful thing. What should I do?"

"You'll get nowhere with George Simpson. And nowhere with the board, it appears."

"I want justice. If it takes ten thousand pounds, then I'll pay ten thousand pounds to bring those scoundrels to justice."

"You have strong feelings, John." It was a mild rebuke.

"James, for once, say what you think."

The second in command smiled suavely, and dabbed at his runny nose. "I think you'll do what you'll do, and any admonition on my part would be wasted."

"What about the rest? Simpson wants to undo everything I've built."

"He's the governor, and we have naught but to obey."

"Do you think the forts should be abandoned? Taku, Sitka, Stikine, Simpson, McLoughlin, Victoria, Nisqually, Umpqua, and the one at Yerba Buena in Mexico?"

"Sometimes men at loftier elevations see things we don't, John. They see the Americans coming, they see the pounds and shillings—"

"You didn't answer me. I asked for *your* opinion. Should they be abandoned?"

Douglas smiled. "We can't always have what we believe is right."

McLoughlin chopped off a harsh response before it escaped his throat, and sank into his seat, peppered with doubts. Maybe his superiors were right.

But he needed to justify himself: "If I had failed to rescue the Americans in their distress, I would be no better than a murderer. I did it because we had to. There's been little expense for the company. These are loans, and I expect repayment. The business is lucrative."

Douglas smiled silently, irritating the chief factor.

"How are we to feed these people? We can't. But by lending them seed wheat, selling plows and the rest, we'll help them feed themselves. You know exactly what would happen if the Americans starve. They'd lay siege to this post and pillage our stores. That's what desperate men do."

"It makes perfect sense, John," Douglas said. "But of course so do the directors and Simpson. They aren't about to surrender. Every time we help these Americans, we're losing our grip on this country."

McLoughlin sighed. Douglas was the enameled, nimble company marionette. But did he have a will or a soul? Did he believe in anything? Did he think there was a God, or a devil? If only Black Douglas would resist him once in a while, or speak his doubts, or remind him of his duties! But Douglas was a man of liquid opinion that could be poured handily into any beaker.

Simpson had directed Douglas to start work on a new Pacific Department post, up on Vancouver Island, which was unlikely to become American territory and therefore a safe haven. That was just one more misery that the doctor would soon endure. The thought of this great Columbia River post, a fortress he had built and rebuilt, overseeing every sturdy building, every wheatfield, every vineyard and orchard, being casually abandoned was as much as a man could bear. Suddenly the world was whirling out of control, and he was reeling.

"I might retire. I've money enough," he said.

"Where?"

"Oregon City. My claim there."

"The company's claim?"

"It's going to the Americans, everything south of the river. And they don't let companies claim land. Only private persons. So I'll claim the falls and pay the company something when the joint occupation ends, to keep it in company hands."

"If you can keep it," Douglas said.

McLoughlin nodded. He'd chased off a Yank carpenter who threw up a shack on his claim, and then he'd tried to get one of Jason Lee's ministers, a man named Waller, off the land, but ended up letting the Methodists build a store there, and he even gave them five lots and some timbers he had cut for his own building. He wished he hadn't, but big, grinning Jason Lee had assured him that everything would be all right.

"Oh, I've something to report," Douglas said. "A little tiff last night. Among our guests."

"If nobody was murdered, I'm not interested."

"The Irish lady, O'Malley, pitched her roommate, Electra Reese, out the door last night. The grieving widow, you know. She was quite put out, so I banished Mrs. O'Malley to the pantry, since there's nowhere else. And advised her to move along shortly."

"I'm sorry. I like her."

"Well, she has a temper, and we can't have that here. I think she'll stay for the Christmas mass and then abandon us."

McLoughlin smiled. He rarely found humor in anything these days, but the thought of the young Irish lady pitching the uppity blond Reese out of the room tickled him.

"James, how much do the Reeses owe us?"

"I'd have to check the accounts."

"Do that. Mrs. Reese seems to be buying out the store, and I lent her brother-in-law a considerable sum. He wanted to outfit and look for land."

"I'll get the figures, John."

"I think I'm going to cut her off. It's enough that we shelter her. Of all this latest bunch, the Reeses trouble me the most. He's been talking against the company, against me. And agitating for some sort of rump government. Word comes back to me."

"Shall I have the honor of telling Electra Reese?"

"No, I'll do it."

Later, with ledgers in hand, the doctor summoned Electra Reese. She appeared at his office elegantly gowned in fawn wool handsomely tailored to her thin form. She was not one for the rustic life, and he wondered why she had come west.

"Are you happy here, Mrs. Reese?"

"I am now, since Mr. Douglas solved the one misery in my life."

"So I've heard. Word reaches me that you do not entertain kind thoughts about the Hudson's Bay Company."

"It's a fine company, sir."

"But its employees are not satisfactory. They are . . . French, mixed blood, Kanakas, colored, Catholic?"

She stared, inscrutable, not the faintest sign of emotion on her glacial face.

"And they live wickedly without benefit of the clergy?"

She fidgeted, her hands plucking at her blond hair.

"Including the chief factor?"

She gazed out the window. He discerned only disdain in her eyes.

"James Douglas is a Canadian justice of the peace, and he's duly authorized to perform civil marriages. He married Marguerite and me some while ago. This summer, in the midst of a certain grief, I read a book that offered me consolation. It's called *The End of Controversy*. I'd been a lifelong Church of England man, Anglican, but turned to the Catholic Church. Marguerite and I have accepted the faith. At the same time, Father Blanchet sanctified our marriage. He's the missioner down at Champoeg. Are you satisfied? Or does it concern you that Marguerite is half Swiss and half Cree?"

Tight lines formed around her icy lips.

"Have you something against the Roman church, Mrs. Reese? And something against the honorable company?"

She turned to leave.

"No, please, not yet. I've learned that you've spent over forty pounds at the store without offering any assurance of repayment. Two hundred American dollars, on top of Garwood Reese's heavy debt. The total comes to two hundred pounds. I've asked my people not to permit further purchases until there's been some substantial repayment."

He watched Electra Reese swallow back rage.

"Since you're unhappy with us and our hospitality, I think it's time for you to make arrangements elsewhere."

Now, at last, she showed signs of agitation. "But I'm a widow . . . I'm not well. The trip, it made me sick."

He saw calculation in her gaze. "Yes, and putting a sick widow out would be one more strike against the company, eh? Make arrangements, Mrs. Reese."

"But I don't know anyone."

"Don't know anyone! You came across a continent with a wagon train, a hundred people. Six or seven months of intimacy. And you don't know them? Or maybe you didn't *want* to know them. Is that what you're saying?"

She compressed her lips.

"I think you're right," he said. "You don't know anyone."

She stood suddenly.

"We'll help you find someone," he said.

"Are you through with me?"

He nodded. She glared at him and walked away.

19

Garwood Reese seethed with ambition. During his sojourn at the Falls of the Willamette he met Destiny and shook hands. The course of empire would be decided right there, in a burgeoning village thousands of miles from the seats of power.

Everywhere Reese looked, he found American settlers turning the hamlet into a town. Whether it would end up as Oregon City, as McLoughlin was calling it, or the Falls, as the Methodists were calling it, he didn't know. But Americans were plucking lots from McLoughlin's company and throwing up rude dwellings, some of them so close to the cataract that he wondered how anyone could sleep, or even conduct business. Sometimes a breeze blew cold mist, whipped from the tumultuous waters, over the whole village. He sensed energy here; pulsing, roaring, bullying force that would cut wood, mill grain, and build empires. Here was the jewel of the Pacific!

On the island, a new firm organized by the Methodists, the Island Milling Company, was building a sturdy sawmill using the very millrace that McLoughlin had blasted years before. The audacity of it amazed Reese.

He wandered out to the island and talked with the crew erecting the structure, barely able to converse over the roar of tumbling water.

"Won't Hudson's Bay stop you?" he asked a millwright.

"How can they? We claim it too," the man replied. "And besides, he's building his own mill, right over there. This race'll power several mills. As far as we're concerned, he's the trespasser."

"But wasn't he here first?"

"Not so anyone could notice. He never *did* anything. He never built a mill. Besides, possession's nine-tenths of the law. I'll tell you something. No claim here's worth the paper it's written on because there's way to protect it. So whoever puts the land to use and holds it has the advantage."

"And that's Waller, I gather."

"Yas, yas. He's claimed the whole thing, waterpower, town site and all, and he'll make it stick. But the milling company's a separate enterprise, plenty of men in on it. I've a share myself. Best thing the mission ever did. Waller's a shrewd man. Business sense. Keen eye for the dollar. Makes you wonder why he chose his calling. Claimed this privately, for himself, not for the mission. Now it's Yank property, no matter what the English say."

"I'd like to meet him."

"He's living in that wood house next to the store, and that's a story too!" The millwright grinned. "He begged the timbers from old McLoughlin, put up the house, and now he's got old McLoughlin on the run! He also begged a few lots from McLoughlin for mission purposes, and got a start that way, never putting up a penny. That's how to squeeze McLoughlin. Just tell him it's to advance Christian religion and the old duffer smiles and gives you whatever you ask."

"I saw a surveyor working on lots this morning."

"Hudspeth. An American. McLoughlin hired him. He staked out all of these, and he's still got most of the town site to go."

"I know him. He came out here this year."

"Well, it don't matter who surveys the lots. Waller, he figures Hudspeth's just doing the job for hisself, not McLoughlin. That minister, he's going to get aholt of those lots, and he don't let nothing get in his way, especially them British."

Reese retreated to town, found the reverend's house and knocked on the door. The reverend was home and accepting company. Reese found himself in a dirt-floored cottage, but nonetheless a substantial building compared to anything else in town.

Waller turned out to be a merry man with a brightness in his eye and a sly wit. The reverend was perfectly willing to answer Reese's questions.

"Mr. Reese," he said, with a grand sweep of a hand, "this is mine. I've claimed it and my claim's got more force than his. McLoughlin's trespassing on my property." He laughed. "That'd be news to him!"

"But how can you claim it?"

"Why can't I? What's to prevent it? I'm here!"

"What's to prevent me from claiming it?"

The reverend turned serious. "I'd say that'd be immoral, especially snatching it from another American. This will all be part of the United States soon; that's why my claim's good. That's why the British claims don't count for anything, and I just ignore them. We're all united about Oregon. It will never end up in British hands."

"Maybe McLoughlin will have something to say about that."

Waller laughed. "Let him howl!"

"How big is this town site?"

"A square mile. At least McLoughlin and I both agree on that. Plenty of lots. Plenty of mill sites on that millrace. Plenty of land for commerce. That gristmill he's putting up . . . let him. It'll be mine just as soon as we get the boundary line settled."

"Are there any other places on the Willamette River where a town might be started?" Reese asked, getting to the heart of it.

"Sure, anywhere along here. It's all fertile valley land, like Frenchmen's Flat. But the Methodists have got this place and all the other good ones . . . you thinking of starting a town?"

"I was counting on it."

Waller squinted. "You going to be my rival? Take business from me? I think you'd better not, Mr. Reese. This is Methodist country and not one of us would buy a lot from you. I'd see to it. Are you a Methodist?"

Reese shook his head.

"I thought so. Never heard of you. Well, this is mission country here. And we're organized. And we're running it."

Reese saw his hopes go a-glimmering, but he smiled. "I imagine I can be of service to you and your mission colleagues," he said smoothly.

"What do you do, Mr. Reese?"

"I am a man experienced in public office."

"There aren't any here!"

They both laughed, but Waller leaned forward earnestly. "I'll tell you something. This place, right here, is going to be the capital of Oregon. This is where it will all be decided. This is where Americans will form a government and drive out the British. Right here!" He jabbed a finger toward the floor. "You work with us, the mission people, and you'll have a government position soon enough. We need patriots here, not opportunists."

"How long will that be?"

"Just as fast as we can push Congress into acting."

Reese sat there, seeing his hopes drain away. He had counted on opposition from the Hudson's Bay Company; he hadn't given a thought to the powerful Methodists, and hadn't even dreamed that these missioners, led by a clergyman, would be commandeering the best town site on the river. Nor had he considered himself a rival of these Americans . . . until now.

"Reverend, how can a man get ahead here? I'd like to own a parcel of lots."

Waller laughed. "Sonny boy, you're too late, 'less you snatch 'em from Hudson's Bay."

"What about a government? Someone should organize one. I could do that. I know how governments work. You'll need a clerk. Need someone to record claims."

Waller leaned forward again. "Mr. Reese, when the Methodists decide to do so, we will do so."

Reese hastily excused himself. In the space of a morning, his dreams of a livelihood had tumbled down, demolished by a bright-eyed clergyman with the instincts of Commodore Vanderbilt.

He spent the next day wandering the nascent town, talking to the surveyor, Hudspeth, talking to settlers, talking to Abernethy. He garnered all sorts of odd information, but all he got out of it was the certain knowledge that he would not be able to get a living by selling lots. And unless he joined the Methodists, he would not get a position in whatever makeshift government they formed.

He braved the December rains to venture upriver to Champoeg, and found a sleepy hamlet there along with the Catholic mission. Not a place for the likes of Garwood Reese. He pushed onward to Mission Bottoms, and saw the well-organized Methodists in their lair, and continued upstream to the new settlement of Chemeketa, where Jason Lee's people were building another mission and a milling operation. And everywhere he turned, he saw that he was too late to go into the town-lot business for himself.

The Methodists had beaten him. Odd, how they had come west to Christianize the Indians and turned, instead, to getting and spending. But Abernethy had explained all that one morning:

"We found that you can't just convert 'em," he said. "They don't convert. We tried hard. They want white men's magic. Guns and metal and power, and that's what they think the Good Book's all about. So we've turned to business, long as we're here and this is a fine place to get ahead."

Slowly, Reese made his way back to the Falls of the Willamette, knowing that his survival depended on currying the goodwill of the missioners. For all practical purposes, he would have to conjure himself into a Methodist . . . or starve.

20

John O'Malley was winding up a long cold day peeling and notching logs when he learned that Jasper Constable was looking for him.

Wearily, he washed in the trough beside the dormitory, and set off to find the dominie, who was usually lingering about the warm mission offices, reluctant to leave.

"Ah! O'Malley, there you are," Constable said, peering over his wire-rimmed spectacles. "Have a fine day, did you?"

O'Malley nodded.

"Jason Lee tells me you're going to Fort Vancouver, and you've asked for the rowboat. Is that so?"

"I am leaving in the morning."

"Good. You'll have a passenger, then. I've been asked to officiate at the Christmas Eve services."

O'Malley nodded. "I will be leaving early, soon as a bit of light shows me the way."

"Ah, that early?"

"Long trip. But of course, if we take turns rowing—"

"Oh, I'll leave that to you. My mind leaps and jumps but my muscles don't. And I've a sore throat I'm watching out for."

"You are a fit man."

"A scholar, sir. You don't learn rowing in divinity school."

O'Malley smiled sourly. This had little to do with health, and much to do with station. This divine had just hiked across a continent and was hard as iron. "Before dawn," he said.

While he was in the building, he stopped at Lee's lair and exchanged the ten dollars of wages on the books for a letter of credit. He would buy cloth and needles and thread for Mary Kate at the mission store at the Falls. Clothing was what they needed the most.

He visited the mission kitchen and talked the Indian women out of two loaves of bread for the journey and then returned to his dormitory bunk.

The boys accepted him now and grinned at him.

"I am going to Fort Vancouver for Christmas, lads," he said.

"Bring us good things, Mr. O'Malley," said his next-door neighbor, Ah Moc Moc.

"A wee something for each; that I will do if I can."

He wasn't sure he could manage even that. The boys were not going to their tribes for Christmas and would continue to receive instruction, except on Christmas Day.

He discovered the next morning that Constable had beaten him, and was standing beside the overturned rowboat in the frosty hush. The reverend had acquired a greatcoat and was bundled in it. O'Malley had only the ragged coat on his back and was suddenly grateful he would be rowing.

He flipped the boat, dragged it to water, added oars and the loaves, helped Constable step in, and shoved off into the swift-moving Willamette. He would not have to paddle hard.

Mist rose from the river, blurring the shorelines, and dampening sound, even the small gurgle of his oars as they bit the water. The predawn sky hinted of sunlight and he was glad he would not row through snow or rain.

The reverend occupied the rear seat of the flat-bottomed boat, facing the future, slouched deep in his warm black coat, his eyes gazing upon things unseen and mysterious. O'Malley sat amidships, facing the past, rowing steadily in the utter silence of the quickening dawn, slackening when his arms ached. They faced each other, but to the dominie O'Malley was invisible.

A frosty breeze eddied about the Irishman, chilling him, so he rowed harder, letting the current steer him along the gloomy shoreline.

"We are both a long way from home this Christmas," he said.

"What? What?"

"Home."

"My home is wherever God sends me."

"Well, right now, I do not have a bit of land, nor a house to call my own, nor a sheep or a cow, nor a tree or grass. But I will be home for Christmas, for home to this man is wherever his bride may be."

A rim of blue tinted the eastern sky.

"How is Mrs. O'Malley?"

"Haven't heard. But she is there at the fort, with a roof over her and food on the table. She is homesick. Home is Clonmel, County Tipperary, and her family, the Burkes, and her pa, and her brother and sisters, and the good whiskey-sipping Father Riordan . . . and Oregon is like Pitcairn's Island, and the United States might as well be Madagascar, but she is going to be all right when the wee one comes along and starts her cooing. It is better here than there."

The minister nodded. "Home is where the church sends me. But Fort Vancouver's a beastly place, run by a beastly company, lost to vice and lust and greed. The cardinal sins are all flourishing at Vancouver, and I think they want it so. I go because I'm called, and not because they've earned respect."

"They saved my life and Mary Kate's and the little child she carries. That is good enough for me."

"Well, I'm grateful of course, but that doesn't excuse the wickedness or remove the stain." The minister tapped his breast. "Right here I have a draft for one hundred thirteen dollars. I got it from Jason Lee. It'll pay off my debt to the Hudson's Bay Company, every last penny. I didn't want to be saddled with the slightest debt to them. So I prevailed on Lee. It's an advance on much of my salary for the next year. But I'll be free, you see, to take a stand, as any good man must."

"A stand?"

"Against the company. I won't owe them a penny."

"Not a pence. But maybe you owe them four lives, a decent burial, and the means to start over."

"Oh, that always had commercial overtones, O'Malley. Save a man and you've got a customer."

"Do you really believe that? Dr. McLoughlin told me that he did it out of conscience."

"Well, after a manner, I suppose. Do you know what a parable is?"

O'Malley smiled. He was tired of rowing so he let the current tug the boat.

The minister leaned forward earnestly. "Suppose a great storm came up and threatened to capsize this boat. Suppose the Serpent himself appeared suddenly, quieted the waters, and let us make shore, sparing us from certain death. Would I be grateful? Oh, in an abstract sort of way. The Serpent spared me, after all. But I would be mindful that the Serpent did it for his own uses. He thinks he's bought my loyalty, you see? But he hasn't. So in the end, gratitude doesn't apply to the case. I will still rebuke the Serpent, eh?"

"And who is the Serpent? Hudson's Bay? How do you reach that conclusion?" O'Malley asked combatively.

"That scarcely needs demonstrating."

"No, please demonstrate it."

"Some things aren't visible to you, I suppose. But I can understand that. You've been busy sawing and hammering."

"Well, have they helped your Methodist mission? And the others? The Presbyterians up on the Walla Walla?"

"Yes, but for obvious reasons."

"Have they rescued numerous Yanks?"

The minister nodded, obviously bored with the inquisition.

"Did they lend Yanks the means to grow grains, lend livestock, lend tools?"

"The devil always gets his due."

"How about McLoughlin, then?"

Constable pondered that a bit. "I concede he has some virtues. And yet no decent man could possibly work for so rapacious a company or consort with a squaw. No, he's imperiled his soul."

O'Malley felt the stir of anger percolating upward in him.

"And therefore you owe him no gratitude. Did you feel that way when he hurried us into his parlor, rejoicing that we were alive, offering shelter and food and comforts?"

"No, I don't feel any particular gratitude. They waited too long to rescue us, not wanting to go to the expense. He wanted to spare the company the last pence. It took a sleet storm to spur them to act. And then they were too late. They dithered; that's what I've heard.

"Please don't look so shocked, O'Malley. And don't misconstrue my remarks. I am humbly grateful for deliverance. I thank God for the rescue. Let Him have the credit. Hudson's Bay was merely the instrument of Divine Providence. *The Hand of God!* It can inspire even the most faithless to good works. He can soften the hearts of hard men, as he did that November day. So I am simply careful to give thanks where it is deserved."

O'Malley started rowing again. "I will be grateful to the man for as long as I have breath in me," he said.

"I would expect that of you, my friend. It is an obvious sentiment. I've come to accept the view of Garwood Reese, who's been saying that whatever the company does, opportunism is behind it. Even rescuing Americans. Charity or mercy played no part in it; a desire not to look bad was part of the motive; and settling a population who'd buy goods at the company store was part of it, and profit was all of it. That Reese! He's a shrewd man, and a formidable one!"

O'Malley laughed.

That ended the talk for the moment. A golden glow radiated from the east, and with it came color to the quiet world. They passed ducks and geese, spotted a doe on the riverbank, watched crows circle and listened to them complain, and rejoiced when the horizontal rays of sun bathed them in warming light.

They did not again debate weighty matters, but Constable made hearty observations and spread kindly thoughts upon the silent waters.

"Why, what a masterpiece of a morning," he exclaimed. "How often I observe that God is the perfect artist."

O'Malley focused on his rowing. The minister was spreading enough bonhomie for both of them.

They drifted past Frenchmen's Flat in a low bright sun, and O'Malley could see blue smoke rising from distant chimneys where the French Canadians were homesteading. Then, around a sweeping bend, Champoeg hove into view. The tree-lined banks obscured the village, but the Hudson's Bay warehouse stood bankside, with a small pier and boats nearby. A little distant, beyond the latticework of naked branches, rose the spire of St. Paul's mission, Father François Blanchet's project, the westernmost Catholic post in the Northwest.

"Say, my friend, why didn't you go there instead of our mission?"

"Can't speak French, and they would not be able to pay me. Father Blanchet does not have a sou. You Methodists have money from your mission board and your enterprises, the mill, the store, the farms. I need cash so I work for you."

"Well, how do you know that?"

"I talked to Catholics at Fort Vancouver when I got there."

"You've been helpful to us. Learning the trades fast, I'm told. We're dreadfully short of help. We're going to serve the whole American population, you know. I have to agree with Lee; we can't do much with the Indians."

"They are good sweet boys, sir. Well behaved. They only want understanding."

"How would you know?"

"I am one of them."

"Ah! You're fond of little metaphors. I'm more sober myself, but levity is permitted."

"There are better virtues than sobriety, Reverend," said O'Malley. "I incline toward gratitude, myself."

21

Christmas Eve! Mary Kate O'Malley waited impatiently for John. She knew only that he was coming. She didn't know when. She hovered about the fort's gate, peering down the long slope to the river, aching for the sight of him.

The coldness always drove her back to the kitchen, and then she would pass time helping the Hudson's Bay cooks prepare the feast. She ached for some clothing, anything that would let her endure the winter. But she had only the rude dress she had sewn, and one change lent to her by some of the Canadian women.

Cleanliness had always been a problem there in that public kitchen. But every night, after the last pot had been scrubbed, she had the kitchen and pantry to herself, and then she made liberal use of the remaining hot water to give herself a bath, or even wash her hair in the darkness. It wasn't so bad; at least that's what she told herself. Food, warmth, a roof over her head. But she was growing heavy with child, and she found no comfort sleeping on the plank floor.

Now, this Christmas of 1842, she had scrubbed herself as best she could for John, washed her dark hair until it shone, and tied a borrowed red ribbon in it. And waited. All that dragging afternoon she waited, rushing out the gates whenever the fort's bell signaled the arrival of a bateau. It grew dusky in that solstice time, and still John didn't come.

He must come! He had sent word he would!

Then, finally, in twilight, she hiked into the broad fields below the post and did see him in a group of new arrivals, their breaths steaming the air. He carried a bundle under his arm. With him was the minister, Jasper Constable, the one who had been on the Oregon Trail with them.

She ran, feeling the cold air whip her skirts, her arms outstretched, the weight of her child in her, ran into his outstretched arms and felt his arms embrace her tightly, and felt his laughter, and the bristle of his cheek, and the thud of his pulse.

Only after a long hug and whispered lovesongs did she discover Constable staring everywhere but at them, as if the embrace of a husband and wife were unseemly. Which, she surmised, was exactly what he thought.

"Merry Christmas, Reverend," she said.

"Yes, yes, indeed, the sacred time again."

"The happiest time."

John had a strong arm about her and was half carrying her to the post. They were walking amid a whole group of people, including voyageurs, all of them gathering at this seat of empire for the holy days.

John looked grand; lean, weathered, his eyes bright and filled with love, his brown hair unkempt, his ragged coat all that stood between him and freezing temperatures.

"And what have you in that bundle, love?" she asked.

"Cloth, my darling. Broadcloth, flannel, cotton sheeting. Needles and thread. Enough for a dress for you, a shirt for me, a good winter cape for you . . . and some wee things for the baby."

"Oh! What a gift!"

He grinned.

They penetrated the post and were at once surrounded by the high stockade and dozens of buildings that stayed the wind.

Constable halted. "Thank you, my good man," he said. "I presume you'll row me back?"

"Imagine so," John said dryly.

"Good. Now to find McLoughlin. I'll pay him every cent, and make him give me a receipt. I've been waiting for this for weeks, this moment. Never let it be said that a Methodist minister didn't pay every last penny of debt."

"He will be pleased, I'm sure, sir."

"Will he? Rather not, I'd expect. He prefers that we're all beholden. Well, Merry Christmas. Tomorrow, eh?"

They watched the stiff and stately minister trudge toward the company offices.

"He is a good man, is Jasper Constable," she said. "Paying up and all. I hope his wife is well, and they are bearing their loss, and the boys are fine."

He smiled mysteriously, odd lights in his eyes, and nodded.

She was leading him toward the dining hall, that being the only place she could have a minute with him. Soon a gong would announce the feast, and the hall would fill. She had some things to explain, such as what constituted her dwelling now.

The aromas of roasting beef and potatoes and the yeasty smell of bread met them as they entered, along with smoke from a dozen oil lamps. She led him to a bench at a trestle table, and they sat.

"Now here, my colleen, is a bit of Christmas, all I could manage, anyway," he said, pulling fabric from a gunnysack. Navy blue broadcloth, nankeen, green flannel, yards of white linen, a thick textured wool, some white cotton flannel.

"Oh! John O'Malley," she said, seeing skirts and shirts and a cape in her mind. "Where did you get them?"

"The Methodists have a store at the Falls. We stopped a bit."

"You rowed all the way?"

"No, the mission rowboat is beached above the falls. We caught a company bateau from there to here. I am not even tired."

"O'Malley, you I love."

"And you I love also. Is the little one . . . ?"

"The little one is coming along, O'Malley."

"And you?"

"A bit of sickness in the mornings."

"Have they treated you well?"

She laughed. "That I will tell about later."

"Something is wrong?"

"I am warm, fed, and safe."

He stared at her, trying to fathom what had changed.

She wanted to hug him again, but cooks and serving women bustled through the big room, preparing for the crowd.

"Tell me, my love."

"It is nothing for the eve of Our Lord's birth, O'Malley."

He waited, gently, and she relented.

"I live in the pantry; there is no other place to put me."

"But you were billeted with some of the women—"

"Electra Reese . . . did not want me there."

"You were not good enough for her, Mary Kate?"

"She was not good enough for me! One night I pitched her right out the door, and in her wrapper too."

An expression more comic than concerned built in his face. "Oh! And then what happened?"

"James Douglas came and moved me. He thought perhaps I would prefer to leave after Christmas. That is how the man put it. His words are like soft butter."

"And what was Electra Reese doing that got your temper up?"

"Making a servant girl of me."

"I would say maybe you tried for a while, Mary Kate, and the more you tried, that being your sweet nature, the more the woman took advantage."

She squeezed his hand.

"And you have worked for your keep every day, while they gad about and sponge off the company. Is it not so, because we agreed to do it?"

"I have, O'Malley." She leaned close. "I heard some gossip. "Electra Reese spent forty pounds at the store getting herself up, and finally Dr. McLoughlin cut off the credit. And she has been saying terrible things about him ever since."

"But does he know you've been earning your way?"

"Of course not! How would the chief factor, who runs an empire, know what one small woman does here in his kitchen?"

"Does Douglas?"

"No. He was not listening when I told him. Nor Ogden neither. Only the French Canadians and the breed women. They know, and they like me."

"It is not fair or right, Mary Kate."

"O'Malley, it is Christmas," she whispered.

"I have got to get you out of here."

"I am all right."

"A scullery sleeping in a pantry!"

"O'Malley, do not be worrying about me. You go make some money and get some land and be thinking of our baby."

"No, I am going to get you out."

"There is no place."

"Somewhere there is a place."

"I wish we could go back to . . ." She pushed a thought away.

"I will not have the English treating you this way."

A gong sounded, and the dining hall quickly filled. Mary Kate swiftly plucked up the fabric she treasured so much—cloth her husband had won with weeks of brutal toil—and hid it in the pantry.

She knew most of these company employees, single men as well as the married, who lived in cottages strewn about the fields beyond the fort. All were gathered here for the Christmas feast.

Dr. McLoughlin himself appeared, his crown of white hair haloing his ruddy face. She knew he had come to bless the food and welcome guests. He and Marguerite, James and Amelia Douglas, the Ogdens, and the HBC clerks, along with the minister, Jasper Constable, and the priest, Father Blanchet, would dine later at the chief factor's bright and commodious home.

She watched Electra Reese, on Garwood's arm, settle at one of the tables, looking sour. The French Canadians gave her wide berth, but the Brownells joined her. A few others who had been a part of the overland party joined them, but most of the congregants at this feast were the Montrealers of New France. She tugged O'Malley to a table whose company was entirely French.

The White-headed Eagle arose, and his looming presence was enough to quiet the crowd.

"We welcome you all," he said in a low voice that carried to every cranny.

"Our Hudson's Bay people, and our guests. Our good cooks have prepared a fine wassail feast. There'll be some Madeira for you this evening with your meal, and a punchbowl and carols later.

"Now, our friend the Reverend Mr. Constable of the Methodist mission will conduct services in the chapel at nine, and Father Blanchet will celebrate the Yuletide mass at eleven. Now I will bless this food, and then you may begin. We wish you all the most blessed of Christmases."

Dr. McLoughlin intoned a blessing, smiled, and walked out.

"Father Blanchet will help us," O'Malley said. "Someone here will translate. After mass."

She loved O'Malley for his devotion.

Later, when she listened to the Latin-song of the Christmas mass, and watched the candles gutter in the darkness, and watched Father Blanchet lift the Host, and studied the wondrously carved crèche at the altar, with the little Holy One upon the hay of a manger, and the Blessed Mother looking over him, Mary Kate thought of the angels singing of their joy, and pushed aside a pang of sadness.

22

James Douglas surveyed the guests in John McLoughlin's bright-candled parlor that Christmas Eve and wondered how many of them grasped that all this was doomed. He particularly wondered whether the doctor himself understood the future.

Present on that festive evening were about thirty people, all of them senior company officials and their spouses, excepting only Father Blanchet and the American minister, Constable.

Doomed.

Douglas had recently been given the title Chief Factor by the directors in London. That was the very title held by McLoughlin, the only difference between them being McLoughlin's seniority. And the doctor received an annual five-hundred-pound bonus as well, for administering the northern plantations near Puget Sound.

Douglas didn't mind. The future was his. Sir George Simpson had asked him to build a new western headquarters post at Vancouver Island, on the Strait of Juan de Fuca. This great fortress on the Columbia would be abandoned. *Abandoned!* Its usefulness had diminished radically in recent years. The beaver had been trapped out and silk tophats were in fashion. For a while more HBC could thrive in this area, but only for a while. The Americans were swarming in and the boundary settlement might well put the headquarters inside of the United States. And finally, as both Simpson and the directors had pointed out, the bar at the mouth of the Columbia was hazardous, and the company needed a post with better sea access.

John McLoughlin had resisted the change with all his formidable powers, while Douglas had gently, discreetly, opposed him and hewed to the wishes of the directors and Governor Simpson, even corresponding privately with them.

But that was not much on his mind this festive evening. He was more interested in plumbing the mind of that rather odd American minister, Constable, so he maneuvered suavely through the evening until he caught the man alone, spooning up some plum pudding and staring dourly at the half-breed women, boisterous French, Cree clerks, others of various hue, and at Father Blanchet in his Roman collar and black suit.

"A festive party, is it not?" asked Douglas, as smoothly as long practice permitted.

"Yes, indeed, quite a feast!"

"The McLoughlins entertain every Christmas. Buffet, of course. Too many to sit at table. Marguerite has good help from the Canadian women."

A buffet table groaned under beef, ham, potatoes, puddings, breads, and wines. The doctor rarely drank, prohibited drinking and punished drunkenness, but he always relaxed his rules during dinners and holidays, when there was good port or Madeira on hand. The Methodist minister had not touched the punchbowl or poured a goblet of port from the cut-glass decanters.

"Yes, yes, they must have got the recipes from the English and Scots."

"It was good of you to come this evening. The company sends out Anglican clergy, but they don't stay long, and don't like the constricted life."

"This is scarcely rough, Mr. Douglas."

"Not here, in the chief factor's house, but everywhere else life is without amenity."

"Yes, it's hard. The mission's scarcely able to accommodate us. But we endure, in heath or illness. We have a calling."

"I like the Reverend Wilberforce's epigram. Have you heard it?"

"I can't say—"

"If I were a Cassowary on the plains of Timbuctoo, I would eat a missionary, Coat and bands and hymn-book, too."

"Oh! You Anglicans! Where did you ever hear that?"

"I read, Reverend. I hear your mission board's threatening to shut you down. Is it so?"

"Yes, it is so. We've harvested no souls, sir. The savage bosom yearns for magical power, not union with God. Mr. Lee now believes we must serve other purposes. He's appealing the decision."

"Ministering to settlers."

"Yes. Thousands are coming, you know. Every year, from now on."

That startled Douglas.

"Thousands, you say?"

"We're the vanguard, sir. We estimate between one and two thousand next year."

"I see. And how will all these countrymen of yours be fed?"

"God will provide."

"I hope they don't confuse God with the Hudson's Bay Company." He laughed softly.

The minister looked faintly annoyed. "It will be planned out, I'm sure."

"This post feeds its hundred, but only with a struggle."

Douglas wished that McLoughlin had heard the exchange. Fort Vancouver was doomed, destined for the scrap heap. The doctor had seen the post rise in a wilderness. He had built well, with solid British rectitude, built for three generations: thick beams, massive posts, huge planks, stout iron hinges, cedar shingles; built a lucrative business from beaver pelts, and then sea otters and salmon and sales of wood to the Sandwich Islanders, and trade with Cathay, only to have that imperious bastard, Simpson, tell him to close it all down and sell it for scrap.

Douglas sympathized, but prided himself in being a company man. What Simpson and the directors wanted, Douglas would suavely deliver. There would be a new post far enough north not to be threatened by Yankee migration; the trading posts along the coast would be replaced by a steamer trading from coastal village to village. And the money-losing post in Mexico's Yerba Buena, run by McLoughlin's son-in-law, would shutter—just as the governor insisted.

The Americans were swarming like hornets, and there was little the company could do about it except delay matters a few months or years, twisting and turning like a condemned man dodging the gallows noose. That and try to make a profit from it. If you're going to croak, you may as well sell tickets to the hanging.

"I think you're going to get what you Americans want, Mr. Constable. A nation stretching from sea to sea. Just as Canada will, to the north."

"It's our destiny," the minister said. "A nation pure in its intentions, devout, modeled on the clear principles of Christian canon, free and white. The City on the Hill."

"Except for the slaves?"

"God willing, they'll be free someday. They'll be eager to return to Africa."

Douglas doubted that. His mother, a Barbados freewoman, had no desire to return anywhere. British Guiana was her home. And he, part black, had no wish at all to leave this world. His father, a Scottish plantation owner in British Guiana, had sent him to the best schools England could provide, and he took secret delight that he was far better schooled than the white oafs who drifted through. Even now, deep in the American wilderness, he read from his library of English classics almost daily.

McLoughlin loomed.

"Ah, there you are, Reverend," he said. "It's a quarter to nine, and I thought you might want to prepare. I'll have a man take you to the chapel. We'll bell your flock in ten minutes."

"Yes, yes, thank you, Doctor. I hope my voice lasts."

The missioner hastened away.

Douglas watched him leave. "I've learned something, John. Did you know that one to two thousand Americans are coming out here next year?"

"I've heard it too, but it's just rumor. Are you sure?"

"That's what Constable says."

"All missionaries?"

"No, they've given up that pretense entirely. This is empire, John. American empire, Uncle Sam wearing Methodist britches."

"We'll steer them south, then."

"We can't be feeding and rescuing an entire migration."

"No, of course not. I'll speak to Jason Lee. They're going to have to raise plenty of grain next summer, and get some clothing and shelter and pasture and hay ready. Write Simpson. He must be informed of this intelligence."

Douglas fashioned a snare. "Some are going to arrive destitute and desperate. You'd best be thinking what to do," he said.

"Our Christian duty," McLoughlin replied. "I think they'll repay us, don't you? Do you know what Constable did when he arrived this evening? He marched straight to my house and gave me a draft for the provisions he'd gotten from the store. It's on a Philadelphia bank, and I'll forward it to London for collection. So there you are. The better class of these Americans are perfectly ethical. One account cleared in a matter of weeks."

Douglas absorbed that uneasily. Why did Constable, with his miserable missionary pittance, act so swiftly? Douglas thought he knew, and mentally put Constable in the camp of the company's most venomous adversaries. The company's flesh was too dark for the reverend.

A bronze bell clanged its Yuletide summons, and the Protestants among Dr. McLoughlin's coterie set down their goblets and gathered their capes and slid into the frosty night. Douglas gathered Amelia and followed the crowd headed for the well-candled chapel. From the mess hall, carols lifted lightly into the night.

The chapel bulged with company men as well as the Americans from the surrounding area. He found a bench for himself and Amelia and discovered the two Reeses a few seats away. He shared John McLoughlin's utter distrust of Garwood Reese and his distaste for Electra. But his distaste was nothing compared to Electra's disdain for the whole rabble in the chapel, written prettily across her glacial face. Douglas discerned within himself an odd wish to seduce her, like a merging of the antipodes.

Constable, in his black robe and a white stole, appeared on the stroke of nine, and welcomed them all with raised arms.

"Come let us rejoice!" he exclaimed hoarsely.

The service was impeccable and joyous.

23

Mary Kate O'Malley tried to be happy. Her husband sat beside her. The Christmas mass soared. She had precious calico and flannel to turn into skirts and blouses and a cape, and little things for the baby. This was the evening of joy, and the harbinger of peace on earth. She felt the stirrings of her child.

And yet she was not. Happiness seemed to belong to another world, a greener place far, far away, lost in mists of memory. She slept on a pantry floor in a public room.

But she tried. She listened to the Latin and uttered the responses. *Gloria in excelsis Deo.* She studied the crèche, thinking of her own baby. She peered through the candlelit darkness, seeing the honeyed faces of French, breeds, Indians, and there, to one side, the towering figure of John McLoughlin, his white-crowned head a foot above the rest, and short Marguerite beside him, and one or two of his children. She wasn't sure of that. Maybe grandchildren.

But Mary Kate felt heavy with desolation, and not even John's sturdy bulk beside her could vanquish that.

Then came the benediction and it was over.

"I am going to talk to McLoughlin," John said.

She shrank back. What would the chief factor do but brush them off?

He tugged her anyway, threading through the French-babbling crowd.

"Sir?" he said to the towering man, who was helping his wife throw a shawl over her shoulders.

"Why, yes . . . O'Malley, isn't it?"

"I need to talk to Father Blanchet. Could you translate for me?"

"I think he understands a bit of English . . ."

"I need to find a place for her." He gestured toward Mary Kate. "She is well along and has only the pantry for a home. I was hoping he could find some family on French Prairie to board her. I can pay them. I work for the Methodists."

McLoughlin lifted a hand. "Wait." he said. "Marguerite, I'll be with you directly."

The man who held empires in his palms lumbered toward the priest, who was greeting the last of his congregation at the doors. She could see the pair talking earnestly, the priest gesticulating and nodding. Then McLoughlin led Father Blanchet to the O'Malleys and introduced them.

"Father says there are many families among the Montrealers who would gladly keep your wife for you and want nothing for it."

"I will pay something."

"It's not necessary. These good French are eager to bless your Christmas. He invites you to come upriver with him tomorrow. Put everything in his hands, he says, and our Lord will provide."

"I must take the Methodist home, Dr. McLoughlin."

"It can all be arranged. Our voyageurs will be going. They can take your wife with them."

Mary Kate felt the stirrings of hope as she watched her husband thank the smiling priest and shake his hand.

"And where will you be tonight? Not in the pantry," McLoughlin said. "There's a small sacristy here. Right over there. It is yours, this sanctified place, this Christmas night, in the House of the Lord. Father Blanchet is a guest in my home, and you would be, too, but we haven't space." He smiled. "It's not a manger."

Mary Kate held back tears, curtsied as she had done always in another world, and thanked this giant of a man.

Blanchet smiled.

The thin priest studied them closely, probably wanting to say something to them, but then he nodded to McLoughlin and the pair of them left the church.

Mary Kate hastened to the mess hall to fetch her blanket and the tick she kept rolled up in the pantry, and ran back, feeling the nippy air on her cheeks.

Christmas had come late to her, but it had come, sweet and aglow and warm.

By the light of a guttering candle, they laid their pallet on a plank floor, in a somber sacristy redolent of wax and incense.

He clasped her hands. "This is a holy place, Mary Kate, and we will be minding ourselves."

"I will be minding for the baby's sake," she shot back.

Even so, they managed to make her small blanket warm them both, and she fell into the sweetest slumber she had known since they had reached Oregon.

Christmas morning they breakfasted heartily in the mess hall at a late hour, and then John went off to find the minister while she gathered her few things into a bundle. What did her worldly goods come to? A blanket, the clothing she wore, some cloth and needles and thread.

That morning the singing voyageurs paddled them and other guests up the Willamette to the Falls, and then took the priest and herself clear to Champoeg in a canoe. She said adieu to John at the Falls, where he slid the Methodists' rowboat into the river and set off for Mission Bottoms with Constable, his steady rowing much slower than the voyageurs' paddling.

She watched the rowboat recede into the distance as her canoe shot ahead, its fragile bark carrying them weightlessly across the waters.

A Christmas sun broke through the floured sky that fine day.

The priest did not speak, but he smiled occasionally, all the while examining her curiously. She smiled back. She felt she was among friends. She wrapped herself in her thick Hudson's Bay blanket, with its carded wool, and felt quite warm enough.

The river broadened and so did the valley it traversed, mostly flat on the east but hilly on the west. Snow crowned the uplands, but not this dun-stained plain. She saw occasional homesteads now, and supposed this was the farming area where so many Hudson's Bay men had retired instead of returning to Quebec or Montreal. Then, at a sweeping bend of the river, she beheld a small settlement, marked by a tall steeple, and she knew this would be her home and the place where her child would cough and sputter to life if all went well.

"Bien," the priest said.

The voyageurs steered for shore, and pulled up at a dock. They leapt out, and held her arm tightly as she stepped up from the wobbling canoe. The priest sprang out nimbly, and they all stood on the squared timbers of the pier while the priest thanked the voyageurs in voluble French, and blessed them.

He turned to Mary Kate and steered her to the bank, where they watched the men dart the canoe into the current that would effortlessly return them to the fort.

"Allons," he said.

She plucked up her bundle and followed him up a pathway that led to a flat well above water, and the little settlement of Champoeg. He led her into the compound, and into a rectory, where she found another priest, this one younger and sad-eyed.

"Père Modest Demers," Blanchet said.

She curtsied. Demers offered his hand and she shook it.

"Madame," Demers said. "Joyeux Noël."

"And to you, Father."

He turned to the other priest and they talked at length in French, occasionally glancing at her.

At last he turned to her. "Many French families here. Maybe two hund-red souls. The *père*—father will go look and talk. You are fam—famish—hon-gray, *oui*?"

"Yes . . ."

"Bien. I am also. Come."

He led her across a field to a comfortable cottage with smoke curling from its fieldstone chimney, and knocked.

An elderly woman answered. "Ah, Père Blanchet!"

For a minute the two talked, and then she nodded her guests in.

"Madame Foucault," he said. "Madame O'Malley."

Swiftly, Mary Kate came to understand that this elderly widow cooked and cleaned and washed altar cloths for the mission, and that this warm little cottage would be her home for a while.

And this was paradise.

The woman and the priest conferred at length and then the priest left. The woman smiled, peering with one eye at her guest because the lid of the other drooped, sucked her chafed lips, and motioned toward the kitchen corner of the single room. There she began a meal, inexplicably humming, as if this surprise on this Christmas Day had at last brightened her dull life.

Madame Foucault began chattering in a tongue that melded English words into her French, and Mary Kate discovered she could understand some of it. The fathers would consult good families and find a home for Madame. In Champoeg there were many families, some from the Red River region of Canada, brought by the Hudson's Bay Company to populate Oregon and keep it from the Americans. *Oui*, some grew fat upon their farms because the soil was so good and the rains so perfect.

Ah, yes, her late husband was such a one, from the Red River, a métis, French and Indian, until a year ago he died of a twisted colon after falling off the porch. Ah, indeed, and this was the first Noël without him. Now she devoted herself to the priests, and they cared for her.

When Mary Kate offered to help, the old crone shooed her away. Soon an omelette was sputtering in her skillet, along with bacon and cheese and herbs. Bread emerged from somewhere, and newly churned butter. Then this feast was heaped upon a chipped plate and laid before the younger woman.

Erin had come to Mary Kate. And for the first time, Oregon didn't seem as alien as the South Pole.

1843

24

Brownell's luck, that's what it was. In November he and his family had danced from a doomed raft onto a rocky riverbank without wetting a shoe, and hours later the Hudson's Bay boatmen had plucked them up, as if they were awaiting a hack in Boston.

Now a Yank brigantine was dropping anchor off Fort Vancouver. Brownell knew that brig, the *Golden Hawk*. He had been aboard it a dozen times. It belonged to Cushing and Hargreaves of Boston, and Devers Cushing was its master. Brownell had done business with the firm for years, buying whole cargoes dockside, or dispatching cargoes to Canton in the same bottoms.

And here they were. He watched as able seamen reefed the sails while others lowered a longboat that would bring the master and perhaps a mate or boatswain to shore. Cushing was an exacting master, and this trim brig had been holystoned down, enameled up, and varnished until it gleamed.

Brownell recognized the master's enormous white beard, which spread like a lobster bib over the breast of his blue coat. There would be a happy reunion soon.

But of course that would come after Cushing paid his respects to Dr. McLoughlin, who stood beside Brownell at the pier. No matter that they were rivals, or that Cushing was doing his utmost to whip the British monopoly at its own game; and no matter that Dr. McLoughlin's able traders had probably been trying to whip Cushing at every coastal village where pelts might be discovered, by ruthlessly undercutting the Yank on the price of trade goods, and paying extravagant prices for the furs.

"Do you know who it is, Brownell?"

"Yes, Devers Cushing from Boston. I know the man well. He'll be wanting to trade, I imagine."

"Ah, Cushing. He's been here before, but I was on leave. An able man, and one to squeeze a profit from every voyage."

"I've bought entire Whampoa cargoes of his on the piers of Boston. Are you going to buy anything?"

"I doubt that we will, but we'll see. Of course we prefer British products, but we're always short. I suppose he'll drive a hard price."

Brownell smiled.

The white longboat, rowed by six motley crewmen in black turtleneck sweaters, set off from the brig and swiftly covered the twenty yards to the company pier. The red-faced white-thatched master cut as fine a figure as the White Eagle himself, Brownell thought, perched like an emperor among his servants.

Maybe, just maybe, this was salvation. Brownell had done nothing but idle at Fort Vancouver because he was not a hewer of wood, beast of burden, sawman, plowman, herder of animals, or preacher of the gospel. Why sweat when a few calculations and some nimble footwork could win him fifty times the prize? Besides, the post was civilized. Fireplaces warmed rooms and some even had cast-iron stoves. Meals were varied and spiced and generous. He and his family were temporarily crammed into the house of a voyageur who had returned to Montreal for a year, but that was the only hardship.

Felicity had raged at him and her new life, but then suddenly discovered the post had children but no teacher, and from that moment she had a mission. She had opened the small schoolhouse, corraled her children and every child in the vicinity, and taught. Her irritation at him had not much diminished, however. She was merely waiting for him to go back to Boston—without her—or make something of himself here in Timbuktu. She would not go back; that was clear. She also made it clear, day after day, that by teaching in her little school, she was repaying the company for putting them up.

Dedham had become her echo, oozing with an adolescent's aversions, including the newly discovered disdain of his own wastrel father.

At least Roxanne wasn't finding fault with him. She had furtively whispered to him that if he went back, she would too. She didn't like Oregon. She didn't like Hudson's Bay. She didn't like the rains. She was always sick and sometimes whiny. She wanted to see her friends in Boston.

She was all Felicity could handle, rebelling at school, complaining about being stuck in a cold and crowded fort, and openly taking her father's side in every contretemps. She was an adoring twelve-year-old, and he basked in her adulation, but didn't fool himself about it. She simply had a daughter's crush on her father.

Brownell had whiled away the wintry days playing euchre or monte and scandalizing Methodists. He was excellent at cards and often made a bit. He organized horse races, hunts, and fishing trips, and wagered on the results. He openly admired shapely native women. For fun, he proposed to start a brewery, and made sure his proposal funneled into shocked ears of the Methodists at Mission Bottoms. He was, after all, a venture capitalist. He could turn a profit from anything, whether the queen of diamonds or a keg of rum or an entire bottom of Kwangtung silks. And now Opportunity was arriving in the form of a captain who probably would be looking for venture capital.

The master recognized both men as the longboat hove to, and soon was shaking hands, first with the formidable chief trader, and then with Brownell.

"Abel! I never expected to find you here!"

"Neither did I," Brownell said ruefully.

"And what is it you do?"

"Stare down the river, awaiting brigantines from Boston."

"We'll talk later, eh?"

This was properly McLoughlin's moment, and Brownell had the grace to step aside. He only hoped that the master of this familiar ship would not cut a deal without first talking to his Yank friend from Boston.

"Mr. Cushing, by all means, let us repair to my house and sip some Madeira," McLoughlin boomed, artfully steering the master away from Brownell. If there were deals to be done, McLoughlin wanted and demanded the first crack at them.

Maybe that was fine. Brownell watched the White Eagle shepherd the master up the long muddy pathway to the fort, and then through the distant gates. A ruddy boatswain, with a hook embedded in cork for a left hand, was commanding the seamen.

"I'm Abel Brownell, from Boston. And who are you, sir?"

"Blackie Blackwood, sir."

"And what's Mr. Cushing carrying?"

"Oh, more than I can say, sir. He's had a time of it. There's hardly a pelt to be had. You'd think the British had spies in every village."

"In a way, they do, Mr. Blackwood. They'll go to any lengths to keep business in their hands, including paying someone in each village to steer trade toward the company. And what goods did you bring out?"

"We've a hold full of manufactured goods, cotton and wool yard goods from the Lawrence mills, tinware, implements, knives, muskets. His design was to collect pelts and head for Whampoa, trade them at a good price—the yellow devils pay almost anything for a good pelt—and then carry silks and spices back to Boston."

"Ah, yes, the classic three-way trade. How long's he been out?"

"Mr. Cushing? Most of a year now, sir. We had some trouble rounding the Horn, and stopped at Valparaiso for a new mast."

"He's not heading back to Boston, is he?"

"Not if he can help it. Say, haven't we met?"

"Boston, yes. Several times. On the wharfs. I'm Brownell."

"Yes, I remember. You've cleaned our cargoes right out of the hold a few times."

The exchange proved to be valuable. Within minutes, he had learned everything in the *Golden Hawk*'s manifest, and what it had brought: less than a hundred sea otter pelts, some pickled salmon, one pack of beaver pelts, miscellaneous furs, including doe and elkskin, some buffalo hides, and some bearskins. Not a good voyage—so far. But Abel Brownell, financier, was about to make it a fine fat voyage for Devers Cushing.

Brownell drifted to the fort and waited for the master of the *Golden Hawk* to finish his call on John McLoughlin. The pair were closeted in the chief factor's office a long while, and Brownell began to wonder whether his chances were so bright after all. But at last Caleb Cushing emerged into the sunlit yard, and Brownell corralled him.

"Ah, so it's Abel Brownell! Last person I expected to see here, of all places!"

"I'm adventuring, Devers. In fact, I'm looking to do some business."

"You are, are you? Well, what have you in mind?"

"Buying out your entire supply of trade goods, for starters."

Cushing stared sharply at the other Bostonian. They walked out of the gates and into the windswept fields surrounding Fort Vancouver, heading back to the brig.

"I just turned down McLoughlin, and maybe I'll turn you down too. McLoughlin offered half what I want; he thought he had me over the barrel. His agents arrived in every coastal village ahead of me and bought up the skins at premium prices. And now he wants to buy my goods for about what I have in them. Damned Hudson's Bay Company."

"Devers, let's talk. You mind if we ride out to the brig so I can see your stock?"

The master gestured Brownell toward the boat.

A little later, the crew pulled the longboat alongside the brig, and the master and Brownell clambered up a rickety Jacob's ladder to the deck. Cushing produced a manifest, and they toured the hold, looking at the wares. Cushing knew the fur trade well: tinware, knives, muskets, powder and balls, blankets, trade cloth, awls, chisels, cookpots, cured shoe leather, fishnets and hooks, some readymade boots, harness and tack, twenty casks of whiskey and ten of rum, rope, sailcloth, bond paper, and two crates of windowpanes packed in sawdust.

"I'll take it all. What's your price?"

"You have a warehouse?"

"I'll get one. Are your men able to row the longboats a few miles to Oregon City? There's a whole town rising there. I'll pay what I must."

"Maybe I can sail up the Willamette a ways."

They settled on a price of three thousand five hundred, which was what

Cushing wanted, to the penny. But in the deal Brownell got the use of the longboats and crew to act as lighters to the falls of the Willamette.

"I'll write a draft on Stoughton and Bates. You've dealt with them many times. Now, Devers, I'm not done. I'd like to charter your vessel; or if not that, have you act as my agent. There are hundreds of settlers here; a thousand coming next summer; and probably more in the following years. And this is a land entirely without manufactured goods. I'll give you drafts with which to purchase all sorts of goods, especially fabrics, and bring them here. That includes silks and nankeen and whatever else might sell here if you go to Whampoa as well as the Sandwich Islands. There's not much to take westbound; McLoughlin has the furs locked up. But there's two sawmills at the falls, and a market for good Oregon lumber in the islands . . ."

"Done," said Cushing.

They worked out the details in short order. By the time the noon hour rolled around, Abel Brownell knew that he was in business, doing in this Timbuktu just what he had done in Boston; that he would get rich in Oregon, and maybe Felicity would warm up to him again, and even Dedham might discover some minor virtue in his father.

25

The sight of that dazzling white brigantine out of Boston bobbing at anchor off Fort Vancouver did nothing to melt the frost in the cramped room shared by Abel and Felicity Brownell.

At first she supposed he would book passage on that merchant ship to Boston for his family. But if he did, she would not go. She was not the woman he had ripped out of a comfortable and busy life on Louisburg Square without so much as asking her if she wanted to go. Neither were the children he had yanked out of school the same. In fact, now they were almost adults.

But it never came to that. He told her that he was back in business again, doing what he always did, using his Boston capital and investment partnerships to turn profits in merchant shipping. That didn't appease her much. She did not see self-obsessed Abel Brownell through the hazel eyes that had observed him so adoringly in Boston.

Abel didn't seem to notice. Suddenly his whist and euchre games vanished; his lounging about the Vancouver mess hall with the fort's loafers and boasters stopped; and he was scurrying about like a man just one step ahead of the devil's pitchfork. He vanished for several days, gone to Oregon City, he said, to find a suitable place to stash thirty-seven tons of merchandise. A fortune, he called it. He was impossibly cheerful and dashing and healthy, which annoyed her, even as it enchanted Roxy.

She kept on teaching. The work suited her, and it provided the means to keep her restless son progressing at something instead of turning into a lounging, card-playing wastrel like his father. Most of her students were French Canadians, and some didn't speak English. That, too, was fine. They taught her French and she taught them English. She pillaged the chief factor's library and read to her charges hour after hour.

Sometimes McLoughlin visited the schoolhouse, standing quietly at the rear, listening and nodding. Other times he questioned the children, the giant white-crowned man gently encouraging the scholars, speaking both French and English to them. How she adored him. No matter how crushing his burdens, how grave his cares, he still found a moment each wintry day to encourage the children . . . and her.

But Dedham was bored and suffered a procession of fevers. She could not match the level of instruction he had enjoyed at the Boston Public Latin School. After months on the Oregon Trail, hunting and fishing and horses and wilderness were his realities; scholarship wasn't. He sat like a caged wildcat in that board-and-batten building, pretending she wasn't his mother.

Abel shuttled back and forth between Oregon City and the fort for a month, scarcely bothering to attend to his prickly wife, and she rather liked that. His rank inattentiveness bought her some liberty. He was whistling, humming ditties she suspected were bawdy seamen's songs, engaging in long flamboyant consultations with the French Canadians, squinting at the goods in the HBC store, spinning jokes, and making her envious.

The family had split asunder, with Abel and Roxanne on one side, herself and Dedham staring across the barricades from the other. And the master of the house was still making his own plans, unaware of the upheavals he was causing in her life and the lives of his children. My God, Oregon!

The *Golden Hawk* sailed one blue February dawn, its frosted canvas stiff in the cold and sluggard air. She did not attend its departure, though most everyone else in the post watched Cushing run up his pennants and sheets. It rode low in the water, its belly full of new-sawn planks and timbers from the mills up the Willamette.

Abel headed up the Willamette again, and when he returned a few days later, he announced that he had bought a house.

"How did you manage that?" she asked.

"Filthy lucre. I traded some gold I got from Cushing's safe for a letter of credit and some interest. He obliged me, and I bought a house with gold. A simple box of a place, but a house. It's half done."

"Are there windows?"

"There will be. I have some panes packed in sawdust. Right now, just shutters, or linseed-oiled white cotton that lets in light."

"A stove?"

"No, fieldstone fireplaces wide enough to throw heat into the whole place."

"Furniture?"

"We'll have to import some."

"Space?"

"Half the house is full of the merchandise I bought. But we can cram in. I sold some right off to Abernethy at the Methodist store. He grumbled and whined, and scratched his skinny rear, and didn't want to pay my price, but he didn't want that heap of stuff I took off Cushing's hands sitting around in my hands either. I sold him twenty panes of glass for fifty dollars!"

She liked seeing him at his business again. But she had no inclination to move to that raw place where everything was being thrown up by the immigrants who came west with them.

"I think I'll teach, Abel," she said. "In a year, when this Oregon City place is civilized—"

"I need Dedham."

"To keep shop for you? I'm giving him an education."

He paused. "He won't need one. Not here. Dedham and even Roxy can help this family start a business in Oregon, as long as you don't want to go east. I could have chartered that brig to take us clear to Boston."

She was hoist with her own petard, she thought. Now they were Oregonians, and it had been her doing.

"All right. Take him," she snapped. "And if he doesn't succeed later in life, because he's not schooled, we'll know where the fault lies."

"Felicity—we're here. We walked across a continent together. Let's stay together."

He stood before her, the card-shark capitalist, bronzed and lean, with light dancing in his eyes.

"I wish to teach until summer," she said. "Then you'll be ready for me and I'll have given these children a full term. Take Dedham if you need him, but not Roxy."

"She won't be happy."

"I don't want her running wild, unsupervised, while you're too busy to look after her." There was more to it she didn't voice. She was envious. Roxanne adored him and barely tolerated her.

Sometimes she thought the children were all she had, especially when Abel was off on his wild gambols, hunting, fishing, racing, sailing, absorbed in his own life and scarcely aware she existed. And now her son would be leaving, too.

"I'm going to put him to work on the house. Hardly enough manpower in the whole valley."

"You bought it from someone?"

"One of the mission people. He liked gold better than a lot with a framework of timbers and some plank walls with holes in them, a stone fireplace, some doors on leather hinges, and a leaky roof of cedar shakes."

He approached her in the stillness of the dark room, until she sensed his warmth. She had dreaded this moment. There wasn't a fiber left in her that yearned for his embrace. She felt his arms slip around her and press her tight, and she let herself be squeezed.

"Felicity—"

"Yes, that's sweet, thank you," she said, pushing him back.

"It's been so long—"

"The children might come any minute." It wasn't true. "You go build a good house with glass windows and grass around it and trees and a carriage shed, and get us some good neighbors, and import some good Queen Anne furniture, and a pinochle deck, and—"

He kissed her. She stood stiffly. A corner of her responded to him; most of her didn't. He did not see her tears.

He laughed suddenly, that old soft chuckle, and let her go. "When I got here I thought I had been quite mad, pulling us up by the roots, thinking life would be some sort of magical dream here. I guess I was. Mad as a hatter."

She liked that in him. He had a disarming way of airing his flaws and laughing them away. She kissed him and gently pushed him back. She was not yet ready to resume a marriage she doubted would survive the rigors of Oregon.

He looked a little sulky, but accepted her rejection.

"Cushing's going to look in South America for glass. There's been plenty shipped, but some of it gets broken. I have enough panes for the house, but no glazier. I told Cushing to bring all he could get, and we'd both make a killing."

Good. Abel's mind was back on glass and bricks and lime and mortar and doors, and profits, and not upon Felicity's still-handsome, thin figure. She envisioned her body as a vessel of pain now—thanks to half a year of walking through wilderness—not a vessel of pleasure or love.

"I wonder where that Irishman is. He's a glass man. Maybe he can make it. I'll set him up, and we'll both profit."

"He's working at the Methodist mission. His wife got into a scrape here, and she's in Champoeg somewhere."

"I'll find him."

She held him at arm's length that night. He launched amorous sallies all evening, like a field marshal of seduction, and she kept resisting, until he laughed and turned his back to her. "Glass," he said. "You're holding out for glass. It's glass windows or celibacy."

She smiled. How could she not? Abel Brownell was a man beyond fathoming, and just when she thought she knew him, she discovered she didn't. He defied the world's wisdom. Did elders preach industry, sobriety, hard work, diligence, and regular hours as the source of wealth? Abel got rich by sleight of hand and luck. Did the world condemn recklessness? Abel laughed at caution and turned recklessness into piles of gold. Did the sages condemn rank emotion and praise reason? Abel bet fortunes on his instincts and turned impulse into bullion. Who but Abel could shipwreck his family on a river raft, in sleet, and get rescued an hour later? Who but Abel . . .

In the morning he dashed off, this time for the Methodist mission, no doubt to put that Irishman in business. She returned to her teaching, somehow infused with his energies, and trying hard to preserve her indignation. But mad Abel was seducing her again, just as he had long ago in Boston.

26

Garwood Reese held them. His elocutionary powers had never been finer, though he feared his voice might give out in that dank cold. This was the perfect time, the perfect place. And his was the perfect cause.

Several lanterns flickered in the drafty Champoeg warehouse, adding neither light nor heat, but enough Americans had gathered in the building to warm it sufficiently. They stood, or sat on splintery crates and heavy bales of furs, their breaths steaming in the fetid air, their truculence as dark as the wintry interior.

"My friends, my fellow Oregonians, it's time to organize a government," he said softly, understating the feeling coursing that room, as he gazed out upon their shadowed faces. "We're all suffering. We can't get title to the land we've made our own. There's no court to settle our disputes. There's no justice system. We're without a peace officer. Who protects the honest man and his family? We struggle to get ahead and find ourselves losing ground. Where are markets for our wheat? Where are goods we can afford? Where are competing merchants, striving to win our custom?"

He paused, knowing they all were thinking what he was about to say. "We've been in thrall to Hudson's Bay Company too long. They charge us outlandish prices but pay us little for our wheat and use imperial bushels to measure it. They don't stock what we need. Who can even afford a sheet of paper? They're a monopoly, dominating the trade and appropriating the best land, including waterpower sites . . ."

He paused, one beat, two beats, three. "Let us do two things: organize a provisional government on our own, regardless of who says nay, and let us petition Congress!"

These American men, gathered in the Hudson's Bay Company warehouse at Champoeg, listened silently and Reese wondered why they weren't cheering. The Canadians had boycotted the meeting at the behest of Father Blanchet, the toady of John McLoughlin. So this was purely an American affair, which was how Reese wanted it. He didn't want arguments, didn't want objections, and didn't want pieties. He wanted a unanimous vote, an American eagle's cry to all who had ears.

Out there in the dimness stood men he knew, men he had cultivated carefully through the weeks and months of his life in Oregon. Joe Meek and Doc Newell, respected mountaineers who had settled in the valley. Old Joseph Gervais, one of the original Astorians. The mission people, almost to a man, including Abernethy and Waller. That Irishman, O'Malley, who probably would vote with the Americans, for who hated the English more? Some who had come west with Reese, such as Abel Brownell and Jasper Constable, who had recently expanded in the middle, which gave him a certain dignity. A few adventurers and miscreants, but mostly yeoman farmers, salt of the earth.

"Do I hear a motion to form a provisional government?" Reese asked.

"Yeah, sure. Maybe we can agree on who has title to what." That was Doc Newell.

Reese didn't wait. "Are we agreed? All right, then. We'll appoint a committee to draft the laws. Now, do we petition Congress?"

"Reckon it's time. I ain't sure I own the soil I plow," said one.

"I'll draft a petition," Reese said. "We'll get Congress to deal with Hudson's Bay Company. They have no right to their land."

"Neither do we, not until it's settled whether this is the United States or Canada. Fair is fair. Just is just," a man said.

"Friend," said Reese, "I understand your concerns. But the fate of the republic lies in balance. The Stars and Stripes must fly here, right here. Senator Lynn's introduced bills that would make Oregon a territory, and give each male six hundred forty acres. All we have to do is claim it."

"Yeah, well, McLoughlin's got one town site locked up, and all the waterpower."

Reese laughed. "That can all be dealt with. For one thing, Congress has never recognized the right of a company to preempt public land. Only private persons can do it. And there's a few other little items up my sleeve."

"Such as?"

"With a provisional government we can write the land law we want. We can protect the mission people, and we can write HBC's claims right out the window. Who says foreigners can hold a town site like Oregon City if we say they can't?"

Men laughed.

"Done, then," said Reese, not wanting a debate. "We'll draft a petition, and we'll organize a government—"

"Hold up, Garwood." Abel Brownell was speaking. "Is that how you want to treat our benefactors?"

"Benefactors! What have they done for us except exploit us?"

"Saved our lives," Brownell said quietly. "To be specific, your life and Electra's. Took you in, warmed and fed you, and lent you the means to survive, all on good terms. And you don't have to repay until you're ready."

That annoyed Reese. The man had no sense of destiny.

"Abel," he said softly, "can you name one American business that McLoughlin hasn't tried to grind into the dirt with his imperial boot?"

"Farming. He gave people wheat and implements on credit, and lent us breeding pairs of cattle, hogs, sheep and horses, and we can keep the increase."

Reese knew when to bristle, and now he did. "And meanwhile he's tried to ruin our sawmills, drive out our salmon fisheries, preempt the best town sites and waterpower, whip our fur traders, undercut our merchants . . . I say it's time to boot Hudson's Bay Company clear back to Hudson's Bay. Why are you in with that bunch, eh?"

But Abel Brownell, fort loafer, would not be quiet. "Most of the men standing here would be dead, along with their families, were it not for John McLoughlin and his colleagues." Brownell spoke forcefully, and that astonished Reese, who had pegged the man as a wastrel.

Reese couldn't deny that, and didn't try. "Yes, a random act of kindness. And the price? Bondage. We're serfs, raising wheat for McLoughlin, indentured by debt. This is feudalism. In the United States, we're freemen, not serfs! We're the cheap labor he's always wanted. Let us be free! Scarcely thirty years ago they tried to stomp out our liberty for the second time! There are men among us who remember, who fought, who paid with blood and treasure!"

Brownell laughed. He had an amiable chuckle that simply neutralized rhetoric, which irked Reese. "I think Dr. McLoughlin and his colleagues did what they had to do, as men of conscience," Brownell said softly. "Garwood, how much do you owe HBC? Let's just get some things out in the open."

Reese knew to the penny. "That is not public business," he snapped. "Now, let's put things in perspective. We need a land law. We need a court system and a jail. We need to let Congress know how isolated and desperate we are, so we need to petition—"

"I reckon we do," said Joe Meek. "I guess we should think on it, too, and write up something fair and proper, lest we make ourselves worse than the Canadians. I'm for what's fair and proper. So are most good men. For starters, there ain't any of them Canucks here, and they got just as much right to choose how we do all this as we do. They was here first." He squinted at the rest, daring them to disagree. "Most of 'em claimed land and settled roundabout before we even heard of Oregon. We gonna rob them? You gents gonna boot them out and take their farms?"

Reese realized the veteran mountain man was speaking with natural authority, and needed to be conciliated. "Meek, we're going to write the fairest, finest, truest laws you ever did see," Reese said hoarsely, his throat deviling him. "We're Americans!"

The ripple of laughter was rewarding.

"Long as the law's fair and square, I'll be for it," the mountaineer said.

"It'll be so fair and square and American that Congress will sit up and agree with us," Reese said. He looked around for support, and wondered why all those on his side, the preponderant majority, were so silent.

"Spalding, don't you mission people think it's time to assert your rights in Oregon?"

But it was the formidable Jason Lee who responded. "It's time for a provisional government. But remember, Dr. John McLoughlin is our friend and benefactor, and I will stand by him."

Reese didn't argue that. The important thing was naming the committee. Whoever was chosen to sit on the organizing committee would control the destiny of Oregon.

"Gentlemen, fellow Oregonians, I think it's time to appoint a committee, and I beg leave to do so. Is there a unanimous vote?"

"What about the French?" someone asked.

"They chose not to come. Blanchet, he scared them off," said another. "So it's us. Our meeting, and our government."

The lamps guttered in a frosty draft, and Reese was anxious to conclude. "Here's my list: I appoint Reverend Alvin Waller and George Abernethy to represent the Methodists. I appoint Joe Meek and Doc Newell to represent the farmers. I appoint, for Oregon City . . ." He decided not to appoint Brownell, who'd gone soft all of a sudden. "Sunderland and Macgruder. And for the old-time settlers, Gervais . . . and myself as chairman."

They laughed.

"Do I hear approval?"

A throaty roar lifted in the cavernous room.

"Opposed?"

"I'm opposed," said Brownell.

"And I also, friends," said John O'Malley.

Reese stared. The Irishman against organizing the territory? The Irishman? What right had he?

"Sorry, O'Malley, this is limited to American citizens."

"I think we should put O'Malley on the committee," Brownell said. "I think all sides should be heard."

Reese shrugged. "What say you all?"

"Put him on it," Meek yelled. "And Brownell too. And Father Blanchet. That's the only way Congress will listen to us. Otherwise they're going to get word that this here meeting—"

"Yes, yes, statesmanship. Good point, good point," Reese said. "Father Blanchet, O'Malley, and Brownell are in."

"Not I," said Brownell.

"Not I," said O'Malley. "I'll not be serving on it."

"Very well. I believe our business is done, then."

Men gathered their hats and greatcoats and blankets and drifted into the moonlit night. Reese counted it a good night's work. He had his committee. He knew who would resist. He knew who was kowtowing to Hudson's Bay and McLoughlin, and that was valuable knowledge. As soon as a government was organized, he would break them, and their allies as well.

Funny, he had walked clear across the continent with Brownell and never suspected the man was soft. He was supposed to be some sort of financier, hardheaded and tough. He was supposed to be some sort of patriot and visionary, inspired by all those Oregon-boosters in Boston. But now Brownell was playing some sort of private game.

Reese hurried down to the riverbank, where two bateaux awaited the men returning to Oregon City. He chose the one with Brownell in it, wanting to talk.

The oarsmen, mostly Oregon City carpenters and millers and clerks, set the boat loose and let the cold black current tug them downstream in the frosty night. Men pulled their blankets and coats tight around them.

"A good meeting, eh, Abel?"

"Yes, to a degree. Some sort of temporary government would be valuable, providing the Canadians are included and equally represented. Their claim to Oregon's as good as ours."

"Who are you for?"

Brownell murmured so low that Reese could scarcely hear him.

"You know, Garwood, there's two or three ways to get wealth. One is with hard work. One is by risking capital, which sometimes earns a profit, sometimes not, I assure you. And the third way is to use political means, laws and courts, bureaucrats and taxes, majorities, committees, obstruction, and propaganda to take things away from those who got wealth by working for it or risking their capital. The better classes prefer to work and invest and earn."

A dozen others in that bateau were listening.

27

Abel Brownell discovered he was sitting upon a fortune. It didn't surprise him. He had been incubating fortunes all his life. He was, that sun-garlanded morning, in a testy mood because no one would finish his house for him, and he had fewer manual skills than a turtle.

He was increasingly worried about the safety of his mountain of manufactured goods, which filled a lean-to at the rear of the building, and much of the rest of the house. So far, the denizens of Oregon City seemed honest enough; they were mostly connected with the mission, and looked after by the Reverend Mr. Waller, and the lay missioner George Abernethy. And so the goods sat in their back room, unmolested.

But Brownell knew that state of affairs could not last. He wanted workmen in large numbers but could find none. Since little cash floated about in Oregon, he would pay them in goods: blankets, cooking pots, tin cups, molasses, sugar, coffee. And then one fine, bright April day, salvation arrived.

Before him stood two men in bizarre dress. They wore fringed buckskins gaudily decorated with quillwork, moccasins, brightly colored shirts, and fur-lined hats each displaying the tastes of its owner. About their necks hung peculiar necklaces, one of them of bear claws. Their beards were long and unkempt, and their eyes bright and watchful. He had heard of these border men, late of the mountains, now settled over on the plains west of the Willamette River. And he knew the names of these two, though he had scarcely spoken to them. Each carried a gleaming, well-oiled rifle along with powder horns.

"You the old coon they call Brownell?" asked one.

He owned to it.

"I'm Joe Meek, and this old boy is Doc Newell. We quit the mountains when the fur business dried up."

"Yes, come in, if you can call this inside. And how may I help you?"

The mountaineers stepped into his half-finished house, squinted about, discovering mountains of barrels and crates.

"You the gent that bought all them goods off the *Golden Hawk*?" Meek asked.

"I am."

"What did you do with it all?"

"Sold some." Brownell wasn't about to admit he had the bulk of it just feet from their eyes. These gents weren't Methodists.

Meek lifted his furry chapeau, fashioned from a defunct raccoon, scratched greasy hair, peered about suspiciously, lowered his rifle butt to the plank floor, and leaned into it, all of which puzzled Brownell.

"We've been farming on the Tualatin Flats. Six of us, actually, took up homesteads, borrowed some seed wheat from McLoughlin, and scratched the sod with borrowed oxen and plows and all. And we've been putting up cabins, getting started in this country, grunting and hauling and chopping until we're half worn out. The thing is, we're plumb *thirsty*."

That sailed past Brownell.

"You probably can dig a well out there, serve you all."

"*Thirsty,*" Meek said.

Newell spoke up. "We was just thinking, old coon, that a man buying the cargo in the hold of a brigantine, he's likely to have a few things that might quench a man's *thirst*."

Epiphany bloomed in the mind of Abel Brownell. "Oh, I see. And if I have, what would you offer for it?"

Meek and Newell glanced at one another. "What do you have?"

"What do you want?"

Something like piety bloomed in Newell's face. "Something spirituous? Something not available over at that Methodist store, and not available over in the Fort Vancouver store? Something to wet a man's whistle?"

"Ah," said Brownell. "Maybe we can do business."

"Have you a quart? A jug?"

"No, afraid not."

"A pint?"

He shook his head.

They looked crestfallen.

"Well, we just thought we'd ask. We haven't seen a jug for nigh on two years. Not since leaving the Rocky Mountains have we seen a small glass of spirits. We're, ah, not Methodists."

"How about a cask?"

"A cask?"

Brownell could see visions of sugarplums dancing in their eyes.

"One barrel. Thirty-two and one half gallons, Pennyslvania corn whiskey, cured in oak."

"Cured in oak, you say?"

"Cured in oak four years and hauled around the Horn."

"But you're not going to break it up and trade a tumbler or two?"

"How many of your mountain colleagues have you?"

"Six, including us."

"That should do nicely. You fetch them. If the wheat's in the ground, and your cabins are up, and your wives aren't suffering, you perhaps have time for some temporary labor. I'll need you several weeks. You see, I'm the perfect fool. I hustled west without possessing a single skill that you gents have in abundance. I'm no hewer of wood, sawyer, packmule, carpenter, mason, or even a storekeep. When I got here, my entire instinct was to sail out on the next ship. Back to comfort! Stuffed mattresses and pillows! Back to coal stoves, cooks, maids, and butlers."

Newell chuckled. "You poor devil, didn't know what ye were in fer," he said.

"I want you to finish the house and build the store. And to spare you the long trips back to your farms, I'll feed you and put you up here . . . if you don't mind sleeping on the floor."

"And what's to be payment for all this labor?"

"One cask of hundred-proof Keystone State corn whiskey, cured in the barrel. Thirty-two and one half gallons."

They stared like men who had lost their senses.

"Do we have to wait a month?" Meek asked.

Brownell laughed. The men laughed too. Pretty soon they were wheezing and hollering.

"You'll finish this house and put up a store down the street, and then you'll have your reward. I'm afraid that if I let you tap that keg, I'll never see you again."

"Mr. Brownell," said Meek solemnly, "I swear on a Methodist Bible that if you permit us a kindly sample this very night—just to make sure this is the true article—we will all report for work tomorrow morning, rip-roaring and ready to go."

"Better make it the day after tomorrow," Brownell said sagely. "Brother Meek, Brother Newell, return here at dusk, bring your bedrolls, bring your mountain friends, bring your ladies, and you shall be rewarded with a sample of what is to come."

"You sure ain't a Methodist," Meek said.

"A sample? One swig?" Newell sounded doubtful.

"One gallon jug. Leaving approximately thirty-one jugs for you to transport back to your homesteads on Tualatin Flats."

"By Gawd, you're some," said Meek, extending a horny paw. We'll be back at sundown. Oooh-ha! Heeee-ar!"

Brownell didn't own a jug. Not even a bung starter, so he hastened to the Methodist store, which was increasingly dispensing material rather than spiritual comforts. He studied the shelves, under Abernethy's watchful eye.

"What you looking for?" the missioner asked.

"A crockery jug, preferably one gallon, and a, ah, mallet to open a cask."

"A cask of what?"

"Well, that's what I'm going to find out. It could be vinegar, could be anything. Maybe lamp oil."

"I hope not spirits. We have kept the mission and Willamette Falls dry, for the sake of ourselves as well as the Indians."

"I'm not a Methodist, Mr. Abernethy. And the place was named Oregon City by Dr. McLoughlin, who surveyed the town and the lots, including the ones this store sits on. Not the Falls."

"This is a mission town, don't forget it. We've laid a claim to it."

"So has Hudson's Bay, and they were here first, and selling lots first."

"Well, they'll likely quit the country once we outlaw foreign ownership."

Brownell grinned. "Maybe we're the foreigners, George. That's how they see us."

"Well, we'll drive 'em out soon as we're organized."

Brownell despised that sort of talk. "You too, eh? You don't like competition, is that it? If you don't like what others have done, take it from them at the ballot box! Tax it! Outlaw it! Then you can have it!"

Abernethy glared, wheeled away, found a crockery jug used to store cream, and laid it on his plank counter.

"Five dollars," he said.

"Five dollars!"

"Comes around the Horn. Five dollars."

"You sound like that clerk at the HBC store. You need competition. Guess I'll provide a little. Maybe I can meet people's needs better than you. Everyone's complaining about monopolies. How about yours, right here? Competition, that's what they say they want. So I imagine you're in favor of competition, right?"

"Don't, Abel. This store don't hardly make money. We don't want another store in here. Use some sense; one store can survive, but two stores, and HBC up in Vancouver, it's too much competing, and we'll all go down."

He squinted. "It won't go easy for you if you do," Abernethy continued. "The missioners dominate this valley. An absolute majority, in case you're interested. A government is being formed right now. This is going to be temperance territory, a sweet land, and we'll find ways of handling people that don't fit."

"Sounds like a Methodist version of Hudson's Bay to me," Brownell said.

"We're the majority," the storekeep said, as if to settle any issues once and for all.

Brownell left Abernethy's store without buying anything. In his back room he found a white porcelain pitcher and a bit and auger, which would do. He contemplated Abernethy's blunt threat, and decided Oregon was too big to be anyone's monopoly. Not even the Canadians could dominate it against the tide that had started to flood in. But he knew how the factions would soon form: the Methodist party, the French Canadians, and a few independents like himself and John O'Malley.

He spent the rest of that day buying city lots from the HBC agent in town, Jacques Babeouf, paying for each with notes written on his Boston bankers. He didn't want to barter the precious manufactured goods he had just acquired and planned to sell for five or ten times their cost.

At the sawmill he bought timbers and planks for his store from Caleb Magruder, and ordered cedar shakes for the roof, to be delivered within two weeks. He found a stonemason, Arthur Knight, ready and willing to lay a fieldstone foundation for the store for some of those goods in his house.

Except for nails he was ready. There was scarcely a nail in Oregon, but any good joiner could dowel and glue and dovetail wood together, and do a better job than a carpenter. Maybe even a few wild, hairy, wolfish mountain men could master the trades with the right inducements.

They arrived just after sundown, paddling a pirogue across the Willamette River twice to carry the throng. Six wild border men who hadn't even a nodding acquaintance with a razor, four full- or half-blood women with glowing eyes and honeyed breasts, and three infants in cradleboards.

No lamp lit the interior of Brownell's house. Through the unshuttered windows, the last blue of the day limned the western mountains. They settled in a circle on their buffalo robes and blankets, while Brownell placed the filled pitcher in the exact center of their robes and handed Joe Meek a tin cup.

Meek took it, reared back his head, and howled a wolf song. He sipped, smacked his lips, and passed the cup.

Brownell heard the music of saws and hammers.

28

The tidings reached John O'Malley at dawn of a March day, before he had even abandoned his rude bunk to begin the day's toil. His friend Honoré Duquesne had burst into the Indian boys' dormitory and shaken him awake.

"Vite! Vite! Madame . . . nous allons!"

Mary Kate's time! He dressed swiftly, found no one to tell he would not be working that day, and followed Duquesne down to the riverbank, where his canoe was beached. The man had paddled upriver through much of the night.

Mary Kate had found a home with the Duquesnes, who owned a farm outside of Champoeg. There she had sewn clothing for them both and helped Giselle as much as she could while awaiting her child. It helped that Giselle had birthed three children of her own, and a midwife lived but a mile away.

Mary Kate had stayed at the mission for a few days until the Canadian women of the settlement had gathered her into their bosom, finding a home for her and sewing vast amounts of swaddling clothes and cutting precious cotton cloth into diapers.

For all this O'Malley felt grateful and vowed to repay as soon as he could. He now possessed forty-seven dollars in credit on the Methodist ledgers, and while he could not convert it into cash, it would buy valuable things at the store at the Falls of the Willamette, as the Methodists stubbornly called Oregon City.

He thought that the Methodists were good people, as kind and helpful as he might find in Ireland, but empty of passion. What was it about their religion that froze feeling? He wondered whether he would ever see an angry Methodist, or a howling child, or lovers madly embracing, or a group erupting into laughter around a table. He liked Jason Lee the most because of his cheerful friendliness and good humor. Nothing fazed Lee. He liked his Oregon Trail companion Constable the least: a cold man, chock-full of righteous theology, bent upon conforming the wild world to his vision.

The bright spring sun swiftly warmed the morning as they paddled down-river. Champoeg lay quietly in the tender glow. He felt at home there in the shadow of the mission church. He had tried hard to visit Mary Kate and attend mass on Sundays, but the long trip was not easily managed, and exhausted him on his one day of rest.

But now, a child! They beached the canoe and overturned it, and began the two-mile hike to Duquesne's farmstead. O'Malley had eaten nothing, but he had learned to endure during the hardships of wilderness life and travel. Reaching his wife was the main thing. They hiked through pastoral fields, stepping gently on tender shoots of new grass, passing bright blooms in the rising warmth of this new day.

John O'Malley wanted to cry with joy at such a gentle warmth and such a benevolent glow, but anxiety about Mary Kate, and worry about the birthing, drove him grimly onward.

When they reached the Duquesnes' sturdy log home, a lengthy rectangle, O'Malley was fairly flying and Duquesne was laughing at him.

The door stood open, and in the darkness and solemn peace of the household, he heard an infant's wail. The place fairly bulged with women, and they beamed at him as he hurried through the soft dark to a blanketed-off area. There he beheld Mary Kate, the swaddled infant at her breast, her silky dark hair disheveled, weariness and joy in her flushed face.

"O'Malley, we have a boy," she said.

"A boy! And you?"

"I am tired."

"And is he a proper boy?"

"He is well formed and perfect."

The tiny infant, swaddled in white flannels, lay asleep on her bosom.

"Mary Kate, are you well satisfied?"

"John O'Malley, hear me now. We have made a child destined for blessed things."

"Has Father Blanchet come?"

"Soon. And what will you be naming our boy, O'Malley?"

"What name pleases you, Mary Kate?"

"A saint's name, so we might have someone in heaven looking after him. Shall we call him Patrick?"

"Ah, love, Patrick and more. This is a child of Oregon. Across a continent we came to be here in this Oregon."

"Oh, John, do not name him for that!"

"Would you take Oregon Patrick O'Malley?"

"Not Oregon! Patrick Burke O'Malley?"

"Oregon! It sings, Mary Kate. It says where our son is born."

"Oh, please, John, not that name . . . It is not right."

He saw that the name rattled objections in her like old leaves in the wind, as if he and she had violated some ancient ritual of Erin.

"This is a land greener and sweeter than home," he said doggedly.

"No!" she cried.

"You'll take to it, Mary Kate. Our boy's the future, not the past, and Oregon's all tomorrows, not yesterdays."

She closed her eyes, and he could see the exhaustion in her face. "Oregon Patrick," she whispered dully. "All right, then, it is what you wish, John."

She spoke so darkly and submissively that he wondered about her health.

"Was it hard?" he asked.

She nodded. The nod bespoke hours of grueling labor. Then she was asleep. Giselle drew him away with a nod, and steered him outside so his wife could doze in silence. The chatelaine of this château could not speak English, but her smiles said more than words anyway. Duquesne beamed. The other women settled watchfully on the shaded porch. They would not yet leave the mother and infant, and he heard the name Oregon pass from lip to lip. Was it disapproval he sensed? They had seen her sadness.

Giselle brought him a steaming bowl of oatmeal, which he wolfed down, suddenly feeling starved. He did not know what to do, and so he sat, savoring this soft spring morning, along with his baby boy and his wife, who had passed through torment and was now resting. New life. He owed that child and his wife a happy home, a secure home, a home they owned without debt, without rents upon it, without taxes and tithes to alien churches, without burdens, in this lost paradise called Oregon on the shadowless side of the world.

A home.

He had spent some of his free Sundays exploring. The good farmland east of the river had long since been snapped up by the Methodists and these Canadians. But several times he had rowed across the Willamette and explored the hilly pastures to the west, some of the slopes timbered but others open and lush. The Methodists ran cattle and horses there, and had some sort of claim upon it. These animals had been part of the stock brought up from California by an American named Ewing Young, who had prospered and then died. For the want of heirs, the Methodists had divided the livestock among themselves, since they were as close to being a government as existed.

Now, as O'Malley sat on the porch of the farmstead, he could see across moist fields to Champoeg, and across the river to the rising pastures beyond, which rolled upward as they distanced from the river valley. Those lands, he had learned, had been Young's pasture. Now they were no one's. Young's house had long since been dismantled, the precious timbers salvaged by the Methodists. But the land remained: eternal, lush, well watered, and garlanded with promise.

Something stirred in John O'Malley. A wee child needed a home. He would stay close this day, but tomorrow he would stake out a homestead. One square mile was what the settlers said the government of the United States would accept—if in fact this southern part of Oregon went to the Americans. One square mile he would claim. One square mile, an unimaginable amount for an obscure young man from Ireland to think about, a duke's estate. It would support him and Mary Kate and Oregon Patrick and many more who would occupy a cradle in his home.

A cradle. He had none. And not a stick of furniture, not even a bed for Mary Kate to lie upon.

He dwelled that day in the haven of the Canadians' farmhouse. The women let him hold the infant, and he peered into that soft, wizened face wondering what sort of mighty man he would become, what any man might be in a republic, where he could hold property and pay no rents and choose his governors.

He decided he would take another day off. That would be a day without pay, but more important things mattered. A claim, a home for Oregon Patrick O'Malley . . .

He spent time with Mary Kate, who awakened and slept, who clutched the infant to her freckled breast and slipped into sleep. Several freshly sewn dresses, long enough to wrap the child, stood ready, a gift from the Canadian women.

Later that day Father Blanchet arrived, all smiles and solemnity, and christened the child at once, and John O'Malley knew that now Oregon Patrick had been given the key to heaven. He and Mary Kate would raise their son strong in the faith, dutiful to the church and its canons, and the child would be a loyal and dutiful son of Oregon as well. Honoré Duquesne became, at that moment, the godfather. But Mary Kate had stared silently, without joy.

Well, he thought, she'd come to love the name. That's all it was; a name.

The next day O'Malley held once again the tiny burden in his arms, kissed his beloved goodbye, and then hiked back to Champoeg. He paused at the mission to borrow a compass. He paddled across the river in a fine, fair dawn, and walked slowly upward until he stood atop vaulting slopes, rich with spring grass weaving under the zephyrs. He found a spring and a pond that showed signs of livestock use around its muddy periphery, and half a mile south the foundation of a large house, rudely mortared in places, and a dug well in a crease of the hill thirty yards from the foundation. This was pasture, not crop land. He stood there in the shimmering light, gazing eastward across the river to the prairies filled with sleepy farms, gazing down upon the mission just across the river. This was his new Erin.

That day he paced out his square mile. Just there the river ran almost east and west, so he located a southeastern corner bankside, and built a fieldstone cairn. Then he paced one thousand seven hundred sixty steps upriver, and built another. Then he paced one thousand seven hundred sixty steps due north, on the compass point, built a cairn, and again due east and built a cairn, and then south back to the river. He paddled across the river, and returned the compass. Then, in Father Blanchet's presence, he wrote a claim, carefully describing the metes and bounds, and dated it. Blanchet witnessed and dated it also. One copy O'Malley left with the fathers. The other he would cache in the riverside cairn.

When he returned to the Methodist mission, Jason Lee was the first to congratulate him. "The boys told us," he said. "And how is your wife?"

"She is well, and we have a bonny son we have christened Oregon Patrick. I want to thank you for employing me, sir. But now I have to make a home, so I will be leaving."

"Leaving? We need you."

"Leaving, sir. I would like a chit that would let me purchase goods at the mission store."

"Oregon! How did you choose that name?"

"For Oregon we sailed across the sea to Boston, and then down the coast to New Orleans, and then on a river packet to St. Louis, and another to Independence, and then we walked across plains and mountains, and we found no such place except in our imaginations, so we have named a child for what will be someday."

"No such place?"

"Aye, sir, no such place. Only the vision. Here there is little more than wilderness, and we came looking for Eden. So we will make our own Eden and call it Oregon."

"Yes, an Eden, Mr. O'Malley. That is a true thing. We shape our own Edens."

Lee drafted a note in the amount of forty-seven dollars and fifty cents. "May you and your family be blessed by God," he said.

O'Malley stayed that night, supped one last time with the Indian boys, told them he was now a father, that he would be leaving at dawn and that he had treasured their friendship and all they had taught him, and then fell into a deep sleep.

"Come visit me. You will always be welcome, my friends," he said. "There will always be a meal for you, and for your families. You will always have friends in the home of John O'Malley, and don't ever forget it."

29

Joe Meek, Doc Newell, and their friends completed Abel Brownell's half-wrought house and raised his emporium with amazing dispatch, and were duly paid off with the remains of the cask. The prize had been much drawn down during the construction, but that had not slowed the progress one iota nor impaired the quality of their craftsmanship. The capacity of these Arcadians for spirituous drink flabbergasted the Bostonian, and he recognized in them a kindred spirit: these were gents who turned wisdom on its ear.

"Mr. Meek, what are you going to do next?" Brownell asked, upon the final tour of the new store and its contents.

"Go hunting, I imagine. Hunting for old boys to share a little juice each evening."

"And tend your wheat?"

"If the wheat's coming, that's fine; if it ain't, that's fine. If I raise wheat, I eat; if I don't, I don't."

Brownell laughed. The mountaineers loaded their gear, including the sloshing cask, into a pirogue and negotiated the river, leaving Brownell suddenly lonely. Their wild natures and irreverent souls had appealed to him. But he would have to keep them at arm's length from Felicity, Roxy, and Dedham.

He spent those first cheerful hours organizing the store. The building stretched from the front of the lot, square on the clay street, to the rear. Two small windows and a door admitted light to the front room. The rear room, a storage area, was not windowed. Meek and his minions had constructed a rude counter and some shelves, but most of the staples off the brigantine would simply lie about in sacks on the floor.

He loved the scent of new-sawn lumber, and the yellow gleam of the unvarnished wood. The remaining casks of whiskey and two hogsheads of rum he rolled into the storage area in back. He would sell spirits, but not from the front room, which might offend the ladies. And he would require his customers to bring their own jugs.

He intended for the building to be much more than a retail establishment. It would function as his warehouse, a place to hold future cargoes he intended to purchase from any trader venturing up the Columbia. And he would whole-sale merchandise to any who wanted it, including the Methodists and the Hud-son's Bay Company.

He had never kept store, didn't intend to, and planned to employ clerks. But on this day, at least, he rummaged about, happily shelving items and turning the fragrant rooms into an emporium.

He was thus occupied when a party of missioners entered his new domain. He knew them all. George Abernethy, lay missioner and store clerk, and now his rival, stood among them. Three reverends, including Alvin Waller, decorated the assembly. But most amazingly, Garwood Reese was with them.

"Gents?" he asked.

"Brownell, this is a temperance community and we're going to levy your spirituous drink," Reese said.

"I beg your pardon?"

"Stand aside, we're going in."

"By what right?"

"By the right of this community to prevent spirituous drink from ruining our people."

"That's no right."

"By the right of the law. The government prohibits spirituous drink in Indian country," said the Reverend Mr. Waller.

"Yes, but this doesn't happen to be the United States or its Indian territory."

"It will be, and that authorizes us."

"Garwood, show me such a law that governs us here and now."

"It has always been the law of the mission, and the committee is now drafting the articles of government."

"This is not mission property."

"That's a matter of some dispute. We claim it," Waller said. "I personally claim it."

"The Hudson's Bay Company was here first, surveyed and sold it. Now you get out. This is my private property. I will sell what I choose. I don't plan to sell it to Indians and demoralize them. I do plan to sell it to whoever else wants it."

"We saw the debaucheries here. Your drunken mountaineers and their drunken women and brats. We will not permit that in the Falls."

"They certainly weren't drunk, and even less debauched. They sat around and spun yarns. And what law do you cite? Have you formed a provisional government or enacted ordinances?"

"It doesn't matter. We are herewith, in the name of the committee formed to draft a provisional government, levying on your spirituous drink."

"Out!"

But they would not leave. Brownell blocked their passage to the storeroom, but Reese and the divines pushed him aside and plunged into the dusky room and located the casks and hogsheads along a rear wall.

"Men, do your duty," Waller said.

"This is totally illegal and I'll see you in—"

"Some advice, Brownell. Oregon's ours, not yours. Abide by our counsel, or leave it," George Abernethy proclaimed. "Abide, or we'll levy the rest of your stock as a fine."

"This is mob rule!" Brownell stationed himself at the storeroom door. "Not one item belonging to me passes here," he said. "This is theft. Outlawry."

They ignored him. At the door, two of the divines simply shouldered him aside, using breathtaking force that spun him back into the store, and then rolled the whiskey casks out to the clay street. The massive hogsheads of rum followed. Four hundred dollars of whiskey, worth three or four thousand on the retail market.

Brownell watched helplessly as they loaded the barrels into a dray and headed for the river. He could scarcely believe what he was experiencing. Without the faintest color of law or justice, they were confiscating his property and congratulating themselves.

How odd that urbane Garwood Reese was among them. But maybe not so odd for a man with political ambitions. Brownell did not doubt that Reese enjoyed spiritous drinks. He and his sister-in-law hadn't turned down John McLoughlin's wine that long-ago hour when the haggard survivors of the long trek to Oregon were received and warmed and fed in the chief factor's parlor. Garwood Reese was no abstaining Methodist, and his only religion was Garwood Reese. But he knew where to find allies.

"Watch your step, Brownell," Reese said. "This lot and your other lots belong to the Reverend Waller, and he might decide to reclaim them."

"Is that a threat?"

"No, just an effort to help Oregon form a proper and loyal government and become a territory of the United States."

They left Brownell there, seething in the doorway. He watched them drive their funerary wagon down to the river, tap the bungs, and pour several hundred gallons of Pennsylvania and Cuban distillates into the Willamette.

So that's how it would be.

He and Felicity would not have a friend in this Methodist town. He would preside over a store people shunned. She would invite neighbors into their handsome new home and be rebuffed. Now he had enemies.

He choked back his rage, and devoted the next minutes to bolting the lacquered Brownell Mercantile sign on the front of the new building, all the while wondering if a single soul would purchase a single item in his new shop.

For once his facile mind deserted him. He needed to move swiftly, yet couldn't discover a course of action. He retreated to his own new house, now squatting so precariously on a lot not secured by any legal title, and began devising ways to prosper in Oregon.

Within his home, at least, a quart of the Pennsylvania bourbon remained on a shelf, so he poured a stiff and well-deserved libation, adding branch water and some pond ice, and settled back to think things through. This wasn't Boston. He could not summon an array of allies and resources, from bankers to merchant princes. He could not go to the law, sue, or file a criminal complaint. And yet he felt confident. Somehow, it was all a game. He would outwit these righteous pirates just for the fun of it.

Yes, one ploy would be easy: a letter on the next outbound vessel or Hudson's Bay express, billing the Methodist mission board in Pennsylvania for his losses, along with a complete description of what had transpired. But that was just a nettle. A copy to a certain gentleman in Congress, with a request that it be put in the Record. Yes, that would help.

The land was the thing. No one had any legal hold on it, including the missioners. But there were other forms of property, and maybe he could purchase what he wanted from Dr. McLoughlin.

He left the next morning for Fort Vancouver, arriving late that day, well in time to brace McLoughlin in his lair.

"Ah! Brownell, is it?"

The chief factor rose from his desk, towering over Brownell like a snow-capped mountain, and shook hands.

"Yes, sir. Come to do a little trading."

"A bit of trading, you say? You wouldn't want to sell me two hogsheads of rum and a few casks of Pennsylvania whiskey, would you?"

Brownell smiled. News traveled fast, especially into the funneling ears of the company. "You've heard about that. It was done without a pretense of legality. No law empowered them to do it. They said whiskey's not permitted in Indian territory, but this country is not United States Indian territory."

"Spirits are a dangerous thing, Mr. Brownell. We sell none to the Indians. Except to permit my people a little wine at meals, I have forbidden its usage. It causes trouble. A few years ago we forcibly persuaded an American of dubious character, a Mr. Ewing Young, not to make a still, and I would do the same again. Jason Lee and the Methodists stand right beside me."

"But you agree that no law exists covering the matter."

"No law exists; that's correct."

"Doctor, since possession of land rests on such feeble guarantees, I am interested in the rivers. Your company possesses numerous vessels that ply the coast and haul goods and furs up and down the Columbia. Several are sloops. I wish to purchase one for my business operations, namely, a floating merchant store. Yes, in competition with you."

"Why would you expect me to sell you a sloop?"

"Several reasons. I have completed a fine store in Oregon City, with which I propose to pay you for the sloop. You can go into business there against the Methodist store, and compete on better terms because the Methodists depend entirely on chance purchases of cargoes while you get regular resupply."

"And what would you do with the sloop?"

"Store my merchandise in it. The goods are no longer safe on land. And live in it if I am forced to. And maybe sell from it."

"But you have a fine house. I'm told it's a most attractive place."

"If they let me keep it. The missioners seem to think that they can levy upon whatever they wish. That's a curious word, *levy*. It means *steal*."

McLoughlin steepled his hands. "I see.. I'm not able to sell you a company sloop without Governor Simpson's permission, which he is unlikely to give, not even for cash payment."

"Lease?"

"No, I'm afraid not. I'd only open the door to more competition, and I'd never hear the end of it from Montreal."

"I see. Well, Devers Cushing's probably returning from the Sandwich Islands now with a full hold. I'll wait for him."

He rose to leave, but McLoughlin stayed him.

"Some of the Americans are forming a provisional government. Do you know anything about it?"

"I attended the meetings. It's Garwood Reese's little tarbaby. I told him that people who organize governments with which to confiscate the property of others belong to an inferior class."

McLoughlin's eyes lit momentarily. "They didn't invite us, and we didn't participate," he said. "A provisional government must represent the whole people or it lacks force."

"My sentiments exactly, Doctor."

"I'm told you and O'Malley voted against it. You two alone, among the Americans."

"We did."

"For that, you'll suffer. I'll amend that. For that, you have already suffered."

"Greatly."

"Perhaps we can make common cause, even if we compete," the chief factor said.

Abel Brownell smiled but made no commitment.

30

MAY 9, 1843

The Americans are organizing a provisional government. They met again at Champoeg, and defeated the Canadians on the issue by a narrow margin. I am resigned to it because it might quiet the turmoil about property rights. My son Joe is on the committee to draft the appropriate laws and will be defending our interests. Perhaps some good will come of it, though I am not sanguine.

Earlier, these same settlers, the Methodists included, sent a petition to their congress that aggrieves me almost beyond what I can endure. It was an indictment of the Honourable Company and of me and my policies, and requested relief—from me. Its contents were nothing less than scurrilous. I will do no favours for any who signed it.

It accused us of attempting to claim the waterpower at the falls, and interfering with their milling company. But they failed to mention that we had claimed it first and built first. They complain about our use of the imperial bushel, which is larger than theirs, but neglect to say in their petition that it brings them a better price for their wheat than we would pay for one of their bushels.

They complain that we lend breeding cattle instead of selling them, though we have so few that we can do no other. And they assert that if a cow dies, we charge them for it, contrary to fact. What would they prefer? That we lend them no kine and buy none of their wheat? We have offered them the means to build herds if they have the patience, but the policy offends them.

They complain about the prices of our goods, and yet from

the beginning we have sold the Methodists the items they need for their store at a fifty percent discount, going against our own interests to help these American men of faith to establish themselves here. I hear their store is in trouble, not because of our prices but because Jason Lee has extended so much credit and not been repaid by his own missioners.

The list goes on, and I will not detail it here. I look in vain for some recollection of our succor, but find none. We are now The Enemy in all respects. It was the work of those most impassioned against us, and I need name no names. I like the Americans and will continue to cooperate any way I can. But some small faction of them manages to inflame the others, and the canards dishonour the Company, and me.

I have no means of replying, and hope that my silence will thunder in their ears. I don't know what they expect Congress to do, but there is an underlying whiff of casus belli here. The abominations visited upon them by the Hudson's Bay Company may, they hope, cause the Yankee regiments to form up and settle the Oregon Question by force.

These Americans! They're so suspicious of the advice our traders give them at Fort Hall and Walla Walla that they ignore it, to their mortal peril. What do they take us for? Do they really imagine, when Pambrun sternly warns them not to raft the Columbia, that we are misleading them for our own mercenary reasons? I'm afraid some do think just that. I work assiduously to develop the friendship of the levelheaded ones.

I have asked Father Blanchet and others who are our friends to work closely with the Americans on a provisional government. I now can see the need for one, especially as a means to control crime and property disputes. We have friends among the Americans, such as Abel Brownell, whose sense of fairness and justice is manifest to me, along with his good humor and a certain worldliness lacking in some of the less fortunate.

I think that Jason Lee, among the Methodists, will work positively in our behalf, aware that the very success of his mission has from the start been built upon the welcome and succor we offered that good-hearted man.

So, with friends on the committee that is drafting the operative laws for the disputed area, we should emerge more secure than before. I hope I am not being overly optimistic about these Americans. My instinct is to like and trust them.

Narcissa Whitman of the Presbyterian mission has been with

us this spring, in poor health and seeking the ministrations of our post physician. Marcus hastened east last year, upon receiving the news that his church intended to shut down the mission at Waiilatpu.

The Whitmans, like Jason Lee, confide in me that the native bosom is not yet ready to harbour the worship of a great unseen God, and perceives of Christian religion in largely magical terms, personal power to be discovered in the Great Book. They despair of making one true convert.

At any rate, Narcissa has warmed the post with her grace and beauty and devotion to her Indian charges, even though they test the Whitmans to the limit. I worry about them, and dangerous intimations about their safety reach my ears. The Cayuses are a treacherous tribe. But my alarms go unheeded.

Marcus is returning with the overland wagon train this year, reputed to be enormous. I do not know how we can feed them, nor do I fully grasp the implications of this sudden invasion, and how it will affect the Company. But I will, as always, extend the hand of charity and friendship, and if possible, turn this sudden immigration to good account in the ledgers by selling goods and city lots, and purchasing valuable grains and pelts.

Almost nothing has been repaid, and the risk is my own. The London directors have made that clear. And while they do not oppose ordinary charity, they do not see the need for us to equip our rivals. They turn a deaf ear to my argument, which is that we are obliged by ordinary Christian charity to rescue those who might otherwise perish, and that we are equally obliged to lend them the means to survive once they arrive.

If a thousand starving Americans are devoid of food while our granaries bulge with wheat, I have little doubt they would storm us and empty our larders without a second thought. All this I have conveyed, but George Simpson doesn't agree and rebukes me for what relief I do provide. I am not in control. I have not the power to stop this tide of Americans, nor the power to keep them south of the river, nor prevent war, nor assure an adequate supply of food for all these new people, so I am but a marionette here, jerked upon the strings of history, caught between the Company and conscience.

One of the few who has repaid us is the Reverend Constable, but in a peculiar manner, and I suspect the payment was made less from obligation than from a wish to wrestle with the Company without being stricken by conscience.

Our principal antagonists, the Reeses, borrowed the most and have paid nothing back. Electra Reese still tarries here full of discontents. I have repeatedly asked her to find shelter elsewhere. What a pallid creature she is compared to Narcissa Whitman. Mrs. Whitman, even ill, is ten times more a presence than Mrs. Reese, who is quite well though she malingers. Since Reese has his hand in that scurrilous petition, it behooves me to eject Electra from our confines. I think I shall do it, and then stop my ears against the complaints that will trail in the wake. When he comes, I will present him with an invoice.

There is about Electra Reese something that offends me right to my centre, and that is her great disdain for people of color and for Catholics—indeed, for anyone who is not Electra Reese. She treats my beloved Marguerite either as someone to be ignored, or as a servant. She scorns social commerce with any of the wives of our voyageurs, full- or half-breed. I have learned, bit by bit from our French-speaking employees, that Mrs. Reese did a great injustice to Mrs. O'Malley, ridiculing her and driving her off.

Douglas unwittingly compounded it by asking Mrs. O'Malley to leave after the altercation. Little did he or I realize that the woman had faithfully helped in the kitchen and mess, and made herself useful a thousand ways to our people, as a way, she said, of repaying obligations to us. The fault was entirely that of Electra Reese, thin and venomous woman that she is.

Ah, if only the Americans would behave as nobly as this fair Irishwoman! I will make it up to her and her husband. They owe us for blankets and some small things we supplied them at the time of their rescue, but I shall cancel that debt and let them know that the ledgers are clear.

Simpson is a thorn in my heart. He presses me to close all the coastal posts we have opened, and even to shut down this one, which I have laboured two decades to erect. I have sent Douglas north to begin work on a new headquarters at Vancouver Island, as instructed, and he is making progress. I understand the need for a headquarters in Canada. But I would sorely regret closing this post, even if the boundary line should place it within the United States. We are, after all, a company in business and should be able to do business among the Americans, on American territory. But the governor would have it otherwise.

As for other questions, I am vexed. The Company does nothing to punish the murderers of my son, and Simpson grows testy and arrogant about it. With Ogden and Douglas gone much of the time, I am too alone. We will lose our fur trade with the coastal tribes if we rely on Simpson's miserable steamboat, the *Beaver,* which costs more to fuel than we expend on our forts.

I have been here two decades, and know the business, yet now they want to undo my work and scorn my knowledge. I confide this bitterness to this journal, but try hard in my public mein to show no sign of it, just as I conceal my rheumatism, which wracks my body. It is best to hide my sorrows, ignore the nettles, and meet the incoming Yankee tide with affection and cooperation.

31

Rose Constable had lost fifty pounds on the Oregon Trail, in the process becoming strong and slender—and pretty, though she could barely admit it to herself. She knew her body had changed, but she had been slower to understand that her person was changing as well.

Before she had arrived in Oregon, she had been Jasper's dutiful wife, accepting correction, accepting his dominion—and also his criticism.

He had often reminded her that she suffered an excess of feeling and unseemly passions, and she had guiltily resolved to do better. But her feelings always betrayed her, and Jasper's patient sufferance of her weaknesses shamed her into a sense of her imperfection, and a desperate yearning to please him someday, somehow. Now . . . she would see.

Jasper was against passions, and for a serene and unruffled composure. Passions, he always had said, were the savage child in us; we needed to grow into a mature and even-keeled life, and instill these virtues in our children, draining away their volatile savagery and replacing them with Christian serenity. So she had carefully hidden her fevered passions from him, and over the course of marriage had concealed almost all the rest of her as well. If her husband thought it was unseemly to discuss what lay in the heart, she would keep her heart to herself.

She had never supposed herself to be pretty, and scorned thinking about it—until she reached Oregon and discovered, in the looking glass, a lovely figure and sun-browned face she scarcely recognized. She was fetching! During his early ministry, they had coupled rarely and without passion. He had some sort of prissy and ethereal understanding of the mating act: it should be seen as a spiritual assay, gotten past swiftly, and without displays of sentiment. It should be veiled and holy and devoid of lust, humor, and joy, done in furtive secrecy.

She had felt lonely and vaguely cheated each time, and blamed herself for not living up to his spiritual ideals.

Then one bitter day Damaris died of the cold, which was a metaphor for everything wrong in the Constable family. Only a few yards distant, the Irishman kept his wife alive by pressing himself upon her icy body, but Jasper Constable could see only the unseemliness of it and not the life-saving reality. She had thought it unseemly too—until Damaris died, and she realized that Jasper might have saved the girl with hugs, sharing his own body warmth instead of standing apart, letting ice drape them all.

She dated her independence to that moment. Never again would she blindly submit to his will. She would do what she must do. But for months she denied this dangerous vine of independence sprouting in the parched soil of her heart, fought it, conjured up guilt about it, and let Jasper rebuke it when its smallest tendril pierced into their life at the Methodist mission.

After the first of the year they were given, at last, a three-room cottage, with a tiny bedroom for the boys, another slightly larger for themselves, and a common room with a small cookstove. She should have been happy. Instead, she seethed with discontents and worries. Why were her sons so quiet and listless, and above all, why did they not seek friends?

She nurtured, in the utter secrecy of her heart, the wish that her boys would be less dutiful and more . . . like boys. Something was crushing their spirits, turning them into somber adults when they should be playfully rambling the world and wrestling and getting into boyish trouble. What was this crushing thing that was bleeding life from her and the boys—and from Jasper himself?

She felt starved, and her mind turned again and again to the O'Malleys, and the way the young man saved his wife. Was there no tenderness in Jasper other than the bland and holy kind? Was there an iota of feeling in him? Oh, to be held, to be touched, to be kissed, to be fondled, to be admired, to be admitted into his heart and private thoughts and dreams! Oh, to be married to a man who wasn't an utter stranger! Were his fingers so numb that he did not feel the smoothness of her breasts? Would he ever let her yearning hands wander over him, make him her own?

Constable devoted himself to his circular letters, the sole means of publication in such a place as Oregon, and sent a new one winging to the faithful each week, which proceeded from home to home on an established circuit, and theoretically ended back at the mission about six weeks later. Their tone swiftly shifted away from religious exhortation, and toward factional politics. There was a growing Methodist party intending to establish a Methodist Oregon, and Jasper became its voice.

One evening, she nerved herself to speak up. "Dr. McLoughlin's a good man, and you mustn't attack him so," she said at table, right in front of the boys.

Her husband stared, slackjawed, at this effrontery.

"You don't know the issues, Rose. We must avoid sentiment."

"We would not be here, any of us, but for him."

"I believe I have spoken. Perhaps I didn't make myself clear."

She weighed her response, and chose not to retreat. "You made yourself perfectly clear. The fact is, I disagree with you. I think John McLoughlin's claims to the waterpower and Oregon City are valid because he was here first, did the improvements, and fought off claim jumpers. I think it's just fine to have Catholics in Oregon. I think—"

The reverend lifted a white hand. "I will discuss this with you later in private. Mark, Matt, put this out of your minds."

The boys nodded, staring uneasily. She wondered what the boys were to put out of their minds: talk of McLoughlin, or their mother's sudden independence.

She continued, in a voice that cracked under her tension. "No, boys, I want you to grow up with generous spirits, and I especially want you to welcome and admire our benefactor. The doctor made this mission possible, invited Jason Lee and his people to settle here, helped us start our Methodist store even though it would compete with his own, sheltered our newcomers and all travelers, lent us goods, gave us livestock, let us use his boats, kept us alive, saw us through bad winters, lent us his voyageurs, delivered our mail in his expresses, doctored us without charge, invited us to preach at the fort, defended us against his own superiors, and he's entitled to our respect and the security of his property."

Her outburst amazed her more than it did Jasper.

"I entreat you not to speak further about it," he said.

"I will say what needs to be said." Heat boiled in her.

He pressed his eyes shut, as if to calm himself, and then started in:

"You are letting sentiment twist your thinking. McLoughlin runs a ruthless monopoly that bleeds us all. You are speaking of a man who permits wine at his table, allows himself to consort with people with . . . dubious connections to one another, and whose real motive is entirely commercial, though it be veneered over with a shallow piety of the sort that seems to appeal to you. People associated with the *Pope*. People connected with the established Church of England, who warred upon Methodism and other sects from the beginning. People in theological error so grave—"

But he only built bonfires in her. "Do not condescend to me, Jasper Constable. I will not have it."

He looked puzzled, disconcerted, at sea. But he settled himself, and began softly, oleaginously: "You are being childlike again, my dear Rose. Control those passions and you'll come to your maturity."

"I will be myself!"

"Perhaps you would prefer to go east for a spell."

"I am staying here and raising our sons as they need to be raised."

Oddly, he retreated and she watched him deflate. "I'm not always sure what's right," he conceded. "Matters take a complex turn when it comes to judgment. I acknowledge a debt to McLoughlin, but it's canceled by his weaknesses, so I don't—"

"You know exactly what's right. Your conscience shouts it to you. It's just that you don't listen!"

He stared at her, amazement in his face. "I do listen, always . . . I am a divided man, simply searching for the right."

"Then search harder," she snapped.

They subsided into pained silence, with the boys glancing furtively from one to the other. What had simmered for weeks was now open warfare. Rose felt hot and furious and totally unrepentant, and knew she wouldn't budge an inch.

That would not be the end of it. She knew exactly what was coming, and braced herself. Jasper would begin her reformation, with sighs and gentleness and copious Christian charity buttered thickly over her indiscretions. He meant well and was a good man. He had his vision of service and devotion to the Lord he truly loved.

And yet she found herself choking on his views, unhappy with his ways, and she knew this wild place, this Oregon, lay at the root of it. She remembered what Dr. McLoughlin had predicted so long ago: that Oregon would transform them all. She had dismissed the idea then; she would always be faithful to the things that inspired her. Now she understood.

As she scrubbed the plates, her thoughts ran furiously. This was not really about the Hudson's Bay Company; it was about an unhappy marriage. Her husband lived in some distant land where thinking, feeling women weren't welcome, where ordinary warmth, affection, and the sharing of the day never occurred.

It was not merely that she was a drudge; this wild place required drudgery from both sexes. It was that she had no one to share her life with. She resolved then and there, as she poured heated rinse water over her chipped saucers and bowls, to do something about it.

That evening, in the dubious privacy of their tiny bedroom, separated by plank walls from the boys' room, she slipped into her thick flannel nightgown in the guttering light of a candle, and awaited Jasper, who had stepped outside. When at last he came in, she took the first step in her campaign.

"I want you to hold me tonight, Jasper. You never hold me. We are married, you and I. Let us be lovers."

He turned, startled, as he unbuttoned his shirt.

"Rose, you are suffering from some sort of distraction," he said softly.

"No, I am asking you to make a marriage out of our vows. I am left out of your life."

"Shhh!" he rasped, gesturing toward the plank wall. "It's unseemly."

A fury unloosed within her. "Unseemly! Is that all you can think of?" she snapped, knowing the boys would hear every word, and relishing it. "Our dear Damaris died because you worried about the unseemliness of holding her when she needed warmth to live! The boys almost died because you would not hold them, or run with them to keep warm, but made us sit miserably apart, while sleet was murdering us!"

He stared, shocked. "Rose!"

"Unseemly! Unseemly!" She shouted it. "Let us be unseemly!"

She hadn't meant to rage at him, but there it was: the accusation that had festered in her bosom, built within her all these months, and now had exploded nakedly. She began weeping, knowing that she had slipped out of control like a child, just as he accused her of doing.

Tears slid down her cheeks. "I am sorry, Jasper," she said.

But he didn't melt. "You have accused me," he said.

She wanted to flee the implications of what she had laid before him, but the dam holding back all her feelings on that subject had just burst, and she returned to it with new fury.

"Mr. O'Malley saved his wife and no one was embarrassed by their embrace—except you. I thought it was beautiful, the way he twisted the water out of her skirts while she shook, blue and desperate; wrung every drop, found a place for her to lie down, and then pressed himself upon her, giving her his own warmth. She would have died . . . like Damaris."

Jasper controlled himself admirably, as he always did, the perfect and mature Christian minister, ever forgiving, understanding, and kind. He smiled benignly. "It behooves a minister of the Gospel of Christ to be seemly at all times, and I count it one of my triumphs that on that day I acted calmly and quietly, not blaming God or Nature for the disaster, but only malign fate. I grieve our daughter as much as you, my dear Rose, but we must always be obedient to God's will."

"God's will! She might have lived," she cried. "You could have saved her. God had nothing to do with it. All she needed was love."

32

Garwood Reese was well satisfied with his work. For weeks, he had steered the committee drafting the organic law for the provisional government, and now his work bore fruit. He had a solid majority of Methodist missioners at hand, and a scattering of voyageurs and HBC men in opposition. His early intention of staking out a town site had long ago vanished in a bout of bilious fever and bitter weather, and now he was pursuing his true vocation, politics.

The sole model available to the committee was the organic law of Iowa contained in a lawbook that found its way west, so that became the prototype of the Oregon legislation. But with differences. The Oregon version provided for a three-man executive committee in place of a governor, and a nine-member committee instead of a legislature, and it supplied no means of raising taxes, entrusting the treasury to voluntary subscriptions.

Reese had been living hand-to-mouth in Oregon City because McLoughlin would extend him no more credit, which was just one more mark against Hudson's Bay and its chief factor, in his book. But Abernethy, at the Methodist store, had kept Reese afloat, and supplied a place for the politician to bunk. Out of all that rose a seething need to revenge himself on the company, and he knew exactly how to go about it, and in a fashion that would enchant his Methodist friends.

"Now we should turn to the land law," he said at one meeting. "I've drafted a model statute. I'll read it to you. As you can see, this confirms all your holdings. It's in accord with the bills introduced in Congress by Senator Linn of Missouri."

He had their attention, but the Canadians looked skeptical. It was the turmoil about land that had driven the settlers to create a provisional government in the first place. He was proud of this one. At last, he could do some good for Oregon.

He read them the material confirming their right to own the 640 acres they were squatting on, and then he read them his little Ode to Joy. No private person, he said, could hold claim to "extensive water privileges, or other situations necessary for the transaction of mercantile or manufacturing operations."

He noted, with amusement, the concerned expressions of his colleagues, and continued reading. "Provided that nothing in these laws shall be construed as to affect any claim of any mission of a religious character, made previous to this time, to the extent not more than six miles square."

Ah, that was more what the Methodists wanted! It eased McLoughlin out of his mill holdings at the falls of the Willamette, and also his town site at Oregon City, while at the same time confirming the Methodists in theirs by giving them the right to an entire township, 23,040 acres.

Even though McLoughlin's son Joseph was on the drafting committee, he failed to grasp the implications, which delighted Reese. The youth listened peacefully to the debate, which was perfunctory. None of the Methodists were about to reveal that the very ground under McLoughlin's new saw- and gristmills would be snatched from him, along with the entire surveyed and divided town site of Oregon City.

Reese enjoyed the prospect. If enacted, half the town site would fall to him as payment for his leadership of this committee—a deal he had worked out with Abernethy, the Reverend Alvin Waller, and others. That was fair enough; he had true leadership skills. He had focused all the Americans on the malign power of Hudson's Bay Company and then congenially welded them, with praise and encouragement and vast outpourings of good humor, into a disciplined faction.

The motion carried.

That day, Reese wrote a guarded letter to Electra, exulting in their good fortune. If the organic laws were adopted by the citizens of Oregon, and he didn't doubt that they would be, old Dr. John would be unceremoniously scuttled. Of course he didn't quite say that, not in a letter destined for Fort Vancouver, but he did dwell on the changing tide of fortunes that had come to the Reeses.

"Now, my dear Electra, we shall be regarded as the Liberators of Oregon, and have at our disposal scores of city lots to sell, to the benefit of our own comfort and affluence and honor. My heart and conscience are at ease."

He had other clauses buzzing like hornets in his head, which he and Electra had discussed at length, but just now he wished to avoid certain controversies, and they would have to wait. He was well aware that Washington would take notice of the proposed provisional government only if there was a clear showing of widespread support.

That evening he paced Oregon City, enjoying the eddies of spring air, the muscular river, the benched land vaulting upward from the narrow valley. As always, he noted its swift growth, the timber frames of new buildings going up, the new outbuildings, the cottages with newly planted lilacs, the humming sawmills spewing planks and timbers, one operated by McLoughlin, the other by the milling company operated by the missioners. In short order it would be all American, and there would scarcely be a swarthy French Canadian in sight, much less the ludicrous coat of arms of the Hudson's Bay Company flying from any staff in the town.

He thought joyously of the huge immigration even then heading west, reputed to number a thousand or more by express couriers traveling back and forth to the States. Hundreds of Americans wanting his city lots! The committee had about completed its work, and the next step would be to publish it and call a mass meeting to ratify the work. That would come in July.

He spent the next weeks assiduously circulating the proposed laws, and was rewarded on July 5 with a huge turnout that whooped the provisional government into existence at a campfire meeting. It did not matter to the clamorous Methodist missioners that, earlier, John McLoughlin had given the Methodists five lots in his town site with which to build a store and church and mission buildings. That had all been explained away by Reese, who had argued that the lots weren't McLoughlin's to give to anyone.

An election was set for May 1844, to put the officers in place. Until then, McLoughlin would still hang on to his properties, but plainly, the monopoly was facing the guillotine. Reese's spirits bloomed along with his waistline. It was vastly satisfying to him that he had organized the Methodist faction and led it to its triumph. Hudson's Bay was whipped, and Oregon would be settled by Americans, not foreigners.

He heard later that the chief factor was deeply disturbed by the new laws, an intelligence that Reese found satisfying. Let the monopolist worry! Oregon would soon belong to the United States, not the foreigners. He took to roving Oregon City, telling the world that McLoughlin was roaring like a wounded bear, and that the great blow against foreign influence had been nurtured in the bosom of Garwood Reese himself. He had found his political wings and now was soaring over the landscape of Oregon, finding a home there at last. All was well, except that he was dead broke, and could not yet sell Oregon City lots for sustenance.

Sometimes he wrestled with his own conduct: was this the way to treat a man who had saved his life? He had bad moments, when he despised himself for the opportunistic man he was, but these scruples he overcame, shoveling his self-contempt deeper and deeper into the pit of his heart until not even he knew it lurked there.

He waited impatiently through the summer's heat, thinking about the vanguard of the migration from the States and how he could lure them into his own faction. But he was living on a pile of debt and growing irritable. Everyone else in Oregon was sinking roots, building homes and barns, plowing fields, planting wheat and orchards and gardens, creating wealth *ex nihilo*.

He resolved at last to go to Fort Vancouver and offer his good offices during the transition to provisional government. John McLoughlin, after all, deserved some respect.

The next day he strode through the river gate in the twenty-foot picketed wall of the post, past sunbaked buildings, to the chief factor's offices. And there found McLoughlin hunched over his ledgers, his crown of white hair tied back with a ribbon.

McLoughlin peered up, his gaze glacial. But Reese had expected that. The White Eagle stood but did not offer a hand.

"Have you come to pay the company what is owed, Mr. Reese?"

"I haven't a penny, Doctor."

"Then I have no business with you."

"Oh, I think you do."

The chief factor waited, granite-faced, his stare drilling through Reese.

"You're about to lose your Oregon City property, town site, and mill. It's a pity."

McLoughlin nodded curtly.

"I'm concerned about that. It's a blow to you, rather unfair, I think, considering what you've done for us all. I can spare you that loss."

Reese found he could scarcely bear the impact of the chief factor's gaze.

"It's like this, sir. If you'll deed to the Methodist mission all the unsold lots now, before the provisional government invalidates your claim to them, I will contract with you to pay you a hundred dollars apiece as I sell them to the immigrants as they arrive."

McLoughlin's gaze did not release Reese.

"You'd have some gain instead of nothing. There's profit in it for you and your company."

The White Eagle didn't blink.

"As for the mills and the right to the water powering them, if you deed them to the mission now, ahead of time, I'll make sure you share the profits fifty-fifty. It's all in Article Four of the new organic law. You've lost your claim to it. I can spare you such disaster."

McLoughlin's face stained deeper and deeper red. Wordlessly he rounded his ancient desk, clasped Reese by the scruff of the neck, and dragged him toward the door.

"You are assaulting me! It will go ill with you!"

McLoughlin didn't stop at the door of his offices, but wrestled the helpless

Reese down the broad stairs, across the dusty yard, past gaping employees, and finally out the front gates, which suddenly loomed high above Reese, forbidding and imperial.

"Wait here," said McLoughlin. He wheeled back into the post, and Reese heard nothing for several minutes. He stood irritably in the fierce July sun, cursing McLoughlin, the company he ran, and every toadying, swart, stupid French employee of the great enterprise.

In due course Dr. McLoughlin returned, with elegant Electra walking imperiously at his side, dressed in a white summer frock and looking as if she were going to a parade. A Canadian lackey toted a heavy carpetbag stuffed with her things, and a heap of fancy female clothing over his shoulders.

"Garwood!" she said. "This beast is making me—"

"Oh, Mr. Reese! You will never set foot here again, either of you. And you are not excused from the two hundred pounds owed to the Hudson's Bay Company. If honor doesn't suffice, I trust that conscience will."

He wheeled away, leaving the pair of them in the hot sun.

The whole world, it seemed, was watching.

33

A sullen peace descended on Oregon, and John McLoughlin devoted it to the pinched business of dismantling his fur-trading empire. The coastal trading posts, so painfully erected and staffed, had to go according to his superiors, and so he closed them and began shifting his men, pensioning some, sending others back to Canada. Some were the sons of men he had started with; men who expected to work for Hudson's Bay forever.

The Americans were furiously settling the Willamette Valley, throwing up farmsteads, weeding their wheatfields, and raising homes and stores in Oregon City. They came to him for a thousand items, little of which he had in stock, but he gave them what they needed on credit—at least those who had not fashioned that mendacious petition against him and the honorable company. There were some, like Reese, with whom he would not do business.

On his occasional forays to Oregon City, he was amazed at the progress these industrious people were making. A substantial town had mushroomed along the bank of the river. The evidences of commerce and prosperity were everywhere. But even when the settlers began scything and winnowing their first wheat crops, he saw very little by way of repayment of his innumerable loans, though now and then some stiff-backed settler repaid him in wheat because no cash existed anywhere in the area. He credited that man and shook his hand heartily, but on the whole the debts owed to the Hudson's Bay Company increased that autumn.

The monsoons drifted in, and the cast-iron skies pelted cold rain upon the post, blackening the high stockade and turning the yard into a moil of mud. Spirits blackened with the rain. What worried him most, as he stood before his hearth, letting the radiant heat comfort his buckling old bones, was the oncoming migration. Would they perish? Had they died in frightful numbers? What must he do?

The impending arrival set him to warring with himself, and he sometimes paced restlessly around his office, not noticing the curios on the shelves or the ledger books. Business and charity could not go hand in hand. He was a wily businessman whose abilities had so enriched the shareholders that they had divided a twenty percent profit among themselves most years. He could not foster American rivals without destroying all he had built.

But to stare into the pinched faces of a desperate family, famished and ill-clad, cold and destitute, bone-tired and sick . . . to peer into the blue face of a wailing infant . . . An honorable man would do what he had to do.

Then one somber afternoon, about teatime, the first of them tied up at the riverfront. He hastened out to meet them, carrying an umbrella against the nattering rain. They had come in one of the company's own bateaux, or "mackinaws" as the Yanks called them, so many on board that the river rose almost to the gunnels of the flat-bottomed scow.

They stared up at him as they debarked, gaunt, squinty, wind-burned, sun-blistered, starved, bedraggled people, men and women, children, families.

"Welcome, welcome," he cried. "Come warm up, and let us visit! And whom do I address?"

A reddened man of pleasant demeanor, apparently their spokesman, drew nigh. "I'm Peter Burnett of Missouri," he said. "We're mostly Missourians."

"Well, you have news to share. You're the first this year. Come, come, out of the rain. Now, are any ill? Is there any difficulty we should attend?"

"We have sick people," Burnett said. "Bilious fever, colic, dropsy, and a broken foot all swole up and busting out the flesh. And we're all starved. This last water passage, why, we found nought for our stomachs."

Indeed, they looked starved and fearful. They stared at him like frightened does, ready to bolt. "I'm John McLoughlin, in charge here. Come, come, warm up. You're half-frozen, I imagine. I welcome you. The company welcomes you. Come, come!"

He and various traders and clerks and company men hurried the destitute Americans up the long gradient to the gates of Fort Vancouver, while other company men carried their gear. He led this subdued group into the shadowed mess hall where a fire crackled in a fieldstone hearth, and a good shake roof turned the rain.

They sank onto the floor before the fire, pooling water upon the planks. The women, especially, looked worn almost to despair, and the children clung to them, soaked and uncomfortable, one yellow with jaundice.

McLoughlin set his cooks to work. There would be broth and gruel shortly. He summoned Forbes Barclay, the post physician.

"Now who's ill?" he said. "Our post physician, Dr. Barclay, will be with you directly."

Several people raised a hand. "Here, here, you gather here and he'll see to you."

Marguerite arrived bearing some blankets, and they eyed her cautiously, studying her brown face and black eyes and strong-boned cheeks. She handed blankets to the shivering children and smiled as she did so.

"This is my wife, Marguerite," he said. "If any of you women need female assistance, she'll be glad to help."

"I have some spare clothing," Marguerite said.

But no one moved. Still they did not speak. Was it because they believed all those canards about the Hudson's Bay Company, the ogre of the Northwest? Well, if so, he could allay that ugly reputation here and now.

Peter Ogden wandered in, along with several of the traders from the store. McLoughlin introduced them all. They nodded and huddled about the fire.

"Now, Mr. Burnett, tell us about your passage," he said. "How many of you might we expect?"

"Nine hundred, sir. Unless there were losses . . ."

"Nine hundred! Are you mostly connected with the missions?"

"No, we're homesteaders, people looking for a new life."

"And who guided you?"

"Marcus Whitman, most of the way. He was a great help to us. He told us we could do it, and we did."

"Ah! Dr. Whitman! And what's his news? Last winter he hastened to the States fearing his board of missions would close down Waiilatpu."

"Good news, he told us. His entreaties reversed the mission board. And so he's back."

"Ah, good, good. You were in capable hands on the trail. Are the rest far behind?"

"Some are. The ones driving herds."

"Oh, oh, there's peril. The winter storms . . ."

"We fear for them. They may need your help . . . that is, if your company is willing—"

"Mr. Burnett, if any one person perishes for want of help from us, my heart would be heavy. I am bound by faith and honor . . ."

Forbes Barclay arrived, bearing his pigskin bag.

"Ladies, gentlemen, this is our physician, Dr. Barclay. I do not practice, myself, having no skill at it after long neglect of my education. You who are in need, this is your man. If you need to consult privately, he'll see to it in our little hospital."

The infirm rose. A gaunt woman smiled at him, at last. A small fracture in the ice, but a beginning.

"Now, Mr. Burnett, while we await something from the kitchen, please tell us more about your trip."

"We didn't expect a reception like this!"

"I'm glad that we can improve upon our reputation."

"We heard that you would turn us away from your doors."

McLoughlin slowly fashioned an answer. "There are, at present, about two hundred of your countrymen settled south of here in farmsteads, or in Oregon City, or at the Methodist mission . . . Most of them found the means to survive at our company store. We've made loans, though we don't wish to do so."

"Well, then, we've been misled. Some of those fire-eaters in Congress . . ."

"So we've heard. And now you know better. But how was your journey? Trouble with Indians?"

"Very little, and that was only some pilfering." Burnett grinned. "Mostly trouble between ourselves. This is a caravan of fractious and thin-skinned individualists! We formed into companies on the model of the Santa Fe traders, drew up our laws, and I was elected captain. Only first thing I knew, whilst we were still in Kansas, I was deposed." He laughed at himself.

"A commonplace occurrence, and I'll wager there were few rules that survived too."

Burnett nodded. McLoughlin thought he might like this man, who spoke with humor and grace, as a good folksy politician might. The man was showing some education too.

He soon discovered that this huge migration had soon cleaved in two, with those driving cattle trailing well behind because they were slower. There had been more than the usual squabbling among these contentious Yankee frontiersmen and their families, including some fistfights, but in time the harsh conditions, alkaline water, swarms of gnats, dysentery, and rank hunger subdued them. They had suffered badly crossing the rain-swollen South Platte, and by the time they'd reached Fort Laramie they had jettisoned nearly all the household goods and farm implements they had toted, so naïvely, westward.

At the venerable fur post of Laramie they found little to buy, almost no livestock to trade, but pressed on in the heat of summer, suffering from famine, drought, mosquitoes, flies, the disappearance of game including the plenteous buffalo, and straggled into Fort Hall, only to have the company trader, Richard Grant, tell them they would have to abandon their wagons and acquire packhorses and packsaddles, which the post did not have.

"Abandon the wagons! Can you imagine it? How the women did wail!" Burnett said.

"Grant gave you sound advice," McLoughlin said.

Burnett smiled wryly.

Whitman, he said, had encouraged them onward, arguing that this company was so large that its men could cut their own roads, which is exactly what they did. A large party of axemen chopped the way west ahead of the chattering wagons. And thus, amazingly, they surmounted the Blue Mountains upon a new road hastily hewn through the forests. They recruited at Waiilatpu, resentful of Marcus Whitman's prices, which were double St. Louis prices.

It was near there, at the Hudson's Bay post, Fort Walla Walla, that this vanguard of 1843 bought every company bateau available, and began voyaging down the river.

"Others are coming shortly?"

"We're a day ahead of the next lot. They've been slowed down by overloading. And dealing with the rascal redskins for portage. What a thieving lot! We're lucky to be alive!"

"And now the rest are caught in the monsoon rains. And, I'm afraid, the snow. Oh, Mr. Burnett, we shall hear of tribulations, but at least you're safe. Now I have a question for all of you: why did you come here?"

He peered about, hoping for an answer. Finally, a gaunt man with silvered hair spoke up.

"We heard it'd be Eden," he said.

"Eden, sir? It's wilderness."

"We came because we were called."

"Who called you? The propagandist Hall Kelley?"

"You have to hear Oregon a-calling, hear the music, and then you'll know. The heavenly music, the music of the spheres. We heard the voice crying in the wilderness, and we came."

That mysterious summation, which baffled the chief factor, was punctuated by the appearance of two cooks with a great iron pot of oat gruel, tasteless but nourishing, life-giving, and warm.

Dr. McLoughlin stayed on hand, seeing them wolf down the simple fare, seeing the pinched and tearful faces of the children relax, seeing sleep overtake infants, women begin to smile and stroke their children, and the frightful nightmare of a continental crossing begin to fade.

The cost to the company, so far, was virtually nothing. But John McLoughlin knew that the cost to himself, in future suffering, would be profound. Nine hundred vagrants. But what else could a decent man do?

34

John O'Malley would look back upon those early months of 1843 as the time of promise. He had little idea of how to get a living in a new land, but he was mastering useful trades. At least Mary Kate and little Oregon sojourned comfortably in Champoeg with a French Canadian family, but how long could that last? She called the child Patrick, and clouded up whenever he called the baby Oregon, but he didn't mind.

Some days he roamed his claim-land, amazed at its infinities and the bold green of its pastures, the spring blossoms that garlanded the sloping fields, the pine scents and aromatic brush. He would have loved to put Cotswold sheep on his rainbow land, but he could afford none, and gray wolves would butcher them within a week. Other days he hacked fitfully at good straight firs so that he might build a log cabin. But he soon discovered the amount of sheer sweat required to put up a log home was awesome, and he marveled that these Yank frontiersmen could manage it so easily.

He dreamed of ordinary comforts, a place of his own rooted deep in the good earth, a great boisterous family, and enough put by to bring to this sweet land his brothers and sisters and cousins and aunts and uncles. He dreamed of half a dozen more lusty children, with Mary Kate their proud matron.

He dreamed of becoming a sage, consulted in Oregon for his views on great issues, such as freedom and slavery, property and rents; and a lyrical voice in behalf of this new land and the new republic, where he would be a citizen, not a subject.

But they were only dreams.

Then one day his trail companion Abel Brownell approached him. Would O'Malley be interested in clerking in the new store at Oregon City? He could pay little: fifty cents a day and a bunk in the storeroom, but it would be a start. If he did well, there would be more.

"Selling bores me," Brownell said. "I'm an entrepreneur, not a merchant. You run the store, and we'll see about the future."

O'Malley didn't hesitate. "I will start today, and I will be selling all you have on the shelves and then some, and all you can skim off the ships," he said confidently.

Too confidently. He knew the Methodist settlers hadn't forgotten Brownell's attempt to sell drams, nor had they forgiven his liberalist voice in the affairs of the settlement, and clung to Abernethy's mission store. He knew all about shunning.

But it was Abel Brownell's gift to laugh at the fussbudgets.

So John O'Malley became a clerk. There were days when not a customer walked in, and he did little but stare out the window into a bright world; days when he wondered whether he was daft to be there, perched on a stool behind a plank counter, exiled from the whole town, when he could be getting ahead in some populous place like New York or Boston, where so many of his countrymen were settling.

Was it not true that almost a quarter of the population of New York City was Irish? And an Irishman with connections could flourish there, with the help of a political machine called Tammany? Ah, how Mary Kate would love that! She had never stopped grieving Ireland.

But almost imperceptibly, things changed. Goods trickled out the door because people needed them. A little cash and a few hides came in. One day Brownell suggested that the rear room be turned into an apartment where John and Mary Kate and the squalling boy might live.

A flood of joy filled O'Malley, and he set to work cutting a window in the dark room. He rode down to Champoeg, paid his boarding debts from his slim purse, and brought Mary Kate home in a canoe, their squirming baby cradled in her arms. O'Malley thanked another Mary, the Virgin, for his great good fortune, while his wife clung to him in tears.

From then on, things blossomed like roses in June. He persuaded Brownell to buy a wagon from among the few available, and a dray horse and harness, and after that he left the store to Mary Kate, loaded up the wagon with shrewdly selected goods and set out to visit the most distant farms and settlements, drumming pots and blankets and knives and grindstones and taking whatever he could in trade: wheat, oats, hay, potatoes, deer hides, mink, ermine, wolfskins, if he couldn't get cash. These he traded to the Hudson's Bay Company for more goods for the store.

He had a knack. His Irish humor and raconteur's gifts served him well, for lonely settlers were eager to visit with the melodic unruly-haired Irishman, and if he took the time to spin some yarns, spread some news, or tell a good knee-slapper, he would make a sale of some sort. He had the blarney-gift, and he learned to exploit it.

Brownell watched the gloomy balance sheets change bit by bit, and nodded. O'Malley was selling on credit or barter, but he was selling. Abel and
Felicity had settled into the big house on the terrace above, and were living
about as well as anyone in that rude town could manage. Often, they invited
the O'Malleys in for a supper, and Mary Kate marveled at the wonders of
Felicity's kitchen, the wood range and oven, the spices from Boston, the varieties of bread and cereal and meat and vegetables she came up with.

The Brownells could talk and talk about Unitarianism and Thoreau and
Longfellow and Emerson and Transcendentalists and never be dull, and never
bore John O'Malley, and he in turn never bored them with his tales of Ireland
and landlords and rent collectors, or his sometimes perilous adventures selling
from a wagon. Through all this, Mary Kate sat quietly, and O'Malley could not
read what was in her mind. But he sensed she would rather be among her own.

Then one day Devers Cushing anchored the *Golden Hawk* in the Columbia
off the island above its confluence with the Willamette, and Brownell and
O'Malley raced downriver in a bateau to see what the squinty bib-bearded
master had brought to Oregon.

"Abel, I've plundered the Pacific," Cushing announced. "If you have women,
I have the pretties. Sandwich Islands, Whampoa, Sidney, Yerba Buena . . ."

"We don't, but this fall there's going to be plenty of newcomers. I'll bet
on it."

Cushing eyed him. "Then you'll get rich. Come, come, look at my manifest!"

They clambered up a lurching Jacob's ladder onto the holystoned teak deck
of the brigantine, and headed for Cushing's snug cabin.

"I fear I'll lose two or three of my crew," Cushing growled. "They're
restless. Before we dropped anchor, I promised them a bonus for the next leg,
but God only knows if I'll keep them. I've got some tough bosuns, who'd lief
pluck up the miscreants out of the piney woods. I'll tell you what, Brownell,
the only thing saves me is temperance. If they could get some grog in Oregon,
I'd never see the lot of them again."

"You're lucky," Brownell retorted. "The Methodists poured my spirits into
the river!"

"They did? And you let them?"

"Six to one, and all I had on my side was virtue." He laughed wildly.

O'Malley smiled. He had heard the story too many times to count.

He loved ships, and gazed ecstatically at the clean lines, the furled sheets,
the capstan, the white-enameled trim, the raked Maine pine masts, the Yankee
pennant fluttering from the foretopmast. An Irishman, never far from the sea,
carried this mysterious passion in his blood, and he surrendered to it.

They settled upon varnished benches in the captain's cramped cabin, and
Cushing opened an iron strongbox and handed Brownell the manifest.

Kegs of nails, more window glass in sawdust, sash windows in crates, cartons of hammers, saws, knives, chisels, adzes, axes, and awls; manila rope, rolled linen sailcloth; bolts of broadcloth, flannel, linen, nankeen, calico, gaudy China silk; threescore New Zealand blankets, fifty yards of oilcloth, ribbons, a chest of tea, kegs of coffee, molasses, sugar; snuff, tobacco, ten grindstones, fifty skillets, thirty pots, a hundred pounds of harness leather, horse and mule harness, shoe leather, a keg of salt, linseed oil, white enamel, turpentine, cordage, oakum; lime, mangoes, and papayas; three kegs of good Chilean gunpowder, boxes of percussion caps, lead, powderhorns, maize, vegetable seeds, rosebushes, lilacs, two gross of hinges and door hardware, reams of paper, sacks of hard candy, fifty decks of playing cards, a small cask of Scotch whisky, sewing needles and thread, wax candles, iron lamps, tin utensils and cups and bowls, crockery tableware, iron knives and spoons and forks . . . and a litter of cats, wild and snarling in a bamboo cage.

The list dizzied O'Malley. In one stroke, the sun-chastened, red-fleshed Cushing had brought to Oregon more and better goods than everything in the Methodist and Hudson's Bay stores combined.

"It's a fortune if you can sell it proper, Brownell," Cushing said, tamping tobacco in his pipe. There was a faint question mark in his comment.

"This fall," Brownell said. He turned to O'Malley. "John, we've got to move all this truck up to the store with bateaux and the ship's longboat. I'll put you to it."

"I'll put Peters, my bosun, on it," Cushing said. "I've got a fourteen-man crew and I'll put ten on. We'll do this and I'll pay my respects to John McLoughlin. I've a few trinkets for him from China."

It took two days. And meanwhile, Brownell and the ship's master dickered and talked and tapped the captain's locked-up spirits, and what they said was obviously not for O'Malley's ears.

The seamen unloaded boat after boat of goods into the Oregon City store, filling it to the rafters. And when that was crammed they unloaded into the O'Malley apartment, and when that was stuffed, into the parlor of Brownell's house until Felicity and the children could scarcely navigate, while poor Mary Kate stumbled around mountains of goods and squalling fawn-colored blue-eyed cats whose gratitude for escaping the confines of the ship amounted to an eagerness to bloody everyone who came close. But cats would bring a fine price in rat-infested Oregon.

Even before the goods were stored, everyone in Oregon City rushed the store, frantic to purchase items that had yet to be priced. They gathered, pop-eyed; gaunt women in bonnets, men in rough homespuns and decrepit boots, sharply watching the unloading, their mouths pursed and their thoughts hooded from their neighbors.

"Hinges! What'll you take for two pair?" asked one gent.

"I don't know yet!"

"I'll give ye two dollars cash!"

"Well . . ."

"Two-fifty! Cash on the barrelhead!"

That seemed extraordinary. "All right," John said, wondering whether the manifest would show the cost to be more than he sold them for. But he could scarcely halt the frenzy, and finally he simply sold to the highest bidders in that auction.

But then, at dusk, Abel Brownell finally arrived from downstream, with the manifest in hand.

"Devers has sailed. I told him to do it again, and gave him a note on my Boston financiers. I had to scrape bottom this time, John. Nothing left now."

Dread stole through O'Malley. "I have already been selling, sir . . . to the highest bidder. People were mad to buy."

Brownell frowned—until O'Malley showed him the hastily penned ledger that recorded each transaction, and the amazing box of banknotes and coins and gold, the heaped pelts, the bushels of wheat bagged in burlap.

Abel started laughing and wheezing. "John," he said, "you've sold this stuff for around a thousand percent profit, and mostly for cash too. They must've shaken it out of their moneybelts."

That evening, John and Mary Kate and little Oregon Patrick enjoyed a wildly delicious curried chicken dinner at the home of the Brownells, amid barrels of ten-penny nails and rainbow mounds of cotton flannel.

Brownell poured some good ruby port from a cask gaudily labeled "vinegar," filled the glasses of the adults, poured a tiny glass each for his adoring daughter and silent son, and proposed a toast.

"Here's to the new company, my friends," he said.

O'Malley lifted his glass, while he and Mary Kate exchanged glances.

"Here's to Brownell, Cushing, and O'Malley, Importers."

John O'Malley's glass stopped midair.

"Well, drink up, drink up!"

"But . . ."

"Don't but me. You have ten percent; Devers and I each have forty-five."

John O'Malley sipped, trying to process all that.

"What do you think we've been hammering at in that hot cabin, eh? I wanted you in. Not only did you sell when I couldn't because no one walked into the shop, but I like your politics. From the hour you voted against the swindle of old John McLoughlin by Reese and those ungrateful brigands, I knew you were the man to run a business with us."

35

There wasn't anything wrong with the baby she called Patrick. He had been healthy all of his brief life. He lay now in a basket, his pale face artfully hidden from the relentless sun with a cotton flannel receiving blanket. This land agreed with him, and he had flourished in the clean air and spacious wilderness, rarely colicky, and usually content.

There wasn't anything wrong with her either. She sat in the wobbly canoe feeling the sun heat her and the zephyrs toy with her dark hair, which had bleached slightly as the summer progressed. She could not endure bonnets, the standard headgear of the American women, and so avoided them.

Nor was there anything wrong with John O'Malley. He looked almost boyish as he paddled the canoe up the river toward a picnic bower he knew about, where his little family could enjoy the shade of stately ash and smaller box elder trees. Happiness radiated from him, and she marveled at it. His long trek west and endless labor had hardened him, and now he pulled muscularly at the paddle, and with each stroke she felt the surge of the bark canoe as it glided upstream against the quiet current. He had a bright future, and it made his eyes shine. Together, they would prosper and grow with the new settlement, and find respect and veneration in their old age.

There was nothing wrong with Oregon. This sweet and good land seduced her. Every ripple of the river shot sparks of light toward her. The forested banks hid deer and eagles and small creatures she could not name. The land was there for the taking. No landlord's stone mansion frowned upon her or John, no crabbed and imperious agent came for the rents, no king's constables patrolled this wild country.

Nor was anything wrong with her life. The very day after Captain Cushing's cargo had been stored, Mr. Brownell had offered to build a cottage for the O'Malleys. The storeroom at the shop was desperately needed. John had agreed at once, even though he would assume some debt to the new company. But Brownell had been generous, offering the hardware, nails, and glass at cost, and advancing the amounts needed to buy a lot and the lumber and employ the carpenters.

And now that was finished too. They had moved into a little nest of their own up on the top bench above the river, with a fine view of the falls and the valley. It even had a bedroom in it, and a kitchen stove. It had white shiplap sides and a shake roof, and generous windows that let the misty Oregon light pour in and brighten the two rooms. She had planted roses and lilacs and hollyhocks, but they would not bloom until next year.

There was nothing wrong with that. There was nothing wrong with anything else. Father Demers or Father Blanchet usually stopped to serve the handful of Catholics in Oregon City while en route between Fort Vancouver and the mission at Champoeg, so she was neither lacking the sacraments nor the consolations of the faith.

There was nothing wrong with anything, which was why she felt shame wash through her whenever she thought about her life. She was not happy.

On this Sabbath afternoon, John was taking his small family on a picnic. She watched uneasily as he steered the canoe through some treacherous eddies. She did not trust the fragile and unstable craft, so she sat very still and held the sleeping baby tightly.

"There now," he said, pointing at a grove of willows on the bank. "There is a small bit of heaven."

She did not want heaven. She wanted Ireland.

He steered the canoe to a graveled strand, and hopped out easily, dragging the canoe a few feet up so she could step out upon dry shore. She lifted the baby and handed it to him gently, and stepped out. He beached the canoe and followed with the wicker picnic basket.

They were utterly alone. She glanced about her, not liking the aloneness. That was the whole trouble with Oregon. There were no people. There were none of her kin, none of her family, the Burkes of Clonmel, no cobbled streets and brick homes, no pubs on every corner and no teasing uncles.

"I have been here before," he said. "See how the river rounds this headland? See the ashes? How many times have Indians or settlers made a camp?"

"It is beautiful," she murmured. The baby stirred, so she plucked him out of his basket, amazed at how heavy he was, how swiftly his little body had firmed and grown.

John went back to the canoe and fetched a tattered piece of sailcloth that would do for a ground cover and maybe slow down the ants.

"Find a place your heart desires," he said.

"My heart does not desire."

He stared a long moment.

She strolled the glade, choosing shade for the sake of the baby. She marveled that some found solace in wilderness. For her it was empty, even hostile, and often dangerous. Even its beauty offered no refreshment to her spirit. Wilderness was not half so lovely as a garden. Why could she not find happiness in this robust land? Why was she always yearning? Why was John O'Malley not enough, not nearly enough?

That thought plunged her into the usual shame. What would Father Blanchet think, her husband not enough for her? What would he say if she told him that melancholia afflicted her very soul?

He would gently scold her in his laggard English, and shake his head, and urge some contrition upon her for even thinking such things. Did she not have everything? Even health? And not a child buried yet? Shame!

John drew apart the linen cloth, and pulled out the sourdough bread and cheddar, all that they had brought with them. He broke a piece of the bread and handed it to her, and one for himself. Then he pried some cheese from the wheel, and shared it. She saw he had appetite and was relishing the meal.

"In January, we will have our first payout for the partnership," he said. "We will do well, I think."

She ate, watched the dreamy-eyed baby, and stared at the kingfishers swooping over the purling waters. It was his dream, not hers.

"Someday, my love, we will have a big white house on that land. I want wood and windows and white paint. In all Ireland, there never was such wood. But here there is good strong wood, and sunlight, and paint, and we will have glass no matter what the price, and we will have a lawn mowed clean by sheep, and a brood of our own . . ." He peered at her. "Mary Kate, is something wrong?"

She sighed, fussed with the baby's blanket, and smiled at him. He stared back, solemn and wise in his helplessness.

"I am just a bit lonely," she said. "No, that is not true. I am homesick, and I want to go visit for a while."

"Visit? Ireland?"

"I have not seen my father or my sisters or brother for . . . it must be two years. They do not even know about him!" She pointed at Oregon Patrick. "Do not even know!"

"The letter will get there soon," he said.

They had entrusted a letter to Captain Cushing. That and other mail would be transferred from ship to ship crisscrossing the oceans and eventually reach their destination. But it might even take six months or more.

"I have no news! I do not know whether Agnes has a beau; whether . . . who is alive and who is not. And whether Pa is ailing or not, and making ends meet or not."

Her father was a county clerk, a man with a salary, taking the queen's shilling like some soldier boy, but not earning much, especially to feed a family of seven. When he couldn't feed his brood, he wrote poems. When his loyalties to the Sassenachs were tested, he retreated into himself and quietly helped his cousins and friends with a coin here and there, no matter that his children suffered. In the pub he railed at Dublin Castle, and the British, and all the while he suffered the shame of taking their coin, and sometimes drank to maudlin excess because of the injustice of it all. She loved him, and understood his trapped soul, for it was like her own.

"That is not possible, the trip," John said.

"I am sick of here."

"It is just a slow time. One more year, and you will not even remember being lonely."

"I cannot live here any more. I need to see Liam and Ann and, and . . ."

She fought back tears. This tidal wave of feeling threatened to wash her to some far shores of the heart. She had to stop, remember she was married, remember she had a duty!

He caught her hand. "Someday we will go back to the old sod, I promise."

"I need to go now! There is no one! I am alone all day! When I lived with the Canadians we could barely talk! You are away all day, sometimes weeks. I have no friends. There are not any people for me. Women friends? What women! The women think I should be cleaning their pots and pans or brooming their parlors. There are no women. Just me."

He smiled that fine, clean, bright-hearted smile of his, that promised so much, and she caught herself and smiled back. "Give me a wee while, Mary Kate, and we'll invite them all to come here. Your whole family."

"Here! To this empty place? They would hate it!"

"Ah, no, colleen. They would see people with enough food, land for anyone, a chance to get a living, and no rents or taxes or tithes to a state church. They would see a chance to be themselves, to make their lives, to try to be anything they want. This is a sacred place, Mary Kate. The United States is, anyway, and this will soon be a part of it. Sacred and holy, I tell you!"

"No," she mumbled, "do not send for them. Not a one! They would see people like us cut off, lonely, starving for our kin worse than anyone ever starved for food. They would see us for what we are, all alone and not a friend here, and dying day by day."

"We have friends."

"*You* do! *You* do!"

He lifted the child to his lap. The boy was restless, and she knew her open anguish had sounded tocsins in his small soul. A wee child was so quick to pick up anything, including the sadness in a mother's heart.

"I do not know what to say, Mary Kate. But I have a dream. There is no land in the old sod; it is ridden with rents and trouble. I want to bring them here, hundreds, thousands, people like us. I want them to take up this free land, this good soil and mild climate, and bring Ireland here. Do not go home, Mary Kate; you will be on a barque heading east when hundreds of your kin and neighbors will pass you going west, if I have my way."

She wanted to cry out that she could not wait that long, but instead she clasped his hand and drew it to her lips, and toppled him onto the sailcloth, laughing, and kissed him soundly. And then the picnic began, and she hid her heart from him.

36

Electra spent the spring of 1843 perfecting torture. There was nothing else to do, and the more she tortured Garwood the less she felt tortured, so she worked at it.

Garwood's garret in Oregon City served to shelter them both. He had no funds for anything more, and no prospects either. They had partitioned the room with a piece of ragged salt-stained sailcloth salvaged from a schooner, giving Electra a cubicle scarcely larger than her cot. Garwood's homemade canvas cot lay just beyond the fragile wall, and one homemade chair, a crude table built from rough-sawed planks, and a sooty tin stove filled the rest of the room, which occupied a gloomy attic above a harness shop.

An unglassed window provided light, but it could be shuttered against the rain. The hovel drove her mad. Garwood drove her mad. If she used the chamber pot, he knew of it. If he did, she listened. If he snored, it kept her awake. During the long gray days of the monsoon season, they had stared sullenly at each other, coughing, sniffling, hoarse-voiced, headachy, feverish, waiting, waiting for something, anything.

So she began tormenting him, and honed it into such a fine art that she invariably drove him out into the slop and rain and cold which, she thought, immediately improved the air inside. What else was there to do?

"You have no prospects. Why don't you go to work, like other men?" she asked.

"I have large prospects. It just takes a little time . . ."

"We're penniless. Why don't you hire out, like John O'Malley did?"

"Because I'm not fit for manual labor, and besides, it wouldn't look good."

"Well, then, start a business. Warren worked. Imagine that! He walked to his chambers every day, drafted contracts, wrote wills, filed suits, defended people in court, and got paid. He was useful. Why don't you become useful?"

"When the time comes—"

"When the time comes! I mean right now! What ever happened to your town site scheme? At least that was a business venture, and not just politics and factions and rousing the rabble. There's no Tammany here."

"I've told you, there aren't any good sites, Hudson's Bay got them, and we can't afford a surveyor. Besides, I'm not made for outdoor living. I'm going to hold office, and then you'll see more than enough to support us."

"An office in a government without taxes!"

"That provision was merely a stepping-stone to get hard-pressed settlers to agree to be governed. Soon there'll be paid offices, including a justice of the peace, a governor, sheriff, and clerk. At the very least, I'd be a judge, and earning a good piece, but I have my eyes on something better."

"And when will that be? We're starving, and our credit's no good. You could clerk in Abernethy's store. At least you could bring home some soup bones! While you wait for an angel to descend and anoint you with the governorship of Oregon you can snatch the spoils."

Garwood looked pained, which was good. Maybe if he was pained enough to walk out of the garret, he would earn something. She wondered how she ever got wrapped up with the Reeses. She must have taken leave of her senses. She had never wanted to come to Oregon anyway, and it now amazed her that she had acquiesced to the scheme.

"I am preparing a campaign for office, which requires meeting people and sharing my ideals."

"You don't have any."

He glared. "Electra, why don't you find something to do?"

"I just might. Maybe I can scrub floors, since you won't."

She watched him wrap his cloak about him and plunge down the dark damp stairwell and into the gray world. The clay streets of Oregon City were quagmires, each silvered puddle a treacherous sinkhole. Maybe he would vanish into one, drowning in mud, which was a fate devoutly to be wished upon all politicians.

She varied the argument, but at least she got results: when she couldn't stand him any more, in that shabby, dark, smelling room, she drove him out.

She had driven him out of the rotten room twenty times, but it didn't do any good except to let her bathe in privacy. At least Warren had a profession and some dignity. All Garwood really wanted was to get paid for doing what he loved most, which was telling everyone else how to behave and what to think, and spending everyone else's tax dollars.

She had come to her own conclusions about his politics. It was a perfectly familiar variety back in New York: use the ballot box and laws and taxes to whittle down people in power, or people with money, and then divide the spoils. It beat working for a living.

From the moment he had arrived, except for that town site foray, he had been angling toward the leadership of a faction. He never even considered going into business or finding gainful employment. Since the Methodists were the majority, he ingratiated himself among them, and agitated for the triumph of the Americans over foreigners, namely the Hudson's Bay Company.

Meanwhile they starved, accumulated debt at the store, and gained nothing. Her brother-in-law had not even stirred himself to go out and claim his own square mile and record it. It was as if he didn't want to dirty his hands doing the world's work, but was content to dirty his hands in other ways.

She had wondered that season whether he would attempt to take advantage of their intimacy, but he made no gesture, and pretended that the miserable shared room, and unavoidable moments of dishabille, meant nothing. All very proper. Just the way for a solicitous brother to treat a new-made widow. And yet she knew that one of these moments, things would take a new turn. He had designs on her. She was shapely, comely, and an asset. It was only a matter of time. And while she waited, she could keep him at bay with her barbs, her sole amusement in that ghastly attic.

But the rains let up, and a shimmering spring emerged, and with the sunshine came freedom. She could escape that wretched hole, the miserable cooking on the tiny tin parlor stove, and waltz into a sunnier world. She didn't much care what he did, as long as he stayed away from her.

Sunshine was liberty. It was warmth and dryness. It was social commerce too, because she met people she hadn't seen all those wet months. Sunshine dried up the filthy puddles so she could walk from one end of town to the other without sullying her skirts. So she fled that noxious room, with its dirty linens, its subterranean lusts, which she was absolutely certain percolated in Garwood's body. She felt nothing toward him, and hoped she never would.

Then, one glowing April morning, she watched a Sandwich Islander named Kanaka Jim tenderly plant flowers. The Hudson's Bay Company had imported twenty or thirty Kanakas from the islands for menial labor and she had watched them toil around Fort Vancouver while she sojourned there. But this one had left the company and was doing odd jobs in Oregon City. And now he was planting.

If there was one thing the settlers cherished, it was the flowers and shrubs that blossomed miraculously in Oregon. For years, John McLoughlin had assiduously begged seed, ordered slips and plants from afar, talked ship's masters out of any fruit, vegetables, or flowers they might have aboard, and had gradually nurtured a veritable nursery around the post. And now the settlers were eagerly planting slips and bulbs and seeds gotten from McLoughlin, to turn Oregon into the world's most sublime garden.

She sat on a stump and watched Kanaka Jim wield a spade and hoe. The taffy-colored man smiled at her but said nothing, probably uncertain about addressing a white woman. He was planting a small lilac bush beside the Brownells' comfortable house. He wore the remnants of a gray union suit, so rent with holes that his smooth brown flesh poked through, and she could see his muscles ripple as he toiled. Not an ounce of fat hung from him, and his muscled flesh glowed sleekly in the sun. He must be very strong, she thought. Almost like a young horse.

She reminded herself not to speak to the colored man. She didn't even like to be in the presence of anyone but whites. But this man, singing softly to himself this glowing morning, radiated good cheer, and so she settled on the stump and let the cheer wash through her.

She wondered about him. She'd heard they were wild men, dangerous when drinking, but mild as children when sober, which was why McLoughlin never permitted them a drop, even of wine. Did he have a woman? She didn't think so. All the Kanakas in Oregon were male.

He completed his hole in the moist loam and settled the little bush in it. She thought it was a bad time to be planting a lilac, when it was nearing bloom, but that didn't bother him. He tamped the warm soil around its roots, and then watered it with generous buckets of water carried up from the cold river.

He stood, leaning on his spade, admiring his work.

"You like flowah?" he asked.

"Yes. We need more."

"I plant for you, yes?"

"No!"

Angrily she stood, glared at him, and headed down toward the waterfront.

She stood on the bank of the river, hearing the steady roar of the falls above and feeling its mist in the breeze, wondering why she had been irritated at him. He hadn't done anything. But of course he had: he had presumed to speak to her, a white woman. That was insulting, and if he did it again, she would report him to . . . someone. Not having a proper sheriff made matters difficult.

But she paused. She had been abrupt. Maybe she could let him know that he offended her only a little. She wouldn't confess to rudeness. She was an expert at rudeness and used it to great effect, especially on Garwood, who had gradually become so inured to it she had to keep upping the ante.

She wrestled with herself, thinking all the while how absurd it was, how imbecilic. This, after all, was the season of her liberation from that wretched room she had shared all winter with a conniving weasel of a man whose dream was to conquer the world without doing a lick of real work, apart from the diligent flummery of the tongue.

She wheeled, suddenly, went back to the gardener, who was collecting his tools.

He was not friendly this time, and bore her scrutiny with careful indifference.

"I don't have any land, so I can't have a garden," she said.

He nodded.

"But if I had land, I would hire you to make a garden."

He hummed softly, and walked away, and she watched his taffy-colored flesh ripple, upset with herself, with Garwood, and especially with Oregon. She wanted a garden and could not have one.

All that November of 1843, John McLoughlin welcomed the Americans. Their numbers astonished him. Day after day, ragged new groups would arrive in crudely made boats, or on rafts, or with pack trains or on foot, bearing only a knapsack. Fort Vancouver was usually their first stop, though he discovered that some of these industrious Yankees had cut a cattle trail around the south flank of Mount Hood and entered the Willamette Valley without coming close to the Hudson's Bay post.

A few with horses managed to arrive with their goods in hand and solvent. But most arrived destitute and in grave trouble. He heard so many tales of starvation, dying oxen, disease, overloaded wagons breaking down, lack of game to sustain them, bad advice, and tragedy, that they blurred together in his mind and evoked melancholia.

One large clan led by three brothers, Jesse, Charles, and Lindsey Applegate of Missouri, lost a boy when their raft upended in rapids. But the Applegates were hardy frontier stock, and were among the few who arrived in Oregon solvent and able to pay for the purchases they made at the company store.

They were affable people, and took pains to make McLoughlin's acquaintance.

"I was leading the second column—we called it the cattle column because we were all driving livestock and were slower," Jesse Applegate explained in a deliberate Missouri manner. "We sent the cattle over the new cattle trail, and built rafts at the Columbia rapids."

"Our traders try to warn people against—"

"Well, we were late. The faster folks got hold of all the boats and canoes and packhorses, and all we could do was build those rafts, which we did, but this old river . . . it cost us."

"I sorrow for your family."

"I got one boy who made it. He could swim and he rescued another little fellow riding with us, and that's a good branch off this rootstock, I'd say."

"Please consider our resources at your service."

"Just being here in this place, with a roof overhead and a store selling things, and a doctor . . . that's all we need for now. I don't cotton to what they've been saying about your company. Your traders along the way—Fort Hall, Fort Walla Walla—they did all they could and then some. They went out of their way . . ."

"It is what I asked them to do."

"It won't be forgotten, not by an Applegate."

McLoughlin advised them to head for Mission Bottoms where there might be shelter because Jason Lee was moving some of his operations south. He liked Jesse Applegate, and sensed that the Missourian liked him.

He rejoiced that here and there, one or another of these Americans was discovering that the honorable company wasn't Satan, and that the chief factor didn't wear horns and carry a pitchfork. The attitude puzzled him. Where had it come from? What tainted well was poisoning the American mind? Was it mad Hall Kelley, himself rescued from illness by McLoughlin even though Kelley abominated the company?

The chief factor couldn't say. But at least he could do everything in his power to dispel the canards. The lies affronted him and undermined company business. He decided not to let them circulate unrebutted, so he welcomed each group heartily in his own parlor, advised them where to find tillable land, warned them away from trouble, offered them immediate help if they needed it, and offered credit for the seed wheat and farm implements they would need to get started—payable in harvested wheat, in due course.

Nine hundred Americans this time, and that was only the beginning of a tide that would wash through the Northwest. There had been only five hundred Americans and Canadians altogether up until this moment. The tide would change the balance ever more, and the only question now was where the line would be drawn separating the two nations.

He wished Governor Simpson could see with his own eyes this amazing crowd of lean, brown, trail-hardened, resourceful people, including innumerable children, who had walked a continent and would be hacking farms out of wilderness, and raising the Stars and Stripes. He wished the governor could examine the limited wheat reserves in company warehouses and the potential hunger of so many, and then he might grasp just why McLoughlin freely offered the settlers credit for seed and farm tools.

They thronged to his gates suspicious, keen-edged, and ready to make enemies. They grumbled about his prices even while stocking up on what they needed to avoid starvation and penury, all on credit. They wanted Missouri prices, and nothing else was good enough for them.

One of the immigrants, William Beagle, arrived ill, with typhus fever. McLoughlin set him and his family in a small house outside the post, put Forbes Barclay in charge of him, and accepted nothing in payment. Slowly, Beagle recovered.

The amount of debt he carried on his books mounted ever higher and now exceeded thirty thousand dollars. He found himself in grave financial peril and yet he continued to offer them loans and help, for no decent man could do any other. But in his darkest moments, he saw his secure world crumbling. Once he had been able to steer them south of the river, into country that would fall to the Americans, but now they were fanning out in all directions, even toward Puget Sound.

"What do you make of it?" he asked Peter Ogden one drear day. Ogden was no friend of the Americans and could be relied upon for clearheaded, slightly sardonic advice.

"The game is lost here. But we can delay the inevitable," Ogden said in his peculiar high voice, a voice he had possessed since childhood, a voice unaffected by puberty. "I worry about you more than the company."

"I worry about myself. But who can turn down these starving people?"

Ogden grinned in a way that suggested that he knew someone who would.

"I see some good in it," McLoughlin persisted. "The Crown will lose this land, but the company can profit . . . if these people pay their debts and try to get along."

Ogden laughed skeptically. "What did you get for helping the last batch? They're going to take away your town site and water claim. This year's bunch will be worse."

"Peter, let's set that aside. I may be an addled old man. I may be softening. Maybe I'm superannuated. Enterprise belongs to the young, not to men who lean on canes, and hurt like the devil, and keep an eye on the throne of God. I may be undermining the very business I struggled to build in this wilderness. I may be an old fool, surrendering to sentiment . . ." He straightened up. "But it's my policy to help the desperate, and I would grieve the loss of any life we might prevent."

"Actually, so would I," Ogden said quietly. "We have no good choices."

There was a grandness in Ogden that transcended his petty feelings, the chief factor thought. Ogden would rescue the most distasteful of people, if it came to that.

And it did come to that. One bleak December day, during a howling storm, an American named James Waters burst into the post, shivering and dripping and wild-eyed.

"Sir," he said, rivering water in McLoughlin's office, "there's people dying upriver, dying like flies in the cold and snow. They're starved, and the river's flowing hard, and they're freezing and getting sick. Some have some money; they ain't all poor, just starving out. I'm thinking, you load up blankets and food and canvas and such, and we can sell all of it and save lives too."

"How many?"

"Plenty, maybe the last hundred or so."

"They're perishing?"

"If they ain't already."

McLoughlin sprang to action. This December desperation was all too familiar.

"Henri! Pierre! Tous les hommes!"

His men swarmed in, and he directed them to load the canoes first, because they were fastest, take blankets, flour, fat, haunches of meat, flint and steel, tinder, canvas, anything that might preserve life.

"Make haste! Vite! Vite!"

He raced to the river where the bateaux and canoes awaited them, his white hair flying, his heart and soul in anguish, as his snow-flecked men loaded bundles of goods from the store into the canoes and boats. Waters joined the Canadians, ignoring the steady snow and sleet while goods were stowed under cover. And then the flotilla took off, the canoes propelled by the muscular strokes of the voyageurs, darting straight into the current and up the solemn river until they vanished from sight.

McLoughlin sighed, suddenly let down when the last of his rescue armada vanished into the murk. He wondered whether he had just signed his resignation. Would the directors in London ever understand his squandering of so much labor and marketable goods on rival Americans, most of whom would do their utmost to drive the company out of Oregon?

No, they never would.

He limped slowly up the long slope to the post, leaning into his gold-knobbed stick, feeling the sleet collect on his neck and chill him. If he could grow so cold in a half hour, how must the bereft, starving, snowbound immigrants be faring?

He entered the drafty comfort of his spacious home and collapsed into a wing chair. Marguerite found him there, settled beside him and stroked his hands, gentleness in her ample face.

"I fear I have just destroyed everything," he said.

"John, what choice had you?"

No choice. He knew that once the hearthfire warmed his old bones; he would begin a long letter to Simpson and the directors, and express it to Montreal. He decided not to justify himself: if they did not see the need in ordinary human terms, then they would not see his action as defensible at all, and he would await his fate. In this missive there would be no justification of his conduct, nothing but a recital of what he had done and what it would cost.

"You have taught me, we do not live for bread alone," she said, "but by the word of God."

Marguerite comforted him. He was a white man becoming more Indian; she, mostly Indian, was becoming a white woman. Somehow, they had found common ground, such as now, where loss and profit and love and faith and sacrifice had all come to equilibrium. He clasped her hand, thought of his living daughters and son, and knew that the world was a good place.

"I love you all the more for what you have done for those who might be suffering, and for those who might thank us with harsh words and complaints," she said. "This is what makes the White Eagle a man greater than other men."

He squeezed her hand. "If we have saved one life, it will be worth it, whatever our fate."

38

Terrible news that November day. Jasper Constable hurried to his cottage to tell Rose.

"The mission might be closed!" he cried. "Word came with the emigrants."

She was scouring a kettle and set it down. "Come tell me," she said, leading him to the only two chairs.

"A letter from the mission board. They're sending a man, George Gary, around the Horn to examine us. Jason's upset. He's talking of going east to make his case before the board, leaving at once, winter or not, and his wife expecting too."

"It is serious, then."

"Yes. This man Gary has the power to close us, depose Lee, and take over if he chooses. Even sell out. It's mostly a question of money, but also results. We haven't a single true Indian convert. Yet they've sent thousands a year to us, year after year. All's lost, Rose."

"No, nothing is lost."

"But we may have to go east."

"No, Jasper, we won't go east."

That was more of Rose's strange talk, an attitude that bordered on resisting him. He had suffered it silently, praying all the while that she would cease this turbulence that afflicted his family. But so far, his prayers had wrought nothing, and if anything, she was becoming even more independent. Wild Oregon was subverting her vow of obedience. He wouldn't mind going east one bit if only to subdue this cancerous thing.

"Rose, if the mission closes, there won't be a nickel for us. There's four Methodist ministers in Oregon—here and The Dalles and Oregon City. Lee administers, and I'm the one without a congregation. My task has always been to encourage sound doctrine. How will we survive?"

"Survive? Anyone can survive here. There are needs everywhere. We shall fill a need."

"Rose, you don't understand. We can't support ourselves. Not even with a thousand new people pouring in."

She replied patiently. "Perhaps Mr. Gary, when he comes, will keep the mission going. Or Jason will persuade the board when he gets back East. It's too early to worry."

"We must plan! Find passage! Not be stranded here!"

"I think we should stay."

"But there's not even a newspaper. How shall I spread my views?"

She smiled at him. His heart always melted before that smile. It was a new sort of smile, an Oregon-born smile filled with good humor.

"Perhaps God doesn't mean for you to spread your views."

That flummoxed him. How could she say such a thing?

"But Rose. It's all I can do. I've never had a church."

"Then maybe you should learn new things."

"But I can't just become a . . . carpenter."

"We know a carpenter who became . . . a Teacher." She sat quietly, but without budging. "Oregon City has no school. They tell me that two hundred children have arrived, and more coming. I shall start a school. Will you join me?"

"But Rose! I'm a clergyman, dedicated to serve—"

"Help me start a school. We'll charge a little bit, and we'll get by. I know English, reading, and writing, and you know arithmetic and geometry and religion, and we'll find a few books for the rest. You'll teach sound doctrine, and we'll have chapel each morning."

He knew he would have a tough time dissuading her. But schoolmastering was no career for a budding theologian. Some moments, when he peered up at the hazy cone of Mount Hood, he knew he was destined to scale heights. It made him humble even to think about where he would take his life and his work.

"Rose, I'll talk to Jason Lee about passage on the next barque. Our work here is done."

"It's barely begun, Jasper. We were brought here for a purpose and now we must find it. How can you even think of turning tail?"

She was beginning to aggravate him. Turning tail. Did she think he was fleeing?

"There's not a day goes by," she continued, "that I don't think of Damaris, and how she would be now, a lovely girl, and how Oregon stole life from her when it was only just beginning, and how she lies there at the fort. We owe it to Damaris to stay and turn Oregon into a garden. I dream of gardens and lilacs and hollyhocks, and vineyards, and apple orchards, and cottages with happy families in them. Until we make Oregon a garden, I won't rest content, and neither will her sweet and innocent spirit."

He sighed. Marriage used to be so easy. She had always supported him, encouraged him, nurtured him. And now this independence was growing like a weed, choking out all the roses he had planted. But he wouldn't chastise his wife. Forbearance was a virtue, and kindliness, and patience, so he would endure until she came to her senses.

"I think I'll go to Oregon City," she said, "and see about a school. It'll be called the Damaris Constable School, in her honor. I'll talk to Felicity Brownell—"

"Not her!"

She didn't budge an inch. "Felicity taught at the post, and John McLoughlin thought she was excellent. She could teach along with you and me."

"But Abel Brownell . . . he wanted to sell drams, Rose. Drams!"

She laughed. "Other people see things differently," she said. "Others aren't so strict."

"I'd rather you didn't go. The boys need you here. We can barely manage without the loving touch of a good woman."

She smiled, and in that smile lay a steely will he knew he could never defeat.

"I'll go explore, with your blessing, and see," she said. "I want to start a school. So many children now, in such need. Imagine growing up unable to read and write, unable to read the Bible or a newspaper. Unable to read your essays and letters and exhortations. Would you write your circular letters for the illiterate? What a pity that would be."

He sighed. She had a winning way. "After you see how impractical it is, hurry back. The boys and I'll manage somehow. But we'll miss your pies."

So it was settled.

Within the hour he cornered Jason Lee in his office and shut the rickety white door.

"Jason, I must know! Will they shut us down?"

The big man leaned back in his chair. "They might."

"But why?"

Lee's eyes lit merrily. "My accounting. I keep forgetting to keep books. But mostly because we haven't a single authentic Indian convert for all our labor. I need to go back there to the board and explain why. In person. It can't be done by mail. I'll be leaving shortly."

"Now?"

"By snowshoes if I must. Everything's at stake. Whitman had to go back to keep his mission going; now I'll go. It can't be helped."

"What'll you say?"

"We failed to convert the Indians because they're not ready. And because of the Catholics, spreading confusion. Have you seen that big painting of theirs, with the main trunk of the tree ascending to God, and all the branches leading to hell? Including ourselves? No wonder the Indians are confused."

"I've heard of it."

"The work of our Jesuit friends. But my main message is perfectly simple: there are over a thousand settlers here and more coming, and we need to serve them."

"Will I find myself without means?"

"That'll be up to Gary. I will say that you're the most likely to lose your post."

"Well, that's plain, and I'm grateful for that. Rose wants to start a school at Oregon City. She thinks we can manage."

Lee laughed heartily. "Not for a living, I hope. There's hardly a cash dollar in the Willamette Valley. You'd take your pay in rotting vegetables, wheat, eggs, seven-day clocks that survived the trip, cast-off clothing, and homemade lye soap."

"That's what I've tried to tell her, but she's determined."

"She's a great lady, Jasper."

"What would you advise me to do?"

Lee shrugged. He knew better than to suggest farming or any ordinary labor. "Well, just take heart, and wait until I return. Maybe I'll have good news. I'll also speak to the board about you. They owe you passage, at the very least. Maybe there's some other mission, somewhere . . ."

"Get me a press, Jason. Beg one back East. Just get it. Some fonts and paper and ink. Talk the board into it and have it shipped here around the Horn, a whole outfit. I'll start a paper. We'll shape opinion here. We've a Methodist party, a mission party, and it needs a voice. I'll get advertising. I'll go in with Garwood Reese. He has nothing but good to say about us, and nothing but patriotism in him, and nothing but a desire to make Oregon a state in the Union and get rid of foreign influences."

Lee frowned. "I think you would not want to start a paper with him. He is not a kind man, especially toward our friend McLoughlin."

"That's exactly the reason for a partnership with him."

Lee stared out the window a long while, saying nothing. Then, "Jasper, unless a complete printing plant and plenty of paper shows up on the next schooner to sail upriver, you'd best put that out of mind."

Lee yawned, his usual way of dismissing someone who lingered too long in his lair.

It had been a grim interview. No prospects within the mission. The school idea wouldn't support a family of four. There was no chance to start a publication. And Jason Lee had candidly said that he, Jasper, would be the first to be cut.

So much for Oregon, he thought. He would pressure Lee for funds to take the next bark around the Horn, and go back to the States where his voice would be heard and his views would be printed and disseminated. Rose would not resist once she knew it was the only choice.

Or would she? He remembered Felicity Brownell's steely determination to stay, even when Abel was ready to head east. The one thing Jasper knew for sure was that he couldn't count on Rose.

39

Far up the Columbia, Peter Skene Ogden found a camp of shivering Americans trapped by snows, starving, and unable to continue. Four families, sturdy pioneers, thinned to bone by the long walk, and fighting for their lives.

He rode in one of the advance canoes, propelled by his toughest men, who kept dipping their red paddles into the icy river long before the December dawn, and even after dusk, usually in brutal cold. Farther behind, his voyageurs poled and paddled and dragged three flatboats upriver, collecting these desperate emigrants from their huts and hovels along the banks of the river.

These scarecrows rose and shouted as his canoe hove into sight, danced and wept. But some among them lay ominously quiet. Their camp had a fire going. Others didn't. The river had tolled away everything they possessed, even their flints and steels and knives and hatchets.

He nodded to his voyageurs, and they thrust the canoe toward the south bank, where a copse of willows in a bottom defied the barren land. It was not a beauteous place, and even game avoided its rocky shoals. But the trees had meant warmth, and warmth had kept these from perishing—for the moment.

A black-bearded Yank stood on the shore, waiting as the voyageurs homed in. Soon others rose from their beds and struggled to the riverbank.

"Godalmighty, I guess you're about the welcomest sight these eyes have ever seen," he said. "Have you food? We're about done in and boiling shoe leather for our soup."

Ogden sprang out while his men steadied the fragile vessel. He had to avoid piercing the thin hull of the bark canoe, and had stepped from the loose floorboards to land in one quick plunge.

What he saw appalled him. The snowbound camp suffered from neglect. These people had been too weak and sick to shelter themselves, and their few filthy items lay scattered over the muck and snow. Mud caked their clothing and even their chapped skin. They clutched rags to themselves, their only escape from the elements.

"Ogden here. We brought some flour and lard, and we'll cook up some frycakes."

"Food!" a hollow-eyed boy cried.

They were a sorry lot, skinned down to bones, gaunt and dull-eyed, the women prematurely aged by one season of travel.

Somehow, the promise of a meal energized even those in worst condition, and they rose from their pallets and crowded around him.

"We've blankets," Ogden said.

"And you'll be charging us a pretty penny, I suppose," said Blackbeard.

The suspicion evoked a passing annoyance in Ogden but he pushed it back. "If you can pay, fine; if not, we'll help you anyway and hope that you'll pay when you're settled and able to."

"Fancy price, I imagine."

Not even rescue from certain death allayed the man's suspicions of the Hudson's Bay Company. Ogden ignored him and directed his men to lift some blankets and sailcloth out of the fat belly of the canoe. These people had a decent camp; they simply were famished and half-dead. Their suspicions had been fueled by years of mendacious tract-writing back in the States, and he understood their suspicion even if he abominated it.

"I didn't catch your name," he said.

"Hawkins, Abner Hawkins, from Arkansas, and most of us are Razor-backs."

The voyageurs were chopping wood, scraping away snow, building up the fires, heating a skillet, kneading the frycake dough. The Arkansas women looked too weak to help, but no one asked them to. One was weeping and clutching three shivering children to her. LaBouef handed her two gray blankets, and she wrapped herself and one child in one, and the other two in the second, sobbing as she did.

"We've some mackinaws—flatboats—coming soon."

"What's the price for that?"

This time Ogden paused. "More than you'll ever know," he said, which was a literal truth. He and John McLoughlin would not reveal to these truculent emigrants just how much the company would expend in labor and goods to rescue them. Nor would he tell them that the chief factor bore the burden on his own shoulders.

A gaunt black-haired woman bearing a wailing baby approached him. "Could he be first?" she asked softly.

"He'll be first," Ogden said.

"Oh, you're a gift from God," she said.

He nodded. "It was conscience that drove us, yes," he said. "But the gift is from the Hudson's Bay Company."

"Well, may He bless you ever more."

Emile Laroche brought a handful of dried apple slices from the post orchard, and handed them to her, smiling gently.

"Oh, oh," she said, and let her baby gum a piece. "Oh, bless you."

Ogden checked to see who was ill. About half were, he judged. Catarrh, fevers, one knee injury, goiter, dropsy, bloody flux, headaches. But food might remedy some of that. This was typical: his men had discovered a dozen camps like this one, varying in desperation and competence. It amazed him that some of these emigrants had come so far with so few skills and such little ability to make use of the natural world. Not a one had tried fishing in a river filled with fish. They had not built a snare or hunted ducks or geese, though they had fowling pieces. They knew nothing of natural foods, such as the starch in the roots of the cattails that lay frostbitten within their sight.

In one camp a dead girl lay wrapped in an ancient blanket. His voyageurs had buried her while the living eyed his men sullenly, all but accusing them of letting the child die. But it never came to that. How odd they were, coming here to fight the British and the company, while assuring themselves that the British and the company would buy their wheat and produce and sell them whatever they wanted at bargain prices.

He watched his voyageurs fry up the bread and pass it out as swiftly as it cooled. The parents fed the children first, no matter how much they themselves starved, and Ogden admired that. These were good people, but opinionated and obtuse and boneheaded. He would quiet their suspicions.

John McLoughlin had given Ogden one final word before they set off to rescue these people: "Treat them well. Give them no ground to hate the company. I fancy that if we treat them well, we'll have friends, and with friends, we'll be better off . . . but I know you'd do that anyway."

Ogden agreed. He would do that anyway. There were things an honorable man must do, and rescuing these Yanks was one of them.

They ate and ate again, and then Ogden called a halt. He needed to preserve flour for people upstream.

"A flatboat will be here by evening. Are there any more you know of upstream?"

"Some," said Blackbeard. "Half a dozen, pretty sick, couldn't keep up. Maybe ten miles up, at a place where a creek comes in."

"All right. We'll need to get to them. We can't spare more food but we'll leave you some tea you can boil up and give to the sick. You'll get more help when we start for the post."

The woman with the quieted infant snugged to her bosom approached, hugged him with her one free hand, and kissed him on his stubbled cheek. He saw the tears welling in her brown eyes, and he touched her face.

"That's the finest thank-you I've ever received," he said gently.

Ogden's men swiftly built a hut from willow poles and sailcloth and carried the sickest into it. It opened upon the fire and would catch the radiant heat. Then they eased into the skittery canoe, and soon were paddling upstream again, their rhythmic strokes driving the light vessel at amazing speeds against the current. They would reach the last of the Americans, probably caught at Willow Creek, a little after dark. He hoped they had a fire going.

A chill wind sucked the heat out of them, but his voyageurs had lived in nature all their lives and ignored it. They reached the creek well after dark and found nothing. They beached the canoe, shouted, built a signal fire, boiled and ate gruel, and hiked out in several directions looking for the lost. But after an hour's hard search, which included gunshots, signals, and shouts, they concluded that this last batch had either died or found passage, or headed back to Fort Walla Walla. The latter was the most likely.

His voyageurs proposed to drift back to the downstream camp and spend the night among the living, and so they did, making an easy trip of it with the current helping them along and a rare winter's half-moon guiding them. They glided in to the firelit shore, and found the company bateau tied there, and the camp secured in the strong hands of his weary Canadians. Most slept, huddled in their thick new blankets.

Ogden felt a moment's euphoria. All told, they had rescued eighty-seven and buried three. Over twenty survivors were children. These were people of a different and rival nation, but sharing the English tongue, and often were literally cousins of those to the north.

The two other bateaux had already headed downriver, carrying their precious cargo into the very bosom of the Hudson's Bay Company, where they would find the shelter they needed so badly.

The next morning, with his human cargo safely cached in the forty-five-foot hull of the flatboat, his men steered the craft home. He followed in the canoe. The voyageurs portaged around rapids near The Dalles, carrying the heavy bateau on their shoulders while the emigrants toted the rest and helped the sick.

The weather was lowering again, and Ogden feared another snow before they landed at Vancouver. But the snow held off, even though the air grew damper and meaner as they drifted west.

Blackbeard, Hawkins, huddled close to him on that leg.

"I guess we heard wrong about your company," he said. "We heard you was one mean outfit."

Ogden grinned. "We still are."

"You can't fool us."

Ogden rummaged his mind, wondering how to respond. "Times change," he said. "Not long ago we drove out all rivals by whatever means we deemed honorable. Especially you Yanks. Usually we undersold or overbought until we drove your trading ships off our coast without furs or profit. We gave gifts to the chiefs, bought their loyalty, told 'em to trade only with us. That policy's never changed, though the times have. This land, south of here, will belong to the United States. We hope to keep the rest. You're coming. More will come year after year. We've been trying to delay that, and to profit from it."

"Not much profit in rescuing us, I reckon."

"That's what the directors think, and what the queen's men think."

"But you did it."

"The chief factor, John McLoughlin, did it at his own risk. You owe your lives to him, my friend."

40

The Hudson's Bay warehouse at Champoeg might not be a Fanueil Hall, but it would do, thought Garwood Reese.

He waited upon a crude dais for the rustic Oregonians to file in this bitter December evening. Guttering lamps lit the cavernous building and shot smoke through it, but did not drive out the cold. A good crowd would do that.

This would be Oregon's Cradle of Liberty. And here Reese would make his bid for office.

Beside him sat his sister-in-law, wrapped tightly in a black shawl, her uneven teeth clamped against the cold, and plainly not enjoying herself. But she saw the need. The pair were down to their last shilling, and the Methodist store was about to cut off credit. This rally would cure their distress.

Actually, this would be a crucial moment in Reese's career, and he was well aware of the difficulties. In the space of a few weeks, the white population of Oregon had trebled. These new people didn't know him, and scarcely knew about the provisional government that had been whooped into existence last summer, or that an election of officers was looming in May. But that was all to the good. He had a silver tongue, and he would sway these newcomers and lead them to support his Methodist-backed faction.

He was tempted to circulate among them, but chose to sit quietly, enduring the cold, wrapped tightly in his Hudson's Bay blanket, like so many others who lacked greatcoats. His abused vocal cords would not endure much banter.

"I'm catching the catarrh again," Electra said.

"All for a good cause. Your presence is essential."

"For what? These are all men."

"Exactly."

She stared at him, faint disdain in her pale face.

Slowly the dark chamber filled. There were no seats; this would be a standing crowd, ready to bolt if the proceedings grew tiresome. But at least a faint heat rose from the crowd, along with a fetid odor of breath, tobacco, unwashed feet, and moist wool. The guttering lamps cast wavery light over the assemblage.

At last, when the warehouse seemed to gain no more men, Reese nodded to the endlessly energetic George Abernethy. The clerk and political gadfly rose, hushed the assembly with a shout, and welcomed them.

"Now, we've called you together to take a hand in Oregon's future," Abernethy proclaimed. "We have an election coming. And here's the man who's going to be one of our governors."

A faint clapping rippled through the dark room like gravel falling on tin. "What do you mean, governors?" a man shouted.

"The organic law of the provisional government provides for a triumvirate to run the territory."

Reese heard some muttering. He would address that. The triumvirate was his own concoction. He knew he would not be governor if the Methodists prevailed because they would elect one of their own. So he had devised the triumvirate.

"I give you, gentlemen, Garwood Reese!"

Reese shed his blanket, stood, and bowed, letting the ripples of acclaim wash up to him.

He raised his arms and lifted himself to the balls of his feet. "Gentlemen, consider this rude building, so many leagues from our republic, the Cradle of Liberty of Oregon! For here, a free American government was born last May."

No one challenged that, though there were French Canadians among the throng.

He cleared his sore throat, so that he might speak with that sonorous sweetness that stretched out and touched each of his auditors. "My friends, my friends, those of you who've been with me in Oregon from early times, and my new friends who have been pouring into Oregon in recent months, welcome, welcome," he said. "Bless you all. Tonight, my fellow Americans and hardy settlers, we shall discuss the birth of a territory, the inception of a state, the proudest ornament of the republic. But not quite yet. We've some hurdles to overcome first.

"The future is in our hands. We are the masters of our fate. Here we are, gathered into a band of farseeing, upright pioneers who intend to shape this great new land into the finest, sweetest, most sublime branch of the United States!"

He felt them stir. He was in good voice after all, and had mighty things to say, things that would pierce souls and move minds and awaken dead hopes.

"But first let me introduce my beloved Electra Reese, my boon companion and soul mate."

They were sure taking her in. How did a woman so rare end up in wild

Oregon? She threw back her shawl and stood, letting them stare at her statu-
esque form encased in a tight fawn dress, and her ice-blond features, and then
sat down. The faintly amused look she bestowed upon him did not escape his
attention. She had suffered no illusions about her value to him.

He paused, gathering the strands of thought, letting them anticipate his
words.

"You have toiled a great distance," he began, butter soft, "on the wings of
a dream. Something drew you to this bountiful land; something larger than
riches or power or annexing this country to the republic . . . You came to plant
a garden. Yes, a garden! Oh, the colors! Magenta and blue and violet and
primrose; lilacs, roses, sweet peas, magnolias. The blossoms of beauty and hope.
To subdue the cruel wilderness and impose the intelligence and wisdom of
mankind upon the good earth and make it bloom!

"And that means land . . .

"Ever since I came here, I've heard this word, *garden,* upon the lips of
settlers. Not just wheat and oats and barley, but petunias and marigolds. Not
just barley, but beauty. Not just material wealth, but the ethereal things that
delight the soul and heart. A garden. We all came to make gardens . . . we've
come to turn wild and cruel Oregon into an Arcadia."

He had them. The deep silence told him that they were paying close
attention. He knew he had touched on something. He had heard them call
Oregon a garden, and he had understood the metaphor. He settled back on his
feet, rocked slowly, as if contemplating what next to say, but actually just letting
his opening sally settle like a good soup in the belly.

"There are some who don't want to transform Oregon into a garden, into
an Eden, a paradise of flowers and fruits and grains. You know them by name.
There are those kings and dukes and earls of the wilderness who want merely
to pillage the wild forest for furs and pelts; who are indifferent, if not hostile,
to the harmony and beauty wrought by the hand of man.

"You know of whom I speak. They built great posts here, fashioned a trade
with the hapless savages who bartered valuable pelts for trinkets, and even now
agitate the redmen against us. And those of whom I speak drove away Americans seeking to plant a garden in a wild land . . . Emperors of the wilderness,
sweeping out of the cruel north, seeking to keep the land useless and dead,
beyond the cultivation and civilized uses of Americans. They don't . . . want . . .
gardens.

"It is my profoundest desire to drive them out, drive away foreign influence, so that we may hoe our gardens, so that our lives may be abloom with
hollyhocks, lilacs, roses, and forget-me-nots, and that most fragrant of all flowers, fulfilled dreams.

"That, my fine friends, is one of the legs on the tripod of my agenda. I
will now discuss the other legs.

"One. We need a sure and secure means to hold land and resolve land disputes. That question gnaws at the souls of us all. Until this land belongs to one nation, and is not disputed by two, none of us can be absolutely certain that the fields we prepare and plant, the homes and shops we build, the factories and storehouses and mills we erect, are our own. The land under our feet is disputed. The very earth might not be our own, though we have staked and claimed it!

"Therefore, my fellow gardeners and settlers, let us proceed swiftly to a means of registering land, one square mile for each American, and make our work so enduring and fair and just that when we enter the republic—for surely we will—our holy temple will be accepted, in toto, by Congress, and our land will be measured to our own bosom."

Reese knew he was doing well. They stood, silently, absorbing every word. He spoke for a court enabled to settle land and other disputes, the need for a sheriff and a jail, the need for men to be secure in their property and persons, the need for a militia to cope with Indian troubles . . .

"I am standing as a candidate for the governing committee," he said. "But I am also standing upon the platform of the mission people who first settled here. I am standing not just for myself, but as the founder of a coalition, a party if you will, dedicated to resolving the most urgent matters through voluntary means, on a provisional basis until the contesting governments draw the boundary lines. A party of Christian missionaries of the Methodist persuasion, men of pure and disinterested intent.

"To achieve these things, some modest funds are required. We have formed a provisional government that rests on voluntary subscription of funds instead of taxes, for we know not whether we have the authority to tax any man. You are free from the tax collector. But so, too, must each of us subscribe to funds with which to influence other settlers; to make sure that sound policy triumphs; to see that good men are elected to office.

"Toward that end, my fellow Oregonians, I am simply passing the hat, entrusting the future of this territory to your generosity. All funds collected will be employed in the pursuit of annexation by the United States, the pursuit of a provisional court system to resolve land disputes, and in pursuit of a justice system. I will have Electra, here, circulate among you with a beaver, and I trust that you will dig deep; pull up those precious coins you carried across a continent, and purchase leadership, security, annexation, and the blessings of your gardens with the funds."

He nodded at Electra, who stood, grabbed a borrowed beaver, and began her imperial progress. He watched closely, for this was the crucial moment for the Reeses, and was rewarded by the sight of men digging into their britches and pulling up coins.

He sighed gently. "Ah, this is a great moment, my friends. Let us recognize this very moment as the birth of a territory, a state, the instant remembered by history. Let historians look back upon this moment as the flowering of Oregon! Now, while Electra circulates among you, I would be most pleased to answer your inquiries, but of course keep them short."

He watched Electra; he watched her hold out the hat, not departing from the reluctant, but holding it there until they were shamed by the stares of their neighbors into digging up coins. Manna, wealth, capital . . . rent, food, amenities for the Reeses. She had a knack, and a seductive smile.

"A question." The voice rose from the rear, and a well-formed young man approached.

"I'm Jesse Applegate," he said. "Recently arrived here; a lawyer. I'm wondering how a government can exist without taxes, and I'm wondering why you've chosen an awkward three-person executive, as well as a nine-member committee instead of a legislative branch. It doesn't seem workable."

"A good question, Mr. Applegate, very good. It's republican government, you see. Divided power . . ."

"No power, with a government that can't levy a dime to run it. I think— and I'm speaking for almost all of us who arrived this fall—that maybe this provisional government ought to be redrafted along more accustomed lines, including a small tax, capable of supporting a real government, not a paper one."

The stir among his auditors swiftly told Reese that indeed Applegate had put his finger on something. And Applegate represented some nine hundred newcomers.

"Ah, Mr. Applegate. Certainly something to consider. Let us hear your specific proposal at the next gathering here. Prepare an agenda for us. And meanwhile"—he eyed Electra's progress through the mob—"meanwhile, we shall collect the funds to bring all this about."

The hat was burdened. It was time to adjourn.

41

That very night, the moment arrived that Electra Reese dreaded most.

Garwood was ebullient. They had pocketed two hundred and thirty-seven dollars from settlers eager to create some sort of provisional government. A lot of money, coughed up from small purses carried clear across a continent.

"At last, at last," he cried, once they had returned to their garret in Oregon City. His first act had been to pour the notes and coin out upon the table, light a lamp, and count it. This heap, like all the money in the United States, was a motley collection of private and national banknotes, Spanish and Mexican reales, gold, shillings, and small coins, especially two-bit and one-bit silver, and state banknotes.

"Now I can pay Abernethy something," he said. "And live on the rest. I'm launched. This was a great night, Electra, the most important of my life!"

She didn't share his enthusiasm. And she knew intuitively what was coming, and shrank from it.

"Yes, now I have my feet on the ground; I'm a recognized leader. I'm en route to high office. High, high office . . . do you know what that means?"

She nodded. It would mean a proposition when he got around to it. But that would come later. Right now, his mind was afire with emoluments, majorities, honors, power, and titles. Especially titles. Judge Reese. Senator Reese. Governor Reese.

He looked so animated; almost agitated. "I held them in the palm of my hand," he said. "I could feel it, feel the energy. I said the right things. Set the right tone. I talked about their hunger to settle on land they owned. I talked about the monopoly, and its grasping, greedy ways. I talked about the good old United States of America, and getting foreigners out!"

She had heard all this before. She saw it slightly differently and with clear vision: the settlers wanted the easy pickings. They wanted Fort Vancouver, with its tilled fields and orchards and gardens and warehouses, delivered to them like a roast suckling pig with an apple in its mouth. They wanted to pluck up McLoughlin's surveyed lots; commandeer the millrace he had blasted at the falls; snatch the Canadians' cleared, plowed, and settled farms around Champoeg. Drive out the foreigners! That's what the settlers said, but there was more, carefully unspoken: grab their developed property! And that's what Garwood was actually promoting as feverishly as he could. He wanted about fifty city lots all for himself. It amused her.

"I'll have rallies. We'll pass the hat. I've found the secret, the way to unlock their coffers. We'll rally here, and in Champoeg, and at Vancouver, and out in open fields if we must. Campfire meetings, feasts, picnics. We'll go down to Chemeteka and rouse the Methodists. I'll show them how to dream and hope. I'll forge them into a majority! Even the newcomers who've never met me!"

"Along the way, you might consider staking a farm," she said. "Land, lots of land."

He stared at her in amazement. "A farm? What would I do with a farm?"

"Sell it. Good land is disappearing fast."

He shrugged. "I'll get around to it. There's more than anyone could ever want, and maybe it'd be valuable someday. Now, improved land is something else. Take this town site. It's just land. But when it was divided into lots, it acquired some value."

She laughed, unkindly. "You are very obvious."

"There's no government here. People improve land at their own risk. I have as much right to the lots under our feet as anyone else, and I intend to take what's there for the taking."

He counted his loot once again, separating state and national banknotes, heaping coins into piles. "We'll move into larger quarters at once," he said.

"Where? Within the last two months, nine hundred people arrived here, all without a roof to shelter them."

"I have ways."

She doubted that. Garwood liked people to believe he had his hands on mysterious levers and cords; he needed only to tug a cord or pull a handle and things would happen. Connections. Quid pro quos. That's what he called them.

"If you have ways, move us out. I'll know in a week what to think of you."

He beamed, pouring oil on troubled waters, and she knew the moment was fast approaching, and she would need her wits about her.

"I'll talk to the Methodists," was all he said.

He turned suddenly serious, and she braced herself. He wasn't a bad man; just one for whom the virtues didn't always apply. She had lived in such intimacy with him that she knew the odor of his breath and the metronomic regularity of his bowels. He was brighter than Warren, less educated but more insightful, especially about the chinks in the armor of others. Including hers.

He settled on his cot, leaving her to sit at the table rife with booty. The lamplight wobbled. The air in that malodorous attic warren offended her nose. The shabbiness of the place revolted her.

"It's time we talked, heart to heart," he said.

"I'm sorry; I lack one entirely."

He smiled benevolently. "Soul to soul?"

"Mine's in captivity."

"Body to body?"

She sighed. Seduction was in the air, and she was curious about how he would tackle it, or her.

"You've had a miserable year," he said. "Oregon's a miserable place, without comforts."

"You might have provided some with gainful employment. I don't believe you devoted one day to gainful employment the entire time, except to run around and look for town sites."

"I was gathering strength in my loins."

She laughed, and he smiled.

"You've been widowed for a year. You've grieved a proper time. Poor Warren's gone to his reward and you miss him, I'm sure, but now it's time to consider the future. The glowing, joyous future."

"I don't remember him, so it's hard for me to miss him. There are people whom you can't remember the moment they're out of sight, because they leave no impression."

He processed that. "Well, poor Warren, he was fortunate in love."

She laughed unkindly. "Yes, all the while he was drafting torts and frying other people's fish, I relieved him of his earnings as fast as they came in, all for a few favors."

He cleared his throat. "Ah, yes, favors . . ."

"If you're angling me toward your straw tick, you'd better do it with more grace, Garwood. Your approach is pure lickspittle."

He lit up. "That wasn't a no."

She smiled. She had perfected the glacial smile, intending to convey disapproval from her pale blue eyes while posing like a Dresden figurine. She knew her exact effect on males. Only those most attracted to her weathered that frosty weeding-out.

"I know this is a bit premature. I've not yet secured the office that will reward us with prestige, power, and a cornucopia of comforts. But it has occurred to me that, given the brightness of the future, you might consider my hand—"

"It's not a hand that has performed the world's work, Garwood. It's a pink, soft, useless hand, given to dipping into other people's tills."

"It's very well versed at caresses, my dear. It beats a farmer's horny hand."

She laughed. At least Garwood didn't take himself gravely. She feared he might. The conversation had an unreal quality, and was so laden with overtones and undertones she found herself examining nuance rather than what he actually said.

The lamplight guttered in the draft. Garwood's lust filled his face. Shadows leered across it.

"I'm not ready for marriage," she said.

He began to deflate, smiling all the while.

"I take no pleasure in the nuptial embrace."

He stared.

"It was an ordeal to get through, but a good trade for Warren's wealth."

"Ah . . ."

"However, you might be more adept than poor Warren. It's never too late for a poor widow. Maybe you can teach me something."

"Ah . . ."

"But not in marriage. I have no wish to marry. We don't need to, you know. Everyone thinks we're married. There's not ten people in all Oregon who remember we aren't, and they probably think we did, long ago. And you've already encouraged the notion that we are."

"Not marry?"

"If we're going to do this, we should just take up with each other, like all those oily Frenchmen at the fort and their lice-ridden red sluts."

"But they're married, most of them."

"Not until a priest showed up. Do you wish to take up with me?"

"I would prefer marriage."

"No. I may wish to go East someday without carrying baggage. Oregon's an appalling place. If you wish to take up with me, without the slightest commitment, then we might come to some agreement or other. Now that you show signs of being able to support me, I would consider it."

He gazed blankly. "Agreement?"

"Of course, my dear Garwood. I'm not going to hand you my perfectly lovely body, slim and peachy and unmarred and creamy breasted and exquisite, as you well know from peeking at me several hundred times this past year, for nothing."

He waited.

"A quid pro quo or two, Garwood?"

"That's politics," he said.

"Yes, you have the right idea. There are several things. One is that I will not be bound to you, nor you to me. If you wish to empty yourself upon a red woman or the wife of the next judge, that is your privilege . . . and I reserve the privilege to myself, and you will say nothing and never once object. Never!

"Another is that you will keep me in great comfort, for if you don't, I'll leave. I want gardens. I want flowers and fruits and orchards. You'll give them to me."

"Done," he said, without hesitation.

She smiled, amused, and began undoing buttons, one at a time, her fingers fiddling. Men would promise anything to have her. He stared, transfixed.

42

THE YEAR-END MEDITATION OF JASPER CONSTABLE

Year's end is a good time to sum up and consider the future as well. I've neglected to spend time by myself, in retreat, but mean to do better. But now, with my loved ones abed and the lamp extinguished, I will let my thoughts run.

I've been in Oregon over a year now and find myself sloughing off old cocoons, to my own astonishment. I came here expecting to transform a godless wilderness into a spiritual garden, to employ a figure of speech. I intended to subdue the savagery in the native breast (and in the bosom of the Canadian ruffians who live here), not imagining that any of the savagery would be my own. I came here dissatisfied with the venal and corrupt world, and ended up dissatisfied with my flawed self.

Events have greatly humbled me, and the man I thought I was no longer exists. I'm filled with remorse and mortification. In truth, I don't know how anyone endured me, most of all Rose. It is a miracle that she abides with me. That she does, and that she continues to love me, gives me hope that there is some small kernel of redemption for me.

I arrived here with my own sense of mission burning within me. I wanted to teach, exhort, and shape this island in the wilderness into the nearest thing to paradise permitted to fallen man. I had imagined that I would be lecturing the eager Indians, using simple English of course, upon the meaning and truth of the Trinity, or the Commandments, or the Golden Rule. I supposed that during mission staff meetings, I might be consulted on the theo-

logical issues and nuances. I supposed that I would publish inspi-
rational letters to be circulated among our followers.

And of course I fully intended to drive out those branches of
religion less perfected than my own, as well as the corruption
broadcast wholesale by the Hudson's Bay Company.

I found the mission spending most of its time and effort on
subsistence. Yes, food and shelter! I had scarcely realized that a
mission located in wilderness, thousands of miles from manufac-
turers and markets, must subsist itself. There is no butcher shop or
baker around the corner or greengrocer or hardware merchant or
clothier or carpenter or blacksmith.

When I arrived, I discovered, much to my disapproval, that
the Methodist mission of Jason Lee was largely composed of trades-
men and mechanics and farmers and carpenters and joiners and
hunters. The missioners themselves were few.

How swiftly I learned that my small stipend would buy little
because nothing was to be had for cash. And so Rose and I, like
everyone else, devoted much effort to raising vegetables, keeping
a fresh dairy cow borrowed from the fort, helping with harvests,
chopping firewood, spinning and weaving and sewing, cobbling,
scrubbing clothes, splitting shakes for our roof, laying flagstones on
muddy paths, and all the rest that comes with even the most min-
imal civilization.

So the year slid by with survival paramount. Where was theology in this? Where was paradise on earth? It was present, though
I did but little see it until recently. My initial indignation toward a
mission that did so little missioning swiftly evaporated, and I began
to comprehend the need for carpenters and farmers and why Jason
Lee brought them.

Still, the dream did not immediately abate, and I spent time
with the Indian boys, listening to Solomon Smith and others teach
them, and contributed hours of teaching, rejoicing at any small
advance in their understanding of the faith and its complex tenets.

Yet here, too, reality chastened me. The boys' lack of understanding did not rise from the want of dedication of the mission
by Jason Lee or others, but from factors we can scarcely comprehend, not least language, and the great absence of words and con-
cepts that are alien to the savage mind. What's more, there are boys
from six or eight tribes in our school, each with a different tongue.
How might we reach them?

So, imperceptibly, I began to agree with Lee and the rest that
the outreach to Indians would take generations, and that the mis-

sions should turn to serving the growing white population while not abandoning its original purpose. I still try to teach the Indian boys, and I love them dearly and am glad the Lord has given us the chance to plant holy seeds of faith within them, though I am not sanguine about the result. The Indians are restless. I hear talk of troubles at the other missions, and I wonder what will come of it all.

But oh! I found myself humbled in other ways through this year of transition. Rose has taken to this wild land better than I, and I confess I resisted that change and even saw godlessness in it, a view of which I am now ashamed. The heaviest of all my grief lies with my own conduct. I contributed to our own dear Damaris's death, and I cannot escape that terrible realization and the anguish it fosters in my bosom, which will never go away for as long as I exist. I relive that moment of shipwreck over and over, shocked and appalled at my own priorities. What more was required than an innocent embrace?

For I had elevated respectability above even mortal peril, as if the good opinion of the world mattered most of all; even more than death. It was respectability that prevented me from hugging the girl to my bosom, or pressing her between Rose and me, to share our own body heat with her and thus keep her alive. I remember how shocked, scandalized, I was when I saw John O'Malley pull off most of the wet clothing from his trembling and coughing and shaking bride, throw it aside, and lower himself upon her to save her life.

What did it matter what people thought? Was he expending lust upon her or acting in any way unseemly? No. If what he did wasn't exactly according to the canon of proper public conduct, so what? Mary Kate O'Malley survived and gave the world a child. Damaris died, and all because of my fear of scandal.

Oh! What a thing to live with. I cannot bear it. I wonder what Rose thinks, in the chambers of her heart. Will her own pain and loss fester between us? Respectability! The Pharisees' virtue, condemned by Christ! It is a miracle that the rest of us didn't perish as well, for the heat was out of us and I was all for dying respectably a coffin's length from Rose.

I will never be the same. Worse, respectability still courses through me, and I cannot overcome it. I still look at Jason Lee, in his rough frontier clothes, looking more the cheerful carpenter than the minister, and find myself pushing back disapproval. When will I ever be able to put aside my stock and black frock coat, both literally and figuratively? Oh, Oregon, how you have bared my vanities and exposed the cankers of my soul!

Nor is Oregon done with me yet.

Rose, my Rose. Here my thinking divides. Is she a woman loosening herself from the bonds of marriage, the headship of the husband? Will she reject the direction I provide? Will she disregard the proper instruction of our sons? Or is this change, like the rest, rising from some flaw or failing deep within me? Am I the poor husband and father, overly strict, too jealous of my own direction to see the virtue of other ways? She troubles me. She is not the woman who set forth with me to pierce the wilderness and be vessels of Christian salvation beyond the outermost rim of civilization. She is *beautiful*.

She grew. At first, on that long and arduous trail, she floundered, but as we progressed, day by day, driving our oxen and making what small comforts as we could as we crossed the prairies, she strengthened in body and soul, no longer doubting her abilities and no longer depending on me for direction. Is this good? What is a woman, a mother and wife? Is this a Rose in bloom?

Ah, Oregon. I plunged into your bosom brimming with certitudes, and now the whole of my seminary training seems to be ash. What has this wild land done?

Perhaps the thing most painful to me is that she now acts as conscience, and has even rebuked my conduct. She rebukes me! This is particularly true in the matter of politics. She said something to me the other day that shocked me to my bones. I'm not ready to accept it whole, but it needs prayerful consideration, and that for certain.

It came, as usual, when we were contending about public affairs in Oregon. She has become adamant, even outspoken, on matters scarcely of moment to most women.

"Jasper," she said, "the Methodists came here to serve God, and now are serving Mammon." I bridled, but then she reminded me forcibly, and not even out of the earshot of Mark and Matthew, that our mission people were conniving by tricky political means to secure property they had no right to claim because John McLoughlin had claimed and developed it before us. I remember staring at her, as if at a stranger.

She didn't mention my colleague, the Reverend Mr. Alvin Waller, but she was certainly referring to him, and Abernethy, and the faction that wrote the clause disfranchising the Canadians. I had, out of loyalty to our Wesleyan heritage, stoutly supported all this, meaning to drive Hudson's Bay out of Oregon, along with all its vices and iniquities.

And then she raised the simple issue of justice, and I am stricken with doubt. John McLoughlin has been a most charitable and Christian gentleman, and we would not be here but for him; neither would several hundred other Americans, found perishing and rescued by his company.

Could it be that the good doctor, who began his career serving Mammon, first with the fierce North West Company of Montreal, and then the only slightly more scrupulous Hudson's Bay Company of London, has abandoned Mammon and serves Christ, albeit through a papist prism, while we Methodists, so eager to serve the Lord and spread the Gospel among the deprived tribes, have abandoned our mission and now serve Mammon? And grasp at wealth by all political and devious means we can conjure up?

The issue leaches me. I must ponder this and seek illumination. And if I am bled, I must stand up and be counted, no matter whether I lose everything, including membership in Wesley's great Reformation church, my rock, and my salvation. The new year will tell whether I am to be an outcast in wilderness, for the sake of my soul.

1844

43

Life was too easy, and therefore boring. Abel Brownell stared at the relentless rains dripping from the eaves of his Oregon City home, and felt trapped. He was alone this gray day, which only made matters worse.

The rain-spattered river, the sullen slopes, the silvery puddles on the streets did not evoke lofty thoughts, but quite the opposite.

Felicity had, with great effort, established a school and was now teaching at it, along with two other women. She had dragooned Roxy and Dedham into it, resuming their long-corked education on pain of exile and corporal punishment. His children were, indeed, among the seniormost of the twenty-seven rapscallions occupying hard plank benches in her torture chamber.

He thought about going to the store, but O'Malley didn't need supervision. The Irishman was consistently squeezing more sales out of the enterprise than Brownell's most sanguine estimates, and gaining a loyal gaggle of customers, especially from among the newcomers who crowded every cranny of the city. No, going to the store would accomplish nothing.

Unless his business collapsed under a heap of settler debt, he saw no end to the bonanza, which was what bothered him now. He was bored. Oregon offered no diversions. Life had always been easy. In Boston, he had scarcely worked at all. All he needed to do, really, was buy and sell cargoes, commission voyages to China, send vessels down to the Caribbean for rum, and otherwise enjoy himself.

He still was unsure why he had come to Oregon, herding his family from one extremity of the continent to the other: yes, he needed something to conquer, something that would indeed be a challenge. And yes, the overland trip did challenge him and his family, almost fatally. But now, in Oregon, life was easier than ever, and he was restless again. What on earth should he do with himself? Where would he go next? To sample the spice markets of Zanzibar? To look at the honey-fleshed women of Tahiti? To talk to the offspring of mutineers on Pitcairn's Island?

What was the matter with him? Why couldn't he settle down? Why was he prowling his precincts like a caged lion? What energies lay just under the surface, waiting to erupt? He burst into the kitchen, stuffed kindling into the cookstove, and set some water heating in a teakettle. He would have some good Oolong, which the Methodists scorned along with coffee, anything spirituous, tobacco, dancing, wagering, and cards. He had concluded that he, a Unitarian, would rather kiss the Pope's ring than be a Methodist.

The memory of Abernethy and Waller and that pious cabal darkening his door and confiscating his casks of rum and whiskey still rankled. He paced the kitchen, waiting for the tea to brew, waiting for the rain to stop, remembering why he didn't like the missioners, and laughed at them when he wasn't irked at them.

Ah, Boston, civilized and pleasant, with every amenity! He and Felicity rarely missed a Sabbath at the First Unitarian Church because they so enjoyed the warmth and wisdom of William Ellery Channing. Sunday after Sunday he talked of fostering humane living; seeking new and more generous ways of life in the young republic.

And if not Channing, then he and Felicity headed for any venue where Ralph Waldo Emerson might be lecturing, there to imbibe his wondrous Transcendentalism. And if not Emerson, then Bronson Alcott or George Ripley, the founder of Brook Farm, an experiment in divine harmony.

All that ferment had enriched their lives. Boston graciously offered them endless self-improvement, a freeing of soul and mind from ancient authority to focus on the divine and perfect within each mortal. What was the American republic, if not a great reaching toward . . . not utopia, but simply the best life that each of us might devise?

He stuffed brown tea leaves into a strainer and steeped them, all the while excited by something that lay just beyond the horizons of his thinking. And then he knew: Oregon was the Great Experiment.

For a year, he had puzzled out his motives and had yet to understand why he had plucked up his family and come to this remote and mystical place. *Mystical,* that was it. This Oregon was not the frontier, but an island in a wilderness, detached from the civilized world. The actual frontier, the area just beginning to be settled, ran through barely organized Wisconsin and Minnesota, Illinois and Iowa, Arkansas, and on down to the Mexican province of Tejas, where Stephen Austin's Yank settlers outnumbered the Mexicans three to one. The republic had scarcely leapt the Mississippi River. But here he was, clear out on the Pacific, driven by something he couldn't quite fathom. Could it be, at bottom, Ralph Waldo Emerson's Transcendental ideas?

Abel Brownell sipped Oolong and leapt to great insights. Oregon was not merely a settlement; it was paradise being born. Here, in this Eden, the future of the republic would be shaped. What was achieved here, not on some border with the old, but separated from the old by thousands of brutal miles, would fashion a new and better world.

Excited, Brownell reached for a precious piece of paper, for this was too important to commit to a slateboard. He was reaching for something barely discerned and in the chaos he could not limn its outlines. He found the sheet, his stoppered ink bottle and pen, and sat next to a window, watching the gray veils of rain hide Oregon from him.

And wrote nothing.

He was no closer to answers than before. Whatever Oregon was to become, it eluded him.

And so Abel's day passed, lost in reverie. Roxanne showed up mid-afternoon, changed her clothes, and vanished. Felicity appeared later, lugging readers she protected with her umbrella. She set the books down, undid her black cape and hung it on the coat rack, removed her satin hat, and headed for the kitchen to start a meal.

She had been doing that all along, cooking mornings and evenings, teaching, catching up with her household in spare moments. She looked tired.

"You made tea," she said. "Why don't you bring me some?"

He began puttering. Serving tea was a great oddity in his life. There had always been servants. "Did your day go well?" he asked.

"John Battle has catarrh. I hope the rest don't catch it. Nellie Castle started crying and wouldn't tell me why. Roxy kept whispering to Willis Goude, just aching for me to discipline her. What did you do—if anything?"

He sensed a certain tension in the question. She had, from the beginning, assaulted Oregon with every ounce of her energy; if she was no longer to be a lady of leisure on Louisburg Square, then she would be a wilderness dervish.

"I've decided what I want to do," he said, waiting for her to brighten, but she didn't. "Business bores me," he explained.

"There's more to life, majestic alps to climb, spiritual doors to enter."

She was staring at him from granite eyes.

"I'm going to dedicate myself to things beyond myself, and thus achieve my own transcendence. Here we are, in a beautiful wilderness . . . a place to begin anew."

She took the teacup he proffered her and sipped, a wry amusement building on her face. She usually forgave him his idle ways.

"Like what?"

"Making Oregon the Athens of the West."

She hiccuped.

"I wish to found a college. Not just yet, of course, but when conditions permit. And schools . . ."

"A college."

"Yes, with professors, the best to be gotten, people with new ideas, big dreams."

"A college, a Harvard in Oregon. I suppose you'll endow it."

"Not now, but in a few years. The firm's doing so well—"

"I see," she said, heading for the horsehair sofa. "Now it's colleges. What a puzzle you are. In Boston, you were feverish to come west to sample the savage life. Once you got here, you were feverish to go east. When you got your business going, I thought you'd settle down, but I was mistaken. Now you're bored and want to found universities in the middle of a wilderness, and have magpies in attendance."

"Not right now; I was just thinking about it."

"And tomorrow you'll decide to become a Trappist monk and, with many a sigh, tenderly tell us before you leave that we aren't enough."

He stared.

"I thought so!" She laughed, but her amusement was laced with something darker. "It's raining, so you want to start colleges or sail to the South Pole or consult the oracles at Delphi."

"What does rain have to do with it?"

She reached across to him and gathered his hand. Hers was cold. "The Oregon rain falls like iron bars, imprisoning you three or four months of each year. You're a free spirit. I should let you go. You're a frigate bird, soaring across oceans, and here I am, burdening you with small domestic cares, mundane things, children's foibles."

She sipped the tea and sighed. "I'm tired, and now I have to cook, and there's not enough stove wood in the box, and the dishes aren't washed, and I wish you'd endow me with some servants before you endow Oregon with colleges."

Emerson and Channing and Alcott fled the room, along with *The Dial* and all its spiritual essays, as well as Tahiti women and hot spices from Zanzibar and the odd ducks living on Pitcairn's. "I'm able to," he said. "John O'Malley's something of a genius."

"Please do," she said, not unkindly.

That's how it was, he thought. Felicity was not unkind to him any more. She was even smiling, if only one of those patient, long-suffering, probationary sort of smiles.

And then he stood. "I'll chop some wood," he said.

44

John O'Malley wanted a happy ending to the story, but there wasn't one. Life did not offer many happy endings. Something was wrong with Mary Kate. The change had been so subtle he had not noticed at first. Now he noticed nothing else.

She had shrunk. Something had fled from her; her youth, and then her strength. But more than that, something had slipped from her mind. She had become very quiet, ruling her household in silence, feeding and caring for the little boy as if the tasks were onerous. The baby fretted, starving for a mother who had absented herself. She hadn't a friend in the world either. She never visited anyone; never invited anyone.

"Mary Kate, what is the matter?" he had asked again and again.

She had always just smiled, a flash of the old brightness in her eyes that always faded moments later.

He had wanted more children; now he wondered whether she had become barren. Often, when he reached out to her in the night, she had turned aside, and when she didn't turn aside, she accepted his lovemaking with resignation and passivity. The joy had fled from that.

She never complained. He heard not a word of self-pity or distress. No wheedling or begging, no negotiating, no demands. On the surface, she seemed serene and reserved, going about her daily tasks with ease. But he knew that was not what lay in her heart.

He talked to her often, tried to awaken dreams in her. Dreams were a staple of the soul, as important as food and air to all mortals, and yet he could discover no dream at all in her. Once she wanted to gather her family about her in Oregon. Now she never talked of it, and yet he knew she pined for her kin, pined for Erin.

Only when Father Blanchet or Father Demers happened by did she brighten, and he wondered whether his wife might simply need the company of Catholic people, the very sort who were her brothers and sisters, parents, aunts and uncles, neighbors and grandparents, friends, united in the woof and weave of the parish.

So he had encouraged the missionary fathers to stop by, and asked them to spend time with her, brighten her, praise the infant, offer her spiritual consolation. That always helped. He saw remnants of the old shine return to her eyes, and sometimes she even laughed softly, and plucked up the fretful child if one or another priest was admiring the boy.

And yet the moment the priests left, the melancholia crept back into her. How often he had watched it, this transformation, as if a dark fluid were slowly filtering through her. And then she would turn her gaze to him and it would be bleak, or worse, it would barely acknowledge his presence in the room. Her very presence darkened the brightly lit cottage and dimmed the rooms. It was an odd thing; how could feeling wrack such ruin upon a snug, sweet home with flowers abounding?

Still, she neglected no task. There were meals on the table for him. The baby was never ignored, and lay in foundling clothes that were always freshly scrubbed. She toiled, she kept house, she mothered, and yet she had vanished from his household, and lived some distant place an infinity away.

John O'Malley suspected he knew where.

One January day, when the rains pelted Oregon City and the drops were turning to sleet, he braced her as she droned in the dark kitchen, performing rote rituals with dead hands and a dead heart.

"Mary Kate, darling, you are not a wee bit happy here."

"Why do you say that?"

"It is plain."

She did not reply, but continued to peel potatoes that had been stored in a cellar through the fall.

"I have not touched you for months," he said, "for that is your wish."

"I do not want children."

"Ah, no, it is the embrace of your husband you do not want, Mary Kate!"

She lowered her gaze, as if she did not hear what he had said.

"Once you took me in your arms. Once you reached out to me. Once you cooed and crooned and sighed. Am I so bad a man now?"

Her gaze slid away again, but she drew herself up upon the stool. "Maybe someday," she said lightly.

"Ah, maybe never. I yearn for you, and sometimes I am wild as the roses."

She did not reply, but peeled methodically, finding refuge in her task.

"It is Oregon that wounds you!"

"I am content."

"It is Oregon. All I asked was for you to wait, but it was too much. Each day there is less of you to see, less of you to touch, and less of you to hear. You are as quiet and bleak as a peat bog, or a lough at midnight. I do not know what to do."

"You are happy in your work," she said. "Do that, then, and leave me be."

"I will not leave you be! I am losing you! Christ's wounds! Something has fled us. Where are you at dawn, when the world is young and sweet? Where are you in the bright days, when the boy Oregon Patrick lifts up his arms? Where are you at supper, when the man bound to you forever sits across? Where are you at the hour we blow out the candle, when your lover comes to your side, with a joy that is holy and true and sacred? Where are you now? Where, Mary Kate?"

She sighed, but otherwise did not acknowledge his outburst, and he felt shame steal through him. She had shamed him into baring his soul, turning his concern into a whine.

The baby began moaning. In a few moments he would sob. The little boy sobbed and coughed too much, and O'Malley feared for his life. Wee babies needed a lot of holding. Fearfully, he lifted the little one and rested him in the crook of his arm, and he quieted at once, his solemn brown eyes peering upward at the person who was not his mother.

"It is Oregon," he said. "Mary Kate, tell me true now. Would you like to go back?"

She shook her head, and he didn't believe her denial. She was being dutiful, knowing how much he loved this land.

"If I die, Mary Kate, then would you go back?"

She stopped peeling. "Do not . . ." she whispered.

He wrestled with himself, with his own dreams and plans. "I was hoping to start on the big house soon, on the land I claimed, a big sunny house with high ceilings, windows to the sky, sheep on our green hills and many a good sweet child at our table. I just was seeing my way clear to begin it. Tara I would call it, the hill of the palace of the kings of Ireland. Tara, in honor of our people. Tara in Oregon, where each man in this republic is a king, and you and I would be king and queen. Tara of the New World, Mary Kate. A white house upon a high hill for you."

Her hands resumed their rhythm, and a purple curl of potato coiled away from its white flesh. The child stirred in his arms, pushing himself rigid and then relaxing his small body.

"There are no profits now; most of what we put across the counter goes onto the credit sheet, so our profits are deferred. But the customers do come, they pay a bit on their debts, they seek us out and dicker and I make some agreement, or they go to Fort Vancouver and make an agreement there, so the money does not come in. But a little does; and most of it pays off this cottage, and buys us the meat and drink for our table.

"And yet, now and then, I get ahead a little bit, and think about starting

our house on the hill, on six hundred forty acres of land, a square mile, Mary
Kate. A mile for people just starting out, like us!"

The child squirmed.

"Ah, how I would love to see brothers and sisters for you, my little boy.
Ah! If your ma would only like that too."

"John, do not speak that way to me."

He stared. At least she said something.

"Would you like to be among Irish people here?"

"Oh, John, do not talk of it. Do not think of me."

He leaned toward her. "I think of you. I think of the colleen I knew, the
one who smiled and flirted and ran her hands through her hair whenever I
came near. I do not see her now, Mary Kate."

The baby complained, and Mary Kate set down her paring knife and held
out her arms. O'Malley slipped the child to her.

"Tell me who to bring first, then," he said.

"What?"

"Two I will pay for, and it will not put us much in debt."

"We must not! Not debt!"

"This is not some cottage on a quarter of an acre, and there is no agent
coming for rent, and no one is putting us out if we do not have it, Mary Kate.
Who will it be?"

She clasped her mouth, stricken, and he saw a wild pain in her eyes.

"Will it be Liam, or Betsy, or Agnes, or Thomas? Or someone else?

"Oh, oh, John, do not say—do not talk like that!"

He rejoiced. That was the first sign of life he'd seen in his bride for half a year.

"I will ask for Betsy and Agnes," he said, naming Mary Kate's two younger
sisters. "Unless they have been promised."

It wasn't likely.

"They will not come. Who would come here? All this way? And no chap-
erone, unless . . . no, John, it is not possible. And Pa would not allow them."

Again she spoke, again he felt animation, force in her voice, as if she were
returning to the husk of her body and mind and cleaning out the chambers
with a broom.

"Maybe Liam too, for a man to look after them. It will be a long time,
and many a sunset before we see them," he said.

She rocked the child, the rhythm of her body matching the poetry in her face.

"I will talk to Abel Brownell. I will send a letter, two or three letters, one
with the next Hudson's Bay express, and others by any captain to take the
word across the seas."

He watched her. She was crooning a little song to their son, and he hoped
there would be more songs in her when he brought Ireland to her.

45

That Saturday John O'Malley turned the store over to Dedham and Roxy Brownell, who had been filling in for him, borrowed a trap, and headed for Champoeg.

A thin skein of clouds whitened the sky and chilled the pale sun, bleeding color from the gray landscape until it was all a soft blur, which suited his mood. The dray splashed through talcumed puddles and the wheels cut trenches in the mud, so O'Malley didn't hurry the laboring animal.

He had reached a wall. Was this a paradise, this place that bled heart and spirit from his bride, wizened her, stole her laughter, dulled her eyes, pinched her lips, and murdered love? Was that what Oregon would be to him and Mary Kate? Was it Oregon that was stopping her womb, enervating her hands? Was this Oregon nothing more than a harsh settlement at the far end of the earth, as remote as one could be from Erin, from their flesh and blood?

He meant to talk to Father Blanchet about it, and he hoped the priest knew enough English to fathom the desperation that would soon pour out of him. Mary Kate was dying by slow degrees, inhabiting a body she had shuffled away, waiting for reunion or death. She was suffering no ailment except the worst of all ailments, despair, the most terrible of all sins according to the church, the sin that denied the caring of God; and yet a bleakness she could not help and could no longer fight.

Time was against him. He must do something. Unless some joy revived Mary Kate, terrible things would be visiting the sunny cottage on the bench above the river bottoms. He knew that as surely as he knew his own name.

The dray horse tired of the hard slog through brown gumbo, and O'Malley let it rest. Even his hope of help seemed mired in Oregon winter. As he rested, he beheld several Indians on the river, fishing. Some abandoned their nets and approached him, bearing bows and arrows. He did not know the tribe. They collected around his trap, staring, the young men solemn and vaguely hostile.

"Good morning," he said.

They didn't respond. They pointed at the sack beside him, plainly begging. It contained his lunch and a few spare clothes.

"That's my lunch," he said.

One of the young men waved his bow, which held a nocked arrow. The arrow did not come around to point at him, though it could have in an instant.

"All right, you bloody beggars," he said. He threw the sack at their feet. They pawed through it, found the cheese and bread and spare trousers and shirt, and commandeered them all.

"You thieving devils," he said.

"It's you who steal from us, Mr. O'Malley," said one. "This was our home. Our game is gone and our people are angry. We want to eat."

He stared. The youth who spoke English so well had been one of his bunkmates at the mission, though now he wore no shirt, even in the chill.

"I remember you, lad. I'm sorry. There are many white men here, I'm afraid."

"Yes, and you take everything and teach us your bad religion, making us weak. Go now."

O'Malley was only too glad to escape. Things were changing. These waves of immigration, these settlers fanning out, claiming land, plowing fields, shooting game, forbidding Indians access, were kindling trouble.

He hastened south to Champoeg, and pulled into the mission at midday. He peered into the church and sacristy, rapped on the rectory, but could find no one. He thought perhaps Father Blanchet was up at Fort Vancouver and Father Demers was out in the parish, among the Canadians, bringing his solaces and sacraments to his people.

He unhitched his horse, threw a halter over its head, and led it to a paddock. Then he made one last round of the mission and decided to try again later. It was noon, he was hungry and his lunch had been stolen from him, but there was nothing he could do. He would be here a while.

His land lay across the river, beckoning him.

He walked down to the river, feeling the soggy turf squeeze icy water through his leather soles, soaking his feet. At water's edge he found a rowboat and canoes, as he knew he would, all of them belly-up against the weather. He turned a canoe aright, collected a paddle, and dragged it into the water, stepping gingerly as it wobbled free of the bank. He lowered himself and then paddled across the Willamette, feeling the suction of the current drawing him downstream.

On the far side he drove the prow up on a gravelly bar, stepped out, and drew the canoe well out of the water. He would walk his Arcadia this afternoon, check the cairns, feel his own earth under his feet, and dream of the great white house he would someday build, dream of a house full of laughing children, dream of flocks of white sheep meandering the emerald slopes, dream of sunbursts of wildflowers scattered in rainbow carpets, and springs rising in sweet fern grottoes; dream of high ceilings and towering glass windows that admitted sun and air and breathtaking views, even of Mount Hood in the haze to the northeast.

But on this sullen winter day, what came first to him was the rattle of hammers. Dreading what it might mean, he raced up the steep slope from the river, and then strode rapidly through the gentle hills until he rounded a bend and beheld men erecting a house on the very foundation that was to carry his own.

An elaborate canvas house stood nearby, its rough frame draped with duck-cloth against the weather; home to these people until they could complete a permanent house . . . on his land.

He pushed forward over soaked dead grass, entering an area torn by construction and filled with muck. Three bearded men and a boy toiled at the building, whose squared-beam frame stood almost complete.

The burly men paused, awaiting him. Two sat on the ridgepole, one with an auger in hand. The boy on the ground paused, hammer in hand.

O'Malley took a great shaky breath. It wouldn't do to rile these people. It wouldn't do to shout.

"I think there's been a mistake, friends," he said.

They said nothing.

"I think we can work this out. You're on my claim, you see."

They stared.

"But I don't mean to put you out without paying you for the work done. I'll buy what you've put in here."

At last the older one, a little gray salting his dark beard, probably an older brother somewhere in his forties, slid off the ridgepole, clambered down a ladder, and approached O'Malley.

"Get out," he said. The man loomed over O'Malley, a squint in his eyes, his flesh weather-rouged, formidable and bristly.

O'Malley held his ground. "I claimed this over a year ago. My cairns are on the corners. There's a record of the claim over at the mission. Another in a bottle in the river cairn. I took six hundred forty, fair and proper. You would've seen the markers, for sure."

"We saw them."

"Then you know you're not here properly."

"We're here."

The others gathered around. Big American frontiersmen, lean, muscular, and half a head taller than O'Malley.

"I'm John O'Malley," he said. "I arrived here in forty-two and staked this place, registered it proper. Now, you're building here, and that's the risk you took if you knew this wasn't yours. I'll pay for the timbers, but I'll expect you to leave now, fair and proper. And who'm I talking to?"

"Burgess. We're all Burgess. Sorry, Paddy, you're out a claim. We're staying, and you'd better just turn your tail like a good mick."

O'Malley's Irish was up. "It's you who'll be leaving now. There's a government been voted in to deal with this, and if you cause me trouble now, I'll go to it and get a judgment."

Burgess stepped forward, provocatively, menacingly. "Paddy, me boy, in the United States, them that claims land have to prove it up, throw up a building."

"You built on my foundation. And this isn't the United States, Mr. Burgess."

"It is, or soon will be. And in the States, we don't like foreigners taking all the land. You're fresh off the boat, Paddy, and that's a fact."

O'Malley felt his rage course through his body, clamp his hands into fists. "Get off my land, Burgess. Pack up now, pack up! This is theft, and you'll not be stealing a man's rightful claim. If theft's your business, then you'll answer to your neighbors, answer to the provisional government. Now I'll be seeing you pick up and leave right now."

Burgess laughed. "Paddy, there's four of us and some womenfolk and young ones too. You want to be dragged out by the heels, or you want to walk?"

O'Malley refused to budge. If they were going to throw him off his own land, they would have to drag him off.

"Well?" said Burgess softly.

O'Malley stood, thinking of all the world's predators, of the rent men in Ireland, the grasping and greedy, the lords who strong-armed their way to wealth, and all these immigrants who arrived here itching to steal land held and improved by others rather than clear their own land in a huge and unclaimed wilderness. What was it in some men that coveted what others possessed even when there was a whole world to make their own?

"Time enough, Paddy," Burgess said, grinning through his brown beard. He slammed a fist into O'Malley's shoulder.

O'Malley slugged back, kicked, gouged and fought but it all lasted less than a minute. Four Burgesses pounded him, dropped him into the muck, muddied him, lifted him up and threw him bodily down the slope.

He lay on wet, ice-crusted turf, not hurting a whole lot, but knowing he probably would later.

He heard them laughing behind him.

46

Garwood Reese was captivating his audience. He had honed and perfected his delivery in camp meeting after camp meeting, and now knew exactly how to excite his crowds. He knew the issues. These people were bone-hungry for title to the lands they were settling. He played on that theme in a thousand ways, awakening in them the sense that he, Garwood Reese, running for high office, could resolve that difficulty once and for all.

"Land! Free and clear, patented and deeded, title guaranteed by the government of the United States! Your land under your boots! That sums up my platform!"

They always cheered.

Wherever he went, he took the beauteous Electra with him, and her icy blond presence drew appreciative stares. She would be the first lady of Oregon soon; let them survey and measure her. She rarely smiled, rarely clapped, and seemed so distant that men thought of her as some sort of ethereal goddess, not a mortal woman. She usually wore her fawn dress, tight at the bosom, buttoned to the neck, somehow evocative of all the yearnings of all the males in attendance.

He had hit upon the campfire meetings as the way to build a party, promote his candidacy in the May elections, and above all, garner abundant funds easily and without lifting a finger. He had gone from dire poverty to luxury, or what passed for luxury in rude Oregon. Wherever settlers gathered, he set up meetings, small or large. The warehouse at Champoeg became a favorite site because the little town was central. But at other times he had rallied his Americans in Oregon City, Salem, which was what they had renamed Chemeteka, Mission Bottoms, and even Fort Vancouver, where he largely concealed his purposes behind bland rhetoric.

He had developed a fine speaking voice, a flair, a mesmerizing style, in which he sometimes spoke in his clear baritone, and other times softened his words to a whisper that nonetheless drove to every corner of the halls in which he spoke. He had, he knew, a commanding timbre in his voice when his throat wasn't sore, a way of galvanizing the attention of every auditor; sometimes trumpet, sometimes trombone, sometimes spilling words as gentle as a harp's string.

This particular evening he was campaigning at Mission Bottoms in the old Methodist establishment. Jason Lee had hastened east to plead with his mission board to keep the mission open, and for more funds. But the work continued; a few Indian boys were schooled and instructed in religion. The lay members of the mission increasingly entered commerce, operated grist-and sawmills, farmed, built homes and shops and warehouses, or performed services such as surveying and accounting. The new man, Gary, had arrived by sea and was even now studying the operation to ascertain whether it should continue.

Reese had chosen the student dining hall rather than the larger mission church this time because church buildings had a way of inhibiting audiences. He wanted some whooping. And he had packed it with a hundred fifty people.

His arrival anywhere in the Willamette Valley these days occasioned great interest and triggered spirited debates about the future of Oregon. So here he was, in the jammed hall, where most people stood because the few seats had been snatched. Plenty of twilight breached the open windows, bathing the room in gray light. He didn't know most of these people; they were newcomers. Just a few months earlier he had known most everyone in the settlements. But he did spot a few familiar faces, including several of the Applegates, who seemed to be a political tribe. And his traveling companions, the Constables.

"Now I tell you," he concluded, "that together we can create a new and utterly sublime territory and add it to the union. We can petition Congress to accept us. We can drive out the British, including the grasping monopoly that bleeds us with its outlandish prices and land grabs. Out with the bullies!

"We can elect farsighted people who will lead us to the promised land. We can endow the provisional government with the power to settle land disputes and grant title. That above all. Grant title. Settle disputes. Even as I speak, the very lots in Oregon City are clouded because of a title dispute between you Methodists and the Hudson's Bay Company. It is my intention to drive them out! Drive them clear out of Oregon! America for Americans!"

"Hosannah," cried a missioner.

"What does Oregon mean to you? You've all come from so far away. Do you dream of a good and just commonwealth, as I do? A land of plenty and bounty, as I do? A place where the humblest man can find opportunity, and prosper? A place where there will be wisely wrought laws, as I do? An Arcadia, the envy of the entire world, where we can all live simple, virtuous, clean, joyous lives free from the dark forces that blot every other dominion? Can Oregon be *different*? Different from the entire run of human experience?"

He paused dramatically. "Now, friends, all this requires sacrifice, courage, and means. I am going to pass the hat and ask each of you to consult your conscience. Will you contribute to this struggle, or will you merely harvest the fruits of our enterprise without contributing two bits, or four bits, or six bits or one dollar? Will you support the provisional government and its works with your purse as well as your lips? Will you set an example for your neighbors, so that they admire you as a man of principle?

"I have here a beaver, which my beautiful Electra will carry as she passes among you. Dig deep for freedom. Dig deep for security, and land, and America for Americans! Every cent will be put to good use and accounted for!"

He stepped back, knowing that he would walk away with over two hundred dollars again. It was so blessed to be solvent; indeed, to have a little nest egg put by.

They clapped as he sat down. Electra rose.

But then Jasper Constable stepped forward, waving a hand.

"Ah, Garwood, would you open the meeting to discussion?"

"Why, of course, of course."

"Good. There are things we must consider."

The minister, accoutered in black this evening, with a gray stock at his neck, stepped forward. Reese knew him for an awkward and arrogant man, but surely that would make no difference. Who could be more for the Methodist party than one of its ministers?

Odd, though, how solemn Jasper Constable looked, and nervous too. Well, the man didn't have a congregation, and wasn't used to public discourse. The minister approached the front of the hall, stood itchily on one foot and the other, while this lively crowd settled to hear the word.

"I, ah, just want to take a few moments to ask us to examine our souls and consciences this evening, so that we might each of us do the right thing, the thing most pleasing to our Father and to our nation, and to ourselves, as men of principle and good ideals."

An altogether odd opening, Reese thought. It worried him. The longer Constable might talk, the less money would land in Electra's hat.

Constable stood there, ill at ease, glancing from one person to the next.

"Friends, there is something that's troubling my conscience," he began. "It's a source of great anguish in me. I refer, of course, to the treatment of the Hudson's Bay Company in general, and its chief factor, John McLoughlin, in particular—"

"Hurry up, Reverend," yelled someone.

"Yes, I won't take but a minute. Now, you see, many of us in this hall, and others in all the settlements owe our lives to that company. I do; my family does. Mr. Reese here does, as well as his sister-in-law."

The news that Electra was Garwood's sister-in-law startled some.

"This mission itself owes its existence to the company, which gave it food and supplies, carried its debt, and helped it prosper in every way possible, including the gathering of the Indian children who would be brought to our faith through the means of our school and church.

"Now, here we all are, indebted to the company and to the good doctor for everything we possess, the very clothes on our backs, and yet I find, in the provisions of the provisional government, a most obnoxious clause that nullifies the claims of the company and McLoughlin—"

"Ah, Reverend, that's fine, but now we must close this meeting," Reese said. "Getting dark."

Constable turned quietly. "No, Garwood, I'm not done, and I'll have my say. It won't take long."

"But that's yesterday's news, and there's no need to rehash it, Jasper. We all know about the company. But we're all interested in America. Oregon for Americans. Now thank you—"

"I will be heard," the minister said, in a voice so quiet and yet strong that it commanded attention.

Reese seethed.

"It grieves me to speak against my fellow Methodists, including so many here in this hall, but I must. Conscience requires it. Truth and honor demand it. Let me review some undisputed facts . . ."

The minister recited the whole case, point by point. Reese could scarcely believe his ears. Was Constable mad? Reese studied the crowd, a solid Mission Party group, and saw the fidgeting, the impatience, the polite nodding. This would pass. Tomorrow it would be forgotten.

"And what is Dr. McLoughlin's reward?" Constable asked. "The provisional government's clause that nullifies his town site but grants the Methodists an entire township, thirty-six square miles of land!"

Reese debated whether to shut the man up but decided against it. The evening was ruined anyway and perhaps Constable would hang himself, attacking his own people.

"This, friends, is indecent. It affronts the conscience of every just man. I stand against it."

The crowd was growing restless.

"Those who love goodness and justice, those who are offended by greed and cupidity—"

"All right, we've heard you, Reverend," yelled someone. "You want to defend that bloodsucker monopoly, you just go ahead. We Americans, we'll boot it clear back to England."

Reese stood, laughing, as the crowd's clamor dismissed Constable. The evening wasn't ruined after all.

"Well, now, we'll just pass the hat, and gents, if you want to hold on to what's yours, and support the American way of life, you just dig deep in your pockets and help the cause."

But Constable stood, unmoving, staring quietly at one, then another, then another, of his own Methodist colleagues, and there was a bad feeling in the air.

Some made a great show of contributing; some stared at the hat as it passed by.

47

Rose Constable was proud of Jasper. She watched him respond, after Reese's speech, to a dozen irate Methodists who furiously upbraided him. But Jasper was not to be moved, nor were they able to penetrate his calm.

"Reverend, the trouble with holier-than-thou is that we have to deal with a real world, a world in which the monopoly controls every price, and keeps us poor," argued one.

"That is not a license to steal from it," Jasper responded.

"We don't want Canadians in here!"

"This is not United States territory."

"It will be. We're the majority, so we can take it!"

"Why must you take what's theirs? There's an entire wilderness here, for the taking. Hundreds of thousands of acres."

"The best land's all used up!"

"You mean the cleared and developed land!"

Jasper started laughing. Rose had scarcely ever heard Jasper laugh. This most serious of men rarely laughed, but there he was, laughing sardonically at a lazy schemer who claimed that Oregon's tens of thousands of square miles of marvelous land were taken up.

"Why're you attacking us Methodists? And you a minister? How about them others?"

Jasper sighed and stared at the man, a lay carpenter who had built some of the mission buildings. "No people, no congregation, is exempt from sin, and I take it as my personal failure that I have not inoculated my own colleagues against injustice. I mean to be harder on us than upon others, because I should like to see us freed from the evil that seems to have broken out in this congregation."

Several began shouting and the words that reached Rose's ears weren't pleasant: *traitor, disloyal, no place for you here* . . .

Through it all, Jasper stood like a rock, even while others seethed. Eventually, though, the crowd drifted off, and gusts of cold air entered the dining hall whenever some of them left. The Reeses glared at Jasper. Rose knew they had collected little this time: Electra's hat didn't fill because so many were arguing with Jasper, or weighing his words. The Oregon City couple eventually vanished into the darkness, leaving only Jasper and Rose in the forlorn and darkened hall, lit by the last of a hearthfire.

"I am proud of you," she said.

"I wish I could be proud of myself."

"But you should be."

He gazed solemnly at her. "This will cost us, you know. I don't doubt that I'll be severed from the mission."

"Well, good!"

He looked shocked. "But what will we do . . . ?"

"Jasper, maybe we shouldn't be a part of this mission."

"We've come so far, two thousand miles . . ."

"Maybe we shouldn't be Methodists either."

"Rose, what's happened to you?"

"I don't know. I wish I knew. I'm—just thinking now."

The truth of it was that Oregon was transforming her. She didn't know where she was heading or what she was leaving behind. She only knew that ever since Damaris had died, and ever since she had plunged into this harsh, isolated, lonely life some infinity away from everything she had known, everything that had comforted her and supported her beliefs, she was at sea. And what she had so far confessed to Jasper was nothing compared to what really was churning within her.

"Let's go," she said, drawing her hooded blanket capote tightly about her.

Jasper nodded and steered her into the harsh night. They had lived at Mission Bottoms for well over a year now, and could find their way around, even on a bleak late winter's night. The darkness was a metaphor for her own searching. She followed paths by instinct, rather than by sight.

She tucked her arm into Jasper's ever-supportive arm, and they traversed the grounds to their cottage. They now had a comfortable place because so many had moved to Chemeteka, but Rose did not feel at home. This was an insular Methodist world; Methodist buildings and land, now secured by a scandalous clause in the organic law of the new government. Methodist beliefs, Methodist goals, Methodist teaching of Indian boys, Methodist books, Methodist friends and neighbors, Methodist government . . .

Suddenly, in that icy cold night, she knew she was no longer a Methodist.

The thought shocked her. There she was, clinging to the arm of a Methodist minister, her husband. There she was, suddenly aware, in some epiphany, that she wasn't one of them; that she didn't share her husband's traditions.

And yet she did. Was she not proud of the way he stood up and pointed at wrongdoing, even among his neighbors and friends and colleagues?

What was Oregon doing to her?

He unlatched the door of their cottage and hastened to the hearth to add a log to the dying fire there. She lit a taper and settled into the stuffed sofa that had come by sea from heaven knows where. She had come to cherish such things, having grown utterly sick of the rude life, with its thousand deprivations.

He joined her, wanting to talk, she supposed.

"You were serious about leaving our church," he said.

"Yes, Jasper."

"Why?"

"I . . . no longer believe."

"Believe? In God?"

"In God, yes. He's mysterious and beautiful. But in this church, or any church."

It burst from her, almost before she had the will to bite it back. And afterward, she felt miserable. How must he feel? Had his ministry failed at its very center, in his own home? For that matter, how did she herself feel about leaving?

"Have I done anything—" he asked.

"Not wittingly."

"Then unwittingly."

"Oh, Jasper, I don't know. I just don't know. I'm not sure of anything any more. I'm not sure about civilizing Indians. I'm not sure there should be a mission here. I'm not sure our church is any better than . . . that of the Catholics. I'm not sure what I believe. I just don't know, Jasper."

She felt tears rise but fought them back. She hadn't meant to talk like this, leaking tears. He was right: she let sentiment rule her. She wanted to be a good wife, support her husband in his mission to the world, be his helpmeet, comfort him, hold him, encourage him. And now this, this insidious blackness, this doubt, this pain . . .

He sighed, settled back upon the brown fabric, and squeezed her hand. "You'll find your way," he said.

"I don't know, Jasper. Ever since—"

"If I had been then what I am now, I might have saved Damaris. I've changed too."

She could not stop the tears now, and buried her head in his shoulder. The odd thing was, she loved him more now than before. And she knew it was because he, too, was different after the passage of a year in the wilderness. This rude land had softened his intolerance of other views and that in itself had made him much more attractive to her.

She had married him less for love than for the good life she would enjoy as an eminent minister's wife and helpmeet. There had always been a certain nobility within him; a dignified and thoughtful response to life; a measuring and weighing quality that set him apart and elevated him.

But until recently they had lived secret and private lives, rarely baring their souls to each other or to their sons. She hadn't ever known his innermost passions, nor had he known hers. Not until this wild land had strained and stressed their bond, had she discovered the Jasper she hadn't known—and the Rose she hadn't known either.

"I guess we're on a voyage," she whispered. "I wonder where we're going. I hope you aren't too shocked at me."

He released her. "Yes, I am shocked."

"Jasper, you're a fine man, truly fine. I saw that tonight. I saw you stand for justice tonight, rebuke evil in front of the very people who were transgressing. I saw you stand alone, all alone, and unafraid. There'll be people on your side, but they weren't visible tonight. I just want you to know, whatever happens, just know that I think you're . . . sterling."

She felt his hands tighten on her again and draw her to him. Back East, he rarely touched her; his mind seemed lost in heavenly things, spirit rather than flesh, heaven rather than the world. She sighed and settled into his arms, content for the moment. But doubt crawled through her. What if their differences proved irreconcilable? Indeed, what then?

She snuggled into his shoulder, and then pulled back.

"I don't know what I expected," she said. "I thought Oregon would be some holy place where missionaries sacrificed to bring the Word to Indians. A place apart. Now I think the Indians are doomed and the missions have doomed them."

"Doomed?"

"Have you seen them, I mean really looked at them?"

He shook his head.

"They're angry. All these whites invading their homelands. Their game is scarce now. We've shot it away. They're confused. We promised them things we can't fulfill. They're being crowded out, and it's because of us. Us! We meant to do them good, give them civilization and faith, but we're only hurting them! That's why this mission should be ended. I hope it is. How naïve we were, supposing we held the keys. We don't even hold the keys to our own salvation."

He didn't reply for a while. Then, "When we started out here, I knew exactly what I believed and what I intended to achieve. Things were so clear back East. Now . . . I scarcely know what I should be doing. Rose . . . help me, for I'm floundering."

He seemed desperately uncomfortable, and there was little she could do to help him. They would each have to find their way, and hope Oregon would not betray them.

She held him in her arms.

48

FROM THE JOURNAL OF JOHN McLOUGHLIN

MARCH 12, 1844

These Americans! Just when I conclude that they are a barbarous and unscrupulous lot, they surprise me with affection. Within the fortnight I've had visits from two of them, each quietly offering support and encouragement.

The first visit was from that redoubtable Missouri frontiersman and lawyer, Jesse Applegate. It seems that he and the cohort of immigrants who arrived this past autumn are appalled at the state of affairs here, and mean to throw out the provisional government and start over. To this end they are putting up candidates for the May election, and hope to overthrow what has become known to all as the Methodist party.

What delighted me was Applegate's frank assertion, given to James Douglas and me in my office, that their first order of business, should their slate be elected, would be to throw out the notorious Article IV, which robs the company and me of the real property we've developed at Oregon City. The Methodists are all for the clause, of course, because the Reverend Mr. Alvin Waller has designs on the land and waterpower. That notorious clause was the work of the religion party, if such a term may be used here, along with the adventurer Garwood Reese, who insinuated himself into their affairs and is standing for office as one of the governing triumvirate.

But Applegate told us that unworkable three-headed executive will be pitched out as well, along with the funding of their government by subscription, and his colleagues will prevail in such matters, being a large majority.

Reese is running hard and holding great bonfire rallies, defaming us in the process, but Applegate has quietly gathered a majority without so much as a public meeting, or so he would have us believe. And I suspect he is entirely right. He appears to be one of those natural, levelheaded, fair-minded leaders of men who have sprung out of the great cauldron of American republicanism.

He tells me that the assistance provided by the Hudson's Bay Company has not been forgotten among most of them, and that the prejudices against the company and me that had once inflamed them back East proved to be unfounded. He cautioned that there are and will be haters of the company, but they are at present not a majority.

So here we are: some fair-minded Americans are gathering in my defense after all, and I am reminded how much I admire that obstreperous and impassioned race, even while I keep a wary eye on the whole lot. On the whole, we were impressed by Applegate and were buoyed by the interview.

The next to visit was that endlessly cheerful and hopelessly misplaced financier and visionary Abel Brownell, who is now the company's principal rival, having established a lively trade in Oregon City. I welcomed him warily and retired to my offices for private and frank talk. I was out of sorts, having suffered all week from rheumatism brought upon me by dank cold. Douglas was not with us on this occasion, having business elsewhere.

I have always regarded Brownell as a phenomenon. Just what an urbane Bostonian entrepreneur like himself is doing in unsettled Oregon still baffles me, and I'm not sure he knows himself. He toys with life; it is all for his amusement, and because nothing is serious, he succeeds admirably. And yet there is more to him than that. He talks intelligently of the wisdom of Emerson and Channing and once spent half an hour telling me about Brook Farm. Against my better judgment, I suspect he is a man of honor.

His business with me was, like Applegate's, to offer support. He meandered in one stormy March day, wrapped in a Hudson's Bay blanket capote, and I greeted him warily. The man, looking like a deacon at a mountaineer rendezvous, has, after all, eroded our sales, and as near as I can estimate now controls about twenty percent of the market for manufactured goods in Oregon. So I was surprised, nay, astonished, when he announced that the purpose of this visit was to undo the notorious Article IV if he could, and achieve some sort of justice on my behalf.

Now I swallowed all this cautiously. A man's private purpose is often different from the ulterior one. Not long ago an American government spy, Lieutenant Charles Wilkes was his name, arrived for a "social visit." Ostensibly he was making a Pacific Coast map for the American whaling industry; performing a bit of scientific work. But it was plain he was a Washington snoop, looking over the Oregon country to see what might be seen. I welcomed the man, publicly took him at his word, showed him what we were about, and didn't believe anything he said.

For the year or so that I've known Brownell, I've suspected he may also have very high connections in Washington City, but that suspicion has slowly faded, and during the recent visit I found myself abandoning the idea entirely. His purposes are as transparent as could be, and I found myself enjoying him.

He began, after I bade him to be seated and to take his time, by saying that title to all the Oregon City property, including the lots he had purchased from me, was clouded by the dispute between the Reverend Mr. Waller and me, and therefore the matter should be arbitrated by a panel of men on both sides, with the result binding on me as well as Waller.

In fact I liked the idea. I have few customers for my lots because the title to them is in dispute. My case is so strong that I have little doubt of the outcome.

So I welcomed Brownell's idea, knowing that any body of fair-minded men would find for me. I put Douglas onto it, and he has gathered a panel to look into the matter, and there it rests. Douglas himself is on it, defending our interests, and I could not ask for a better advocate. At last, I see the way to vindication, and ere long I'll be selling lots again, to great advantage because Oregon City is now the capital of the provisional government and is swiftly becoming the seat of commerce in Oregon as well. And for all of this I am grateful to Brownell.

I poured a little medicinal port for Brownell, knowing he enjoys a drink now and then; it is not something I do lightly, because of the pernicious effects of spirits, especially upon frontiersmen, where the straps and bolts of civilization have been loosened. And I took some myself for the rheumatism, which eased the torment a bit. He told me ruefully that Oregon is going to be dry; there is much sentiment for banning all ardent spirits. I think it would be a good thing; he and I differ.

He offered some intelligence that I find nettlesome, if not alarming. The most recent arrivals in Oregon have it in mind to exclude black and mulatto men from the area, and are devising harsh measures to enforce the interdiction. That would be an insidious blow to James Douglas, and one I will protest vehemently if it should come to pass. There are but two or three black men in Oregon, but I fear the proposal may also be aimed at our Kanakas, who have been so valuable to the Company. I'm afraid there is widespread sentiment for it among the Americans, both the newcomers and ones who came earlier.

I will fight it relentlessly. I confess I don't grasp the reasoning or the motives for such proscriptions, and mean to inquire about it. To be sure, Canada does not have slavery nor are Canadians familiar with Africans, so I am inexperienced in these matters and frankly puzzled by them.

I supposed that Brownell could throw little light upon the subject. He is something of a follower of the Unitarians and their broadly humane approach to religious and public polity, but all he could say was that the southernmost of his fellow Americans had a narrow and inhumane streak, and not a few northerners as well.

I relished the interview, and took occasion to praise Felicity Brownell for her efforts at educating young people in the most difficult circumstances. Brownell expressed some ritual pleasure at my compliment, but I discovered no heartiness in it. I vividly remember their arrival, shivering and destitute, and Brownell's sudden confession that he hadn't the faintest idea why he had dragged his family to Oregon; and her amazing reply: "you have made us savages, and savages we shall be," or words to that effect. Savages! The lady has done more to civilize Oregon than anyone else.

They are an odd match: she is industrious and ambitious and carries in her bosom a passion for life and achievement. He is a paradox. Who in Oregon is more successful, yet who possesses less of the ordinary business virtues, such as industry, prudence, and perseverence? Who has benefitted Oregon the most with his enterprise, yet who of all the Americans has spent more time at cards and gossip? And who of them is least stable, least resolute, most restless? Did I not hear him plan an immediate departure by ship, the day he arrived, having discovered that Oregon is not paradise? But Oregon will shape him, just as it shapes the rest of us.

49

Electra Reese watched Garwood collapse into a useless hulk. The May election had demolished him. The newcomers to Oregon had pitched out the Methodist faction and elected a slate less hostile to the Hudson's Bay Company. Save for old Doc Newell, the mountain man, no one in the provisional government had even been in Oregon six months ago.

No more campfire rallies. No money. Nothing left. She was stuck with a man who had no skills, no trade, no profession save for a little political glad-handing. Warren's useless brother. Stuck with a man who shunned labor, would not sully his hands with an axe or hoe or hammer or saw or plow or harness, would not clerk or sum accounts, and would not hire out.

She had never really thought about it before they left New York. Warren would practice law and earn a living. Garwood, well, he wanted to run for office, any office. Warren would make a living; it never occurred to her that Oregon might be a trap, offering a life of penury and misery. But that loomed now as the prospect for her life.

Her sole salvation was that she wasn't really married to him. Oregon teemed with woman-famished males, and maybe she could find one.

Still, he was the devil she knew. And she hadn't met anyone else who interested her. But time and money were running out. She had put away a few pass-the-hat dollars without his knowledge. Such was his enthusiasm that he would have spent every cent on the campaign. She supposed she could eke out a life for a few weeks . . . and start looking.

He didn't deserve sympathy, and she offered none.

One warm May day, a week after the election, when it was clear that he was vegetating, she confronted him as he sat, disheveled and unshaven, in the sole stuffed chair in their possession.

"What are you going to do for a living?" she asked.

He stared, not answering.

"You have no trade, and working for hire is beneath you."

"I'm a public man," he said.

"The public didn't think so."

He looked wounded, which was what she expected.

"I just rode the wrong horse. Next time, I'll ride another horse. The Methodists are done for."

"Next time is a year from now. How are you going to put food in your mouth and mine? Pay our rent?"

"I don't know."

"What do failed politicians do for a living?"

"Electra—"

"You'd better just answer that because you're going to have to feed yourself or beg on the streets."

"Just leave me alone."

"What are politicians good for?"

He summoned something from within, maybe even dignity. "We're a scorned breed but we serve. We galvanize public opinion. We see that justice is done. We expose evil. We fight for the people. We embody people's dreams, and help them achieve their dreams."

She laughed. "You fatten on the public purse, is what you do."

He retreated into sullen silence, but she didn't mind. She felt like slicing and mincing him, just to see whether he would bleed.

"I suppose I'll have to make a living to keep you alive," she said. "Unlike you, I'd do what's necessary, which is more than you'd do."

"Electra—"

"I could become a kept woman and keep us both in style. You could live off me and run for every office in Oregon."

"I almost won. Next time I'll win big, and then we'll see about the mighty Hudson's Bay Company and the British."

He seemed to shrink in his chair, and she felt some unaccustomed sympathy for him. Poor Garwood was lost outside of his world of factions and issues and speeches and coalitions.

"This is wilderness, Garwood. These are hardworking people. If you want to hold office, you'll need to impress them with your abilities. You still haven't answered me: what do you plan to do with yourself?"

"I'll apply for a position in the new government."

"Unpaid."

"I have to start somewhere."

"You'd better find a *means.* I don't have to stay here. We're not married. I can walk out any time, and I will."

"You'd do that to me," he said.

He was full of accusations and not interested in his future or hers. The election defeat had ruined him. He seemed to have no sense of self, save upon some platform or in front of some crowd, and if the crowd didn't like his message, he was helpless.

"Just one week ago," she said, "you were ready to fight wholesale for anything. *Fight* the Canadians. *Fight* for the United States. *Fight* for the whole Oregon country right up to Russian Alaska. *Fight* the monopoly. *Fight* foreign interests. *Fight* for the common man. In every speech, that was the word. Your whole campaign was about fighting . . . and now there's no fight in you."

He looked pained. "Not enough voters wanted to fight."

"I'm not talking about voters! I'm talking about you. Where's your fight? You yourself!"

He looked baffled. She was staring at a ruin. His jaw hung slack, his eyes were dulled. He had crumpled into his chair and slouched in it like an exhausted dog. It had been his idea to come to Oregon so that he might win elections and hold offices. He had talked of it endlessly to Warren, with bright facile arguments, employing Hall Kelley's literature, until Warren was persuaded, and then the two of them worked on her, painting Oregon as a heaven on earth, a chance to live a life other people only dreamed of living; fame, wealth, power, great landed estates, sublimely beautiful weather, healthy climate, lofty mountains, and shimmering seas.

"Would you like to go back East?" she asked.

He didn't reply. That was a maddening new trait. He sat inert, not caring what was said, not even avoiding the nettle when she thrust it.

She was swiftly gaining the perception that she was really alone; this man, her erstwhile brother-in-law and now something more intimate, might as well have died in the Columbia River, for all he was worth to her, himself, and the world.

The odd thing about this was something building in herself: she ached to rescue him. She ascribed it to her womanhood; hers was the nurturing sex. And she fought the impulse, knowing that the veil of ice she wore was her sole protection, and that under that armor of cool disinterest lay a fragile heart.

Her father had been sickly, spending his days in a rocking chair with an afghan over his knees, demanding constant attention from her mother, who was trying to run a boardinghouse to keep the family afloat. And he had been arrogant too, abusing her mother, belittling her, abrading her spirit.

Then he had died suddenly, and it had been a blessing. But his tirades and scorn had worn out her mother, who spent the next years in tears, hating herself, ashamed of her failure to heal her husband, and shuffling through life as if it were a prison sentence. Electra had absorbed it all and vowed never to care about anyone, especially a weak and mean man.

She did a strange thing she could not explain to herself. She walked over to Garwood, knelt before his chair, cupped his ruined face in the palm of her hands.

"I have strength enough for both of us," she said.

She was her mother's daughter.

And yet this wasn't the same. Garwood wasn't mean, nor had he ever abused her. He had collapsed, to be sure. He had come to Oregon for the same reasons that so many came to Oregon, believing in its magic, its ability to salvage a ruined life. But he had only brought his weaknesses with him, especially that odd vanity that forbade him to work at any trade for a living.

He had made a feeble attempt to establish a town site and sell lots, and if he had had any ability he might now be living comfortably on the sales. But that had been a doomed venture, and another reason to blame Hudson's Bay and begin yet another assay of politics as a means of escaping the futility of his own life.

She would need to keep him from politics, for politics was his escape into a surreal world. The rallying, the applause, the rhetoric, the flags and bunting, the cheers, the handshakes, the calculated positions, all that was Garwood's flight from his own fragile and futile self. She suspected most politicians were like that, and only those who were successful in other realms would make any real contribution to the commonweal.

She would, somehow, lead him away from politics. Oregon was rife with opportunity. People cried for amenities. She would help Garwood become, for the first time in his life, a productive citizen. And she wondered, again, why she was going to do it. Why didn't she just walk out?

She simply could not understand herself. Why did she stick with him? Why did she both despise him and nurture him? Why was she full of ambition, yet paralyzed? Why was every impulse within her at war? She sighed, miserably. Life was a mystery.

50

Electra found Garwood Reese a job as a surveyor's apprentice, but Reese flatly rejected it.

"I can't be seen doing that," he said. "It'd ruin my reputation."

"It's fifty cents a day and that would nearly support us."

"That's too little. I simply won't do that."

"Garwood . . ."

The very idea of toiling at demeaning work inflamed his senses. From a leader and public man to that? Never!

"George Washington was a surveyor. You could become one. Washington was appointed a county surveyor, and you could too. Oregon needs surveyors. You yourself planned to turn yourself into one, or hire one, to sell town lots. So here's your chance. You'll learn the business from this man and have a useful trade the rest of your life."

The tirade alarmed him. She actually meant it. She actually believed he should throw away everything he was, and tromp around in the mud taking orders from some tradesman.

"No, not now, not ever!" he exclaimed.

"Then feed yourself! You won't need to feed me because I won't be with you."

He studied her. She meant it. She had been telling him for days that they would soon be starving and unable to pay the rent for their handsome rooms overlooking the falls.

He arose, a picture of dignity, and smiled. "Electra, the world is made up of winners and losers. The losers are content to toil like mules and never question what life is about. The winners see opportunity and grasp it."

She glared at him, her lips pressed into a thin hard line.

"The secret of life is to have friends and call on them in moments of need," he said. "I have innumerable friends. Allies. Connections. People who have received favors from me. The Mission Party is not dead. There are powerful men, like George Abernethy, who'd be glad to help a man who gave voice and power to their ideals. I've only to ask, and they'll find some office for me to fulfill. I was thinking of public notary or clerk, myself, with a remuneration that would suffice until the next campaign."

She plainly didn't like what she was hearing. "I wish you'd forget politics, influence, connections, and public positions," she said.

"Forget it? That's my life's work!"

"Work," she said, and laughed ribaldly.

"This is an unpleasant scene," he said.

She laughed again.

His response was to depart. He brushed his worn trousers, blacked his hightop shoes, buttoned his one clean stock, clambered into his plum-colored frock coat, wiped his high-domed face clean, put a spring in his gait, put a shine in his eye, and remembered the glad handshake and the hearty hello. Once outside, in a glowing May morning, he felt better. Oregon's blooms were rioting in every yard. Even the crudest shanties of the settlers sat in carpets of saucy color.

He would talk to Abernethy. The man had come a long way, from Methodist roustabout to store clerk to businessman to mill operator. He was a leader of the Mission Party, a voice for the total elimination of British influence in Oregon, and an old friend. Like so many who had come west charged with missionary zeal to convert the Indians, he had discovered another calling, and was now shaping Oregon into a great center of commerce.

He found Abernethy at the Methodist store, as always.

"George, my old friend, we've fought many a battle against McLoughlin together, and now I've come for a favor. A public position."

Abernethy waited, a faint smile on his square florid face. "Well, Garwood, what can you do?"

"Anything I'm appointed to do."

"But we lost. That's not in my power. Why don't you go talk to Peter Burnett? He's the gray eminence behind the new government."

"Would you give me a letter?"

"Certainly. What shall I say?"

"That I'm a capable leader and officer."

"For what position?"

Reese shrugged. "I don't know what offices they will create."

"Then I'll recommend you on your public character," Abernethy said, a faint amusement building about his mouth. He found a sheet of foolscap, a quill, and set to work, finally blotting the sheet.

"If I can't hold office, I'd like to start a newspaper," Reese said. "A fine thundering sheet. I know I could sway the run of men. Perhaps the party could come up with the means."

Abernethy shook his head. "Dream on," he said.

Reese had indeed dreamed about it, spending two weeks in his chair, under an afghan, dreaming about a newspaper, a way to campaign endlessly between elections. But the nearest press and fonts and paper and ink were fifteen hundred miles away in Missouri. And even if he had the physical means, he doubted he could find enough advertisers and subscribers to pay the way. Almost no one in Oregon had cash. Who would pay for a copy, much less a subscription? And there were scarcely half a dozen firms in Oregon that might advertise. Still he dreamed. Fiery editorials, great exposés, finely wrought barbs, a drumbeat against the British and the company, week after week.

Abernethy handed the recommendation to him. "Good luck," he said. "I don't suppose you'd want to work for me. I need mill men."

Reese laughed, treating it as a fine joke between old colleagues, and slapped Abernethy on the back.

He headed out to Burnett's place for another conference. Burnett was a self-taught lawyer who had uprooted his family and brought them all west, galvanized by a vision of health and wealth, a salubrious climate and pots of gold at the end of every rainbow. He and Applegate and others now controlled the provisional government and had swiftly undone most of the earlier provisions, including the article depriving McLoughlin of his Oregon City town site and supporting the Methodists in all their rival claims. They had made Oregon City the seat of government, which was all the more convenient. They had thrown out the governing triumvirate too, and were swiftly enacting other reforms.

Reese had thundered against these very men, but there was a certain brotherhood among politicians, and it existed because losers became winners and winners became losers, and the outs and ins needed each other. There were courtesies and rituals, considerations of prudence, and endless building of coalitions that were part of all political calculus. Now Reese was counting on that.

He found Burnett in his law office, which occupied the front of a white-washed Oregon City house. The rear sheltered his family. Some of the structures in Oregon City were dirt-floored one-room log cabins, but more and more of them were whitewashed frame affairs, built with the lumber pouring from the mills.

"Ah, Garwood!"

Burnett rose from his creaking swivel chair to meet his old rival, shake hands, and settle his visitor in the sole chair reserved for clients.

They talked of politics, the new government's broom, the hope of bringing the whole of Oregon into the United States. They avoided the differences between them, for this was a social occasion.

"And what brings you here this fine spring day, Garwood?"

"I am applying for a position in the provisional government."

A pair of bushy eyebrows rose and lowered. "Now that's a novelty," Burnett said. "Why? What have you in mind?"

Reese was determined not to mention need; never admit to need or poverty or starvation. "I'm a public man, experienced in public affairs, and I thought perhaps your people might put me to good use in some spot where I can be of service to the people of Oregon."

Burnett grinned, almost wolfishly. In fact, the grin affronted Reese.

"Why, Garwood, perhaps you've come at the right moment," Burnett said. "We might have a position for you. In fact, I think it'd be the most important position in the government. A position that could provide a fine income for the right person . . ."

Reese could scarcely believe his good fortune. "Tell me about it," he said.

"The new government's making some changes," Burnett continued. "You know, one of the troubles with the former one that, ah, the Mission people put together, was the funding. Voluntary subscriptions!" He chuckled. "Now, of course, when the government is merely provisional, and Oregon isn't even a part of the United States, one can understand that cautious approach. But, alas, governments need money. This government needs cash, not promises. Money to fund a justice system, control crime, adjudicate land disputes, and of course, maintain a militia against Indian uprisings."

Reese nodded. The Mission people wanted no part of taxes; who could afford them anyway? There was scarcely a dollar in cash in the whole of Oregon.

"Well, we've just enacted some tax legislation, and it provides that people can pay in kind—wheat, for example—if they lack cash. Cash, wheat, hides, anything that can be sold to raise monies. We've put a tax on livestock, mills, town property, carriages, and clocks. And we'll have a fifty-cent poll tax. If a man wants to vote, he can support his government. And here's where you come in. We've been looking for someone to collect the taxes. For a percentage, of course. Who better than you, with your golden tongue and persuasive ways? The holder of this most important office of tax collector will get ten percent of whatever he brings to our coffers."

Garwood Reese sat erect in his chair, doing political calculations upon his mental abacus, summing up the favors any tax collector could do for friends.

"Yes," he said. "I'll take it."

51

John McLoughlin was not taking the news well, but then again, James Douglas had not expected him to. So far as the chief factor was concerned, possession of the Oregon City town site and waterpower site was indisputable. He was there first, properly claimed it, defended it, and surveyed it.

But Douglas had run into fierce opposition during the arbitration. Those Americans supporting Reverend Mr. Waller and George Abernethy had bleated that the property was theirs and they would not yield an inch. For days a deadlock had prevented resolution. But at last some of the Americans yielded a bit; only the most obsessed of anti-British men could deny that McLoughlin had a valid claim, but the retreat was grudging and costly.

The compromise painfully hammered out by both sides did acknowledge that McLoughlin had the prior and best claim, and his right to the mill site and town site was sustained. But for a brutal price. The Methodists would get fourteen lots and five hundred dollars as their price for quitting the claim.

McLoughlin sat in his chair, shocked. "You have bound me," he said.

"Yes, I thought it best for your sake to give you one good fever and have done with it."

Douglas knew that the chief factor would accede anyway. He would pay the cash and it would all be over . . . for the time being. And if the issue came up again, the arbitration would strengthen McLoughlin's case. Or the company's case. The chief factor had never made clear whether the town site and mills were his own ventures or the company's and Douglas chose not to ask.

The doctor immediately drafted a note and handed it to Douglas. "Let it be over, then. If you say I've won, then I've won. But it's an odd victory."

Douglas pocketed it. Waller had not done badly for a blatant claim-jumper. He wondered how the reverend squared his cupidity with his religion. But then

again, so many Americans were peculiar that way. When religion got in the
way of avarice or other appetites, religious scruple usually lost.

"There's another matter we need to discuss. It appears that I may be driven
from Oregon," Douglas said, a certain metallic tone in his voice.

"You? How can that be?"

"It seems I'm the wrong color."

"So they drafted the law after all."

Douglas nodded. "It provides that there shall be no slavery in Oregon, and
it also provides that no one with black blood can live here."

"Good God, can they do that?"

Douglas shrugged. "The new law has to be ratified in the next election.
But they've started to circulate the new organic law in Oregon City, and I've
read it. Blacks and mulattos will be flogged every six months until they quit
the territory."

McLoughlin growled. "That won't apply to you. You're a Canadian; a
magistrate of Canada, justice of the peace . . . This doesn't apply."

Douglas smiled wryly. "They may think it does. This isn't Canada."

"This is barbaric," McLoughlin said.

Douglas said nothing, as usual. He considered the Americans worse than
barbaric; he considered them illiterate ruffians for the most part, and vastly
inferior people. He had yet to meet one who could even remotely match his
own erudition, civility, or understanding of the way the world worked. He
knew it was a conceit, but he knew it was entirely valid. Not even his superior,
John McLoughlin, could come close.

But of all this he said nothing. It was not his wont to reveal any of his
true feelings. Flog him! He laughed at the idea. He could, in Canadian proceedings, try them for whatever misdemeanor they committed in all of Oregon,
so long as it was disputed territory, for the Crown had granted the company
that power.

And that turned his mind to another and more delicate matter, which he
was loath to explore although he had little choice. Governor Simpson and the
directors of the company were worried about McLoughlin, and had opened a
private correspondence with Douglas about the matter, knowing he would keep
the correspondence secret.

McLoughlin's recent letters, as well as his conduct, had given them pause.
On the one hand, the chief factor still railed at Simpson for the failure to bring
his son's murderers to justice and the diatribes had become tiresome; on the
other, the chief factor had been wilfully ignoring the governor's instructions,
as well as those of the directors in London. What about all this?

Nor was that all. The possibility of war with the United States was looming
if the boundary question could not be arbitrated, and Her Majesty's foreign
office was wondering just where McLoughlin's loyalties lay. Was he still a loyal

subject of the Crown? And if so, how could one explain his generous support of the United States settlers, even to the point of endangering the company?

And why was McLoughlin defying the directors? Had he not been ordered to close down the store in Mexican Yerba Buena, and had failed to take the step? Had he not been directed to shut down the coastal forts stretching clear up into Russian Alaska, and replace them with the trading steamer? He had not even begun to do so, and why?

Was the man becoming unhinged? Was he so enamored of the empire he had built that he could not endure the change that was being forced upon him by the decline of the fur trade? His world was coming to an end, and yet he was not adjusting to it, and the company's fortunes were declining.

And so they wanted information about the old man; anything that might help them draw conclusions, take actions, for the sake of the company and Britannia.

Douglas did not like the assignment but he would pursue it with his usual skill and discretion. He liked McLoughlin. They had gotten along cordially. But now, indeed, the old man seemed erratic, even unbalanced. And the burden had fallen on Douglas to assess and perhaps resist the very man whose genius had put a twenty percent annual dividend into the pockets of the directors year after year.

"I hear some of the Americans are settling north of the Columbia," he began, ever so gently.

"That is true," McLoughlin growled. "I can't legally stay them because the disputed territory runs to Alaska. But I do what I can to keep them south of the river. Even bribe them a bit, with offers of credit at the store. They get no credit if they head north."

"But it's not working, John. There's been an exodus up to the Nisqually area."

The chief factor sighed. "The best land's claimed to the south of us. They know there's plenty more up north, around Puget Sound. I tell them it's rockier and less suited for crops, but it doesn't stop them. They know about our plantations there."

"Where do you think the border will run?"

"The Columbia if we can help it; the forty-ninth parallel if we can't."

"I suppose we could stop offering credit to Americans," Douglas said.

"And then what? We'd have starving multitudes hammering at our gates!" The doctor pinioned Douglas with a glare. "I don't know what to do. I've lent so much they could ruin me. Yet if I don't, I imperil this post and everything we've built, and future profit as well.

"God knows, we can't stop the migration but we can steer it, shape it to our ends, get tough when we must. And of course plunge right into their councils of government and let them know our view. I shall not suffer their imposts and rules in silence, not as long as I'm a subject of the Crown, and the company is England's."

Douglas noted all that. He didn't really doubt McLoughlin's loyalty, though some in London certainly did. The good doctor was trapped between his deeply felt allegiances and his humanity; between his past accomplishments and the changing future.

Douglas and Ogden knew something that McLoughlin didn't; that the Royal Navy would be examining the area, gathering intelligence, preparing for war against the Americans. The foreign office would not trust McLoughlin with the news, fearing his sensibilities had drifted too far toward the American settlers.

"What about Yerba Buena?" Douglas asked casually.

"Well, what about it!"

"I was just wondering if the governor's directives were now being implemented."

"No," the doctor growled. "He doesn't know what he's talking about. William Rae's building the business; I get good reports." Rae was McLoughlin's son-in-law, an habitual drunkard, depressive, unstable, and the reason George Simpson wanted to shut down the store.

"I see," said Douglas. He would report the conversation, but not because he took any pleasure in it.

"And as for that lunatic plan to shut down the coastal forts and replace them with a wood-eater that requires two days of chopping trees for every day it sails, well, Simpson doesn't know what he's up to. Imagine, shutting down profitable posts! Imagine cutting loose dozens of lifetime employees!"

Douglas nodded and smiled. That, too, would be reported to the governor. The stark fact was that McLoughlin had slipped into insubordination. Business at those posts had declined radically. Closing the posts made sense, but the old man just couldn't surrender what he had struggled so hard to build.

Douglas supposed he'd probed enough for one session. Any more and the doctor might begin to wonder. He retreated from the office, trying to assess just where McLoughlin stood, and what to report to Simpson and the directors.

He understood London's view perfectly. From their perspective, they could see what John McLoughlin couldn't or would not: the fur trade was dead. The beaver hat had vanished and the silk hat had replaced it. Beaver had been trapped out, clear across North America. And Yank coastal traders were buying pelts on better terms than Hudson's Bay could offer.

The company could survive as a merchant and agricultural operation, but not as a fur empire. And even that was threatened by the flood of Americans who mysteriously had waltzed over their own frontier to settle in lands coveted by the Crown. He and Ogden knew something that McLoughlin didn't: if a showdown came, England would fight.

Douglas considered himself a loyal subordinate in his own way. He would treat Dr. McLoughlin with utmost kindness in his report to Simpson and the directors. But there were some things that had to be said and could not be avoided. McLoughlin had escaped harness.

And there was his own future to consider. He would, someday soon, be knighted by the queen: Sir James Douglas. That was in the works. He would, someday soon, be chief factor, and the de facto ruler of half of Canada. That, too, was in the works. And he would, someday, possess a luster brighter than any white man in North America.

But for Dr. McLoughlin's future, he could only sorrow.

52

The green stamp bore a likeness, in profile, of the young monarch of England, Wales, Scotland, Ireland, and empress of much of the world. The letter, not at all bedraggled for its endless journey, had been borne by a Hudson's Bay courier to John O'Malley at the store in Oregon City. It had come across the Atlantic to York Factory, Hudson's Bay, on a supply ship, and then carried in the company's express pouch over a thousand miles of wilderness to Fort Vancouver. And then to John O'Malley.

He saw, in the corner, the name of the sender: William Devon Burke, the father of Mary Kate. It was addressed to him, John O'Malley, Fort Vancouver, Oregon, Canada, all in an angular, orderly copperplate that O'Malley suspected was not his father-in-law's own hand.

He held it a moment, savoring the suspense, the surprise, but also girding himself for hard news, hurt, pain, or grief. This was the first contact since he and Mary Kate had left Erin nearly three years earlier. In that space of time people were born, people sickened, people died.

This had not come with the vanguard of the 1844 immigrants, just then arriving in Oregon in mild and sunny weather, though the Americans had brought considerable mail with them from Missouri, much of it lying in his store for settlers to pick up.

No, this letter had followed the course of empire, traveling in British vessels, in British pouches from the British Isles.

Stiffened at last against bad news, he slit the letter open with a knife and withdrew the single sheet within. It was dated July 24, 1844.

"My beloved John and Mary Kate," it began. "How we yearned of news from you, and then your letter came, telling us of your good fortune and health and happiness and a grandson. And with it the voucher drawn against the Hudson's Bay Company. We rejoiced in your news.

"But it is my sad duty to report that my beloved wife and Mary Kate's beloved mother left this world on September 27, 1843, regretting that she could not one last time behold you both. My sister, your aunt Martha, is also with God, having suffered too long from consumption. A blessing it was for that pain-racked body, though we grieve her loss. She died in January of 1843.

"You have sent for Betsy, Agnes, and Liam. The voucher was almost enough, and I am able to spare a little for the journey. Their bark, a British clipper called *Endurance,* leaves in a fortnight from Waterford harbor, bound for Buenos Aires and Valparaiso, but there they must find passage north to Oregon. Look for them early next year. This letter should go faster, God willing; by Dublin steamer to Liverpool, and across to Hudson's Bay.

"I pray this finds you content and that you are in good health, and the wee Oregon Patrick, what a grand name for such a lad, is growing by leaps, and that he now has a brother or sister or two. We yearn for news. Do not forget us, and be sure to send us news of the arrival of Betsy, Agnes, and Liam. I can hardly bear to see them go across the misty sea, but it is best for them, and for us, and it will be easier to put food in our mouths when they are with you. Things are difficult here, and the world does not know the half of it.

"Your loving father . . ."

Coming! Mary Kate would no longer be so alone! There would be a lad and lasses at their table, laughter, the bright sweet days of youth to share.

He closed the store and pierced into a smoky afternoon, with the pungence of burning leaves on the air, and hastened up the hill, his heart wild and joyous. This precious letter, which he carried with all the reverence accorded the Host, would both sadden and brighten her, return her to the world of the living, and out of the shadows where she had dwelled for so many months, wasting into someone he barely recognized.

But as he climbed the steep path, he found himself worrying. She had been close to her mother. By the time he reached his cottage, he knew this would be painful, but there was no help for it.

He entered, found her napping, the baby in his crib, and sat down on the tick beside her.

"See, love, what is come from across the sea."

She opened her dark and smoky eyes, glanced at the letter, and sat up.

"It is from your father, Mary Kate."

"Is the news . . . good?"

"No, not all of it."

She stared accusingly at the letter but did not take it. "Read it," she said.

She could read, at least enough to parse her father's words. But she didn't want to struggle with them, especially if the news was bad. He sighed, not wanting to read, not wanting his voice to convey the bad news. He wanted her eyes to see it on the paper.

He pulled the soft white sheet, folded twice, from its envelope, and read.

"... left this world on September twenty-seventh ..."

"Oh, Mama," she said. "And I was not there."

He read the rest, slowly, and repeated it. The baby stirred but did not awaken. She sat pensively.

"The lung fever took her. She was only forty-one, John. And now I will never see her again. So far away ..."

O'Malley thought she would weep, but she didn't. All she did was sit there and repeat the dirge: so far away, so far away, so far away. The distances seemed larger and more important to her than the death.

"And my father will go before I see him. He will go, and I will be here across the sea, and I will not see him or pray with him when his time comes, or hold his hand ..."

"We can go back soon, Mary Kate. Soon enough the store will pay for passage. A long visit."

She shuddered. He let her grieve and did not try to cheer her with the news that three of her siblings were even then at sea, somewhere off the coast of South America. That realization would bloom in her in good time. Let her grieve now.

"If only I could stand at her grave now," she said. "But I never will. We were separated forever."

He wished she would weep. He would have welcomed tears instead of her strange retreat from feeling.

"Mary Kate, let us have masses said for the dead. And let us rejoice that Betsy and Agnes and Liam are even now coming toward us, day by day."

"Yes, please speak to Father."

"I will do so. Tomorrow he comes through, and I will tell him. We will have words said for the souls of your mother and your aunt, and that will comfort us both."

The baby was awake now, whimpering, but she did nothing. O'Malley could not endure the neglect, and lifted the child. He needed a change.

"Ah, little boy, you have lost a grandma, and a great-aunt, and your good sweet mother grieves. Come along now, and maybe even a storekeeper like me can clean you up."

He managed, somehow, to perform the unaccustomed task, and handed the child to her. She accepted the baby absently, scarcely aware of him.

"Mary Kate, I think the boy wants a meal."

"Yes," she said.

"I must go back to work. You keep the letter. Read it again and get all the news. Soon you will not be alone."

"Across the sea," she said.

He left the house and plunged into an autumnal warmth, disturbed. Her homesickness had only worsened. Could it be that some people could not put roots down in a new place, but withered away unless they were restored to the one and only place of their heart?

He worried his way down the steep hill to the store, opened it, and fretted away the rest of the day, trying to think of his mother-in-law, and barely able to remember her face or her ways.

He locked after six, and made his way up the steps in autumnal dusk and the sudden premonitory chill of the season.

He dreaded what he would find in the whitewashed cottage with the lilacs growing beside it. But when he entered, she greeted him warmly, with life in her eyes as if she had become the colleen of old.

"Ah, it is you," she said. "See how the boy walks!"

Indeed, Oregon Patrick O'Malley was toddling around, while her glowing eyes tracked the child.

He kissed her intuitively, not having done that for months, and she laughed. He had an inkling that her mind had turned from loss to the arrival of three of her own.

He had not heard her laugh for so long, and her laughter sounded like chimes and church bells to him.

"How far are they, do you suppose?" she asked.

So her thoughts were running that direction after all. "Why, he wrote they're on a clipper. That's a fast ship! Have you seen a clipper, love? A slim hull and a cloud of sail above it, racing ahead even in still air, breathless to get where it is going."

"They left in July, John. Where do you think?"

"Well, I suppose they have rounded the Horn now, and maybe they are anchoring in Valparaiso. Yes, I would say so. Ninety days for that. Those clippers go twelve or fifteen knots in a good wind. Yes, they are on the west coast of South America now, probably waiting for some captain to take them to the Sandwich Islands, and then here. Who knows, maybe even Devers Cushing!"

"Is Valparaiso dangerous, John?"

"Any port is. How old is Liam?"

"Oh!" She did some swift calculating. "Eighteen, almost nineteen now. Agnes is just seventeen and Betsy fifteen."

"He'll be a steady boy and see to their safety, Mary Kate. Do not fret."

"When do you think?"

"Four more months. Maybe five. February or March, if they make good connections."

"And we will make the house bigger?"

He laughed. "Bigger it will be, my love."

"And can we bring others too?"

"Mary Kate, we will not stop until we have brought half of Clonmel here."

She kissed him, and again.

1845

53

FORT VANCOUVER
OFFICE OF CHIEF FACTOR

2 JANUARY, 1845
THE HONOURABLE GOVERNORS
HUDSON'S BAY HOUSE
NOS. 3 AND 4 FENCHURCH STREET
LONDON

My lords,

It is my pleasure to report to you the state of affairs in Oregon at the beginning of the new year, as I regularly do. Enclosed are the annual ledgers.

The Company continues to do a profitable business in the Pacific Northwest, though this is due more to its mercantile and agricultural enterprises than to its fur business, which has declined sharply.

The most important event of 1844 was the arrival of 1400 more Americans in the Willamette Valley, effectively doubling its population. The number of residents loyal to the Company and Crown are now but a handful compared to the numerous Americans, and this is swiftly altering the nature of affairs here.

War is in the air, at least among those of more excitable temperament, though I resist it stoutly. The most urgent of our tasks here is to secure the post against the American threat. Some of them do not recognize our long-standing patents upon land here, and have laid claim to fields and orchards to the very gates of the fort. These I have forcibly evicted, but have taken pains to make our case to the American settlers, and have found them generally sympathetic.

Nonetheless, their sheer numerical dominance has altered the mood here. I am taking steps to increase our safety by building a bastion in the northwest corner of the fort, repairing pickets, and improving our means to combat fire. This has caused a stir among the Americans, who think we are preparing for war, but I assure them we are preparing only to defend the post and its valuables against outlaw depredation.

If Fort Vancouver is to be defended, and if Oregon north of the Columbia is to fall to the Crown through arbitration, then I implore the governors to reinforce our numbers here and give me the means to remain a presence; else we shall be overwhelmed, and all too soon. The security of the post, along with its business, is now a matter of grave concern.

This latest wave of immigration swept out the trail, and fell into the same error as the previous waves, ruining themselves in the narrows and rapids and falls of the unnavigable stretches of the Columbia. We had no choice, for humane and other reasons, but to offer them a helping hand, and at considerable expense I caused my employees to pull the Americans off the banks of the river and bring them to the valley in our bateaux.

Most of these people were genuinely grateful, as before, but most of them were destitute and wished to purchase the most basic means of survival at our stores, and on credit. I could not refuse them credit; indeed, their temper is to storm the fort if we do not accommodate their needs, since our stores alone are what stand between them and death, and desperate men will do what they must.

They have scattered through the Willamette Valley, as the previous immigrants have done, straining housing and taxing food supplies to the utmost. There is not a bolt of cloth to be had in Oregon, and people are patching their rags because there is no other remedy. A number of them, finding the best land of the valley taken up, have decided to head north and farm lands around Puget Sound in the vicinity of Fort Nisqually.

This I have energetically opposed, trying to channel them south of the Columbia so they will not be a disruptive element when the boundary is at last drawn. But I have not been entirely successful, for they have as much right to put down roots in all of Oregon as do we, and they are well aware of it.

So we have plunged into a time of acute change, and only swift action can preserve the security of the Company, protect its investment, and prevent the Crown from losing valuable lands.

We have lost some trade to the Americans, whose mercantile instincts are formidable. But we still dominate commerce in all ways. Our inventories have been built upon practical experience and planning, and we are usually able to supply a want, whereas the American merchants sell a miscellany and are usually unable to fill a need. They depend on the scourings of the Pacific for replenishment, while our orderly planning keeps shelves stocked with desirables that command premium prices. But this will not last, and I expect the Americans to begin importing a broad variety of iron and tinware, fabric, and other necessaries from their eastern states within the next year or so.

This vast influx of Americans has compelled me to tap our stores a year early, and there is urgent need to replenish them as swiftly as you can manage. This ought not to be regarded as a bad thing: these brisk sales will translate into splendid profits as fast as the American debt to us is liquidated.

I am currently carrying about $32,000, American, of debt. Some few have paid us off, but most will be unable to do so until they have broken ground, raised a crop, built adequate shelter, and advanced beyond the frontier stage of mere survival. This is, admittedly, a large and dangerous balance on our ledgers but it is my belief that it will be properly liquidated over time, at good profit.

It also is good business. We have made friends, sold goods at profit, and fostered a climate in which our presence is welcome, except among the hardest-minded few who are offended that anyone but an American lives in Oregon. It is these intractables I worry about: Vancouver is a wooden post and vulnerable to the incendiary passions of any who may wish us harm.

So far, we have steered entirely clear of their provisional government, and I know of no Canadian who has taken the oath, which requires allegiance to the United States. However, there is talk of changing the oath so that we may, in good conscience, as subjects of the Crown, swear fealty to the provisional government so long as it does not violate our prior loyalties. I am leaning toward it, because the Company would thus establish its legitimacy, and its land and property claims would be protected by the joint government until such time as a boundary settlement can be made.

I remain sanguine that the Columbia will divide the nations, though there is increasing talk among our adversaries of claiming the whole of Oregon, clear up to 54 degrees and 40 minutes north, the Alaska line. It has become a byword in their politics, but I think it will come to nothing. They know we have an excellent and prior claim that England will defend sedulously, and I don't think it is worth a war to them. Nonetheless, I certainly urge upon the Company, and the Foreign Office, a much larger Crown presence here, else all might be lost to us. Numbers count, and we are losing ground in that respect.

The Company is regularly accused by the Americans of stirring the Indians against them, an accusation I deny at every opportunity, pointing out that we have gone out of our way to assure the various chiefs and headmen that the settlers mean them no harm. But the tribesmen complain of loss of game, and of being excluded from large tracts, and this malcontent is becoming increasingly dangerous to all white men, British and American alike. The emigrants bring with them various diseases which are mild enough among white men, but fatal to red men, and the epidemics raging through the tribes, killing so many, are stirring future trouble, I fear.

It is true that several of the tribes are restless, seeing their hunting grounds and traditional homelands besieged by white men. They send delegations to me, demanding that the Company remove these Americans. I tell them it is not in my power to do so; they are a different nation. But I assure them that if they conduct themselves peaceably, so will the Americans. Privately, I am not sure of that.

Some of the Americans abuse the tribesmen, but the main problem is indifference. The Indians are invisible to them, and the settlers give no consideration to their hungers and needs and rights. How long I can allay serious Indian trouble I don't know, but danger looms ever closer in spite of my constant diplomatic efforts.

I am particularly worried about the Cayuse tribe, an unreliable and sometimes treacherous band that threatens the safety of the Presbyterian mission at Waiilatpu. I have steadily urged the Whitmans to abandon their mission for the time being and find refuge in the fort, but they rarely heed my warnings. I have sternly told the Cayuses that if any harm should befall the mission, the wrath of the Company should befall them, and the trading windows would be sealed shut against them.

I am proceeding with caution toward the dissolution of our coastal forts, feeling that their stout presence serves to anchor the Crown's claim to Oregon (and would provide naval depots and anchorages as well if war should erupt) and that the steamship intended to replace them is not the most efficient or economical means of collecting peltries or selling trade items.

If this pace is slower than what the governors expect, it is because I am acting from prudence. That is true as well of the store in Mexican Yerba Buena, which now approaches profitability. But if in time these prove to be uneconomic, they will be shuttered as directed.

James Douglas proceeds apace building the new Fort Victoria headquarters at the southern tip of Vancouver Island, and shuttles between here and there regularly. It will be ready when and if the HBC presence on the Columbia becomes untenable. I am confident that it will serve the Company for decades.

But I trust that the present post will not be abandoned by the Company. There are pounds and pence to be made here in commerce with the settlers. I will be working toward an accommodation with the provisional government to assure our property and trading rights. The vexed question of the Oregon City waterpower claim and town site was arbitrated this past year, generally in our favor, and the American claimants have quit. One future difficulty remains: under American law, companies may not claim land; only individuals can.

In that case I may, to clarify matters, purchase the Oregon City claims to put them in my own name, though I would expect them to remain, in actuality, Company property. I hope to conclude that matter this winter, after further discussions with the provisional government.

Your Ob't and Humble Sv't,
Jno McLoughlin

54

Oh, ho! They thought they had pulled one on old Reese, but he knew better. He'd pulled one on them! They thought that the tax collector would be the most shunned man in Oregon, but he saw it differently, and set out to mend his fortunes.

In short order he acquired a pair of high-steppers, a surrey, and a collection of empty bushel baskets, and then he set out, first to the most distant cabins where he could perfect his arts.

He knew he would pull into a sorry yard, discover a one-room log cabin, some cleared land, a lean family wearing rags and wrestling with wilderness. Not a likely prospect for a tax collector. But that didn't faze him.

He would try to catch them at mealtime and get himself invited to the table. But in any case, he would track down the man of the house, usually out in the fields where he was pulling rocks, breaking ground, and preparing for spring planting.

On this February day, it went like this when he approached a ruddy blond man chopping out a stump:

"I'm Garwood Reese, friend. Tax collector."

"Tax collector, eh! Well, you just turn around and be on your way. I don't have a cent for taxes, don't recognize the government because it ain't a real government, and you can't squeeze blood from a turnip."

"Ah, indeed, my friend. Actually, the government's taxing only a few items, like carriages and clocks and livestock, and there's a poll tax of fifty cents if you want to vote. You want a say in the government, then you've got to support it."

"Don't know what it's good for."

"Ah, now there I have you, friend. It's good for your land. It's going to defend your claim against jumpers and scoundrels, and put the strong arm of the law on 'em. How'd you like to be booted out of here by a claim-jumper? That's what the government's for, even if it's a fatherless mongrel that'll disappear soon as we become a territory of the good old United States."

"And how'm I supposed to pay a poll tax or a tax on the clock? I'm in debt and I'll be blessed if I can come up with a red cent."

"Wheat. We're taking wheat. I didn't catch your name."

"Zebulon Grange. I came out in the rush of 'forty-three. Been here over a year and it feels like ten. This Oregon isn't what it was made out to be. I got sold a bill of goods."

"Mr. Grange, it's slow going, I can see that. Nonetheless, you've got some property that is taxable. A seven-day clock in there?"

"There is, but you're not going to tax it."

"Well, all right. Your first business is to put food in mouths, get more fields opened up, build some more rooms on your cabin. Looks like you've got half a dozen mouths to feed. So, I'm not going to tax your clock, and not your horse and buggy either. We'll just let that go. But if you can spare one bushel of wheat—a real United States bushel too, not one of those oversized Imperial bushels that Hudson's Bay uses to euchre Yanks—just one bushel, I'll mark you up as paid, and your poll tax paid too."

"Well . . ."

"I see the granary there; I've a bushel basket right here. We can fill up the basket and I'll give you a receipt, and mark you paid, and we won't even talk about that clock and buggy, all right?"

"A bushel makes a lot of bread, tax collector."

"Oh, how well I know. I'm Reese, by the way. Garwood Reese."

"Heard the name. You with the Mission Party that got whomped last year."

"Oh, that was the beginning of my education, Mr. Grange. What I learned was that Hudson's Bay controls everything here. Everything, including elections! Now I'm just a tax collector, bottom rung of the government, and trying to help all the hard-put folks and keep those scalawags from spending money they shouldn't have."

"What else they taxing?"

"Town lots, but that won't affect you. That's how I'm going to put the heat to old McLoughlin and Hudson's Bay. Every town lot they got, it's taxable, and the more the monopoly pays the taxes, the less we have to get from struggling Americans like you. But we have to get 'em to pay.

"You know something, Mr. Grange? So far, that high-and-mighty McLoughlin hasn't paid a cent. Not one shilling. If they did, I wouldn't have to pester good solid people like you to keep this government going. But someday the good citizens of Oregon, they're going to rise up and pitch out the foreigners, and I'll be leading the pack, believe me. One bushel of wheat, that's all you need to do. Except maybe vote against the monopoly next time."

"Well, all right. It's good wheat, and there's hard work in it, but if it helps me with my claim, maybe it's all right."

"Of course it's all right. Now, Mr. Grange, if things get worse before they get better, you just count on Garwood Reese not to look too closely at that horse or that clock, all right?"

"Well, you sure understand how it is."

"I sure do," Reese said.

He plucked up a bushel and Grange filled it with wheat, exactly level and not a grain more, and Reese wrote out a fancy tax receipt. That's how it would go that day. Later, he would sell the wheat to the milling company, deduct his ten percent, and turn over the balance to the provisional government head-quartered in Oregon City.

No one minded very much, and though he occasionally ran into walls of hostility, the real effect of his tax collecting was to advance his ambitions in every way: he was suddenly self-supporting and making friends everywhere. Next election, he would win easily.

When the weather was good, he traveled. When it wasn't, he worked door to door in Oregon City, collecting taxes for the lots, the various taxable house-hold items, and the poll tax for male voters. He found some actual cash in the city; if not coin, there often was bullion, and if a householder couldn't come up with money, Reese adeptly offered credit, giving receipts even to those who could not manage the poll tax. They were voters, and none of them would forget his generosity and the way he didn't see what was plain to see.

It wasn't much of a living and some days Reese scarcely made a dime, but he was a politician, and reaping another sort of harvest no matter whether he squeezed some cash or wheat out of settlers. One by one, day by day, he had rounded the country, visiting with people, collecting coin and wheat or what-ever else could be sold, and making friends.

The moment came at last to knock on John McLoughlin's door. By the clerk's calculations, Hudson's Bay owed about fifteen dollars for the city lots, mill sites, and miscellaneous property, and Reese intended to get it. And charge McLoughlin fifty cents if the man wanted to vote.

He rode up to the Columbia, boarded the next available bateau—they came and went so often now that a man didn't have to wait long to get across the mighty river—and walked up the long path to the gray, picketed stockade of Hudson's Bay, with its red banner arrogantly flying above what ought to be Yank soil.

The chief factor was a formidable man, and Garwood Reese had to nerve himself to collect the taxes. But it had to be done, and the fifteen dollars would be the largest single collection he had ever made.

He discovered that McLoughlin was at home wrestling with gout instead of working in his office, but was let into the elegant house by Marguerite and escorted to the factor's study, where the doctor lay on a chaise, his white hair disarrayed and an afghan over him. He did not rise.

"Mr. Reese," the man said neutrally. "Forgive me for not getting up. What may I do for you?"

"I'm collecting taxes for the provisional government. The company owes us about fifteen dollars for this year. I have it all here. Twelve thousand two hundred twelve in taxable property; fifteen dollars and seventy-seven cents in taxes, including the poll tax."

He shoved the accounting at the factor, who studied it.

"We are not subject to the provisional government, nor do we acknowledge it," McLoughlin said. "We are a Crown-chartered company."

Reese held his temper. "You have to pay like everyone else, Doctor. It's that or have no government or order in Oregon."

McLoughlin struggled to his feet. "Do you expect us to swear allegiance to the United States, eh? Do you expect me to pay the company's taxes to an entity we've never recognized, eh?"

"Yes, we do."

"Maybe I'll pay the taxes after you pay what you owe the company, Mr. Reese. How much is that, eh? Over two hundred pounds, now two and a half years in arrears, eh? Have you put one dollar upon it? Did you put aside a little from your pass-the-hat campaign to retire your debt? Do you intend to pay or will that sum slide into obscurity whilst you assail the lenders who bailed you out?

"Tell me, Mr. Reese, when will it be? Tomorrow? Never? Should I have sent men and boats up the river to rescue you and your, ah, sister-in-law? Perhaps not. What did we rescue, but a dead carp, eh?

"Tell me this, Mr. Reese. How much have you yourself paid to the government, eh? What for that horse and buggy? Did you pay your own poll tax? Is it an untended obligation, like yours to the company, eh? Are you exempt, eh?"

Reese sighed. In fact, he had not paid his own assessment, which was modest enough: fifty cents for his surrey, plus fifty cents for the poll tax.

McLoughlin towered above him, wild-haired and in obvious pain. "Now, Mr. Reese, hie you across the river and stay there, and keep your connivances south of the river, and don't come back."

Reese staggered back from such a fierce onslaught, but McLoughlin limped toward him, edging the visitor to the door.

"And Mr. Reese, word reaches me that you use every occasion to defame the company and me. You collect taxes by turning wrath upon me and this company, and do your politicking even as you pick their pockets. Some don't like it, and they tell me what you're up to. And then you walk in here, expecting me to write you a draft, of which you'll pocket your judas money. Get out now, and don't return until you're prepared to pay your debts as any honorable man must!"

They had reached the door, and Reese fled, just before McLoughlin filled the entire frame. Twice now Reece had been thrown out. He had never hated and feared any man so much.

But he would bide his time, and then . . .

Two fierce blows struck Jasper and Rose Constable. News came that Jason Lee, sick from hard travel, had died in the East after talking to the mission board. The frontier had worn the man's body down until he perished. Exposure, bad food, exhaustion had all taken their toll. But that was only part of the story.

The mission to the Indians that Lee had founded was being shut down and sold off by the overseer, George Gary. The Mission Bottoms buildings and land were for sale. The mission was debt-ridden and could not sustain itself, and no longer served its missionary purpose.

Suddenly the Constables were cut adrift.

Gary had given the various missioners the chance to buy parts of the mission and its lands, but Jasper and Rose were penniless. It had been a struggle just to survive on a mission pittance and they had used what little they could spare to pay off their debt.

Gary explained that he had no choice: the Methodist Church had debts that must be paid; it would get whatever it could for its properties. There was no prospect of coming to agreeable mortgage terms, especially with Oregon teeming with immigrants desperate for shelter and willing to buy.

Then came the word, in a cold note from the administrator, that they must vacate their cottage by the end of the month. It had been sold. There had been no thanks, no appreciation, no commendation, no tenderness or kindness. Out, it said, and out the door of their humble cottage they would go at the appointed hour.

Constable sat, ashen-faced, at the kitchen table with Rose. The boys were outside chopping and stacking stove wood. He had a family to feed, no income, no prospects, no trade suitable for the frontier, and would soon have no roof over his head.

Jasper's own tangled prayers had caromed off a hard sky and back again, leaving him desolated. Where was comfort and hope when he needed them?

"We're a few days from beggary," he said. "No time, no time!"

"Dr. McLoughlin would take us. He's taken everyone who asked."

"I can't bear to ask him. He's overburdened. He's still harboring the people who arrived last fall."

Rose had no response to that. She didn't want to ask the company for help either.

"Do you suppose we could borrow enough for ship's passage from someone? Maybe Abel Brownell?" he asked.

"Maybe we shouldn't go back."

"Well, that's the question." He reached across the table to her. This was crucial. "Rose, do you want to go back East?"

She shrugged. "Whither thou goest . . ."

"No, Rose, that won't do. Tell me plain."

She smiled. "All right. I would like to see how the story ends."

"I don't follow."

"I am not what I was. I'm not sure where I'm going. But Oregon has changed me and I can't go back to what I was in the East. You are not what you were either. We're on a road together, going somewhere or other. So I want to see what I—we—become."

"And the boys?"

"They're doing better here than back there, I think . . . don't you?"

He nodded. She wanted to stay, then, if they could. "A year ago, I would have insisted we return east," he mused. "Nothing here. Oregon's a chimera, a utopian delusion. But now . . . we're in a hard way. And I just don't know what to do."

"Neither do I."

"You know what? That great man Jason Lee came out here with an axe and saw and plow and built a mission out of nothing, and began a great work in the name of God. I admired him and now I grieve him. And suddenly in death he's my guide and mentor, reaching across the Divide. It's uncanny. Why is he here in my thoughts?"

"Because we're in the same position!" she replied. "We have to start somewhere. This is a huge place, filled with good land. Maybe the best is gone, but there's more. We could find something, something to subsist on. That's all these emigrants do, subsist for a while, grow their own food, spin their own wool, make their own clothes, make a cabin with an axe, get along somehow."

He lifted her two soft white hands. "Rose, I've never set hand to a plow or used a spade, but I'm prepared to try if we decide to stay. The truth is, I'm utterly bewildered. I don't know what to do. Is this paradise? When you're fit for nothing?"

"Let's try farming, Jasper."

It didn't seem impossible to him, not now. "We walked fifteen hundred miles to become missioners to the Indians. We learned how to yoke oxen, how to halter them and put them on grass. We learned how to repair our wagon with rawhide and how to boil beans over open fires, even in the howling wind. We learned to repair our boots and harness. Remember when I had to make a wagon tongue with nothing but a cottonwood log and an axe? We did it because we wanted to come here and convert the Indians."

"You could start a church, Jasper."

He shook his head. He might gather a dozen families in one or another of the new hamlets, but their combined tithing wouldn't feed a dog.

"Maybe we can teach."

"Teach who? The Indian boys are gone. Gary's let Solomon Smith go and he's looking for a schoolmaster position. No school, no teacher, no one looking for a teacher, no family can afford one."

"Maybe Marcus and Narcissa would employ us at Waiilatpu," she said. "I think they have Methodists on their staff."

"I'll ask. But they've had financial trouble too. Pretty bad, I think."

She arose and carried wooden dishes to the wash kettle. "There's a way," she said, "and it'll come clear. Maybe we should just take a step, even without knowing where it will lead. Let's find land and stake a claim and see."

His mind swarmed with reasons not to. What would one square mile of land do, even good land? How would it feed a family that had never farmed? And yet, it was all potential wealth. Oregon was a land waiting to be turned into milk and honey. A land of apples and grapes . . .

Nervously, he eyed the kitchen shelves. Flour in a tin canister. Oatmeal. Some squashes in a bin. Dried apples. A small sack of beans. Some precious sugar from afar. Some milk in a crock, chilled on the porch. Some salt, the product of an enterprising emigrant who was boiling seawater to get it. Some yeast percolating in a sourdough mix.

He had never been seriously hungry, not even on the Oregon Trail. There had always been something. Someone on the trail would shoot an antelope or deer and share the haunch. Someone would kill a duck or a goose. But now . . .

Constable didn't even have a rifle or shotgun with which to make meat. Nor had he ever skinned and butchered an animal. He had never hoed a field, plowed, harrowed, planted, weeded, or culled. Until he came west he had never harnessed a draft animal or saddled a horse. But there had to be a way.

"Well, what can I do? Let's make a list, Rose," he said. He reached for a pencil and the back of an envelope.

Between them, they were able to list an amazing number of occupations that flourished even in frontier Oregon: hunting, grain farming, orchard growing, cattle or sheep raising, shearing of sheep. One could work in salmon fisheries in season. One could be a carpenter, joiner, dyer, greengrocer, tailor, merchant, cobbler, harnessmaker, millwright, mill worker, miller, blacksmith, lawyer, doctor, accountant, surveyor, riverman, ship's chandler, ferry operator, clerk, salesman, peddler, teamster, wheelwright, wagonmaker, cooper, dairyman, logger, secretary, clothier, minister, teacher, law officer, politician . . .

"Which of these?" she asked.

"I fancy an orchard. But it would be years before we'd have a harvest, and I'd have to learn everything there is to know."

"Then we'll have an orchard! Find land! Good south-facing slopes. We'll plant, build a cabin, start up!"

"You and the boys, anyway. Someone has to make a living while we begin. And that's me." He reached a divide and knew it was fateful. "I'll leave in the morning and apply at the sawmill in Oregon City," he said. "I'll saw wood. You and the boys start looking for unclaimed land. A place for an orchard. Maybe land that's been overlooked because it's too hilly for the plow."

He saw wonder and delight in her face.

"Jasper . . . you're a blessing to me," she said.

"Well, fifty cents a day doing mill work won't support us. And there's no place for us in Oregon City. I don't know what I'll do, where we'll stay."

"The boys can work. They're old enough. And so can I. We'll find a way."

He nodded, hope rising within him along with tendrils of faith in the goodness of life, and the certitude of God's gifts. He rose from the table, feeling some modest elation, the result of coming to some sort of decision. What of all his years of seminary, of theological training, of commitment to a great faith?

He stared at his soft hands, wondering if they would endure the rough times ahead, wrestling logs onto a cradle and pushing them past the whining blade again and again, and stacking up the new-sawn boards, and sweeping sawdust, and breaking his soft body for fifty cents a day, ten hours a day.

She came to him and took his hand. "Do we belong here?"

He felt a sudden rush of tenderness. She was searching him out, ascertaining his dreams, making sure their agreement was real and not feigned, not the miserable fruits of politeness and surly sacrifice. He had somehow slipped into a new and wondrous relationship with her.

"Yes, I belong here now." He was frightened, though. "Rose, a year. One more year. If Oregon offers us only grinding poverty, bone-breaking labor, and no hope, we'll go east. Odd, isn't it? Rose, you and I are unfinished business."

She laughed unexpectedly.

"Let's see how we'll end up. Maybe it's what the Good Lord has in mind for us."

"All right, Jasper. We'll see after a year. We'll live just for the day, and not worry. I'll find ways to help. God banished Adam and Eve to live east of Eden, but we're staying."

He laughed uneasily.

Neither of them was very comfortable with the decision. He was torn in a dozen directions. The vision of smooth ministerial life in some town in the East under arching elm trees haunted him.

The next morning he took a canoe downriver to Oregon City, paddled directly to the sawmill at the falls, and applied for work. He knew the operator, Bob Baker. He knew most of the valley's Methodists.

"You? Here?" asked Baker.

"Me. I'm ready, if you can use me."

"I need strong hands," Baker said. "Mill men. You haven't done this before."

"I can learn."

Baker was uncomfortable; Constable could see that.

"Well, I need someone who'll weather the work, Reverend. Maybe you could clerk or something like that, somewhere."

"Yes, I understand," Constable said sadly.

56

They came to him every day; John McLoughlin could not escape them. They were lined up at his office door when he arrived in the morning. Some knocked on the door of his home.

They wore filthy rags, they looked gaunt or ill, they were swathed in grimy bandages, they stood barefoot for the want of shoes, they were sun-blistered, or sun-poisoned, or sun-blinded. They carried infants at their breast, or dragged small pinch-faced children, or carried broken bodies in on a litter. Some were so old he marveled that they had crossed a continent. They came to this office, in this post, because he was their sole hope and salvation, and every hard case wrung his heart.

They asked him for credit at the company store, or medical attention, or food, any sort of food. They spun tales of hardship on the long journey west; stories of destitution, starvation, illness, bad luck, death, orphaned children, madness. They wanted help: a plow and seed wheat, harness, plow horses, mules, beans and flour for their families, fishing gear to catch salmon, clothing and canvas, rifles and fowling pieces, shot and powder, milch cows, goats, chickens, axes, planes, drawknives, hammers, backsaws, ripsaws, crosscut saws, adzes, mallets, chisels, awls, knives, hoes, shovels, pitchforks, grinding stones, ribbons, leather, shoes and boots, cinchona bark for ague, foxglove, diuretics, morphia for pain.

They often wanted what he could not give: calico and flannel and gingham he didn't have on the company shelves, metal items made across the seas. He listened to haggard young men tell of their dreams: just enough flour and beans to live, and an axe and drawknife and saw and shot and shell to build us a home and get us settled, they would say.

"And how will you pay?" he would ask. "How will you pay us back? And when? And on what terms?"

A few said they would sign a promissory note with interest. Most just wanted free credit, unlimited, enough to get started, with a vague promise to pay . . . sometime. Give them a year, two years, then they'd pay in full, you bet. It wasn't just the shelf goods in the store they wanted; they begged for cattle and sheep, corn, fruit-tree rootstock, fishnets, barrels and casks and bottles and crocks. And horses. John McLoughlin could have sold every horse and mule and burro in his possession a hundred times over. Draft horses for plowing; saddlers, dray horses, trotters, packmules. Anything, they'd say, so long as it's got most teeth, one good eye, four legs, and ain't lamed up.

He often spent an entire day dealing with these starving, impecunious, adamant, angry, excited, mendicant Americans. They exhausted him. Most were good people; anyone could see that. It wasn't easy to say no to a hard-luck story. Yet in some cases these reckless travelers had brought their ill luck upon themselves, rafting rapids they had been warned against, traveling too late in season, not guarding their gear against thieves. Many should never have started out in the first place because they lacked the means and the grit.

But most of their difficulties weren't their doing; they just happened. Trail accidents, clothing rotting away, boots falling apart, game nowhere in sight, drought, madness, sickness.

More often than not he couldn't accommodate them, but usually he could do some small thing or two, if only give them a pound of flour. Sometimes he was forced to say no, though he did his utmost to help. His own clerks turned sour, trying to deal with these importuning Americans who wanted more and more and more, all on credit.

He was bone-tired. Even the Hudson's Bay Company couldn't supply the wants of an entire population. A few cursed him if he couldn't help, imagining that he was hoarding vast stores in his warehouses that he was denying them out of sheer perversity. But most regarded him as a hope and a refuge, and in the midst of troubles he heard his name blessed. All this took a toll on him, eroding his health and happiness that winter of 1845.

The unsecured debt in the ledgers mounted. The amount he had loaned lowered upon the company like a thundercloud, occasioning the wrath of the director, who warned him curtly that such obligations were his own and not the company's. And so John McLoughlin struggled between two millstones.

There came one blustery day two people he knew, the Reverend and Mrs. Constable. That surprised him. It was a long hard trip from Mission Bottoms, especially in rainy and sullen weather.

"Ah! So it is you! Come in, warm up! Fire's just right to chase away the damps!"

"Yes, thank you," Jasper Constable said, shepherding Rose to the hearth, where they turned their damp backsides to the warmth. "It's a hard trip in February."

"A spot of tea?"

Constable hesitated, and the chief factor remembered that Methodists eschewed stimulants. "Something else, then?"

"Well, no. We're just here for advice . . . and maybe some simple thing," the reverend said.

"I'll try to help."

McLoughlin meant it. He counted this couple among his friends and allies. Their early hostility to him and his company had vanished, and then the minister had bravely risen in a public gathering, among a partisan Methodist crowd, to defend the company and rebuke those who wanted to cheat it of its property. It had been a courageous act, and had forever changed McLoughlin's opinion of the scholarly cleric.

Constable hesitated.

"Perhaps this has to do with the closing of the mission," McLoughlin prompted.

"Yes, yes it does. We must be out March first. What we're hoping is to start an orchard. Or a vineyard. Stay here in Oregon. We love it, and the reason we love it is because it's no paradise. It's what we make of it. Now that we're here, we think it's home."

"Home? Home? I would have guessed that someplace like Philadelphia would be home for the Constables. But I am delighted to hear it."

"We were wondering whether we might get some rootstock, or cuttings. I don't know much about it, but one has to start somewhere . . ."

McLoughlin paused in his pacing. "Just a moment. Rootstock? Do you know viticulture? Grapes?"

"We want to learn. We've a mind to stake out a claim, like the others, plant vines, and begin the business."

McLoughlin sighed. "Reverend, it's hard to grow a good grape. We've mostly failed here. We don't have the skills. There's a blight that destroys our vines, except when we graft domestic grapes to the roots of the wild grape. And of course you realize it takes years . . . years before you'd see a shilling."

Constable nodded. His black broadcloth suit steamed in the hearth heat. Rose said little but stared tautly at her husband.

"Well, then, an orchard," he said. "Could we purchase some rootstock or cuttings?"

McLoughlin marveled at this couple. "Years, you know. Raise up trees, start others, keep the pests away, years and years. What will you do meanwhile?"

"We don't know. We only know we must start somewhere."

"It'd be easier for a man of your background to take up in Oregon City."

Constable shook his head. "I applied. The mills, clerking, shops, you know.

Finally it came clear that the Good Lord has other purposes for us. And so we will begin blindly, in faith, not knowing where we are being led."

"Are you sure you're being led?"

Constable chose his words carefully. "It is up to each of us to discover why we're set upon this earth, and the purposes for which we have been prepared, and the sacrifices we must make to reach wherever we are going."

McLoughlin feared that the reverend was daft. "Have you selected the land you wish to claim?"

"No, we thought we'd ask you what's best for orchards or vineyards, and where you think we'd find it."

"And when you stake this land, what then?"

"We don't know. We'll need shelter, of course, but maybe we can find that in Oregon City. So many friends, Methodists everywhere. We need only ask, and someone will take us in for the moment. But the first thing is to plant the rootstock, prepare the ground."

Helpless as babes. A man keenly tuned to theology here in a tangled wilderness. Any trade other than ministering would keep him afloat, but not agriculture.

"Perhaps it would be wise to catch the next schooner out," McLoughlin said. "I think the company would provide the means. You were among the first of the Americans to repay us, and in full too. That secures your credit as far as I am concerned."

Constable and Rose glanced at one another, and then, unexpectedly, Rose spoke up. "No, Doctor, we'll stay. I want to see how the story turns out."

"The story turns out?"

"Yes. My story. Jasper's story. I don't think there are two other people on earth who've been so altered—that's such a poor word—transformed by a place. We can't go back. We'd be utterly restless in the States. Our lives will play out here."

"Indeed. But one must be practical, you know. Oh, my. This is a challenge. Now let me see. An orchard, means to survive, someone to teach you . . ."

McLoughlin wanted to help; perhaps he could.

"Yes, yes, rootstock. I'll put a man on it. We've some fine varieties. Cooking apples, eating apples, a few pear trees, plums, whatnot. We've a regular orchard man, Boulieu, and I'll have him teach you. He doesn't speak English, but he'll show you."

"Most grateful, most grateful. What will it cost? We'll pay the Hudson's Bay Company."

"Nothing, Reverend. You're an inspiration." He paused. "Now, I want a promise from you. If you and your family starve, come to me. Send word. There's flour for you here, whatever you need."

"Yes, thank you. Have you some idea where we should go? What land?"

"South of the river. I continue to believe the river might divide our nations. West of the Willamette. Everything east's farmland, plowland. The soil here's gravelly and light, but fertile. I don't know good soil from bad; I'm a fur man, not a farmer. But Boulieu can help. Now tell me, how will you survive after the beginning of March? I want to keep track of you, my friends."

"We thought maybe to go among the Indians, Doctor. I'm not likely to find a white congregation, but maybe the Indian boys at the mission will remember us. I've thought maybe to continue what we set out to do when we walked across the continent. We did it wrong, you know, and now they're restless. But this time it'll be different: befriending them, living among them and sharing their ways. They have elders, medicine givers. Maybe they'll welcome some white ones. We'll plant an orchard and teach and await the fruit."

"Indians? What tribe? How will I reach you?"

"Wherever God leads us," Constable said. "That's where we'll be."

McLoughlin ushered them out. Indians? Now?

John O'Malley worried about Mary Kate, and watched her closely. As February rounded into March, without word of her brother and sisters, her spirits darkened again.

For weeks she had alternated between exultation and despair, sometimes chattering about her siblings who were slowly making their way around the world to this remote shore. Other times she slid back into that melancholia he had come to fear, becoming distant, withdrawn, and unsmiling. A bout of lung fever put her in bed for a fortnight, and when she arose at last, she looked haggard.

Some there are who don't transplant, he thought. Some there are whose roots don't sink into foreign soil. He only hoped that the arrival of Betsy, Agnes, and Liam would cure that, bring a bit of Erin to Oregon. But he wasn't even sure of that.

They pounced on every scrap of news that drifted in on the schooners and clippers landing at Vancouver. But no word came. By now, the *Endurance* should have reached Valparaiso, taken aboard its return cargo, and sailed for England.

But silence veiled January and February.

"It is all right, my love. They are just waiting for a ship to the Sandwich Islands, or waiting there for a ship over here. It is not scheduled transport, you know. It is sit-and-wait, and sometimes that takes months. But they will be along and soon you will all be hugging, just you wait."

"Something is wrong," she said. "I just know."

She said it with such certitude that it gave him chills. But how could she know? Of course she didn't know, unless some fey gift was at work in her.

The rains oppressed him, but so also did the partnership and the business. The store was virtually empty because Devers Cushing hadn't returned to provision it. Just as bad, the customers had no money; they wanted goods, begged for them, but all on credit because they had arrived in Oregon with little more than the clothing they wore. And so the ledgers revealed a deepening crisis: goods not paid for, deep debt, empty shelves, not enough on hand to pay his salary.

Abel Brownell worried too, and in January put a halt to credit purchases. "Cash or barter, John. No more credit."

"Yes, I will insist. And I will hear some sad songs, I suppose."

"We can't help that. Barter for as much as you can, including what you need, and maybe we'll weather this. Get something in return for every purchase."

Thus the gray days drifted by, rainy and overcast, waiting and waiting for Cushing, waiting for word of Mary Kate's kin. But he was greeted only with the cursed silence and the gloom of an Oregon winter. What had started as a promising enterprise was swiftly sinking into debt.

Even Brownell had taken to taut walks along the river, dodging silvered puddles, peering into the wintry mists for signs of a longboat or bateau signaling the arrival of Devers's brigantine.

Then one day Cushing's *Golden Hawk* did drop anchor at the mouth of the Willamette, and a horseman brought the news. Brownell and O'Malley rented a trap and raced downriver to meet their partner, arriving there one drear March afternoon that threatened another downpour. The white ship bobbed forlornly under a cast-iron sky, its sails reefed, rain beading its enamel and glazing its teak deck.

Cushing hastened them into his dank cabin and exchanged hearty greetings, but O'Malley could see at once that the heartiness was forced, and there would be unpleasant news.

The master poured some heated rum into crockery and settled back to talk business.

"I've not a quarter of a hold of goods," he said, once they had settled. "Half the ships on the Pacific are scouring ports for goods to unload here at a fancy price. The fact is, without a regular run to the States or England, I can't supply the store. Hudson's Bay does it right; ships go out on schedule with a carefully planned manifest. A thing like a plow, that goes out regularly, but I can't find an iron plow in the Pacific. What I've got here, it's mostly Whampoa stuff. Some nankeen, which'll sell well, and some silk, which may not. Some rattan and bamboo furniture, spices, tea, teakwood; some California hides and lemons and oranges, and a little bar and sheet iron. A few stuffed chairs and a divan from Monterey . . . but damn me, I can't go traipsing the Pacific, paying a crew, paying insurance, feeding my hands, for this! I hope you've some cash for me, or I'll be facing a mutiny."

Brownell shook his head. "We've been forced to sell on credit."

Cushing sat in dead silence for a moment. Then, "I've a crew to pay!"

O'Malley suddenly found himself privy to the dissolution of a partnership that would end his income, cost him his cottage, and maybe more . . .

Brownell sighed. "I think I can scrape up credit enough for this cargo," he said.

"Credit! It's cash or barter! I've a brigantine here, and it's floating light, and there's insurance and repair and provisions, and what'll I load here?"

"Devers, let's reorganize this. It's going to be lucrative! Ransacking the Pacific doesn't work. What we need is a regular schedule around the Horn, and a regular manifest, so we're supplied with goods we can sell, and customers can count on us!" Brownell said. "You'll run from Boston to here and back."

"And what'll I take back to Boston, Abel?"

That gave Brownell pause.

Peltries were Oregon's only significant export, and those were controlled by HBC. And the take was diminishing as beaver grew scarce. The other prospect was sawn lumber, in demand in the Sandwich Islands, but not a valuable cargo.

"Abel, it's gold or silver or coin."

Brownell grinned. "It looks like you'll have John McLoughlin for a partner, then," he said.

They sipped silently, the master adamant and irritable, Brownell putting a brave face on it, and O'Malley discovering that he was about to become unemployed once again, and wondering how Mary Kate would endure all that.

"Devers, what news do you bring? Of shipping?" he asked the master, in the silence. "Who is en route?"

"Bridesdale, with his schooner out of Gloucester," Cushing said. "He's got a good mixed cargo, I hear. He's a week behind me."

"Any passengers?"

"Didn't think to ask him."

"Where did you see him?"

"The usual. Sandwich Islands. That's where I get the news." He cocked an eye. "Master out of New Orleans told me there'll be another three thousand coming out the Oregon Trail this year."

"Three thousand! That'll double our population!" Brownell said.

"That's what the man heard."

"Do you know anything of a ship called *Endurance* out of Liverpool?" O'Malley asked.

"Terrible thing, terrible," the master said.

O'Malley froze. "Terrible?"

"Clipper, rounded the Horn all right, but hit heavy seas and burned to the bilge. They found flotsam off Madre de Dios Island. Some fishermen found it . . . enough to put the story together. Rough sea must have tossed a lamp. I never light a lamp in heavy seas, never, not even a binnacle lamp . . . say, John, are you all right?"

O'Malley stared in the mist. "Were there survivors?"

"No one knows. None that anyone knows about. Chilean fishing outfit trolled the area for a day, but there wasn't so much as a longboat or anyone clinging to debris. It's cold water, you know. No one'd last long in it."

Brownell stared. "John, that wasn't the clipper with Mary Kate's kin, was it?"

"It was," he said tightly. "Do you know for sure? *For sure?*"

Cushing looked uncomfortable. "No one knows. Maybe they made that archipelago, maybe they're a pack of Robinson Crusoes digging in, but I'm . . . afraid not. Your wife's people?"

"Her sisters Betsy and Agnes, and her brother Liam."

"I'm sorry."

"When? When?"

"November. Late spring down there, but the Horn was still blowing. Straits of Magellan are always tricky, but they got through that. They were out on the Pacific. Very unusual. No, I don't have an exact date. Two masters told me of it, one in from Valparaiso."

O'Malley felt choked and desperate. "We sat and waited, and waited, and waited. It means so much to her. It means life, it means happiness. It means . . ."

He didn't know how he could tell Mary Kate. Or how they would survive. Or if they would survive.

"I have to go," he said. It would be a long, long trail to Oregon City.

58

The dray horse wearied, but John O'Malley whipped it onward, scarcely knowing why he rushed. The last thing he wanted was to tell Mary Kate.

But he hurried anyway, exhausting the nag as it wrestled with muck. The trap splashed through silvered puddles under a weeping sky. There had been no sun, and would be none.

Finally, as he approached Oregon City, he slowed the horse. Dread had overcome him and the reality of telling his wife about her sisters and brother loomed so large and terrible he wondered if he could manage it. Maybe he should have Father Blanchet do it.

Cowardice. He put aside that idea, knowing that somehow he would convey the ghastly story to his wife. He let the horse puff its way uphill and he halted it before the cottage. The horse's sides heaved and rain blackened its dark coat.

"Ah, now, I have half ruined you and I am sorry," O'Malley said, stepping into the muck. His home exuded gloom.

He nerved himself and slowly opened the door, discovering a dankness within. No fire burned in the hearth.

"Mary Kate," he called, supposing her to be in the bedroom, but he found her at the kitchen table, Oregon Patrick on her knee.

"They are dead," she said.

"Mary Kate—!"

"That is what you came to tell me, is it not?" It wasn't a question.

He marveled. How could she know? He himself had just heard the news. But he remembered she was fey; had always been fey.

He sank into the other wooden chair and nodded. "Captain Cushing had word. The *Endurance* never made Valparaiso."

"Last November, the thirteenth," she said.

"No one knows that."

"I do."

"I . . . oh, God, Mary Kate, I am so sorry."

The boy squirmed free of his mother, reached the plank floor, and walked away. Something in her had driven him to a safer place.

"Tell me," she said.

He did, conveying everything Cushing had heard. Fire-charred flotsam, Madre de Dios archipelago, fishermen, no sign of life, no one on the barren and distant shores, news traveling by masters from Valparaiso to the Sandwich Islands to Cushing.

"We are all gone now."

"My darling, we will have Father Blanchet say masses. We will pray for their souls. I will grieve beside you . . ."

"It is death we are talking of, John. Betsy, burnt or drowned, Agnes too, and Liam, all gone, forever. And my mother too, and here I am in this wild place."

She was not crying. She sat there bitterly, accusation in her eyes. The child whimpered and she ignored him.

"I miss them as much as you, my love."

"You hardly knew the Burkes of Clonmel, John O'Malley, and now you never will. There is nothing you can do, not ever, to help me or comfort me, for it is your doing and I will never forget it as long as I live."

Her words struck him like whiplash, and he reached for her hand. But she yanked it from him.

"Weep, my love, weep, for we have received another hurt," he said.

"We! You mean me!"

"I mean we. Trust that I love and care all I could."

"Trust! I wish I had never met you, John O'Malley. Did I know you would be full of wild things? That you would take me away, against my will? That you would kidnap me from my family? That we would sail half across the world, walk across deserts, and settle in the most godforsaken place on earth? Did you tell me that before you asked for my hand, did you? You did not! You made me come here, you with your wild dreams!"

"I did tell you. There is no future in Ireland."

"No future! There is no future for me, for Betsy, for Agnes, and for Liam! No future, you say!"

She was starting to rant, her voice shrill, the sweetness bleeding out of it. She sat stiffly, her body exuding some strange violence he had never before seen in her.

"Mary Kate, peace."

"Peace! How can you say such a thing when my heart lies torn? Dead! And you are at the heart of it!"

"Mary, Mary Kate, it is not so."

"They would be alive now, alive but for you."

"But . . ." He didn't want to argue with her.

"I will get Father Blanchet," he said wearily. Guilt seeped into him. Had he dragged her here against her wishes? Had he so mastered her that she hid her dreads and hatreds of this place? Had he lured her siblings to their deaths? Had his dream meant the ruination of her life, and now his own? A heaviness stole through him. He could not remember such misery.

The lad was whimpering so he picked him up and placed him in her lap, but she fiercely rejected the boy, set him back on the planks, where he blotted up her bitterness. The child began to weep.

"Ah, lad, you need a mother. A father," he added, lifting the whimpering child to his knee. "You are a fine boy, and you will be a fine man by and by."

Mary Kate stared into space, her focus on things he could scarcely imagine.

"I will go to the mission," he said. "Will you be all right?"

"When have I ever been all right here?"

"I thought—"

"You never asked me. You have no right to think anything."

He felt the crush of desolation. "My love," he said softly, "we will go back to Erin just as fast as I can manage it."

She didn't answer. He thought he saw a softening of her face, or was that, too, only imagination?

"I will get a priest, Mary Kate."

"I do not want one."

He paid little heed. A priest would help her.

He slipped into his capote and out into a sleeting world, worrying about the unhappy child and brooding mother. He could not take the exhausted horse to Champoeg; indeed, he had neglected to care for it. He drove it slowly downslope to the livery barn, returning the trap and horse to the hostler. The liveryman eyed the splattered and drooping horse, studied the mud drooping from the felloes, and grunted. Somehow, though, O'Malley was spared a lecture.

He would summon a priest in the morning. By then, Mary Kate would have quieted and would want all the comforts the church could give her.

O'Malley returned to the dark cottage. His wife sat unmoving in the kitchen chair. The boy stared fretfully. O'Malley thought it would be best just to let his wife sit.

Someday the healing would begin; someday she would smile again. Or so he told himself. But he could not shake off her terrible accusations. He had dragged her there. His foolish dreams had stolen her from her family and her world. And now he was the instrument of three deaths. That was more than any man could bear.

They slept apart, she in their room, he in the parlor on the leather sofa. He took care of the child because she couldn't or wouldn't. The next day began a reign of silence that abraded John O'Malley's soul; an accusatory, relentless, cruel silence. Her gaze followed him, her tight mouth scorned him.

He rented the trap again, bundled the boy, and drove to Champoeg and arranged memorial masses. Father Blanchet was away but Father Demers would come at once.

Nothing changed in the next days. She sat and kneeled and stood through the mass in Oregon City, saying nothing. She sat blankly while the good father talked with her, comforted her, and instructed her about the goodness of God and of the world. She scarcely acknowledged her son. The father stayed two days but failed to touch anything in the heart of Mary Kate O'Malley.

John reopened the store to sell the remaining stock, such as it was. Abel Brownell told him the partnership would be dissolved and the store would be closed. The business had foundered on the rocks of debt. The settlers could not pay for what they had purchased.

John took Oregon Patrick with him to the store because his wife had utterly abandoned the little boy. Poor innocent child. Plainly, he would need to take his wife and child back to Ireland. The wilderness of Oregon could not nurture her, though he thrived on it. He dreaded what he would find back there: a life so cramped and limited and hopeless and poor that it would be all he could do to feed his family. And yet, he would make the best of it, and there would be occasional pence to buy an ale in a pub and be among friends and talk politics and revolution.

He could sell the cottage; it was mostly paid for. Somehow he would take her home to green Ireland misted by the sea and more home to Mary Kate than he had ever imagined.

But to save her and his son, he would sacrifice his own life.

59

Jasper Constable would come to look back on that period as the forty days and forty nights in the wilderness. He had a biblical cast of mind, and saw the parallel. They found shelter among settlers. She and the boys were hardier than he had ever imagined. But even as they wandered, the monsoons faded away and a glorious spring burst to life.

Equipped by friends with a tent, a pair of packmules, and enough rootstock to begin a hundred fruit trees, they drifted toward the coastal range, whose eastern slopes, they believed, would be ideal ground for an orchard.

They made little progress toward finding ideal land until they started up the Tualatin River and into the country settled by those savvy mountain men, Doc Newell and Joe Meek, whose hospitality was boundless, and wilderness wisdom encyclopedic.

"You want to grow apples," Meek said skeptically. "And somehow survive while you wait a few years. And befriend some Indians too."

Nonetheless Meek and Newell set aside their farmwork and took the Constables upriver and into the verdant foothills of the coastal mountains, where mist hung in the valleys until the sun burned it off.

"If you're wanting to start an orchard, I'd say you could hardly do better than right hyar," he said, waving an arm at a long, sunny, tree-dotted, grassy ridge north of the river. No one's claimed anything back this far. You want redskins. I'd say about the time you put up a cabin, you'll have a hundred camping on your yard. Tillamooks, Cowlitz, maybe Clatsops, maybe Kalapuyas. It used to be they all had their own turf, only now they're being pushed around . . ." He squinted at Constable. "They're mighty unhappy. This ain't the safest plot of ground in Oregon."

"We hope to befriend them and begin our own Indian school."

Newell frowned. "We can't stop you, but maybe you'd better think it over some."

"Actually, we thought maybe to live among them."

"A few years ago that might've worked," Meek said. "But now . . . I don't know. If I was you, I'd build me a good stout cabin and a hall or church to teach in, and not try to live in one of their camps. You'd be plenty hungry in a coastal village."

"I guess we'll be hungry wherever we go. I thought maybe they'd keep us fed if we taught them."

Meek grunted.

The mountain men helped the Constables pace off a square-mile claim, pile cairns in the corners, and then they cut and barked logs for a few days. When they left, they would carry with them a vaguely located claim signed by Constable that they promised to file in Oregon City with the provisional government.

"You're pretty far from help here," Meek said. "I reckon fifteen miles from my place. But if you send for us, I'll come."

"We'll all come," Newell added. "And we'll be checking on you."

And then the mountain men rode away.

The Constables watched them depart in the tender sun of an April morning; watched until the pair vanished around a bend. The moist air didn't stir; no bird sang. Constable wrestled with an impulse to pack up and run after these well-armed protectors, but stayed the impulse.

He turned to Rose and Matt and Mark. "Let us pray, and then begin," he said. He held his arms open until he had gathered his family into them.

"We thank thee, Lord, for this bountiful land and these sunlit slopes, this Eden you have given us. We will plant our rootstock, and someday they will be fruit trees, and some of what we plant here will be from the Tree of Life. Bring us those we can help . . . and who might help us. For we are without means. Bless us in our work, amen."

It amazed him to see the smiles. Rose's in particular. Something about Oregon was nurturing her, putting a shine in her eyes. And the boys too. That accusation in her eyes, the terrible blaming for Damaris's death, had at last vanished and now when their gazes locked he discovered a warmth in her chiseled face that never existed before. She, who had been so reluctant to come to a wilderness place, was now the most adamant about staying.

"We'll decide where to put the orchard and plant roots now," he said. "When we have every root in the ground and watered, we'll start a garden. Then we'll start a cabin."

That heady day, armed with a spade, they planted all the rootstock they possessed and bucketed water to each planting, and drove a stake to mark each future tree. Someday, perhaps, there would be fruit, and perhaps an income from the apple trees as well as food for their table. But would apples grow on these inclines, prosper in this climate, endure whatever insects lived in these locales? Would the orchard be a living enough so they could pursue their real mission in life?

They decided on a site for a log home and chapel that would double as a school; level land snugged close to a yellow bluff, watered with an icy spring that formed a tiny rill that tumbled down to the Tualatin River half a mile distant. An Eden, if they could keep it; misty in the cool mornings, hotter in the afternoons, but usually mild and mostly comfortable.

The garden proved more difficult. They had no plow; only a spade to break the earth, tear apart the thick sod that armored it. But they persevered, taking turns, and after a few days they had corn and squash and potatoes and carrots started. They would plant more as the season progressed.

Then one dawn, as they slipped out of their blankets, they discovered they were not alone.

Standing there, watching them awaken, were a dozen or so armed Indian males, bows and spears in hand, a cold and impassive curiosity in their faces.

Jasper arose, his heart pounding. He was afraid, though the Indians made no hostile gesture. The boys rose too, obviously scared witless. Jasper stood, nervously, aware that he was wearing only his white union suit, and examined the visitors. They wore mostly native attire, leathern skirts and vests and high moccasins. But one or two wore white men's fabrics, shirts and trousers.

One of the younger ones caught his eye. "Billy? Billy?"

"Methodist," the slim youth responded.

Billy, a Tillamook boy, one of those at the Indian school for a while.

"Billy, remember me? I'm the Reverend Mr. Constable."

The youth nodded.

"What brings you here?"

"This is our land. Not for you. Go away."

"But Billy . . . we're here to teach and help you."

"Go away now."

"But we've started a farm and an orchard. We've planted apple trees. We will share the fruit with you."

"You make the game go away. We are hungry. White men take away the deer and the elk and the fish and all meat."

Constable realized he was being chased out, and that his dreams were tumbling around his feet. "Are these Tillamook people?"

The boy nodded. "Once we were many, and then you come, and now we are few because of the sickness. But we are strong."

Constable contemplated his dwindling supplies of flour and grease. "You stay for breakfast. We will feed you."

He nodded to Rose, who wheeled out of her blankets. She was wearing a shapeless cotton gown, and evoking much curiosity among the Indians. Over this she threw a coat and began gathering kindling for her fire. The dawn light was seductively gentle and made her beautiful.

Billy addressed the others in his own tongue. They argued and then they warily set down their weapons. But there were irreconcilable youths among them, who glared at the Constables and were slow to set down their spears. These were bitter men. Jasper's pulse began to slow. He could not imagine what might come of this, or whether he could convey to Billy his hopes, or whether Billy could translate them into the native tongue, but he sensed he and his family were not in immediate danger.

It took time for Rose to build up the fire, mix the flour and grease and salt in a tin bowl, spread the dough in the skillet, and begin frying the cakes the Indians loved so much, and while they waited the Indians probed the whole camp, boldly examining the tent, their clothing, the spade and hoe and rake, and the mules.

"Billy, let us talk," Constable said, trying to fathom just how much English the youth could grasp.

Billy settled on the grass, his brown eyes unblinking and intelligent.

"The mission's closed but I would like to continue the work," he began. "We have much to teach your people . . . and much to learn from you too. My plan was to start my own school. I thought your people might like to come here, and help feed us while we teach you. But now I see you are hungry and I must make different plans. Maybe I can start a farm. There's some level land here I can plant. We will share the food with you, if you'll help us get started."

The boy said nothing.

"We came here because we care about you. That's why we are a day's walk from other white people."

"Tell the white men to go away. Maybe we will leave you alone. But they must all go away. I have told you."

"I do not have the power to make them go away, but because I am a minister men listen to me. I will be your voice. I will tell them that you are hungry and sick and the game is scarce and you are being pushed away from your homes. I will do that . . . if you will help me here. I want to teach your people many good things."

The youth thought about that, impassively, and Constable hadn't the faintest idea what he was thinking.

"You will help the Tillamook?" the boy asked, at last.

"I will make your every wish known to the government—the chiefs of the whites. The wishes and complaints of your people and the other tribes too. I will be a loud voice among the whites."

The youth thought again for a while. "I will tell them," he said. "We are hungry. We are very angry. Some among us talk of war. No white man cares, or speaks for us."

Jasper Constable imagined, just then, that he had stumbled across the life that God had intended for him. It came as an epiphany, bright and dark at the same time, for he would make bitter enemies among the settlers.

"I care, Billy," he said.

Felicity Brownell beheld a man she scarcely knew. Was this her Abel? His famous luck had run out, and suddenly her husband was a different man, baring traits she had never suspected he possessed.

He had become, by turns, impatient, curt, sullen, and highly critical of everything around him. His affability had vanished. His generosity had disappeared along with it, and she was hearing a streak of blaming and faulting that had never before reached her ears. He complained now of a chronic backache, and lumbago. What had Oregon done to him?

It had begun when Devers Cushing anchored the *Golden Hawk* at the mouth of the Willamette, this time with a scant cargo. It deepened when Cushing refused to unload even those miserable scourings of the Pacific until Abel had paid what was owed on the last shipment as well as the new one. His rage flamed higher when Cushing refused to accept most of the goods John O'Malley had taken in trade, including the wheat.

Then that ruthless old seadog, Cushing, threatened to impound the remaining goods in the store and put liens against the store and the house. Nor was that all: Cushing intended to sell whatever he could to John McLoughlin, and load whatever the Hudson's Bay Company wished to transport to Liverpool or London.

Cushing had been around the world a few times, knew the ways of turning the screw, and was quietly extracting blood from Abel. The erstwhile partner had become the destroyer. The man who had survived pirates, bureaucrats, swindlers, and frauds in foreign ports had no trouble putting heat to Brownell.

"That old pirate's ruining me!" he complained to Felicity. "We'll have nothing left!"

That prospect seemed to alarm him far more than it alarmed her. All his life in Boston, he had waltzed through his business transactions as if they were mere bores, scarcely bothering to sort out details. But his famous luck had held, and with each returning ship, he took his fat cut of profit, until they were saying that Abel Brownell's genius at business would create one of New England's great fortunes.

And now it was gone, and the man she married had somehow gone too. This was Oregon, not Boston, and his casual flyer into frontier life, and his equally casual uprooting of his family, had ended in disaster. No one in Oregon had money, and business could not long survive on credit or barter. Oregon didn't even belong to any nation, so no one knew whether to deal in dollars or pounds, or whether it mattered.

This morning he had shocked her once again: he said he had signed over the house and store to Cushing as partial payment. They could continue to live in the house, but for rent of a thousand dollars a year. That unsettled her.

It was truly the only civilized house in all of Oregon, and sat in white splendor amidst log and rough-sawn plank buildings. Not even John McLoughlin's handsome residence matched it. Now it, too, was gone and the place would go on the market the moment Abel failed to pay rent.

"O'Malley did this to me!" he raged. "Instead of holding out for cash, he put it all on the books. He offered credit to everyone, even the dregs. And he bartered my money away by accepting worthless cow hides and wheat. Cushing won't take a bushel of wheat, so what good is it? He says he's not about to carry wheat to Boston, and there's too much of it in South America. O'Malley ruined me!"

"I thought you admired him for making deals, and finding ways to do business. I thought you told him to—"

"Admire him! I had to keep an eye on him every day. But he still managed to ruin me. Him and Cushing. That man's a pirate even if he doesn't fly the Jolly Roger."

"Last time Cushing anchored, you thought he was the best man in the Pacific," she said dryly.

"I didn't know him very well."

"You've known him a dozen years."

"That was Boston."

"And what's changed?"

"I'll tell you what's changed! Cushing did. He turned on me. He won't carry me."

He didn't belong here. There were no clubs or restaurants or inns in Oregon; no libraries and law offices, no opera houses or parks or gardens where an affable financier could while away time among friends and sycophants. In Oregon he had chosen to do virtually nothing. He fished now and then, hiked, bought and trained two setters, dabbled in politics, rowed on the river, and dickered for land or mill sites or whatever came to mind. But he had shunned the hard work of settlement life, purchasing everything from firewood to gardening instead of soiling his hands with manual labor, axes, hoes, saws, or spades. And now Oregon had retaliated.

"John O'Malley didn't ruin you," she said tartly.

"He didn't follow a single direction I gave him. I told him a hundred times not to give credit but he did."

"Then you should have been overseeing him instead of leaving it all in his hands."

"I knew you'd blame me for everything. Now it's my fault, is it?"

She shrugged. Weeks earlier he had been praising the young man for finding ways to move goods off the shelf, for being more liberal than Hudson's Bay Company, for sorting out good prospects for credit from the poorer ones and limiting the purchases of those who showed little aptitude for life in a wilderness.

She waited for one more thing: some recognition in him that his own indolent habits may have been the root cause.

"We can go back to Boston. Cushing offered to take us," he said.

"What's there?"

"What's here?"

"Here's our future. The children are doing fine. I like it. I never thought I would."

"The children are turning into barbarians. We could put Dedham in college back there."

"With what?"

He glared. "So you won't go back. You won't let me recoup or start over. You won't let Dedham get an education."

Was this the man she had known for seventeen years? "Go back, then. Nothing's stopping you."

"Maybe I will."

The chasm opening up before them startled her. Separation was not something she wanted or had even considered. Divorce was unthinkable, and impossible anyway where there was no government and in a land possessed by no nation.

"Maybe you should settle down, learn the lessons to be gotten from this, and look to our future, Abel."

"Now you're lecturing me."

"No, I don't plan to sail with Devers Cushing. And I don't think you should either. Not with the man you've just called a pirate, the man you think has ruined you. There's a future here, and we can build it together."

"I'm sick of Oregon."

Felicity played her ace. "Abel, Roxy asked me what's the matter, why are you upset and snapping at me?" She let him absorb that for a moment. "I told her that things went bad in business for the first time in your life, and we're penniless and we don't know what tomorrow will bring.

"She loves you so. She's all mixed up, not knowing what her future will be. I think you should talk to her. If you're going back to Boston, you'd better tell her. If you're going to stay and fight and make something of yourself here, you'd better tell her that too, because right now, that girl's almost in tears. This blaming, this . . . I don't know what to call it. But you're crushing a sweet and blossoming girl, who's happy to be here, who looks up to you, who thinks you're the best papa in all the world . . . and who's now so shattered that she can't even bear to be with you, and hides from you."

Felicity knew that would reach Abel. Until recently, Roxanne had adored her father so much she was always finding excuses to be with him, and was always aglow whenever he took her with him on his daily rounds.

Abel stared, stricken. Then he wheeled away from her, preferring his anger. She watched him plunge out the door of the house they no longer owned.

She would remember to speak kindly to John O'Malley, the cashiered partner. Cushing had brought hard news to that family. Maybe she could bake a cake and take it up the hill to that darkened cottage.

What had Oregon done to the Brownells? Not long ago they had attended the sublimely inspiring sermons of William Ellery Channing at the Unitarian Church. Now they were squabbling like alley cats. Were ethics only for men of ease, men unchallenged by hardship and the world's casual brutality? In Boston Abel had been veneered by comfort and prestige; here the veneer had fallen away, and she saw someone not yet grown, someone less an adult than her children. The very thought hurt.

Had she been to blame? Had she hurt and hindered and belittled him? She would think upon it. There was blame enough to spread around. She would see how much she should own.

Captain Cushing set sail one fine spring day and Abel did not see him off. The master had sold his few goods to the Hudson's Bay Company and loaded some peltries and about twenty retiring French employees bound for Montreal, or so she had heard. McLoughlin had been under pressure from the governor to cashier them, and had resisted until this opportunity to send them back to their relatives presented itself.

For several weeks Abel barely spoke to her, and she did not attempt to speak to him. He sulked, walked, brooded, and glared. She continued to teach the gaggle of youngsters who came to the volunteer school, and found goodness in her own life. But things had to change, and soon.

61

FROM THE JOURNAL OF DR. JOHN McLOUGHLIN

AUGUST 27, 1845

This year has been the undoing of me, and I hope I have the
strength to endure. It has unfolded on the saddest of notes, and has
only grown worse for all the McLoughlins.

In June, we learned that our beloved Eloisa's husband took his
life, apparently not long after hearing the news that I would be
closing the Yerba Buena store in Mexican California. William Rae
was not a steady man, and given to strong drink, and enfeebled by
disease. But he was making progress there until the Honourable
Company compelled me to shut that operation down, which I
proceeded to do after delaying as long as I dared.

We grieve for him. Eloisa had been here giving birth to a son,
William, but the infant didn't survive, and suddenly our family was
burying two more, this time in the churchyard of the Mission
Delores down in Mexico. My beloved Marguerite suffers. Will our
grief never end?

But that was only one of many disasters. In March I wrote
Governor Simpson offering to purchase the company's property in
Oregon City, which it was in danger of losing because of an
American law that permits only private persons to claim land. I sent
a draft for four thousand one hundred seventy-five pounds, almost
twenty-one thousand American dollars, for our developments
there, but fully expected the company to quietly reimburse me; I
would be landholder only in a nominal sense, and the development

would continue to belong to the Honourable Company. Indeed, I requested the return of the funds.

Little did I expect, when I opened the express from George Simpson a few days ago, that he had blithely accepted the offer but not my conditions. So I am forty-one hundred pounds poorer, but own a town site if I can hang on to the title when the country south of the river goes to the United States, as it surely will. I have been aware of the governor's malice, but now it is naked, no longer concealed by the velvet glove.

These events were harsh enough, but in this summer of discontent I am facing worse. We had a most difficult time early this year ejecting an American who staked out a land claim at our very gates, square upon our wheatfields and pastures which we put to use every summer to feed ourselves. The man, one Williamson, claimed he had a perfect right to the land, and we "foreigners" didn't! It was only with a mixture of diplomacy and bare-knuckle threats that we got rid of him, in part by appealing to fair-minded Americans.

The episode so alarmed us that Douglas and I have been shoring up Vancouver's long-neglected defenses, building a bastion and strengthening the pickets. We are suddenly vulnerable, and a mob of impassioned Americans could swiftly burn this post and undo everything we have built for almost two decades. Our efforts to secure our property have occasioned much rumour-mongering south of the river, but we have not been deterred and consider the defenses vital to our and the Crown's interests.

My friend Jesse Applegate, newly elected to the provisional government, undertook to meet me in Oregon City soon after that affair to discuss these matters. I traveled up the Willamette, ostensibly to examine our sawmill on the island, but actually to engage in serious discussions with Applegate, a lawyer and a moderate and a man I respect. It turned out that he wanted us to subject the Company to his provisional government *for our own benefit*!

He argued that his government, weak and uncertain as it might be, would be our sole means of securing our property, and unless we submitted the Company to it, we could not be certain of keeping what is rightfully ours.

That certainly was a radical proposition. We had been operating here long before the first American arrived, on a Crown charter giving the Company a monopoly on all commerce. We even have the right to try misdemeanors, and James Douglas is a

Canadian justice of the peace. But here was the Missourian Jesse Applegate, telling me we must submit to this American government.

"But Jesse," I said, "your oath requires allegiance to the United States, which is unconscionable for those of us loyal to England."

He acknowledged our dilemma and had the oath rephrased so that it read that we would dutifully support its laws while remaining a "citizen of the United States or subject of Great Britain." I took the case back to Douglas and we agreed to the virtue of it, and thereupon we sent letters to the provisional government placing the Company under its aegis, subjecting ourselves to its taxes, etc., but also receiving, in return, assurances that our land claims, including the very land under this post, would be secure. Just to make sure, we've had seven trusted employees file claims on our post and properties, seven square miles in all.

There was equity in Applegate's case. From their standpoint, they resented our insistence that we had a rightful claim to the Oregon City town site we had developed, while at the same time we were denying the provisional government any authority over the Hudson's Bay Company as well as any land north of the Columbia. We were trying to have it both ways, and now that is no longer possible.

I thought the matter was thus resolved, but it only worsened my situation. The London governors, quite unable to grasp the business opportunities occasioned by these vast migrations of Americans, including, so we understand, the greatest of them all heading west along the Oregon Trail even as I write, have come to distrust me, and so has Whitehall, if not most of the Royal Navy and Army. I should have seen it coming. I should have read it in the conduct of my colleagues, both Douglas and Ogden, but I was more concerned with turning a good profit for the Company, to grasp what was developing in London until it was too late.

I did, however, foresee some of it, and recently caused to have built a home of my own in Oregon City, a Georgian-style building on a choice location between Second and Third. It is not yet done. I am glad I did, for when it is completed it may well be my sole refuge from these gathering storms.

Although I make no public admission of it, I am cut to the quick that my loyalties to the Honourable Company and Crown are suspect. Everything I did to ensure the Company's security is now held against me. Did I give supplies to settlers on credit, in part to save life and in part to prevent a hungry mob from threatening us? Now it is taken for disloyalty to the Company, and maybe even to England. Should I have let these Yankees perish? God forbid.

I first got wind of this insidious stain upon my good name when a doughty pair of English naval officers, Captain Parke and Lieutenant Peel, who is third son of the prime minister, arrived in these precincts, having traveled by land from Puget Sound where their fifty-gun ship, the H.M.S. *America,* was anchored. They were bearing a letter from its captain, Sir John Gordon, brother of Foreign Secretary Lord Aberdeen, assuring me of the Royal government's protection of Company property. Suddenly, it seems, the cyclops eye of empire is upon us.

But lo, the real purpose was intelligence, and this pair set about to ascertain American strength in the Willamette—by asking everyone *but me* about it! It did not take long to dawn on me that my loyalties are suspect. Captain Parke, in particular, thought that the loutish Americans could be whipped handily with a few barrels of grapeshot, and my efforts to disabuse him of this notion—had he never studied their two revolutionary wars?—only deepened their suspicion of me.

Nor was that the end. Now I have a pair of government spies running about. They showed up with Ogden, of all people. These young and sharp-eyed gents, Harry Warre and Mervin Vavasour, arrived in the guise of sportsmen, toting fowling pieces and wearing checkered tweeds, but their natty attire and hunting equipment ill disguised their mission. They proceeded to buy fine beaver hats, brocaded vests, handkerchiefs, tweed trousers, pipes, and extract of roses at the Company store, making a great show of being dandies and idiots.

But they are Queen's men, no doubt officers, poking and probing about, and they spent several days sketching this post and everything in it, whilst asking detailed questions about the men, the Yanks, and me. Of course they never approached the chief factor, since I am, it seems, *suspect*! But with war clouds once again looming, and this the likeliest field of combat, they are busily assessing strengths and weaknesses for Her Majesty, and preparing for *war*.

Just now these jolly sportsmen are up the Willamette, no doubt weaseling information out of the Americans, who will see what they are up to as swiftly as I did. They arrived with Ogden, and that surprised me. Douglas, yes. I've long had a feeling about Douglas. He has been coveting my position for some while, and in fact is fully able to fill it, being a man of supreme competence and ability. But in these matters he has kept me in the dark. But Ogden! I somehow didn't expect him to be playing Cassius to Douglas's Brutus.

Why do I write thus? Because the axe has fallen. I've been deposed. My long tenure with the Honourable Company is swiftly coming to a close. Oh, they did it with all the civility that London musters on such occasions, but the beheading proceeded anyway. They made Douglas and Ogden chief factors, with rank and authority equal to my own, and proclaimed that this district will be run by a triumvirate, consisting of us three. But of course added that if I should find the matter embarrassing, I might wish to *retire*. They have some grounds there: I ache more and more, my knees quake and my legs howl at me. In London they know I cannot long endure.

They also took five hundred pounds of annual income from me by transferring to Douglas my authority over the agricultural colonies to the north, though I still hold Company stock and share in its profits, and would not be hard-pressed but for the heavy investment in Oregon City, which I never intended. It would be folly to underestimate the inexhaustible malice of George Simpson, knight of the empire, and a bastard in all known ways.

Neither Ogden nor Douglas possess such malice, if I'm not mistaken, but in the end, both have found reason to depose the man who built the Pacific Department of the Company into its most profitable enterprise. Will I be knighted for my services to England, like Simpson? Shall I receive commendation from my Monarch, as well as the lord governors? Ah! The questions answer themselves!

So here I am, distrusted by Whitehall and Fenchurch Street, distrusted by Americans, and my principal assets perilously held in a venue that will surely go to the United States. It is time to think of the future. I am no longer a well man; Marguerite is not young or well either. There is yet time to gather my family about me in Oregon City, and there run my mills and store.

Another burden looms over me: I have advanced the Americans about thirty-two thousands in credit for goods from our Company store, and if they fail to reimburse the Company, that debt is mine to pay, and to do so would largely exhaust my resources, destroy a lifetime's work.

These things I can bear if I must. What I cannot bear is the suspicion among my countrymen that I have not been faithful to the Crown, or to the Company to which I have devoted most of my adult life. I am an honourable man: faithful to God and my church and country; faithful to Marguerite. Faithful to my humane ideals: I have offered a helping hand to settlers of all nations, saving life and making friends. Faithful to our commitment to treat the Indians fairly whilst earning a good profit; faithful to my subordinates.

I will continue to be faithful, even if the world be faithless.

62

Again they flooded into Oregon, these tough, desperate, miserable Americans. And again they sent messengers before them with tales of death, disease, disaster, starvation, cold, and misery. And again, John McLoughlin turned the resources of the Hudson's Bay Company to aiding the unfortunates.

From October onward, the weather had disintegrated into rain and snow and cold, pummeling these exhausted people as they progressed across the Blue Mountains and into the great Columbia basin. At The Dalles they piled up, camped and starved, awaiting four-footed means to get past the rapids and falls, or build a raft, or hire a boat, or employ Indians to portage their goods.

McLoughlin sent his bateaux and rivermen to help out, and a few began to trickle into Fort Vancouver, ragged, driving their bony cattle before them, racing against a wintry death to find food and shelter.

He interviewed as many as he could, including one of the advance guard, who had managed to arrive on horse in October:

"How many, did you say?"

"Likely over three thousand, sir."

"Three thousand! Did I hear you right?"

"I reckon so."

"And are they provisioned?"

"No, they're plumb starved, sir."

"What will they do for food, sir? *Food?*"

"Hunt, I guess."

"Hunt! There's no game left! And the Indians depend on it!"

"Well, we'll get what's left."

"Do you realize that three thousand's more than live in Oregon? And we can scarcely feed ourselves?"

The man grinned slowly, baring gapped yellow teeth. "Guess we'll be eating horses and maybe each other. Or eating Injuns."

McLoughlin shook his head. This skinny newcomer, named Biggs, was a typical specimen, little concerned about tomorrow. But there were a few among the settlers, such as Jesse Applegate, who did. Somehow, there would be food, and maybe there was business in it for the company. He would send the next available schooner south to California to pick up whatever was edible.

This new contingent drifted in, sometimes in great caravans, more often in ragged groups, and he found himself employing his neglected medical skills to keep these worn people alive. Mostly they needed food and rest and shelter against the raw autumnal monsoons now lowering over the Pacific Coast.

The thought that once again he would risk the company's resources, extend goods and food on credit, depressed him, and yet he would not permit any mortal to starve, and would do whatever charity and conscience required of him in these waning days of his tenure.

So great was the shortage of doctors that much of his time was spent treating settlers. The new order of rank with the company did little to relieve him of his management burdens.

He intended to resign at the beginning of the year, and in those moments when he was not coping with the deluge of Americans, he was overseeing the construction of his house in Oregon City, a place within the roar of the falls, and within hailing distance of his gristmill, which he had leased to a pair of Americans. He possessed two sawmills and a gristmill and a store now, and intended to make a living from them and sales of lots.

The house would not be cheap, even with lumber from his own mills. It would cost him over eight hundred pounds, and the outbuildings another three hundred. The doors and windows had been shipped from New England.

In the midst of this, Her Britannic Majesty's Ship *Modeste* arrived, and anchored more or less permanently in the Columbia off Fort Vancouver. This swift fourteen-gun corvette was in the hands of the affable Captain Baillie, who did what he could to calm the alarmed Americans by holding balls, theatrical events, and dinners at every excuse. And yet the threat was plain enough: Britain was baring its teeth.

But so was the United States, for word came that the lower Columbia was being patrolled by the sloop-of-war *Shark,* effectively bottling the *Modeste* on the river.

And still they came, fevered, gaunt, ragged. Many stopped at Vancouver, told their tales of misery, of feuds, of weather, of stupid efforts to raft the rapids, a great replay of the events of previous years but larger and more forbidding. And Dr. John McLoughlin opened the stores and warehouses once again.

They fanned out to the new cities of Salem and Portland, and the older ones of Champoeg and Oregon City, into country indisputably American though two mighty powers were poised to shed blood for it. Because of George Simpson's perfidious games, John McLoughlin, a man who fiercely loved his native land, would soon reside in another nation.

To each and every visitor he cried out a single message: "Food, sir, food! Get yourselves food, for we have barely enough to feed ourselves! Get it from somewhere else, and don't count on game, else you'll be eating your horses, mules, and broodstock."

They listened, at least.

Then came word of an incredible feat, something that only these audacious Americans, who wouldn't take no for an answer, could have done. A man named Sam Barlow, frustrated at the delays at The Dalles and with starving cattle to tend, organized a company to build a tollroad around the southern flank of Mount Hood, through dense and impassible mountain forest. It couldn't be done, he was told, but that didn't stop him! After getting permission from the provisional government, this company of desperate Yanks chopped and dragged a rough cattle trail where no road had ever gone, and eventually linked The Dalles to Oregon City.

And that unstoppered the bottle. Another tide of emigrants surged through, bypassing Vancouver entirely, flooding straight into the Willamette Valley, where they camped everywhere, begged shelter from everyone who could spare a barn or shed or coop. But they had made it, alive, and with living cattle and mules and a few horses too.

Suddenly, the Willamette was a well-populated valley.

Dr. McLoughlin welcomed the Barlow road. He reasoned that it took pressure off the Hudson's Bay Company. Let the Americans take care of one another; let their own merchants run up the credits and dole out the goods for promissory notes.

In the waning weeks of 1845, the chief factor divided his time between relief for the suffering Yanks, building his handsome two-story home, and overseeing the company. He hoped that terrible year might slide into oblivion without further grief, but his hopes were dashed when he finally was permitted by the company to see the Warre-Vavasour report.

The quondam sportsmen were indeed lieutenants of engineers, and pursuing intelligence matters, using Warre's ability as an artist to cover their real purpose, which was to look to defenses and report on the strengths of the Americans. All those fine sketches were never intended to grace galleries or the walls of private homes in London. They had hooked up with Lieutenant Peel, shared impressions, and Peel had then taken their report across Mexico and across the Atlantic, where copies now rested on important desks at Whitehall.

They had made John McLoughlin the goat. It was because of the doctor's cooperation with the Americans, they explained, that the United States now had an insuperable foothold in Oregon. He read the report, forwarded by express from Montreal, with deepening dismay, for it all but portrayed him as a disloyal subject of England, if not a fool.

He felt the slow, pained thud of his heart. Could matters sink lower?

He resolved to defend himself, even if he were on the brink of retiring from the honorable company, and chose to do so in a lengthy letter, which he scratched one bitter December evening by the light of an oil lamp.

They blamed him for being a friend of the American missionaries, and he replied: "What would you have? Would you have me turn the cold shoulder to the men of God who came to do that for the Indians which the company had neglected to do?"

Accused of joining the provisional government, he wrote: "If we had not done this, Vancouver would have been destroyed and . . . the trouble which would have arisen in consequence would have probably involved the British and American nations in war."

And accused of failing to get rid of settlers, he wrote, tartly, that "we have no right or power to drive them away."

The world was full of young, ambitious second-guessers, full of condescending opinions about their elders, and now he would try to rebut these swift, shallow, foolish impressions garnered from a whirlwind tour of Oregon. It mattered to him what Whitehall thought, and what the company thought, no matter that he had become increasingly alienated from them. He was the man in the middle, distrusted by all sides.

Gloomily, he sent his rebuttal in an express eastward, and wondered what good it would do. But he was not one to brood, so he devoted himself to the future: in Oregon City he would have grist-and sawmills, a store, and a voice in the new land. He liked the Americans in spite of all their surly suspicions and rancorous ways.

"Well, Marguerite, we'll soon be moving," he said one December day.

"We will be happy."

"Yes, and I'll have my own businesses. The company still owes me sums, and a pension, and a share of the profits for years to come, but we won't be dependent on it. Free at last! Independent at last! There'll be no lords overseeing what I do, no miserable George Simpson undermining my work."

She smiled. "It's best," she said. "And we'll have our family too. Oregon City is a good place."

"So we are to become Americans," he said. It had never been his intention, and it hurt.

Life had turned to sawdust for John O'Malley, and Oregon had become a prison worse than the land of his birth. He struggled to put food on the table after Abel Brownell closed the store.

First he toiled in the sawmills, earning his half dollar for ten exhausting hours each day, save only the Sabbath. It fed his wife and son, but pushing logs through the whirring blade, watching out for his fingers, grappling logs that rubbed pitch on his clothing, and stacking beams and planks, was a miserable toil, and he wondered why he had not stayed in Ireland.

Then he learned that John McLoughlin would build a great house in Oregon City, and he signed on as a carpenter's apprentice, knowing the skills he had acquired at the mission would not suffice to make him a journeyman. That work was better. The building crew was cheerful, and the chief factor himself visited frequently, his gaze intent upon each man. O'Malley he knew, and O'Malley he welcomed.

Still, this was not the Oregon of his dreams, nor was his life any better. His cottage had become a whirlpool of darkness threatening to suck him under. Land was everywhere, land to be claimed for the asking, but he could not break free to find it and stake it—and defend it against jumpers like the Burgesses. Nor could he do anything with it, lacking so much as two bits. What Oregon was this? Surely not the bountiful Oregon that had fevered his imagination, the Oregon of dreams.

These things he endured, but the hardest of all was Mary Kate's bitterness. The deaths of her brother and sisters had unhinged her. She thought of nothing else and every word she spoke to him became an accusation.

She railed at him whenever he appeared; she cooked sullenly, ignored her household chores, scolded the boy, glared bitterly upon a golden and sunlit world, rued the day she had married John O'Malley, and found ways to make life miserable for them all.

That spring of 1845 the flowers rioted. What was Oregon if not the world's brightest garden? The settlers had planted every imaginable seed, and now these bold blossoms garlanded Oregon City and the fields beyond. Flowers might heal a broken heart, so he brought her bouquets of tulips and daffodils, lilacs and bridalwreath, daisies and poppies and nasturtiums, and iris.

"Here, love, it is some iris to brighten the light in your eyes," he might say.

"I do not want your flowers."

"I will put them in a vase, then."

"You cannot buy back dead people with flowers."

She always looked at him as if he were a worm, the malice visible in her pinched face. If she had stopped accusing him of causing the death of her siblings, that did not mean she had forgiven him, or that she had changed her mind. The bitterness lay behind every glance; the accusation in every gesture.

He worried about Oregon Patrick, a spindly child, frightened and whimpering under his mother's ruthless rejection. Sometimes, of an evening or a Sabbath afternoon, he slipped out with the toddling boy, hiking along the river or dawdling at the foot of the falls, letting the roar and mist boil over them.

"Oregon, lad, you are a fine son, and do not you ever think otherwise."

But the boy's solemn eyes betrayed a sadness beyond anything that O'Malley could heal.

He sought help from the priests. They exhorted her to forgive, to stop blaming, to return to her son and her husband. They cautioned her against mortal sin. They urged her to love. They begged her to accept the good world around her.

"Accept what? This wilderness? I was brought here as bride. Little did I know! Look at it! It is the home of snakes; not fit for some poor woman. What is it but the end of the earth, as far from the world as one can get?"

Then came word that there were other Irish settlers. Some Reardons in Salem, and some O'Reillys in Portland. Ah, at last some people from the old country, people Mary Kate might enjoy! He paddled down to Portland, a tiny new town largely settled by those who arrived the previous fall, and found the O'Reillys, two young brothers, one a cobbler and the other a smith.

"We are putting money by to bring our wives and families," said the elder of the two, named Thomas.

"Would you come visit? I have a wife, Mary Kate, who is so homesick she is out of her head."

"We will stop by, John O'Malley, and cheer her up."

But they weren't able to. Mary Kate upbraided them for deserting their families and for coming to the most godforsaken corner of the whole world. Eventually she tongue-lashed them out the door, and they wandered away, glancing furtively over their shoulders.

"Well, Mary Kate, you did not welcome our countrymen."

"Why should I? They are leading their poor wives into hell."

"It is not hell here! This is a good place!"

"Good place? Good place?" She began laughing wildly.

He found the Reardons in Salem, an older couple from County Limerick who'd been dispossessed of their holdings by their landlord and had made their way to the New World.

"My wife hates it here and cannot forgive me for bringing her," O'Malley said.

"Ah, lad, do not go back there. Do not let her push you. This is heaven on earth," said William Reardon. "She will come around, after you earn a bit. It is bad there. Too many mouths to feed and not a chance to get ahead unless you are Church of Ireland and you have sold your soul to the lords of Dublin Castle. Now, do not let her do that to you. We will stop by next trip down the river and maybe put some light in her eyes."

O'Malley thanked them.

Worst of all were the nights when she lay beside him in the sweet close dark, and yet half a world away from him. How often he had reached, tentatively, toward her only to unleash another torrent of bitterness.

"You will not be touching me," she hissed. "You will never touch me again!"

"God's wounds, Mary Kate! You loved me once!"

He ached to draw her to him, to feel the crush of her body, to feel her cling to him in joy, to experience again her shyness and ecstasy.

Where oh where had all that gone? Night after night he had lain beside her, wild with desire for her, and yet rebuffed by her stiff back, thrown at him as some rampart of soul and flesh.

He had thought that maybe he might hold hands; the simple act of clasping hers to his might unlock the iron gates. And so he had often slipped a hand in hers, and sometimes was heartened when she didn't at first resist. But then she always pulled free and turned her back to him.

He had talked some nights, just meandering through his life, telling her of Dr. McLoughlin's house, of the big windows made in the East, of the skilled workmen building it, of someday finding another square mile of land and claiming it, of his hopes that little Oregon Patrick might grow up straight and true, of his yearning for a brother or sister for the boy, of what the Reardons of Limerick said about Ireland and its deepening grief. It all came to naught. She lay beside him, lips tight and unkissable, heart locked and chained and bolted against the soft commerce of a shared life.

The boy sickened, wheezed and hunted air; coughed up his food, and stared fearfully at his mother, who mostly ignored him. O'Malley feared for the boy's life.

Once, when Dr. McLoughlin was inspecting the construction, O'Malley asked him to look in upon his boy. Together they hiked up the bluff to the darkened cottage, and there the good doctor listened to the boy's heart and lungs, took his temperature, studied his pale flesh, and shook his head.

"This child . . . does he ever laugh?"

O'Malley shook his head.

McLoughlin, who knew of the affliction upon Mary Kate, sighed. "This boy needs a mother and brothers and sisters, that's all. Love's as vital as food and air, and a little boy can starve for any of them." He turned to Mary Kate. "Madam, your hugs and kisses, your love and attention, can put health into this little boy. You're the medicine he needs."

She nodded stiffly, her gaze on the wall, her thoughts a million miles distant.

Outside, McLoughlin confided in O'Malley.

"This boy won't live more than a few more years, John. Not even youth and energy can save a rejected boy. Some disease, maybe consumption, will sweep him unless you can turn things around."

O'Malley nodded tautly.

For some while he had been weighing a plan. He would send her home with Oregon Patrick but would not go himself. He could manage that by selling his cottage. The separation would be permanent. They would live out their days apart. Most of a year had elapsed and she had only grown more bitter and accusatory, and now her darkness was menacing his son.

The time had come.

"Mary Kate," he said that evening. "You are going back to Ireland on the next ship that drops anchor. I am staying here."

"Oh, so you are going to kill me too, like Liam and—"

"Stop that."

For a change, she did.

"I will sell the cottage and stay, for here a man can breathe and here a man can live. I will send you and our son, and send money to you when I can, and you will have the Burkes of Clonmel around you, and you will be happy again."

She glared at him, her silence laced with darkness.

1846

64

For two weeks, McLoughlin's French Canadian boatmen had paddled and poled the burdened bateaux up the Willamette, each carrying a piece of his life. Out of his spacious home in Fort Vancouver came his mahogany furniture, his blue and white china, his crystal goblets, the bric-a-brac of his office and household, including the gifts he had received, the souvenirs, the portraits of his family, the beds and blankets.

As always, his stout and doughty rivermen sang their way upstream, turning hard work into melody and somehow muting the pain of this great severing. For he had resigned as chief factor, though not as an employee of the honorable company, and was transporting the possessions of a lifetime to his new home in Oregon City.

His work was done. He had, once again, seen to the safety and comfort of the straggling settlers of 1845 who, as usual, had been trapped by snow and cold, and impoverished by a murderous river waiting to suck their goods into its belly and spit them into the Pacific. Over the holidays he had overseen the furnishing of his handsome new home, a two-story white building far better than any other in Oregon City.

And now, this sixth day of January, 1846, he was done with that. There remained only the task of bundling up Marguerite, Eloisa, and the children, and bringing them home . . . to a land that would surely become the United States.

He loved Fort Vancouver. Now, as he stood within its gates, he remembered all there was to remember. The first fort had been built farther back from the river, so far back that portaging goods from riverbank to post had been a great hardship. This post was closer, but still respectful of the mighty river's potential to flood the surrounding plain. He remembered how the crews cut logs in the mountains and floated them down the river, and how these great logs were erected into a rectangular picket that would preserve the post from all harm save one: fire.

How hard his Canadians had toiled in those early days, axing and hacking and chopping, rolling logs and raising them up, one by one. They built the store and warehouses, the barracks and mess hall, the chapel and chief factor's home, and bit by bit this bastion of empire turned itself into a civilized island in a wild infinity of forest and mountain and loneliness.

And here he had received the fur brigades, Ogden and his trappers returning, their horses and mules burdened with beaver plews and other peltries, often successful; sometimes not. And here the small sleek ships anchored, ships out of Brighton or Liverpool, three-masters or two, ships that had pushed across the Atlantic, rounded Cape Horn at a latitude of 56 degrees south, and then struggled northward again to the mouth of the Columbia, above 46 degrees north, bearing goods to trade to the savages, and goods to keep the company men alive; and bearing a fortune in furs back to the warehouses of London.

And here, between these good gray timbered walls, he had caused a piper to pipe an evensong at dusk. And here he had entertained an amazing array of notables and adventurers and scoundrels, most of whom he liked.

Here his children were born and grew to manhood and womanhood. Here his life with Marguerite had deepened; here they had remarried, the second time by a Catholic priest who had received them into his church, putting him at one with his voyageurs. Here he had received Governor Simpson, and listened to the dynamic little man undo projects, demand new ones, and complain endlessly about everything.

Here he had served the honorable company with all his might and intelligence, and served the Crown and empire as loyally as any man could. And here he was still tugged by that ancient loyalty and love of England and its might and genius, even if the company, and England, were abandoning him.

He wanted to be alone, so he left Marguerite in the barren house while he toured his post one last time, the low light of the winter solstice matching his gray mood. He walked the pickets, probed the warehouse, opened the schoolroom door, examined the chapel and its altar, wandered out upon the fallow fields, through stubble. All this he had built. Not alone by any means, for Douglas and Ogden had been able seconds, and his multitudes of employees had labored mightily year after year, two decades and more to erect this bulwark of commercial and imperial England.

The chill air didn't bother him. With a mind so rich with memories, the mere temperature of the air meant nothing.

Then he was done.

He returned through the great gates, gathered his black-clad family, and led them down the familiar path to the river, where his burly boatmen waited.

He helped Marguerite board the bateau, and then Eloise and the children, and nodded.

Now, this last time, his boatmen pushed free and paddled across the River of the West, their great sweet voices serenading their employer this one last time.

Mightily, as always, they worked across the river, past the island, turned into the Willamette, passed the little settlement of Portland, and muscled their bateau against the swift current on the pewter river, past dark wooded banks, toward McLoughlin's new home in a new land.

> Row brothers row, the stream runs fast,
> The rapids are near and the daylight's past.

He sat quietly in his greatcoat, the vast mop of white hair pinioned under a fine beaver tophat, the White Eagle coming to roost at last. Now, in the dead of winter, his men worked the bateau close to Oregon City, and he could hear the roar of the falls in the distance. This would be their home. He smiled at Marguerite, who observed all this placidly.

His boatmen drew the craft to a small wharf below the falls, and there the McLoughlins debarked. He embraced each of his men, these loyal, cheerful, laughing, robust employees of the honorable company, but they weren't laughing this time. They stood on the jetty silently, their multitudinous private thoughts carefully masked.

"Adieu!" he said. "Adieu . . ."

Now he saw their tears.

Quietly they clambered into their flat-bottomed barge and loosened the ropes and soon the current drew them away.

His world would never be the same. But the new one would not be bad. The company, in the end, had been generous and he was secure.

He linked arms with Marguerite and they walked to Second Street, well back from this great tributary of the Columbia, to their imposing home, which stood within sight and sound of his mills, and in the midst of his own town site.

He led them in. Servants already had a fine fire in the hearth.

"Ah, John," she said, surveying room after room. "Ah, John . . ."

"I'm sure you'll want to arrange things your way."

"This is our home? It is even better than before."

"Yes, and there's plenty of room for company. For visitors. For Eloisa, for children to grow up . . ."

"Is it . . . are we . . . safe?"

He nodded. There were, indeed, some things to consider. War, for one.

How would the Yanks treat an Englishman if the two nations came to blows? Even if he were to pledge his allegiance to this new nation, as he intended to do, would they leave his property alone?

The church, for another. They were Catholics. He had converted, after a lifetime in the Church of England, bringing his family with him. His neighbors were overwhelmingly Protestants and militant about their beliefs. Oregon, as they saw it, would be a Protestant Arcadia, and they would make life hard for those who didn't fit, including men of color who had been barred from the entire territory in a fit of sheer meanness. Why did these greathearted, fair-minded, generous Americans nurture such flagrant offenses against the very words of Christ?

Envy, for another. He was the richest man in the Northwest in spite of his tribulations. No house as grand as this one existed elsewhere, and indeed, many of those in Oregon City were one-room log buildings with clay floors. The provisional government, now under his old rival Governor George Abernethy of the Methodist store, had guaranteed his property in its organic law, and he could only trust that these fair-minded Yanks would keep their word. And yet the matter worried him, for there was trouble brewing.

"Yes, we're safe, Marguerite. And settled. Here now, let us look at the kitchen, and our bedchambers, and the outbuildings, and you can tell me how well I built."

"You build well," she said. "You always do."

65

Someday, in the rotunda of some domed capitol of Oregon, there would be a heroic statue hewn from veined gray marble and shaped to the image of Garwood Reese. He would be standing with back arched and arms outstretched, caught in a moment of reaching for the stars. And beneath, graven in stone and gilded with gold, would be his name, and the words "The Father of Oregon, Liberator, Statesman, and Friend of the Humble."

There, in capsule, was his life. He debated the word *liberator,* sometimes preferring *patriot,* for his entire passion to bring Oregon into the union could best be described as the highest sort of patriotism and love of country. But *liberator* was a great word also, and perhaps more apt, because he wanted himself to be remembered as the man who, singlehandedly, freed this mighty land from the oppression of foreign influence; who drove out the British and toppled the mighty Crown monopoly, the Hudson's Bay Company, and drove it and its autocratic minions to oblivion.

Yes, *liberator* would be the better word. Father of Oregon and its Liberator. And now, thanks to the stupid arrogance of the British, his great moment was upon him. This would be his finest hour, and he would make the most of it.

Riding at anchor not far to the north was that symbol of British imperial power, the *Modeste,* its cannon aimed down the throat of every American in the Willamette Valley. Already, this season of war, settlers had witnessed a bunch of British spies and provocateurs snooping about, painting pretty watercolors of American property, examining terrain. The queen was baring lion's claws, and all this was pure gold to a man with Reese's ambitions.

This was the moment for which he had lived and suffered, and for which he would someday be forever remembered in the marbled capitol building of Oregon. For a year now he had driven across the entire district, collecting taxes and visiting every settler and homesteader. He often settled for less than was due and made a great point of it, and sometimes even forgave a tax entirely, or grandly offered to pay the tax out of his own pocket, a gesture that won him fanatic support and sometimes tears of gratitude from a hard-pressed or luckless settler. Even so, he duly deposited considerable funds with the provisional government, and in the process found his own pockets bulging with lucre that Electra found no trouble spending.

The thought of her brought a certain darkness into his otherwise rosy fantasies. That ruthless, miserable, unhappy iceberg would not let him alone, and vented her discontents upon him on every occasion. Her social ambitions were so grand they were grotesque. She wanted a home that would put Mc-Loughlin's to shame, and insisted on importing every imaginable luxury, including Sheraton and Hepplewhite furniture, damask drapes, Wedgwood china, Brussels carpets, and Orientals as well.

In vain did he protest that it would not do for him to live in too great luxury while the vast majority of Oregonians endured life in dirt-floored log cabins, eating off homemade tables and chairs, and lying in plank bunks upon hay-filled ticks.

"You promised I'd be queen of Oregon," she said one day. "Some queen. Charwoman would be more like it."

"Electra, for God's sake, give me time. We'll be holding balls in the governor's mansion someday."

"When I'm nothing but wrinkles."

He'd had enough. "Given your, shall we say, temperament, it won't matter to any man whether you're wrinkled or whether your flesh is peaches and cream."

She burst into tears, which utterly astounded him.

"I hate this place!" she said, when at last she had subsided. "What's here for a woman? What does Oregon give me? What does Oregon give any woman?"

"You won't know until you try being one."

"Oh, you beast!"

He laughed. He hadn't intended their partnership to be war, but it had devolved into that, and now he relished the battle.

"Electra, you sit here and complain until I dread to come home and listen to you whine."

She glared coldly at him, some misery and bitterness swimming in the depths of her blue eyes. He both despised and pitied her because she had reduced herself to such pettiness and could not bring herself even to offer ordinary warmth and civility to him, or to anyone he brought home with him.

"The only trap you're in is one you've made for yourself," he said relentlessly. "Maybe, if you try desperately hard, and rummage through your icy soul, you might even find a few shreds of kindness in you."

"Oh!"

"Maybe even some love. Maybe even some charity. You might even make a husband out of me and take me into your bed. Maybe you could even become a mother."

Tears welled in her eyes. "You do not know me. You don't know what I've suffered. I try to be a good woman, but sometimes I . . . am not what I want to be. It's like I'm two people. No one knows me . . . not even you."

He'd hurt her; he could see that. They had replayed this scene over and over, and nothing had ever changed.

Apart from his sham of a union, life had become nectar. On his daily rounds, he had never failed to remind the settlers that the Hudson's Bay Company had put them all in debt and was charging outrageous prices and undermining American commerce. All this talk had its effect. The moribund Mission Party had revived, and now George Abernethy was governor and the earliest settlers dominated. Reese knew how it had happened; he was the éminence grise who had changed things around.

And then, incredibly, that towering mountain of arrogance John McLoughlin had moved like some Oriental pasha into a huge home in Oregon City that beggared every home in Oregon. There he was, the instrument of British imperialism, the man whose bogus land claims had impoverished settlers. There he was, blatantly settling in what would surely become a territory of the United States even if it took a pocket war to achieve it. There he was, John Bull himself, huge and domineering.

For Garwood Reese, the move was a dream come true. Now at last, stripped of the protection of imperial England, McLoughlin was vulnerable. Ere long, he would crush the man and free the territory from foreign influence. It wouldn't take much; not with the honorable company scurrying northward and abandoning its coastal trading posts. The Yanks outnumbered the Canadians five to one, or so it seemed, and each year tipped the balance even more. Those fourteen guns of the *Modeste* would be nothing, nothing at all, against an American militia backed by Washington.

Reese had a new political bludgeon at hand. He was the secret owner of *The Spectator,* Oregon's first newspaper, a weekly published in Oregon City by his hairy-nosed front man, Caprell Blodgett. Here at last was the means to galvanize the populace, to worm into the minds of thousands of settlers.

"The grand pooh-bah of the more or less honorable company has removed himself to our village," it reported. "What mischief is he up to now?"

The presence of John McLoughlin here is going to increase the papist influence upon Oregon. We would hope that Oregon doesn't succumb to jesuitical designs. They were instrumental in the failure of the Methodist mission, casting doubts and confusions into the minds of the red men, and now we have in our midst the prospect of even worse.

The same foreign company that has driven us all into debt by charging monopolistic prices for necessaries now wishes to extend its influence southward, riding upon the mouths of fourteen cannon. But imperial Britain, which does not wish to be taxed or governed, will discover that it can not lightly tread upon the rights of Americans.

And so it went.

One wintry day in 1846 Reese paid a visit upon that erstwhile Methodist storekeep and now governor, George Abernethy.

"I can't stand this waiting. What do you hear?" he asked.

"I did hear something. There's a Yank bark anchored off the mouth of the Willamette. The *Wyandotte,* out of Gloucester, a schooner under Dominick. He brought newspapers. Polk, it seems, doesn't want two wars at once, and he's gearing up to take on Mexico. There's been some outrages down on the Texas border. We're going after California. At the same time, he's bargaining with the British about the Northwest. One war at a time."

"Bargaining!" Reese was aghast.

Abernethy shrugged. "The news is months old. Who knows?"

"But he ran on the slogan 'Fifty-four forty or fight!' "

The governor smiled. "What wins elections is not necessarily good policy. Polk's negotiating to extend the boundary along the forty-ninth parallel, making a straight line from the Great Lakes to the Pacific, save only for Vancouver Island, which the British want. This is it, Garwood! I think we'll see Oregon become American territory within a few months! Including Puget Sound and its great harbor, and all the good farmland up there."

"But that's only half of Oregon."

"It's the best half. It's the half we wanted, including a great port on the sound. Now we'll stretch from sea to sea, and if we get California and the San Francisco bay, we'll see destiny fulfilled."

"And what's to become of the company?"

"Your guess is as good as mine. But one of Britain's hard and nonnegotiable positions is that British property is to be confirmed and left alone. If Polk's absorbed with Mexico, he's not going to quibble."

Reese pondered that. "I'll find a way," he said. "We can't permit that. It's like a serpent in Eden. I want you to begin working on Congress. We need a territorial act that confirms American property, but not McLoughlin's."

Abernethy grinned. "I think that can be arranged if we present our case carefully."

He slapped Reese on the back, a rude gesture that offended the tax collector. But Abernethy was always the rube, and Garwood Reese would endure the man's barbarities so long as the governor was useful.

Well, all this was news, and rather disquieting. He had been entertaining visions of forming a militia to take on the *Modeste*. One good outrage and there'd be a fight. But Mexico intervened. *Mexico!* Still . . . there was always opportunity, and if anyone could turn the news to advantage, it would be Garwood Reese.

66

Thick fog shrouded the *Brighton,* merchant brigantine wharfed at the rude village of Portland. John O'Malley, scarcely twenty yards distant, could not see its masts and yards, and its hull was little more than a blurred black mass across silvered earth.

The *Brighton* was to sail that dawn, but now lay to, waiting for the fog to lift. He and Mary Kate and Oregon Patrick huddled uncomfortably on hard benches in a shipping office. At least it was dry and warm there thanks to a cheerful hearth fire. On board, the cabin would be cold and clammy.

His wife sat immobile, her face a mask, her lips drawn tight. She wore what amounted to widow's weeds, black broadcloth that shrouded her entire body save for her face and hands. If she thought she was attending a funeral, perhaps her own, O'Malley thought he was attending another sort of funeral, the death of a marriage, his dreams and life. For this was a great sundering, and half, nay, two-thirds of his life would soon sail away, bound around the Horn to England, and then to Ireland, where he trusted she would find refuge with her family in Clonmel.

Her response had been explosive and bitter: "Sending me away, are you? And what will we do in Ireland? How will you support me? Burdening my father, are you? Oh, I rue the day you set eyes on me, John O'Malley."

But in time that had subsided. He knew he was doing the right thing. She could not be transplanted from her native soil and she was dying here in Oregon. She needed to put her roots deep into the loam of Erin, or sickness would destroy her and take the baby too.

Even now, as they sat waiting, he worried about the boy, who had scarcely been healthy in his whole three years of life. O'Malley knew the trouble wasn't this great land, but his mother, who had ignored and rejected her son until he found no reason to exist. It would be two lives he meant to save, not one. And O'Malley supposed the cost might be his own life.

He saw no love in her. Like some uprooted weed, she was trying to find nurture when her roots had failed her. He pitied her in a way, when he wasn't feeling wounded by her savage attacks, which cut deep and left him so anguished he wondered how he could bear another day.

He had made the decision, tested it, lived with it, hoped she might improve, and finally concluded she never would; she didn't belong in Oregon and not even in the New World. Ireland was the sole place on earth she could prosper.

He said nothing to the priest of this; he couldn't bear the platitudes about sticking together, families, faithfulness, and all the rest. This was something he had to do no matter what the price. If it meant solitude the rest of his days, yearning for a wife he could never have, longing for the blessed embrace, aching to share his days . . . he could not help that.

The new year had arrived, and still no ship docked, and then, this March, the *Brighton* appeared, unloading a fine cargo of British manufactures and loading Hudson's Bay peltries. O'Malley hastened to Portland, made his arrangements, and awaited the sailing.

Swiftly, he had put his cottage on the market, not surprised by the intense bidding for it among shelter-starved settlers. In the end, he settled for five hundred eighty dollars in gold, and this very day he was homeless. He would go back to Oregon City without a place to lay his head. He had paid the passage to Brighton, given Mary Kate gold enough to sail to Waterford, sent an additional sum by Hudson's Bay express to her father for the support of his wife and child, and kept about fifty dollars to begin his life anew.

There was nothing else he could do.

The terrible accusations had faded, but not the bitterness. It distorted her white face, soured her expression, and burned in her gaze.

He had gnawed at the prospect of returning to Ireland with her and finding work there in his father's crystal glassworks. He might manage it, if his brothers allowed it. But likely they wouldn't. When he had decided to go to the New World, he had surrendered any position he might have had there, for a position was precious. He could not support her or Oregon Patrick in Ireland.

If he went back, he'd be the one doing the dying. He'd be the one slowly suffocating in a land that had lost hope, and where laughter had grown thin, and fear ruled hearts and souls. He could not go back, not after drawing the sweet air of liberty into his lungs; not after standing in a new land, glimmering in the sunlight of opportunity.

The fog was lifting, and soon the ship's bell would summon passengers. He could make out its yards now, and the white haze had brightened under a rising sun. He squirmed on the varnished bench, not wanting to sunder a marriage in this fashion, wanting some tenderness in her eyes, some softness, some tentative smile on her lips, some forgiveness in her face, and in the end, one last kiss. But he could see none of that in her stern countenance.

"Mary Kate, love, the fog lifts, and soon will you be sailing over the sea, and soon will you be embracing your father, your family, and the land you love. Go with God, and may you find whatever you seek."

She pretended not to hear.

"Mary Kate, I did not mean to wound you; I wanted only to give you a sweet life in a new land, but now I know it was not in your heart to accept these things. I am sorry. I pray for your safe passage over the seas, and for a joyous reunion in Erin, and for your happiness. I will provide for you, yes I will, and be dreaming of you."

She stared at him so somberly that his heart sank.

"Well, then, at least I can thank you. For you filled my heart with song, and bore a fine son, and held me in your arms, and suffered our hardships together. You walked across a harsh land with me, and braved the prairies and the mountains and wild Indians with me. You gave me dreams, and in the touch of your hand was a whole universe. You invited me in, at least for a while, and now I will carry those memories within me, in a sacred place . . ."

The hardness was gone from her face.

The ship's bell clanged, a false joy in that misty morning, and he helped her to her feet, and lifted the fretting child to his, and led them through the door of the rough riverside office and across the slop. She lifted her black skirts and stepped irritably through mire, soiling her shoes.

He helped her up the gangway and onto a clean, wet teak deck. The ship still lay next to the wharf, its hawsers tying it to land, and yet there was a subtle change now. This was civilization. White-enameled rails, a white cabin, no mud at all . . .

He led her to the quarter-deck cabin where she would make a tiny home for six months. Her trunk rested there. She would share a single bunk with their child. A small glassed porthole offered light. A chill pervaded the room, and moisture hung on every surface.

"Here you are," he said softly. "All will be well."

"Will it?"

"I believe so. Jonas is a good master, an old sea dog. I made sure of it before I booked passage. He said he'd take personal care of you and see to all your comforts."

She drew the deepest of breaths, peered through the water-beaded porthole to a gloomy land she hated, and smiled.

He had not seen a smile on her face for many seasons.

Maybe, maybe, there was hope.

The bell clanged.

"Better be off, Mr. O'Malley," said a mate, appearing in the door. "We're casting lines."

Tentatively, he gathered her into his arms and kissed her. She endured it, and he took that as a sign.

Then he released her, patted the head of his son, who stared wide-eyed at him, smiled at the boy, and slipped away before he could no longer endure the pain. She was smiling.

Swiftly he strode across the slippery deck and down the gangway, and then onto the earth of Oregon.

The master watched his deck crew free the ship, and slowly the river current drew it downstream. Up in the yards, seamen unfurled sails, the canvas sagging in the slightest of breezes, virtually useless for a while. A helmsman centered the brigantine in the channel, and slowly it drifted toward the Columbia, and out of sight.

It was very still. The few people who had watched the departure hurried away. The world seemed empty. He did not sorrow. He had done his sorrowing months before.

John O'Malley sighed, drew his lungs full of this air of Oregon, and stood unmoving, wondering what to do next. He was homeless and unemployed and without land, but he was free.

The bank idea fevered Abel Brownell. He had to succeed! Everything lay in ruins and he intended to rise, Phoenixlike, from the ashes before he lost his wife and family. Oregon cried for a bank, and he would conjure one out of nothing but a pile of debt and good faith. Storekeeping he hadn't known. Banking he knew.

From the ruins of the old partnership he had inherited a mountain of unpaid credit. Cushing had sailed off with the loose cash and assets, including the store and Brownell's house, and O'Malley had gotten a cottage out of it. But here was the Bostonian, the creditor of five hundred–some settlers who might or might not pay him. He hoped his paper might be worth fifty cents on the dollar, but maybe even that was optimistic.

A bank! Hudson's Bay had done whatever banking could be done in so remote a place, in the ordinary course of business. But money was lacking, coin nonexistent, and because no nation possessed this land, no nation's money was legal tender. Indeed, a polyglot of gold coins, dollars, Mexican reales, pound banknotes, shillings, and other odds and ends passed for money in Oregon, but the real exchange was barter, with warehouse receipts for wheat the most important medium.

Very well. He would use all that to advantage. From John McLoughlin he borrowed a safe, and found a limited silent partner.

"Leave me out of it, Abel," McLoughlin said. "Your bank's better off if there's no link to Hudson's Bay. But I'll subscribe ten percent of the capital if you're going to open with ten thousand in assets."

Brownell then turned to the printers of *The Spectator*, selling them some of his notes for fifty cents on the dollar, and soon they were churning out Bank of Oregon scrip in one-bit and two-bit denominations, and dollar and ten-dollar banknotes, each of which Brownell signed.

He rented the front of a cabinetmaker's store on First Street, added a dark-varnished teller wicket and a private office, and made a rustic bank out of nothing. He put up a gilded sign proclaiming the Bank of Oregon, capitalized at $10,000, and advertised in the paper for depositors. People looking for cabinets, furniture, or coffins could proceed through his bank to the shop in the rear.

He soon had all the depositors he could handle, even from as far as Salem. Mostly they opened small accounts: some deposited gold, some brought United States currency, some had drafts on Eastern banks, some had pounds, some had various foreign coins, especially Mexican reales, or one-bit pieces of eight, some had receipts for wheat, or debt instruments. He accepted all but the most outlandish, and went out of his way to help his customers.

They flocked in, some to deposit funds, others to borrow. He worked alone in his teller wicket, doling out scrip coinage, which the settlers eyed suspiciously but accepted, and sometimes his gray banknotes, each bearing his signature, looking more official than they were. But what else could a bank offer without a country or a currency?

The result was just as he calculated. In the space of a month, Oregon's bottlenecked economy began to flourish as a medium of exchange made commerce possible. Barter all but vanished. In essence, the very act of creating a currency was helping to secure his new loans and repay old ones. He even began to see payments on some of the old debt owed the partnership store.

His Bank of Oregon scrip found its way south to Salem, north clear to Puget Sound, and even into the tills of the company stores, which began accepting it and converting it to pounds at the bank.

Brownell found himself furiously busy. For a man who had always lived life in a leisurely manner, this was acute hardship. He no longer had the luxury of idleness, no longer could control his days and schedules. He was no longer one of the privileged rich, but a man locked in a cubbyhole making sweaty transactions, trying to satisfy clamorous customers, trying to placate settlers wary of a crudely wrought piece of paper that had no nation's guarantees behind it and was backed by very little but debt.

But for all of his pain, he knew the bank was succeeding, a wildly successful and much-needed service in this huge chunk of North America not yet owned by any nation. He noted the paradox: the more his scrip coinage and banknotes penetrated commerce in Oregon, the less shaky it became.

"Good as gold," people intoned of crude currency that was secured by debt, warehouse receipts, land, livestock, and a raft of dubious assets.

He charged a high interest rate, a percent a month, on loans, in part to protect himself against the bad debt which was ubiquitous in Oregon, and in part to earn enough to make a living and pay Dr. McLoughlin his ten percent share besides. Settlers complained, but his was the only bank and they could take it or leave it.

He began immediately to make a living. His own account, at his own bank, waxed large enough to keep Felicity and the children in a small house they now rented. Felicity, at first skeptical, began smiling, and Roxy hung around the bank, adoring her father and making a nuisance of herself.

His first printing of coin scrip proved to be much too little, and again he ran the job presses at *The Spectator*, stamping out Bank of Oregon one-bit and two-bit paper coins, and then he added a nickel scrip as well.

Much to his astonishment, he discovered he had become an admired man in Oregon. Men stopped him in the street.

"Say, Abel, who should be our next governor?"

"Abel, I've been meaning to invite you to run for office."

"Mr. Brownell, we've named our new boy for you."

"A boy? Is he an Abel? How amazing!"

"Well, you gave us money for some seed wheat and a plow horse, and we're eating, so we thought there'd better be an Abel in our cabin."

He had always understood how banks enabled commerce, but here in a wild frontier a bank was a hundredfold more important to humble and desperate people than anywhere else. Maybe they were flattering him because he was the man with the money, the man who could help. But there was more to it. He had, in weeks, won the esteem of Oregonians after falling from grace when the store failed.

He could scarcely fathom it. There were other and more pleasing signs of success. Felicity's gaze was friendlier now and her laughter more cheerful. It had been a close thing. He had brought the marriage to the brink of collapse, only to snatch it back.

By spring, he knew he needed a teller so he could devote himself to loans and collections. Dedham wanted no part of indoor life, having discovered the beauties of wild Oregon, and ached to to stake his own claim to mountain pasture and stock it with a few cows.

"You want to become a banker, Ded? I'll hire you. I need a man in the teller's cage. It'll be a bore, taking in cash, paying it out, posting every trans-action in the ledger book, and summing it all up at the end of the day. But it's a position, and it's the beginning of any life you want to live. In a year or two you'll be able to do whatever you want. Think it over."

But his son didn't have to. Abel started him the next day, hovering over his shoulder and trying hard not to be overly critical. The young man seemed to flourish. Abel found time to work on collections, which were always threat-ening the solvency of his precarious little bank. Tracking down debtors and sometimes seizing assets weren't tasks he enjoyed, but it all was part of banking.

Months passed and the bank flourished.

Sometimes, during a quiet Sabbath morning, or late of an evening before he blew out the lamp, he reflected on his odyssey, which was more than just a trip into the unsettled West. The real odyssey had been his own interior journey from being a gifted, lazy, quick-witted opportunist in Boston who gathered wealth effortlessly to a frontiersman slaving away every spare hour and extracting a living through hard and relentless toil which left him drained at the end of each workday.

In Boston he might have gone on forever, almost, as he was: his swift sharp calculations earning him a comfortable income. But he had paid a price for that, and only now was he fathoming that price. There had been little satisfaction in it, nor any growth of his skills, for there had been little challenge in anything he did. After three years in Oregon, he was so transformed that he could hardly grasp what he had become.

Looking back, he saw a man he didn't much care for, a man thinking of his own whims, dawdling in Boston clubs, gadding about town in liveried coaches, and giving little thought to his wife or children, who were simply fixtures in his self-centered existence rather than individuals with their own dreams and needs. That was especially true of his life with Felicity, his handsome wife, a woman to show off to the world and dress up in the latest Paris gowns. But had he ever known her?

Now, at last, he was embarrassed. He had yanked her out of a cheerful life there in Boston. It was a miracle she had agreed to come at all. But indeed, she had come, walking with him all that way, making jokes out of it all. For her wit was her salvation, and now he knew that the wittier she was on any occasion, the more she was hurting within. And she had joked her way clear across the continent.

She still was teaching, along with several other wives who managed to find a few free hours to drill the ABCs into the swarming children of Oregon City. She got nothing for it; whatever parents could spare went to maintain the log building, buy cordwood, books, and slateboards. He had imposed Oregon upon her and yet she had plucked up a new life in the wilds more easily than he. She had found something valuable to do; he had careened about, bankrupting himself, refusing to change until the last second.

He was no longer the nimble possessor of Brownell's Luck. He no longer needed it.

Jasper Constable was too busy to contemplate life's cosmic jokes. He, the gifted young theologian who could tell the world how many angels could fit on the head of a pin, was now a subsistence farmer in the most obscure corner of a chimerical Eden called Oregon.

Surviving required every bit of energy he possessed. By his calculation it would be five years before his orchard would bear fruit, and meanwhile he had mouths to feed and a family to clothe and shelter.

How to do that was the great conundrum. His world had been stale books, musty lecture halls, dark chapels, battered lecterns, odorous dormitories, cobbled streets, ornate parlors, tepid debating societies, fiery professions of faith, and chaperoned socials at which young seminarians were introduced to pale and pious young women suited to become the wives of ministers.

All of it had proved useless save for the fierce faith that buoyed him when he was especially burdened. Were it not for his distant neighbors, who instructed him in the ordinary arts of farming and helped him build a cabin and a pen for his mules and put in a vegetable garden, he and his family might well have perished.

But help did come to him, mostly in the form of those neighborly veterans of the wilds, Joe Meek and Doc Newell, refugees from the dead fur trade in the Rockies. They hewed down trees and barked them and hoisted them into place until the walls of a cabin took shape; then laid up the ridgepole and rafters while Jasper and his sons awkwardly split cedar shakes. They built a hearth of fieldstone and mortar, and embedded iron hooks in it that would hold cookpots, while Rose hoed the garden and bucketed water to the tender seedlings that would someday become fruit trees. They hunted game for him, and advised him to get a fowling piece for self-defense, though he could not afford anything so costly.

Other help came from an anonymous donor who wasn't a bit anonymous to Jasper Constable. John McLoughlin had quietly sent along a big blue mule, harness, a one-bottom plow, a harrow, and a small wagon, treasures that Jasper immediately put to use.

The land he had staked was not the best for crops because most of it sloped. Yet there were twenty or thirty acres of good bottoms with rich loam that he could put to a cash crop if only he could master the skills. So he hitched his mule and began plowing, learning swiftly how to guide it in a straight line, with pressure enough to cause the moldboard to turn over the sod but not go so deep that it would buck and throw the mule off stride or topple Constable to the ground. For a man with a muscular intellect but weakened muscles, it was not easy, and he could work only minutes at a time before exhausting himself. But slowly his strength built.

He took wild pride in his fields, voluptuous pleasure in the plowed and tilled and planted black loam, where the green shoots of spring wheat poked upward into the waxing sun. Had he, the pale urban seminarian, wrought this miracle? And yet that pride was matched by loss. He was wasting his life. His good mind was atrophied. He was making no progress. He was depriving his family. His sons were not being schooled and would end up illiterate unless he and Rose found time to teach them the three Rs.

Yet work got done. The boys helped. The hearth required awesome amounts of dry wood, and he detailed Matthew to chopping it; the dry limbs and deadwood first, but then they cut a future supply as well from live conifers. The boy blistered his hands and produced barely enough for current needs, much less for the winter. Mark, the younger son, could hoe and weed, or scythe or sickle, or chop kindling.

Jasper lacked so much as a dime. His clothing disintegrated under the terrible beating of farming, yet he could do nothing but hope that Rose could put a patch upon patches. His shoes fell apart, and so did those of his sons. Rose's dresses fell to pieces. But there was no money for new, and little time to sew, for it was all she could do to keep them fed and her rude cabin in order.

He shrank to flesh stretched over bone, and his body never stopped hurting. She thinned too, but somehow became all the more beautiful, tanned and angular. His sons looked like scarecrows. Matt, at least, had taken to fishing on Sunday afternoons, when he was allowed time away from his duties, and often returned with a string of trout. But they never had enough and lacked money even for salt and sugar.

He had not forgotten his dream of helping the Indians, and continuing the very schooling now abandoned by the church, and from the moment he had staked his place, he had tried to make it an active mission.

Through his young friend Billy, who alone among his people could speak some English, he invited the Tillamooks and other coastal tribesmen to come each Sabbath to a riverside grove, there to hear the Word. These were angry and desperate people, rapidly being deprived of their hunting grounds and thus their very food and life. He meant to help them. He could not stop the influx of whites or stop the slaughter of game, but he could bring them hope, a voice in the territorial government, and most of all, teach them agriculture, which alone offered them food and even some coin.

A few men did come those first Sundays; he and Rose never saw a woman among the guests. And there, under arching willows, he built a small altar and offered Christian services, and proffered simple sermons, trusting in Billy's dubious translations. He had hopes of continuing, but then one Sunday, halfway through one of his services, a dour young Indian demanded to speak and this time Jasper found himself listening and learning.

"White men have taken everything from us," Billy translated. "We are hungry. We are sick. Our children weep because they have nothing to eat. You must leave. This place is the home of black bears, who eat the berries. Every year, we came here to hunt bears and we had fat and meat and bearskins. Now they are gone . . ."

Jasper sensed their heat and knew they were not far from violence.

"I will take your word to the chiefs in Oregon City," he replied. "I will plead for you. I will ask them to set aside plenty of land that will be yours forever, good land. But you must also learn to plow and plant for your food, because the world is changing and I do not have the power to stop it."

That caused a stir, and several of the men angrily charged Billy with a reply.

"That is women's work. We will not do it. We are hunters and fishers and warriors. We will not make ourselves small."

"But you must! Am I less a man for working and planting?"

They did not reply, and he sensed at once that yes, in their eyes, he was less a man because he devoted every waking minute to growing food.

For a few Sundays that spring of 1846 they came and then no more, except for Billy now and then, who came to beg a meal and tell him how angry the Indians were, and how they talked of war and driving away the white men forever.

"You go. You're not safe here," the youth said. "Go quick!"

"No, we're here to stay."

Billy absorbed that sullenly. "Big trouble," he said.

"Billy, listen! I've sent letters to Oregon City pleading your case. I've told the white people about your needs. Food, land, safety. I've written the newspaper there. A newspaper is like a book; it sends the word out to everyone. My letters have been published there. We are your friends. We will keep telling them about you until their eyes are opened."

Billy squinted at them, and that was the last time he saw the Tillamook boy. Somewhere west, over the brow of the coastal mountains, an angry people sickened, dreamed, plotted, and starved. And they no doubt thought about the Constable homestead, located much closer to them than any other white men's farms, the spearhead of yet another invasion.

These things frightened Constable but he hid them from Rose and his sons. There wasn't a weapon on the place and he knew he couldn't use one even under siege. How could he, a minister, lift a rifle, peer through its sights at the very red men he wished to convert, and squeeze a trigger? Their sole refuge would be flight, and he hoped Billy might give him warning if it came to that. Flight and faith; the mighty shield of God.

It was then, reflecting upon the failure of his plans once again, that he began to think of his Oregon venture as a vast delusion. He could not imagine why the very word, "Oregon," used to bloom in his mind as a shining and sacred land.

Now it was a place he could not escape. Life had thrust him into this. He could not tell one beetle from another, nor did he know what yellowed some of his greening wheat, or why scale grew on the maize or the tomato plants curled up.

Nor could he tell why his mule sickened and refused to work. It had almost died until Meek showed up with salt and some grain, and trimmed the mule's shoes, and prescribed a week's rest on fresh pasture.

Constable was, as usual, chagrined.

It came down to one of life's mysteries, which he turned over in his mind over and over again. Why was he here, doing things for which he was not fitted, when he should be stretching his abilities, giving himself to the service and life he had always intended?

And yet, in the midst of all this, he was discovering something so precious and sacred that he turned it over and over in his mind, scarcely believing it.

Rose, Rose, Rose. There, in her bright warm eyes, was a love he had never imagined, hadn't earned, and could barely fathom. She loved him. He loved her. It was no mistake. He saw it there upon her gentle face, an expression more precious than gold, a humor in her that warmed his very heart. He knew now that when they had met back East, the sober thing they called "love" had not been love; it had been a very decent and proper potpourri of duty, commitment, affection, and respect.

Now in her sudden laughter, her touching, her cheerful mothering of their sons, her buoyant spirits, her quiet bustle around that one-room cabin in which only a fabric wall made of tattered sailcloth divided the homemade marital bed he shared with her from the bunks of the boys, he and she were blooming with love, and this sojourn in the Oregon wilderness had become an utterly improbable honeymoon.

69

John O'Malley scarcely knew what to do, which way to turn. And he wasn't sure he cared. When he watched Mary Kate drift out of his life, he knew it was the end of a dream as well as a marriage. She was gone, never to return. She was going to Ireland to save her life and the boy's too. He was here to save his life, for he would sicken and die back there.

He walked along a bleak and silent and reproachful shore, not knowing where he was going. He had no home and no prospects. He had to earn his keep or perish and yet he didn't much care. What difference did it make? Was the hunger of the body any worse than the hunger of the heart?

He could not sort out his feelings. One moment currents of bitterness laced him; another, moments of great tenderness. Still others he was filled with malice. And still others, he wept for lost dreams and shattered hopes.

Now he was alone, and there were no consolations. He supposed he ought to tell Father Blanchard, the new priest. Tell him he had just shipped his unhappy wife and innocent son away, and listen to the rebuke. Something in O'Malley welled up biliously against the church. He wanted no rebukes and no platitudes and no reproach and no more guilt. He had enough guilt without having the dominie heap more upon him. And yet he knew he would go to the church first, out of old habit if nothing else, and that meant Oregon City.

He hailed some passing boatmen and for one bit got a ride upstream, and debarked at Oregon City, which suddenly seemed an alien and hostile place. He ached for a public house on the nearest corner where a man could sip an ale and talk with friends, but there were none in Oregon because the fanatic Protestants had abolished spirits, even beer and ale. If there was anything evil about Oregon, surely that was at the top of any list. It was bad enough to be an isolated Catholic surrounded by thousands of Methodists and Presbyterians; worse that they made it a sin to sip a glass of ale with friends.

He felt a crawling disdain for all churches, including his own. He found Blanchard in the rectory and pushed in, something sullen in his demeanor. He didn't care.

The lean and bespectacled father looked up from his writing, set aside a quill, and waited amiably.

"I have put Mary Kate upon a boat for Ireland," he said. "I will not go with her, and she will not return." He stood there defiantly, waiting.

Blanchard motioned him to a chair. "Why?" he asked.

"Because she deserted me, because she was starving our son in all the ways there are, and because she needs her people, and because she was dying of homesickness."

The priest masked his face and settled back in his swivel chair, waiting.

"It is the end of the marriage," O'Malley said. "I am not going back there to die."

"Marriages are forever, John."

"You say so; I do not."

The priest let that slide. "I think in time you'll see it's so. You'll miss her. You'll want your son. You'll want to pick up life. That's what our Lord wants for you."

"It is over and I am not going back."

Blanchard smiled unexpectedly. "This isn't the time to be arguing with you; I can see that. You're in pain. I'm here to comfort you. Maybe we can find ways to heal things. How about in a week? We'll arm wrestle if that's what you want."

"Arm-wrestle, will you? I am not arm-wrestling; I am burying a love and a marriage. I am mourning a wife! She is as good as in the grave! I am not going to wrestle you; I am going to pick up the pieces if I can, and if you will help me, fine . . ."

Blanchard's eyebrows climbed. "John, you go pray, and I will too. When you're ready to talk, we'll talk. I'll be here when you're ready to see me. I'm not here to condemn you or judge you. When you're ready for the confessional, I'll hear you. When you're ready for absolution and forgiveness—"

"I will never be."

He hadn't meant to say anything like that. He had come to this place to find comfort and hope, but here he was, boiling over and taunting the priest and provoking trouble. He could not fathom what was goading him.

"I will be going now," he said.

O'Malley stormed into a cold spring twilight, the old turmoil occasioned by the church upsetting him. He'd never been at ease in those precincts, and now he felt as alien and alone as he felt among Protestants. But some hard cold thing was in him, like granite, and he wouldn't listen to rebukes or pleadings. He had lost Mary Kate long ago, and now she was gone, and nothing would change that.

There remained to him the task of making sense of his life, and finding a job, but he didn't much feel like it. He wandered through the bustling city, feeling the crushing power of the falls pour through him, thinking of Mary Kate, loving and condemning her, kissing and despising her, yearning and rejecting her all at once, until he thought he was mad. But at bottom he knew he loved her and what hurt so much was her cruel rejection of him.

He heard the whine of the sawmill, heard the sawteeth snapping through knots, got a job as a cradle man, pushing the massive fir logs into the blade of the saw, and worked there three days before quitting. He had slept in the Oregon City livery barn, shaved with river water, and wrenched his muscles piking logs too heavy to handle onto the groaning saw cradle.

He had earned three dollars and spent two of them.

He went to John McLoughlin's store and applied for a clerking job, but no one needed him.

"Let me take a wagon then, and I will peddle your goods. I did it for Abel Brownell. I have a way with farmers."

But the manager resisted. "You can go talk to McLoughlin about it but that's not for me to say. I have my instructions."

O'Malley didn't talk to McLoughlin. He didn't want to be beholden to anyone. He wasn't going to accept one nickel of debt or assume one obligation.

He worked a fortnight as a riverman, rowing and poling and dragging flat-bottomed mackinaws or other craft up and down the Willamette River, making six bits or eight bits a day on good days. Then he picked a quarrel with the boss, who owned the boats, and quit.

He thought sometimes about Mary Kate and Oregon Patrick, and where they might be and how they might be faring. Were they weary of the sea and of the tropical heat? Were they well? Were they scurvied? Were his letters and funds safely en route to Ireland?

It did no good to think about them. That was the past.

He apprenticed to a blacksmith for five days and quit. He became a surveyor's assistant and liked the work. Maybe it would lead him to some unclaimed land. Mostly he stood, holding a pole or a chain while his boss peered through a transit, wishing away the wind or rain, and wondering what he was doing. That lasted a while, until he got into a fight over pay and was discharged.

"I want a steady man," the surveyor, Dub McPherson, said. "You had a chance. The whole area's cryin' to be surveyed. I've more work than ten of me could do. People stake a place and want a description of it. All you had to do was let me teach you a bit, calculate and measure right, and you'd have a fine living rest of your life. I don't know what is the matter with you."

"Don't preach at me," O'Malley snapped.

"You got your Irish up."

"Call it what you want," O'Malley said.

"I'd still take you if you'd settle down. You a drinker?"

"I would be if I could find spirits anywhere in this country."

"Well, there's not a drop, and maybe that's good."

McPherson had been more tolerant than most, and O'Malley felt bad. But that job was over and the summer had wasted away.

He'd been discharged near Champoeg and was tempted to go to the mission and maybe find someone he could call a friend. St. Paul's still served the French Canadians who'd retired from Hudson's Bay Company and settled there. But he didn't. Religion would only shame him, and he refused to be shamed. Instead, he rowed across the river and hiked through fields he once called his own; land he had staked until squatters stole it from him. This was his land, and he wanted it back. A breeze rustled the knee-high grasses. From the slope he could look down upon Champoeg, sunning sleepily in the hazy distance.

This had been his dream. He had found this land soon after he arrived in 1842, and now it was gone, Mary Kate was gone, and he had little more than the rags on his back.

He rounded a bend and beheld, above, a small white house occupying the very place where he would have put his, and employing the timbers he had cut, and some of the foundation he had once owned. An emerald lawn stretched in every direction. A barn and outbuildings stood below and to the left. A stolen house, a stolen dream.

The bloody thieves. There was no one about, which suited him fine, because he knew what he had to do.

A great sadness beset John O'Malley. Dreams. That was what this was about. Stolen dreams. They had taken his land from him, knowingly, mockingly. He couldn't even remember their names. But he remembered the thorough whipping they gave him when he had quietly protested, offered to show them his corner cairns, his claim duly recorded at the mission.

Odd how close they had come to his own dreams: their house was narrower and had fewer windows, but it stood atop the very hill, commanded the same views, lorded over a sweep of slope leading down to the Willamette Valley. This was his place, where he and Mary Kate had been destined to live. For this he had come to Oregon.

And yet he was sad, for it wasn't in him to destroy anyone's dreams, and he regretted what he had to do. The rebels of Ireland regretted what they had to do now and then, the protest they were required to make to see to justice. So a sadness betook him as he stared at the silent house baking in the summer sun, with daisies planted about it, and pine shrubs, and potted geraniums on the veranda, and some sheep mowing the lawn.

He saw no one. No horses stood in the paddocks. Gone, then. He walked warily toward the white house and knocked, not even thinking of what he might say if someone should answer. He rapped hard, waited, rapped again, and waited. He wished someone would come, an act of mercy, sparing him what he had to do to a clan of thieves. But no one came. He squinted down the long reaches of greensward toward the distant river, studied the brows of ridges, and saw not a soul.

That saddened him the more, because there was nothing on earth to frighten him away, to deter his dark designs, and he counted it an evil omen upon his life. He rapped yet again to aching silence, and entered. An odd mixture of rustic furniture and pieces brought from great distances stood about:

a brocaded sofa with doilies, an armchair, a fine dining table and chairs, a kitchen filled with utensils and pots and strainers and towels. This house was shadowed and dark. His would have let in the light. A jar of lucifers sat next to the wood range. He plucked up two.

He found the coal oil in the pantry, a gallon crock of it, and lifted it. He poured the coal oil across the kitchen floor, and then soaked a carpet in the parlor, leaving a great black swatch, and then poured the kerosene on the carpet runner going up the stairs. He emptied the last of it on the veranda, around the posts. The pungence of coal oil laced the air.

He felt a great melancholy, and if it weren't for justice he would have forbidden himself to do this thing to other mortals, no matter what their wickedness might be. But in all his days abroad he had encountered injustice, and the knowledge of it was as ingrained in him as if it were a part of his soul. Injustice and helplessness. He had followed the ribbon men's resistance in Ireland, and then the men known as Young Ireland had come along, agitating for justice, and he had quietly supported them too, but thought their cause was doomed.

Doomed causes were the reason he had come here. It was better to begin life fresh and new than to plunge into doomed causes. This would be a doomed cause. It would gain him nothing. It would not set aright the wrong he had suffered, and evil for evil healed nothing.

He scratched the lucifer. It flared and hissed and then settled into yellow flame. He touched it to the pool of coal oil in the kitchen, and watched the flames leap to life. He started the other conflagrations too. Then he stepped into a sunlit day, observing that so far, no smoke escaped the dying building. He walked downslope, angling away from the river road, and when he was half a mile distant he turned back. Now a fine handsome pillar of black smoke rose into an azure sky.

He reached the Willamette River in twenty more minutes, found his beached rowboat and set it afloat. He sat down and rowed himself toward Champoeg, observing the fine black plume that now rose like a question mark in the heavens a mile distant. On the far shore an excited crowd had collected, and some were launching boats.

He knew how this would end, and knew what he must do.

As he rowed, he remembered the name of the family: Burgess. Four Burgesses had pounded on him, battered his flesh while robbing his land. He didn't know their given names.

He rowed the boat to the riverbank, hopped off the prow, and pulled it onto the bank of the river, while the crowd swarmed in.

"What is that fire?" one asked. "You come for help?"

The moment had come. "It is a house burning," O'Malley said. "I believe it is the house belonging to the Burgesses."

"The Burgesses. Yes, that's what it looks like. They went to Oregon City today. The whole clan."

Another asked, "Should we go? Is it too late?"

"Yes, it is too late. They will come back to ashes."

"Ashes. That house! And all within it! Do you know what a tragedy this is? Finest house in Oregon! Furniture brought round the Horn! Was anyone in it?"

"Not a soul."

"And how would you know?"

"I checked."

"And what were you doing there?"

"Looking at the property."

"And how did it start, this blaze?"

They weren't ready to accuse him—yet. Not quite yet.

"A liberal application of coal oil."

The crowd stood, bewildered, suspicious, not giving credence to their own ears.

"Coal oil? Coal oil? Did a lamp fall and break?"

"No, no lamp fell. It was an act of arson."

"Arson! The Burgess place, it was burned down by some madman?"

"Yes, burned right to the ground by an angry man."

The burly inquisitor stared. "And who might that be, sir?"

"That would be me."

Now a buzz sawed through that mob. People could not believe what they were hearing. He saw a farmer gaping at him. Some women, brows furrowed, stared at him as if he were the devil. Some big galoots squinted at him murderously.

"Surely, sir, you're not confessing to a crime?" one asked.

"No, to a dream," O'Malley said. He was tired of this.

"Who the hell are you?"

"I am John O'Malley."

"We'd better get the sheriff," one said.

"That is fine. I will wait right here."

"Meek's a long ways away," another said. "Maybe we better haul this man up there to Oregon City."

"That is fine. Whatever you wish."

The inquisitor was puzzled by this.

"Something don't add up."

"It adds up perfectly."

O'Malley said it with such force and calm that this surly mob quieted, utterly without understanding. In fact, O'Malley didn't much care. What they might do to him scarcely mattered. He hadn't really helped himself. Revenge was the hollowest of all passions. And justice was merely an abstraction.

"Let us go," he said.

But an old Frenchman, one of the early settlers, began muttering volubly. "O'Malley, oui, c'est bon."

It took a half hour for the story of O'Malley's claim and eviction to become known. Indeed, the Burgesses had boasted of taking it from some Paddy off the boat. A lay brother from St. Paul's Mission produced the original claim. Some men rowed across the river and upstream and found the corner cairn. The Burgesses had not bothered to throw out the other copy of the claim that lay in a bottle within the rock cairn.

And yet it didn't suffice. This was arson.

A shame crept through O'Malley. A man should not be in the public eye, but here he was.

After a great deal of shouting and snarling, a group of Champoeg citizens manhandled O'Malley into a rowboat and started for the capital. No mick off the boat was going to get away with arson against good solid Missourians like the Burgesses. In the midst of all this he had learned the Christian names of those who had stolen the land from him. The father was Oliver; the burly sons were Mike, Peter, and Clarence. Mrs. Burgess, Annette, had come with a daughter, Millicent, and baby, Bobby.

O'Malley listened to all that with an odd detachment. He wondered why he felt nothing at all, except maybe tired. They rowed downstream, angry men who looked ready to pitch him overboard and get rid of their problem. There were none aboard who had taken his part in the fracas; none who had his claim in hand. These were all friends of the Burgess family, ready to string up their prisoner upon the slightest excuse. Arson! The man should be hanged like a horse thief!

Some considerable while later, they docked at a wharf at Oregon City, but these burly friends of the Burgesses didn't head for the offices of the provisional government, but toward Oregon House, an imposing inn one level up from the river.

Then, indeed, O'Malley realized that his fate would not be settled by the dubious and temporary government of Oregon, but by the Burgesses, and it was probable he would not survive this day.

71

O'Malley's pulse raced as they dragged him out of the boat and up the slopes. And yet a part of him seemed detached, as if he were an observer watching his own doom unfold.

They treated him roughly, not letting him walk but shoving and mauling him, punching him along, a beast to be beaten and abused, not a mortal. And that, indeed, awakened the keen interest of local people, who began following this strange procession consisting of a dozen burly and angry men bullying the Irishman toward the inn.

The mob caught the attention of Joe Meek, and the sheriff hastened in their direction carrying a double-barreled fowling piece. He had abandoned his mountain attire these days, and was wearing pin-striped trousers, a vest, and a steel star. But what law did he represent?

"What is this?" Meek asked.

"Keep out of this, Sheriff."

"That's John O'Malley. What's he done?"

One of the men turned squarely toward the sheriff. "You'll find out. You keep out of it or you'll be sorry."

That was enough to provoke the amiable Meek, who clung to the party like a burr.

They pushed O'Malley into the inn and found the Burgesses gathered in the lobby, getting ready for their supper.

"Oliver! Bad news. Your place burnt!" said one.

The Burgess patriarch stared, unbelieving. "Burnt?"

"Your house, right to the ground."

Burgess whitened, shock showing beneath his hard dark flesh.

"Nothing left?" he asked.

"Nothing. And here's the man done it."

"Done it? Deliberate?"

The big Burgess sons crowded close, looming over O'Malley like rumbling thunder. The hefty Burgess women began to weep, and the mother sank into a scratchy divan, drawing the daughter to her.

"Who's this man?"

"O'Malley's his name."

"I've seen him. O'Malley, eh?"

"He's confessed it. We all heard it. We saw that house afire clear across the river, just a pencil of smoke going up, and we got a spyglass and saw the house a-going, and not a thing a soul could do, but some of us took off for the blaze, and then this mick's rowing across the river calm as the devil and tells us he done it."

Burgess stared at O'Malley, recognition building in him, and glanced at the rest with swift, sharp eyes that raked the whole crowd, and settled at last on Meek, who stood just apart, watching events unfold.

"And?" the sheriff asked.

"We told you to stay out of this," someone snapped.

"I've known O'Malley for years. He was one of the first to come here." He turned to O'Malley. "Did you burn it?"

O'Malley nodded.

"Why?"

"I think you know."

Meek nodded. "I know."

"We're hanging him, Sheriff. That's what a son of a bitch gets for arson," Burgess said. "And you're going to stand and watch."

A great crowd had pushed into the hotel, and Meek obviously didn't like it. "Clear out," he said, the voice hard and flat. The fowling piece remained in the crook of his arm.

No one moved.

"Tell me your story, John, in your own words."

O'Malley felt himself floating apart from this whole scene, observing it from afar.

"Stealing dreams, that is the worst of all thefts," O'Malley said.

"Enough," Burgess said. The man plainly didn't want certain facts bruited about. He grabbed O'Malley by the collar and started out.

"Let him talk," Meek said, and big black-bearded Burgess discovered he was looking down the muzzles of the piece, just two feet from his chest.

The women were weeping.

"I come from a bitter land where a few hard men steal the dreams of the rest of us. Some enjoy it. Some do not care. A few care and do it anyway. It is an odd thing, how some men like to steal dreams. A man like that, he might see unclaimed land everywhere, a new country just being settled, but he sees a piece of land he likes, and takes it away from the one who claimed it first just to be mean. Beats up the owner, pounds him half to death, and throws the man off his own land. Odd, is it not? That with all the free land everywhere, some dream stealer just wants to make someone else miserable."

O'Malley was finding poetry in his words, and spilled them out easily, and from afar he watched himself orate.

"Odd it is, how some of the race can't see what they do to others, or do not care. That is how it is in my old country, where most dream stealers hate themselves for stealing, but do not stop it because they do not care enough, or they think maybe God is not watching, or maybe the scripture "Love thy neighbor . . . ," words like that get ignored, you know? So they take the prize, and have no mercy, and their souls are like boulders in their chests."

Some of the younger Burgesses stirred, as if to stop all this, but Meek's piece turned and lifted slightly, and in the mountaineer's face was steely resolve.

But O'Malley knew how this would end. Burgess was not listening, nor did he care what the argument was. The man's gaze darted hither and yon, calculation in his alert eyes, intent upon tilting the scales.

"I never much cared for destroying other people's dreams, but some people need the lesson," O'Malley said gently. "How does it feel, seeing a dream vanish?"

"Enough of this," Burgess snapped. "The man's an arsonist, and we'll show him what my clan does to arsonists."

"We'll have a trial," Meek said, as slowly and distinctly as he could into the bedlam. His unblinking gaze focused on Burgess. "We'll do this right. You can bring your charges. And he can bring his against you. I know this story. You took that land from him and threw him off. Now you've paid. We'll let a jury decide who's right."

Burgess laughed shortly. "The man just confessed."

He jerked O'Malley in front of him, shielding him from the bore of the piece. O'Malley felt his back wrench under the anvil weight of his captor's massive hand.

"Put that down, Meek. We'll deal with this."

Meek casually swung the barrel toward the sons. "No, I'll deal with it, not you. You do this, and you'll go on trial for murder, and I'll be after you."

It was a bluff. Meek could not pull triggers in that crowded vestibule without hitting a dozen bystanders.

"You haven't even got a jail," Burgess said. "He's a dumb Paddy. You crazy or something?" He nodded at the boys, who fell in behind. O'Malley felt himself being dragged and manhandled.

"Stop right there and hand him over," Meek said sternly. "You'll get hurt."

But he hadn't the power or authority to stop it, not alone, in a place without a jail and only a makeshift government. Not without several armed deputies. They knew it. They knew he wouldn't fire that buckshot into a crowd.

They dragged O'Malley into the broad street, beside the stately river, hunting for a gallows tree and finding none. The falls roared, drowning their voices. They walked upstream, into the vapor and roar of the cataract.

The Irishman was always their shield, always between Meek's barrels and the mob. Now at last O'Malley felt terror. No longer was his spirit floating somewhere else. He struggled, but these brutes held him easily, laughing at his contortions, twisting him until his neck and arms hurt.

Meek was shouting, trying to bull through, but they repulsed him easily. The roar of the falls deafened O'Malley. They tied his hands behind him with cord, lashing his wrists. They lashed his ankles together with cord. He felt the spray of the falls, and his heart roared with the water. They brought iron to hang on him, chain from the smithy down the street, link upon link, so much weight he could drop like a stone.

"Stop this," a man commanded. O'Malley gaped upward from the ground into the florid face of Governor Abernethy, bland old George from the mission store. Abernethy, his rival, head of the Mission Party, apostle of Protestantism, stepping in against an ugly mob.

"You're too late," Burgess snapped.

"Men, do your duty. Stop this," Abernethy snapped.

After a long pause, a few citizens surrounded the Burgesses and their Champoeg friends and sycophants, ready to spring. But the Burgess party would not be deterred.

O'Malley felt his breath being sucked from him. His heart convulsed.

"Go," roared Abernethy, and a dozen citizens waded in, wrestling against the Burgess faction. On the ground, O'Malley found himself staring up at Oliver Burgess, who was grinning broadly.

Bedlam surrounded the party. He heard Meek shatter bone with his fowling piece, cracking it left and right. One of the Burgess sons howled, and another man went down. But Burgess was grinning, there in the epicenter.

"You got yourself killed," he said.

O'Malley knew then that his last seconds were ticking.

The falls thundered as loud as the blood buzzing his head.

"This is how to put out fire," Burgess said cheerfully, lifting one of the chains.

But O'Malley spun free and rolled into the roaring river. He felt the cold water suck him deep under, and pummel him; he felt himself tumble through the torrent. He hit the surface suddenly, and gasped, sucked air, and was drawn under again. He could not free his wrists or feet, and felt helpless.

Then he surfaced once again, far downstream, and this time he saw running men and heard shouts. He coughed, gulped air, and tried to free himself. Someone waded in, caught him as he raced by, and dragged him to the bank. Another man untied his bonds. He sat on the riverbank, cold, dripping, amazed, and trembling. Governor Abernethy hovered over him, a rifle in hand.

Meek raced up.

"You all right?"

O'Malley nodded.

"Come with me."

O'Malley stood up on wobbly legs, rivering water, and hastened after Meek, who was heading into town. The sheriff dodged between two buildings and finally paused at the government's office.

He led O'Malley in and locked the door behind him.

"I have no way to protect you, O'Malley. No jail, no deputies, nothing. Some citizens saved your neck. If you value your life, you'll get out of Oregon. Burgess and his friends, they're out to get you, and they will if you stay."

O'Malley, shivering, nodded.

Meek smiled suddenly. "I ain't gonna hold you for trial. That was dumb, burning down that place, but I figure it's rough justice."

"Where should I go?"

"Mexico. It's warm; you can walk over the mountains this time of year."

"What is there?"

"Life, O'Malley, life."

Meek found a towel and tossed it to the Irishman. "Few years ago a man named John Bidwell came out here, didn't like Oregon, and headed down to California. Last I heard, he's doing fine, working for a Swiss named Sutter, on the American River. Sutter employs anyone with a skill or two. Go on down there and start a new life."

"But—"

"I'll help with a kit. Wait here."

An hour or so later, Meek returned with a burlap sack filled with provisions and gear.

"This isn't much, but I've seen men go far with less," he said. "There's some dry duds in there. Knife and cookpot. Fishhooks and line. Flint and steel. Some jerky for hungry times."

That night, Meek spirited O'Malley out of Oregon City, and left him alone, under the stars.

O'Malley thought the stars were friendly. They were eternal, like hope. And he was free.

72

The news sifted out of the sea, printed in a newspaper borne around the Horn in a British frigate. In June of 1846, Great Britain and the United States had settled the border controversy and averted war. The 49th parallel would be the boundary, from the Rocky Mountains to the Strait of Juan de Fuca on the Pacific Coast, leaving only Vancouver Island, and the new Hudson's Bay headquarters there, in British hands south of the parallel. Lord Peel's government had called Oregon a pine swamp and not worth fighting about. The United States agreed to respect the ownership of all Hudson's Bay Company property, including the Fort Vancouver holdings, and the great farm plantations around Nisqually.

The tidings reached Provisional Governor George Abernethy in November, about the time the first of that year's immigrants arrived by land. But the overland travelers did not carry the news with them because they were all en route before the treaty was agreed to, and knew nothing of it.

The tidings rippled outward from Oregon City, evoking a great celebration among the Americans. And some animosity too. The calculating, hard-eyed emigrants waiting to devour the well-kept farmlands, orchards, vineyards, hayfields, houses and warehouses and depots of the Hudson's Bay Company were thwarted by the treaty.

Not a few of the Americans, loath to cut and burn forests, dig up stumps, erect cabins, dig wells, build fences, plant gardens, and plow virgin lands to get a living, coveted those sweeping fields which the hand of man had turned to profitable use. And so they grumbled, and chief among the offended was Garwood Reese, the dulcet voice of anti-British sentiment in Oregon. He wasn't simply offended; he was outraged, and penned a screed.

"Now the Crown company is a dagger poised at our heart, a foreign element right in the midst of us," he proclaimed in *The Spectator*. "I am appalled.

The Polk administration has let us down! We must have justice! If I am to serve in any public capacity in the territory, my first order of business will remain just what it always has been: drive out the cutthroat British, who continue to milk and bilk us, set their monopoly prices over all our commerce, and beggar us. The Polk administration sold out, settling for only half of Oregon, ignoring us, letting itself be drawn into a war with Mexico.

"The Hudson's Bay Company and its chief factor, McLoughlin, wrested the best farmland, the best waterpower sites, the best town-site land from Americans, held it by economic force backed by imperial British shot and cannon, divided it and sold it back to us at an unseemly profit, and now escapes scot-free from the natural and heaven-ordained justice that governs this universe."

That won him hosannas, especially from those settlers who had not yet given up the idea of comandeering the company's property. Even twenty acres of cleared, cultivated, productive land like that would put any man at his ease; forty acres of orchard and vineyard, why, that would set a man up with an estate!

But Abernethy didn't like the letter, and summoned Reese to his spacious Oregon City office, one of the few islands of amenity in a state where pioneering people ate off hand-carved wooden utensils, cooked in open fireplaces, filled their rude windows with scraped hide to let dim light into their cabins, and wore homespuns or garments cut from tattered sailcloth because there was no fabric to be had.

"Garwood, we still haven't any word. Nothing but that newspaper report. I don't think you should be agitating and stirring up trouble until we receive official word. It may take a while. Polk's getting into a war with Mexico, and we're half-forgotten up here."

"It doesn't matter what the treaty says," Reese replied. "We still have to drive out the foreigners. Oregon for Americans!"

Abernethy was not impressed. "There's going to be a territorial government formed, and then a state government if we're admitted to the union. Both of those will require acts from Congress. Just be patient. Don't get us into trouble with Polk or Congress—or the British. Especially before we've seen the treaty."

Reese smiled. Abernethy always had been timorous, a mild front man for the Mission Party; a man whose very blandness veneered the rabid cupidity of the old Methodist coalition, the settlers whose hatred of Hudson's Bay Company ran deepest because they owed the most to the British firm and had contested its dominion from the start.

Reese nodded, promised to wait for official word, and departed, his head teeming with schemes.

Everything depended on the wording of the treaty. If the language protected the holdings of all British subjects now living in the United States, that would be a setback. But if the treaty language protected only the holdings of the Hudson's Bay Company, as the newspaper report indicated, that would, indeed, be just fine with Reese.

He knew how to proceed. John McLoughlin held the unsold town-site lots in his name; he held the mill and waterpower rights in his own name. He held the land under his house in his own name. He had filed his claims with the provisional government, all in his own name, and made much of the fact that he had paid the company twenty thousand dollars for the property . . . and thus his holdings were probably not protected by the treaty.

Reese itched to act at once, but knew he must wait. A rash move now against McLoughlin and the French farmers around Champoeg might explode in his face. Nonetheless, as he hurried home through the December chill of 1846, his mind seethed with plans to liberate Oregon from the clutch of the oppressor, and win himself a place in the history books.

The next step would be to send a trusted man to Washington to make certain representations to Congress about the British monopoly and its ruthless conduct. The act enabling a territorial government in Oregon must have language confirming the holdings of Americans, especially those in the Mission Party, and language nullifying McLoughlin's holdings.

He could not even think of that big brute of a Canadian without sheer loathing, and now he saw a way to revenge himself for all the slights and humiliations that Dr. McLoughlin had heaped upon him. The memory of having twice been driven from the chief factor's office rankled as much now as when it happened. Soon there would be sweet revenge. The man was vulnerable; he was a foreigner, a Catholic, a Hudson's Bay executive, a squaw man, a monopolist . . . and a man whose loyalties remained with the Crown!

He let himself into his modest house, at once disliking it for its modesty. A statesman required stately quarters. The place oppressed him, not just because there were several other homes more fashionable, including McLoughlin's, but also because its chatelaine was as comforting as a cold hearth in January.

He found her sipping something amber in the kitchen, and neglecting her disheveled blond hair, her begrimed dress, the dirty dishes, and his dinner. He wondered where she had obtained the illegal spirits.

"Pour me some," he said.

She laughed nastily, but then arose, dug into a cupboard, found a crockery jug, and poured him a generous dollop.

"Here's to the Mission Party and all its rotten laws," she said. "You've managed to support a party that knows what's good not only for its members, but for all the rest of the world. What a strange cast of mind: declare something's a vice, tobacco, spirits, dancing, tea, and then prohibit the rest of the world from living as it chooses. God, Garwood, you sure like to make life hell. How did I ever end up in this goddamned place living with a weasel?"

He smiled and sipped. Good Kentucky, as far as his famished palate could tell. He glanced nervously out the glass windows, but this was late afternoon and no one could see in. The whiskey slid down easily, and he thought only of catching up to her. Who knows, with enough spirits in him and her, they might even enjoy a civil moment. But he knew better than to hope.

"Within a year, you'll be living in John McLoughlin's house," he said.

"Are you going to steal it?"

"No, but we'll have able men in Washington, shaping the enabling act making us a territory, and the law will require that he surrender it and all his property."

"You'll steal it," she said. "You're a dandy, Garwood. A regular Tammany politician. That's what politicians do, you know. Rob the most industrious class, pass some of the boodle to a few grateful idiots to win their vote, and keep the rest. It beats working for a living, and it all sounds so good, justice, equality, virtue . . ."

"We'll only replevy property," he retorted stiffly. "Bring justice to Oregon."

"God, I love your rhetoric," she said. "You can make rape sound like a sacrament." She looked amused, not caring what he thought.

He angered. "I came here with good news. You've complained that I don't provide you with a comfortable life. Now I am sure I will, but I hear no thanks from you!"

She smiled, slowly. "You'll give me a purloined palace, and demand my affection."

"Just once, just once in our years together, speak kindly to me, thank me!"

She smiled. "It's a good house, but that squaw doesn't know how to decorate. When I'm in it, I'll show the world what a good house looks like. You'll have to steal the rest, you know: some good Kazakhstan rugs, some good cherry furniture, some good Limoges china . . . The only question, Garwood, is whether you've nerve enough. If you're going to be a politician, you'd better go all the way and get rich. If you want me to entertain you in my boudoir, you weak-kneed trimmer, you'll make sure that all my needs are fulfilled. If you want me to stop embarrassing you in public, do my bidding."

Garwood poured more fluid from the jug to his tumbler, and raised it. "To the ugliest woman in Oregon," he said, wondering where he had found the courage.

73

John McLoughlin dressed himself in his best brass-buttoned blue frock coat and a freshly boiled white stock. This would be an important occasion, and he would dress appropriately. He eyed the lowering clouds warily and prepared for the worst. At the door, Marguerite handed him his black cape, which he threw over his massive shoulders, and then settled a fine black beaver over his white hair. Then he drew his black gloves over his gnarled hands, and stared briefly at the image in the vestibule looking glass. It was a costume fit for births, deaths, weddings, and coronations. This day would offer none of those, but something quite as important.

She smiled at him, knowing the gravity of this moment, and how he had arrived at it. She knew everything but spoke little.

He plucked up his ebony cane and set forth from his big white house, into a sullen December day, his painful metronomic steps releasing memories as he walked. He remembered all the Americans he had dealt with over the years, such as Nathaniel Wyeth, the Boston merchant with visions of empire; with Hall Kelley, the fanatic who penned scurrilous diatribes against him and the Hudson's Bay Company even while seeking its assistance and succor. He remembered Ewing Young, probably a horse thief, and certainly an adventurer looking for ways to get rich.

He remembered the flood of emigrants who showed up at his door seeking assistance from a company they were determined to hate. Some had been so suspicious that they would not accept the counsel of his traders, and thus added to their miseries. Some had been obstreperous, angry, stupid, and devoid of character.

But he thought of so many others, men he liked, men he admired, men with boundless enthusiasms and a love of enterprise. He thought of other Americans he had initially disliked, but ended up admiring; men like Constable and

Brownell. Oregon itself had transformed them, the trial by fire having burnt away everything weak and dark in their nature.

What a strange breed! Lawless and yet governed by a natural law; adventuresome, warm, impulsive, generous, mad, energetic, chaotic, barbarous, but filled with piety and good humor. They were freemen, and having discovered their liberty, they took every advantage of it, often to excess. But they were paradoxical as well. These contentious freemen were quick to impose their ideas of virtue on others."

On the whole, he liked them in spite of their obvious defects, an excess of passion and enthusiasm, a tendency to set aside moral or ethical considerations at times, and an alarming want of education and civility.

Yes, he liked most of them, and cherished their friendships. Many had thanked him for his assistance. Not a few had repaid, some entirely, some bit by bit, whatever he had lent them. Some had sprung to his defense when he was under siege from one or another politician, such as Reese. Some, like that frontier lawyer Jesse Applegate, he regarded as pure sterling.

He liked to think of these people as brothers. In times past, working as a Nor'Wester, he had been as unruly as they, and as ruthless and reckless as any of the Yankees.

This day would mark a transformation of his life. He had not reached this decision easily. His treatment by the company rankled. The company had more or less shoved him here. George Simpson's knighthood rankled. A man without honor deserved rebuke, not elevation. But those hurts were nothing compared to the suspicion at Whitehall about his loyalty, and the several spies the queen's government had dispatched to Oregon to poke into his business and blame him for the American exodus. He had seen their reports, all but accusing him of disloyalty. He, the most loyal of subjects!

That offended him so deeply, so bitterly, so absolutely, that he knew he could never go home. If that was imperial England, blindered and obtuse, accusatory and arrogant, then he would leave his native land for one more ready to embrace him. He wasn't sure but what this business would be a self-imposed act of exile.

He walked through a cold mist that beaded in tiny drops on his black cape, feeling his rheumatism with every step, and reached, at last, the seat of government in Oregon. He mounted the slick steps and entered the familiar cramped hall, and turned left into a small courtroom, and then the chambers of the chief justice of the provisional government, Peter Burnett, who was the sole magistrate in all of Oregon.

He found his friend Burnett poring over a lawbook through wire-rimmed spectacles, his dark hair in disarray.

"Ah, you're in!"

Burnett peered up, noting McLoughlin's attire, smiled warmly and waved

him to a chair. McLoughlin settled into it, gratefully, and lifted the beaver hat
from his wreath of white hair. His legs always hurt now.

"John, what can I do for you?"

"Let me swear the oath."

Burnett stared, puzzled.

"This is the United States now, isn't it? I wish to become a citizen of your
republic. So I've come to take the oath."

Burnett closed the lawbook and blinked.

"John, I can't do it. I'm simply the magistrate of a makeshift temporary
government not authorized by Congress. I don't have the authority. When
they form a territorial government, someone can do it."

"I see. How long will that be?"

Burnett shrugged. "Anyone's guess. We haven't even gotten official word.
I guess they're too busy fighting Mexico to tell us." He peered at the doctor.
"This is a big step. You're the last person I thought would want to become a
citizen."

"This is my new home."

Burnett seemed taken aback, and McLoughlin wished to confirm his intentions.

"I'm going to become an American citizen, and I do so with great joy and
anticipation. I subscribe to the idea of a limited, republican government. I
embrace your nation, and will do so with absolute commitment and loyalty.
You're surprised, aren't you? The head man of Hudson's Bay coming over.
You'd expect me to retire to London and a life of ease in the clubs. I could
well afford it. But here I am, by choice and desire."

"John, when the day comes, I'd sure like to witness the event. But you'll
have to wait for a while, maybe even for this war to end. That's my instinct,
anyway."

McLoughlin sighed. For this aborted moment had he prepared himself,
with all the care and cleansing of heart and soul that one prepared to receive
the sacrament. And now he could not complete his design.

"Very well, Peter, I'll be sure to invite you. Let me know the moment it's
possible for me to become a citizen."

"I will," Burnett said uneasily. The prospect of the chief factor of Hudson's
Bay Company hitching up to the republic seemed to congest his imagination,
as if the act were too large for the mind to absorb.

McLoughlin did not head into the rain, but turned toward the governor's
office, hoping his erstwhile friend, rival, and now leader of the faction most
set against him and the company might be in.

Abernethy was, and McLoughlin waited for him to finish his visitation
with the Reverend Mr. Waller. Indeed, he had a sense that the pair of them
had been discussing himself, or maybe his properties, now that this half of

Oregon was safely in American hands. He waited in the antechamber, while the pair completed their murmured business just beyond, by the light of a double-chimneyed brass lamp.

Waller emerged at last, nodded curtly, and vanished. Affable George Abernethy, a smile glued to his face, tidied up his desk, popped a document into a drawer, waved McLoughlin in, and offered the glad hand, which McLoughlin shook gingerly.

"Well, what can I do for you?"

"Nothing. I've come from Peter Burnett's chambers. I just wished to tell you that I attempted to take the oath of citizenship, but he felt he could not give it."

"You, a citizen?"

"Yes, sir, a citizen of this republic. I'm looking forward to it. I subscribe to its principles—limited government, liberty, equality before the law. Yes, those are my ideals as well. I will support this republic without reservation."

"Well, ah, that is admirable."

McLoughlin got the impression that Abernethy wasn't overjoyed by the news.

"I should like to know when I will have the opportunity to take the oath of allegiance," he said. "Please keep me posted."

"Well, it depends on Washington. On Polk, you know. He's got the Mexicans on his mind."

"Let me know when this is a territory and when its officers arrive. When there's a lawful United States magistrate, I'll be the first to take the oath."

Abernethy nodded, and then suddenly grinned. "Imagine that," he said heartily.

Imagine that. McLoughlin didn't much care for Abernethy's lukewarm reception, and he understood exactly why the governor wasn't pleased. The Mission Party still had designs on everything that McLoughlin owned or developed, and citizenship would throw a serious obstacle into their confiscatory designs.

That property was considerable. His home on three lots; his store, his gristmill on the island, which he ran himself; his two sawmills on the island, which he leased; numerous unsold city lots. He knew, intuitively, that the old Mission Party cabal had not surrendered.

He smiled bleakly at Abernethy, thinking back on the times when Abernethy came to Fort Vancouver begging for goods to sell in Oregon City, begging for credit, all in the name of advancing Christian religion. McLoughlin had supplied the goods at cost, ignoring his company's own interests. All in the name of religion.

"Governor, I won't take more of your time," he said. "You've already spent so much of it on me."

1847

74

Was this paradise? Rose Constable didn't think so. But it was sometimes pleasant and sometimes rewarding.

The orchard prospered. The apple saplings took to the good earth and flourished. She plucked weeds and brush from them, and sometimes during dry spells painfully bucketed water to the weakest ones. Someday they would offer the Constables a living.

The farmstead grew. Jasper somehow had turned himself into a frontiersman, and built their small paradise from the materials at hand. How strange he looked in his chambray shirt and canvas trousers, with a soiled hat tugged over his ragged hair. His soft round white body had turned into a lumpy, muscular, oddly made frame, sun-blistered and perpetually reddened. He seemed ill at ease in his new body, as if it was an alien presence.

His very nature had changed too. Doctrine had vanished from his religion, shorn by frontier life, and she wondered what remained within; what God he would present to her and the world when this odyssey was complete.

But she must have looked strange to him too. Gone were her prim dresses. Now she wore loose-fitting blouses and generous skirts, straw hats and high moccasins she purchased from the Indians. When she examined herself in a looking glass, she saw a lean, tanned, glowing woman who little resembled the pale one who had trekked out from the States.

In the space of two years, Jasper had mastered a host of skills. He had turned himself into a mason and mortared a stone addition to the log cabin, which became their bedroom. He built a stone springhouse, a granary, and a log carriage barn and storage area, all with the help of Matt and Mark. He expanded his schoolhouse.

But the Indian men stayed away, bitter and angry at this incursion into their hunting domain. Jasper could do nothing to entice them to learn mechanical arts, or agriculture, much less receive the faith or come each Sabbath to his new log meeting hall. We are hunters and fishers, they explained. That is women's work. And we do not like your God, who wants to turn us into women.

But Jasper only smiled and nodded. Time would change all that.

Sometimes they dropped by, even in the depths of the night, demanded food, and then lurked about eating it and putting fear into Rose.

If the Tillamook and Clatsop men scorned the Constables' homemade school, their women did not. Shyly at first, then comfortably, the women appeared at the Constables' doorstep, offering hides, fish, and other gifts. Rose soon worked out a simple lingua franca with them and taught them what little she knew of gardening. Or maybe it was the reverse: they taught her. In any case, they reaped the corn and melons and lettuce and potatoes and tomatoes together, and when they returned to their people on the other side of the coastal range, they always bore the fruits of the farm as well as less tangible things, such as an understanding of the ways of white men, and something of the religion that Rose and Jasper faithfully taught.

But if this was comfortable and placid, it was not paradise. She yearned for more contact with white people, and not even the constant presence of the Indian women eased her loneliness. And she worried about the boys, growing into adolescence without contact with other white boys and girls. And she feared for their education, though she insisted that they devote two hours a day to their lessons, hours the restless boys didn't like and tried to avoid.

The older boy, Matt, had taken a shine to a bright-eyed and flirtatious Tillamook girl named Yo-mah, who came with the older women to sew, hoe, weed, and tell funny stories. He had spotted her at once, hung about, dodged his chores, tried to corral her, walk with her, find time alone with her. Rose had been disturbed at first, even if Yo-Mah's mother wasn't. She hid all this from Jasper, who was rarely around the house when the women were there, and finally decided to let nature take its course. Matt was an honorable young man. It would all come to nothing anyway. But she resolved to take the boys to visit their distant neighbors more often. Matt was far too young to be taking any girl seriously, especially one he could barely understand.

Except for the sudden sullen appearances of the Tillamook and Clatsop men, who stalked provocatively through the homestead and sometimes called their women away from it, things seemed peaceable enough. But she knew they weren't.

Sometimes Joe Meek or Doc Newell showed up with news from the settlements, and that was how Rose discovered that the Cayuse Indians were threatening war and death to people on the Oregon Trail, not to mention the Walla Wallas and Nez Percés, and that both Ogden and Douglas had begged the Whitmans to find shelter at Fort Vancouver until the troubles ceased. Both

Meek and Newell insisted that the Constables arm themselves and see to some fortification, but Jasper and Rose always refused.

The provisional government had enacted a new body of laws governing the Indians. For murder or the burning of a white man's dwelling, the punishment was death by hanging. Whippings for lesser crimes. The new United States Indian Agent, Elijah White, would settle disputes and administer punishments.

"They aren't taking it kindly, Jasper. Not a tribe in the whole area isn't angry. And that isn't all. There's measles among 'em, killing 'em, and they're blaming white people. We survive it, but they don't. No measles around here yet, but if you hear of it, and them dying, you'd better think some about coming into Oregon City for a while. Especially you, so isolated. Mind you, I've been in the mountains, and I can *smell* trouble, and that's what I'm sniffing right now."

He emphasized his point with a wagging finger.

Jasper nodded. "We'll be watchful," he said.

Newell squinted at the missioner, sighed, and rode off.

One day Billy, the youth who had studied at the Methodist mission long before, showed up alone, anger in his bright eyes.

"You go away now. Big trouble coming," he said. "I have warned you."

Jasper did not put much stock in it. The tribesmen had occasionally threatened them, and this was nothing new.

"Billy, we're here to help your people. We have done you no harm, and have shown you good things. You have shown us good things too. You've brought us salmon and furs; we've given you vegetables and shown you how to make cloth from wool. We have taught you about the world to come. Bring your friends, and we'll have a talk."

But Billy simply cut him off with a slashing sweep of his arm, and trotted up the long path toward the fog-shrouded ridges above. The swift, menacing moment vanished, but Rose's malaise about it did not.

"Let's go to Oregon City for a while, Jasper," she begged. "We need to go. We can hitch the wagon and take what we can sell or trade. I'd like some cloth. We need news, we need to talk with people—"

"Oh, pshaw, the Indian boys are just in one of their funks," he said. "Nothing's happened in Oregon. These are not Plains Indians, and they're not warlike. They're used to white people now, and we've friends among them. If anything, we should invite them more often."

But he did not allay her dread or her deepening sense of isolation.

Still, nothing happened. The mission harvested a bumper crop. Wheat and oats and barley filled the granaries, pumpkins and squash and potatoes and yams filled the springhouse. Rose shared the bounty with her friends, the Tillamook women.

Then the women vanished.

The monsoon rains began, a steady gray drizzle day after day, making the mission dark and lonely.

The Constable men cut firewood and began work on a fenced pasture that would contain dairy cattle.

The rain let up in mid-November; the coastal mountains dried out, but fog hung in the valleys.

Then one fog-shrouded dawn, the Constables awakened to a curious quiet, and when Rose opened the shutters and peered into the hazy first light, she beheld a silent army. There, before her eyes, stood fifty, sixty, who knows how many? Some of them had painted themselves red, with terrible white and black stripes daubed on their honey-colored torsos. They bore spears and lances and bows and arrows. Some wore hideous masks. Most were on foot; a few sat horses.

Rose's heart raced. Why, oh why, hadn't they listened to Doc Newell?

"Oh, Jasper!"

He peered out into the gloom, swallowed hard, and closed the shutter. His gaze met hers; there was nothing to say. They could not defend themselves, if it came to that. They lacked so much as a fowling piece.

Wordlessly they dressed and awakened the boys. Maybe there was hope. These men hadn't assaulted the place; they stood there, waiting for something. Nothing was happening, and each tick of the clock affirmed life.

Matt and Mark stared bug-eyed at the armed Indians outside, and stood, paralyzed.

"Get dressed," she said sharply.

Jasper lumbered toward the kitchen, slumped into a chair, and leaned over the table, lost in prayer or meditation or terror, she scarcely knew which. She thought of what she might feed so large a group.

He arose, straightened, went to the door and opened it.

The warriors stood in an arc around the front porch, silent in the misty gloom. No one raised a weapon.

"Yes? Yes?" Jasper said. "Billy? Where are you?"

The youth stepped forward.

Rose barely recognized Billy. He wore ochre and white paint that formed chevrons across his face and body, and in his hand was a long and lethal lance.

"What is this, Billy?"

"Go, now."

"But this is our home."

"This is the home of our bear and deer. Go now."

"No . . . we will stay."

Billy erupted into rage, babbling something, and she could barely understand his ranting, but knew he was talking of other missionaries, the Whitmans, the Cayuse, Waiilatpu, death . . .

And still Jasper refused to budge. Neither of them really grasped what the young man was raging about, the misbegotten words tumbling out of him, half English, mostly Tillamook.

Then the circle of warriors narrowed perceptibly.

"Jasper! Don't resist!"

He nodded. She gathered her stripling sons, and they marched into a cold and damp dawn, step by step, straight away from the comfortable house, straight past the sullen warriors.

Then a headman nodded. The warriors raced into the house and she heard a great clatter. Then she saw the flare of light, and knew that her world, Jasper's world, the boys' world, would turn to ash. But these warriors had spared her and her family . . . for the moment.

Jasper groaned. "Oh, my God," he muttered. "Oh, Lord in heaven . . ." But when he attempted to walk away—he wanted to get help from the neighbors a dozen miles distant—they pinned him to the place where they all stood, with leveled lances. He eased toward his family, and joined them to mourn the death of a dream.

She saw tears in his eyes then, and grief etching his weathered face. He slipped an arm about her and drew her close so they might share their grief together. It was not the first grief they had experienced in Oregon, but it was the first they had truly shared.

She watched the windows of her house glare orange, and knew that all the things she cherished were being consumed. The dolls that the Tillamook women had given her, the wooden plates hewn from cedar, the clothes she had proudly fashioned from old sailcloth . . . the few letters from settler friends in Oregon City. But most of all, the flames were licking at dreams, devouring hopes, defying prayers, mocking faith. She wept hotly, the tears so copious her eyes swelled with them and hurt.

Acrid smoke whirled about. She felt Jasper's strong arm hugging her, lifting her up, willing her to stand instead of slump onto the browned grass. She glanced up and saw the tears coursing freely down his cheeks. What more could a man endure? And she felt her sons gather about her, Matt's adolescent honking evoking a great pity in her. With her free arm she caught Mark, whose hiccuping wracked his skinny frame. He quieted under her touch, but still sniffled.

It took a long time to burn their homestead, their schoolhouse and chapel, and the outbuildings. The wood was damp from the monsoons, and burnt reluctantly, but it did burn relentlessly, slowly, fatally. The crackling yellow flames licked the logs and ate them, mocking human labor and love. The flames caught the beams and cheerfully bored through the shake roof and shot a column of yellow fire and blue smoke into the surly morning.

An hour they stood, drained of tears, aching and solemn, and then another, and then, when the buildings had burned beyond repair, the Indians left, taking the horse and driving two oxen before them. They burnt the granary, scorning white men's food. They began singing and chanting, and then vanished in the morning fog.

It turned quiet and dark. The sun had risen, but she swore it was as dark as an eclipse, their dreams as dead as a burnt-out sun. Everything, including the foodstuffs, was gone. It was probably not yet nine.

"We've got to get help," she cried.

He nodded, and the four started the long hike back to settlement, their mission dream vanquished. But as they walked, she found blessedness even in this frightful morning. This time they had wept and hugged and drawn close. Oregon had given them that.

And she had not lost hope. They would return and rebuild, upon the strong foundations of their faith.

1848

Garwood Reese saw his moment and took it. The horror of the massacre at the Presbyterian mission convulsed Oregon. Dr. Marcus Whitman and Narcissa, a dozen other males dead. Two girls, including Joe Meek's daughter, Helen Marr, dead of maltreatment. Other women and children held hostage by the Cayuse Indians and some malcontents allied with them. An uprising of all the tribes, especially the Nez Percé, closely allied to the Cayuse, in the wind.

Men walked in terror, carried arms, whispered their dread whenever they met. The combined tribes vastly outnumbered the settlers and if united could sweep Oregon of all its settlements. The provisional government of George Abernethy floundered, then gradually developed plans to put a five-hundred-man militia in the field.

Father Bruillet, a Catholic priest, started at once for the Presbyterian mission with only a guide for company, and bravely buried some of the dead and tried to free the hostages.

Peter Skene Ogden, knowing the temper of the settlers and the weakness of the provisional government, didn't wait. He set out for Waiilatpu with sixteen well-armed Hudson's Bay men, and reached the burnt-out ruins ahead of the gathering militia. There his men buried more of the dead and laid down the law: release the women and children, or suffer not only war but the loss of trading privileges with the company. That did it.

The Indians of all tribes had a quiver full of grievances: loss of their lands, loss of the game they hunted, maltreatment by whites, disillusion with white religion, broken promises. But the precipitating cause of the catastrophe was measles, a disease which killed Indians but did little harm to whites. Bitterly, they had observed Dr. Whitman's white patients recovering from the epidemic while his red patients died. Surely this was proof that the head of the mission was poisoning them; that his heart was bad toward them.

And so Oregon convulsed. Joe Meek, a stalwart of the anti-Mission party, led punitive raids, and then headed for Washington City, a harrowing overland trip in winter, to inform his in-law, President Polk, of the disaster and beg for guns and protection, else the whole of white Oregon might perish.

Abernethy looked weak and indecisive, and Garwood Reese moved in, with stump speeches and letters to *The Spectator*. The massacre, he explained, was the direct result of the agitations of the Jesuits, who had been steadily expanding their missions throughout the Northwest. The Jesuits had sown confusion in the minds of the Indians, casting aspersions upon Protestant Christianity.

And the other malefactor, he explained, was the Hudson's Bay Company, still agitating the Indians against white Americans. Did not Ogden rush with his private army to release the captives and herd the Cayuses out of harm's way? Did not the company act on its own, instead of adding to the armed weight of the militia and submitting itself to the will of the government?

All this lodged comfortably in the minds of Oregonians through that winter of 1848, and everywhere he went, on the streets, in shops, in the halls of government, Reese found himself admired as a prophet, the man who had discerned the truth about the horror at Waiilatpu. His future looked very bright. He would hold appointive office high in the territorial government whenever Congress got around to organizing it; indeed, the provisional government's ambassador to Congress, Jesse Thornton, a devoted Mission Party man, would see to it.

When Oregon became a state and elected its first governor, Reese knew exactly whom that would be, and what he would say to the assembled bright lights at his inaugural. He would free Oregon, at last, from the yoke of foreign influence. He felt aglow with vitality and good health. He was young. Even those older than he doffed their beavers when he passed them, surely a mark of great respect. Everywhere it was said that he was the heir apparent, the bright shining star of the Mission Party, the Founders' own choice for Oregon. Did he not have a dazzling woman at his side, the envy of most of the males of Oregon? Was she not the perfect ornament for a statesman and leader of men? Did she not provide him with whatever comforts he desired?

And so his explanation of the horror gradually became the official one in Oregon, and few doubted its accuracy. His star had never shone brighter. For this had he come west; braved the perilous trail, suffered starvation and want, buried a brother, and fathered a state.

And yet, his life was all gall and wormwood. Why could he not be happy? He, who had achieved so much, risen so high? Sharp bouts of melancholia afflicted him, times when he could scarcely rise from his chair and cross a room because of his weariness or soul. Was he a sovereign man? No, the sharp-clawed bitch who shared his domestic life made him miserable. He needed her. His political ambitions depended on her, and she knew it. She decorated meetings, flattered in dulcet tones, ran his political errands, and helped raise funds. Yes, the arrangement was useful.

Yet discontent gnawed at him, clawed him in his reflective moments, and he could not put a name or reason to his malaise. He had fallen into odd habits, and the oddest of all was his obsession with the private life of John McLoughlin. He could not say just when he began to walk past McLoughlin's white house between Second and Third, noting every detail of the place. But he did. Soon his daily perambulation took him past that house without fail once a day, then several times a day.

McLoughlin fascinated him. Often, he dawdled there during the evenings so he could glimpse the family through the lamplit windows, and sometimes he saw the White Eagle himself, hunched with age now but still a massive presence in his gracious rooms as well as Oregon. Sometimes he saw the squaw walking heavily through the rooms; sometimes Eloisa, or her children.

Sometimes he spotted them all at dinner, being served by hired help, McLoughlin bantering with his grandchildren. Sometimes he spotted guests, and it helped him to know who sat at John McLoughlin's table. Sometimes he saw McLoughlin pour medicinal brandy for himself or his company, and Reese gloated at the chief factor's delinquency.

Sometimes Reese strolled by at midnight, stalking past the silent, spectral house in the ghastly gloom, unable to explain to himself why he chose to ramble even late at night, and why his rambles led him to that place, why he peered up at McLoughlin's bedroom, and why his gaze never left the building until it was out of sight. What mad obsession had snared him? How could he free himself from this strange bondage to the retired Hudson's Bay chief? Why was he constantly measuring his own fame and success against a man no longer a potent force in American Oregon? What was this fox in his bosom?

Well, it was nothing, really; just keeping track of his old enemy, a dangerous man who needed watching. What was the matter with that? And yet, his obsessive strolls in the direction of that house were not anything he wanted the world to know about.

Twice he had encountered the old chief factor himself when the man stood in his yard or was setting out on an errand of his own, cane in hand. And those were awkward moments for Reese. McLoughlin simply nodded curtly, his penetrating gaze full of large question marks. Reese suddenly realized that McLoughlin *knew*.

Itchily, Reese concluded the matter had to be dealt with. He could not keep haunting McLoughlin's street on his strolls without being exposed as a stalker.

Surely it was the debt, which had hovered at the back of his mind for years like a black rag, something he didn't want to think about and resented. The crafty company had simply lured American settlers into debt, including the Reeses. So Reese really didn't feel he owed the chief factor a cent. But if paying the debt would free him from this odd compulsion, then he would pay it.

He could scarcely remember what it came to, but it was large, thanks to Electra's extravagance in the Fort Vancouver store.

Yes, pay something, be freed from this terrible obsession, buy off the demons afflicting his life.

He had accumulated some funds after years of collecting taxes, and one March afternoon he drew ten liberty eagles, a hundred dollars in gold, from his strongbox, and headed for McLoughlin's house to perform his exorcism.

But at the door his resolve disintegrated, and he fled.

Instead, he sent a government factotum to McLoughlin's house with the gold, with a note saying it was repayment of his debt.

That very afternoon, the gold coins came back in the hand of a messenger boy, with a note from McLoughlin: "Never, Jno McL" was all it said.

The man had rejected his gold!

After that, Reese tried to stroll elsewhere, sometimes along the riverfront, where the roar of the falls drowned his thoughts. But always, he turned toward the white house and its manicured grounds, unable to avoid it, and knowing that his obsession would not cease until McLoughlin was brought to ruin.

1849

76

A festive day! That dawn old John McLoughlin hurried his family to the carriage and helped Marguerite into it, and then Eloisa, and lastly her children, John, Margaret Glen, and Maria Louisa.

Their coachman set off at a fast trot for the old post across the mighty Columbia. There would be a great celebration this bright May day of 1849. The United States Army had arrived in Oregon, and this afternoon there would be a ceremonial laying of the cornerstone of Vancouver Barracks, just across a sunny field from the old Hudson's Bay post, which the company still garrisoned even though it was not in use.

This was the future, and the old man embraced it. Oregon was now a territory and had a territorial governor. It was an organized part of the United States. He intended to embrace his new country joyously. This fine spring outing, with his family gathered around him, would permit him to meet the new command and also to tour his old post and enjoy the memories that lay embedded in those weathered logs and pickets. What more could an old man ask?

The restless children were clambering over him in the rocking coach, but he didn't mind. He loved them and had made a great point of including them on this adventure so they might see the bone and sinew of their new nation. And he would personally escort them through his old bailiwick and tell them all he could about what he had built, and the wealth he had created for so many, and the greatness of the honorable company, so they might know something of their heritage. He wanted them to know everything about their grandfather and grandmother.

Marguerite sat beside him, placid but unwell. She had come not because of the ceremony, but to see the old Hudson's Bay post where so much of her life had spun out. She had not seen Fort Vancouver for years and this would be a homecoming for her.

They arrived at Vancouver Barracks early in the afternoon after being ferried across the purling river, and walked up the gentle grade to an open field, now dotted with rectangles of white canvas that housed the blue-clad infantrymen. A crowd had gathered at a point in the warm meadow, and in that direction the old man steered his brood. He hurried along, not wanting to miss a thing, ignoring his rheumatism in the rush to partake of the ceremony.

He greeted people he knew, such as Jesse Applegate, Peter Burnett, and Joe Meek, and studied those he didn't, such as the new territorial governor, Joseph Lane. He avoided a few, such as Garwood and Electra Reese and George Abernethy. They had all gathered around a place where a foundation block of dressed stone rested in a shallow trench. Chiseled into it was the year, 1849. At last, under a warm sun, and amid frolicking breezes, the commanding officer, a Major Cavanaugh, signaled to a sergeant, and the lounging soldiers drew up in parade formation. They weren't as gaudy as the redcoats of England, but somehow that was fitting for a nation that called itself a republic.

It all went splendidly. Governor Lane noted the value of an army presence and welcomed the first military presence in the territory. The major responded with some kind words about Oregon, and what a valuable addition Vancouver Barracks would be to the glistening settlements of the Pacific Northwest. Flags and guidons fluttered in the zephyrs. The crowd clapped cheerfully.

The infantry band played "The Star-Spangled Banner," and John McLoughlin removed his shiny black beaver and held it to his chest, his first act of fealty to the nation that now claimed him. Soon he would be a citizen, entitled to all the civil rights and protections embedded in the great constitution of this shining nation. He smiled at his grandchildren. They would be Americans too. He smiled at Eloisa, whose life would spin out in the republic.

"This is a great country, and you will be blessed to grow into manhood and womanhood in it," he said to the little ones.

The ceremony was brief; people had really come to welcome the army, see the soldiers in natty blue, inspect the cannon, and study the layout of the new post. Most of those attending planned to picnic there in the meadows, but McLoughlin had other plans. After much pleasantry he gathered his brood and walked across familiar meadows, once given to wheat and oats and barley, and entered the old Hudson's Bay post for one last look.

How strange and hollow it looked, how like a relic compared to the bright ceremony just a few hundred yards distant. Here was the past. *His* past.

At the high gates stood old Pierre Gaillard, along with his Salish wife, Georgette. They cared for the old post and were still paid by the honorable company. As long as they were present, no one could say the valuable post was abandoned, and no one could claim it.

"Ah, *mes amis,* welcome, welcome," the old gentleman exclaimed in a French-English patois as he greeted his former employer with an effusive hug and much back-thumping, and then pressed his hand into Marguerite's. He doted on the children, learning the name of each, and offering them the run of the old post. Soon the little ones raced off to poke into cavernous warehouses and empty rooms.

McLoughlin learned that these caretakers stayed in what had been Peter Ogden's apartment. So great was the reverence for the chief factor's old residence that none of those who stayed on these days dared move in, and now it stood empty and forlorn, except for the memories that lay embedded within its walls.

He and Marguerite wandered there first, walking through dusty barren rooms, evoking the shards of a life. She held his hand as they wandered through the bedrooms, the kitchen, the dining room, and out again upon the broad veranda. She stayed there while he headed for his old office, the seat of an amazing empire that spanned much of a continent. There, even in those barren rooms, shorn now of all but memory, he felt the presence of colleagues, employees, guests, friends and rivals, and even madmen. There he had studied the ledgers, made great decisions, heard painful news, surrendered to the will of his superiors, saw fortunes rise and ebb. This was all his.

And so that May day, John McLoughlin came to revisit his past. He remembered the utter wilderness, the profound quiet, before the first log had been cut and peeled. He remembered the great task of erecting the first fortress, and then the second one, and he remembered each of the many improvements that he had pursued, year after year.

He remembered the day he had moved Marguerite into the new chief factor's house, and how she had made the spacious residence her own, and had warmed it with love. He remembered the fur brigades he had sent out into the wilds year after year, and the riches they brought back, and the terrible times he learned of death and failure. He remembered the supply ships that arrived from England each year, brimming with welcome news as well as life's necessaries, and even a few luxuries.

And the guests! For twenty years, the post had been an island of comfort and civilization in an empty wild, and he had found himself entertaining hundreds of people who found refuge and nurture within its tall walls. At his dining table had sat Simpson and Ogden and Douglas; the American naturalist Thomas Nuttall; the odd duck Nat Wyeth; the Whitmans, the Lees, and a dozen other missionaries; French, Russians, Mexicans, ship captains, officers in the Royal Navy, and so many more.

He knew, standing there in his barren sun-drenched office, that he had lived a grand life; that he had been privileged in all things, from the happy union with Marguerite to children and grandchildren to achievement, to honor and the possession of a good name, to the blessings of the True Faith.

He was glad he had made the long trip from Oregon City this day, for he had seen his past and future, and knew that it all was good.

EPILOGUE

When President Polk's appointee, Governor Joseph Lane, arrived in Oregon in March 1849, along with the newly appointed U.S. Marshal Joe Meek, Oregon at last was an official territory of the United States.

In May, John McLoughlin went to the new territorial judge W. P. Bryant and began the process of becoming a citizen by swearing allegiance to the United States. He believed that as a citizen he would be treated fairly, and that the controversies still whirling about his properties would be quieted.

Little did he know that Bryant had secretly purchased the clouded title to the Oregon City island and its waterpower from George Abernethy and the Methodist-run milling company there, and fully intended to prove up the conflicted claim by political means. (Later, after he and others had lobbied Congress for the Methodist claim, he sold the island back to Abernethy, and there are those who believe it was a bribe.)

The first legislature, dominated by the Mission Party, sent the young Samuel Thurston to Washington as its nonvoting representative to Congress. Thurston, imbued with all the party's propaganda and cupidity, began to lobby Congress for a land law that would confirm titles of all property in Oregon—except for that owned by McLoughlin.

In a letter to members of Congress, reprinted in *The Spectator*, he called McLoughlin the "chief fugleman" of the Hudson's Bay Company; alleged that McLoughlin had illegally taken the land from Americans; that McLoughlin had forced the Methodist mission off the site by threatening to have Indians attack the missionaries; that he had acquired the claim by violence and was getting rich from it; that he was a British citizen and Hudson's Bay Company man who refused to become an American citizen; and that he was secretly holding the claim for the Hudson's Bay Company.

McLoughlin reacted furiously to these canards, and published his response in *The Spectator* saying he could "scarcely believe anyone would write such a mass of lies." He noted that he had donated some three hundred lots for various religious and civic purposes. The lies so appalled many Oregonians that fifty-six of them sent a letter to Congress protesting the maltreatment of the man who had generously helped so many Americans survive and settle in Oregon.

But it was too late. Congress enacted the notorious Donation Land Act in September 1850, which confirmed all existing land claims in Oregon, except for Dr. McLoughlin's. All unsold lots, including those under his own home and store, were to go to the territory to be sold, the proceeds to go toward establishing a university; the island claim was to go to the rival Methodist-operated Willamette Milling and Trading Company, then in the hands of Judge Bryant and George Abernethy. McLoughlin was to receive nothing, even for the buildings on these sites.

So it came to pass that the connivers had their day, while hiding behind the fig leaf of the public-spirited funding of a university. It did not matter that McLoughlin's claim to the island and its waterpower preceded all others; that he defended his claim vigorously; that his claim was affirmed in arbitration; that when the Methodist mission collapsed, he repurchased at a high price the very lots he had donated to the mission as a way of establishing certain title; that he had paid the Hudson's Bay Company for the claims and possessed them in his own name; that the Hudson's Bay Company had never agitated the Indians against Americans (quite the contrary, it had done everything in its power to protect the emigrants); that the boundary settlement expressly protected the ownership of British-held property; and that McLoughlin had enthusiastically become an American citizen.

All that mattered was that the clique of missioners and their allies got their island and waterpower, and showed the old Catholic doctor a thing or two. But among many grateful Oregonians, the treatment of Dr. McLoughlin was an outrage. The territorial legislature allowed the doctor to live in his "forfeited" home.

After he died in 1857, Oregon, in a fit of conscience, restored to his surviving children at least some of the family property, if the children would make a thousand-dollar donation to Willamette University, the beneficiary of the stolen property.

John McLoughlin never recovered title. In spite of all that, the rest of his life he continued to help destitute emigrants who appealed to him for help.

AUTHOR'S NOTE

The settlement of Oregon has always been a mystery and it continues to perplex historians. What inspired thousands of Americans to plunge beyond the nation's westernmost frontier, cross a dangerous trackless waste, and settle on the Pacific Coast?

Manifest Destiny is the common explanation. The term was coined in 1845, in the middle of the Oregon controversy, to express the inchoate longing for a nation that stretched from sea to sea. That was fine for statesmen, journalists, men of vision, cognoscenti, and politicians, who made immediate use of the term.

But the idea of a nation stretching from the Atlantic to the Pacific could scarcely motivate the heads of families to sell all they possessed, purchase an ox team and wagon, and walk across a continent with their wives and children, parents and grandparents. They did not pull up roots and start a brutal journey for the sake of Manifest Destiny, a phrase most had never heard of. Indeed, many had traveled the long trail before the idea of Manifest Destiny was coined in 1845. They were motivated by more practical and personal considerations: a sweet and fertile and well-watered land promising abundance; a place of dreams.

Such bountiful land was available much closer, on the frontiers of Wisconsin, Iowa, Illinois, and Missouri, and yet these emigrants did not stop there. To be sure, there were the agitations of the likes of the half-demented New England visionary Hall Kelley, whose shrill propaganda stirred the thought of a distant utopia. Other Americans who had been there, such as the adventuresome Boston ice merchant Nat Wyeth, added detail and fleshed out a picture of a splendid land. But these factors, considered separately or jointly, do not inspire a fifteen-hundred-mile emigration across burning flats, empty prairie, malevolent unbridged rivers, and dense forests.

These emigrants were not led there by the pied pipers of Manifest Destiny. They hoped to make a better life in a magical place.

Their exodus still mystifies moderns. Only when the migration is put into historical context can we begin to fathom what was happening. The 1840s were a period not only of religious ferment, but also utopian social experimentation, such as Brook Farm, established in 1841 by George Ripley, Unitarian minister and Transcendentalist; the Owenite colonies; and various socialist communes. The perfectability of mankind, and social institutions, was in the air.

I believe that what drew people to Oregon was precisely its isolation, its awesome, forbidding separation from the rest of the nation. And what so many of the emigrants hoped to build there was something close to paradise, well insulated by thousands of miles of wasteland from a corrupt world. What was there, after all, but a single British company engaged in the fur trade?

The impulse is more sharply etched by the Mormon migration that overlapped the Oregon migration. The persecuted Mormons yearned for a safe haven, and it is no accident that they called their new homeland *Zion*, a biblical word which means *utopia* and *paradise* as well as *homeland*. That yearning for a west-coast Zion may have been less explicit, but was certainly large in the minds of those who endured harrowing difficulties to reach the promised land, the mysterious place of fable called Oregon.

Oregon's provisional government not only prohibited slavery, but excluded blacks from the area, thus making it the most racist of all American territories. This peculiarity has traditionally been ascribed to the presence of Southerners in Oregon, but that makes little sense because the area was settled largely by Northerners.

The more likely reason for excluding blacks is that utopias require a likeness of mind and soul and body among those who participate in them. In the minds of those who went to Oregon to create some sort of paradise, there was no room for a polyglot and culturally diverse population. I believe the racial exclusion clause was entirely the work of Northern emigrants.

Oregon was at first ferociously dry, and its missionary settlers naturally assumed that what was good for their souls was good for all of mankind, including those who didn't share their temperance or their distaste for other of the solaces of the body, such as coffee. Temperance was also in the air in the 1840s, and was part and parcel of the utopian impulse that informed the migration to Oregon.

This novel is an attempt to depict such truths, and to throw light upon the harrowing frontier experience, with all its disillusion and disappointment. It is a story about people heading west with lofty and unrealistic expectations, only to see them founder on the reefs of reality. It is about idealists, such as the Protestant missionaries, whose cupidity and avarice and rank corruption turned out to be the other side of their coin.

The Americans depicted here are largely fictional, and the events in their lives are largely fictional. The Canadians are largely real, and the events and circumstances they faced in this novel are largely real.

Among the most helpful books in the preparation of this novel were Dale L. Walker's splendid *Pacific Destiny*, read in manuscript; David Lavender's *Land of Giants;* the two-volume memoirs of Joseph Meek prepared by Frances Victor Fuller, *The River of the West*; the exhaustive history of the Hudson's Bay Company written by Peter C. Newman, *Company of Adventurers* and *Caesars of the Wilderness*; and two brief biographies of John McLoughlin, *The Eagle and the Fort,* by Dorothy Nafus Morrison, and *Dr. John McLoughlin, Master of Fort Vancouver, Father of Oregon,* by Nancy Wilson. I know of no full-scale scholarly or popular biography of McLoughlin, and believe one is long overdue. The voyageurs' boat song, quoted in chapter 64, was taken from *The Eagle and the Fort*.

I am grateful to my editor, Dale L. Walker, not only for suggesting this book to me and shepherding me through it, but also for his rare expertise about Oregon, which he shared unstintingly.

Richard S. Wheeler
July 2000